P9-CEC-019

Joss knew what was coming. He was going to kiss her.

And oh, at that moment, she *wanted* him to kiss her.

Wanted him to guide her back onto the sofa cushions, to press his big muscled body so tightly against her, to hold her so close and kiss her so long, and so deep and so thoroughly that she would forget...

Everything.

The mess that was her life. All the ways her plans and her world had gone haywire. All the things she somehow had to fix, to make right, though she really had no idea how to do that.

She wanted to tear off all her clothes and all of his, too. She wanted to be naked with him, skin to skin. Naked with her new best friend—who happened to be a man she'd only met the day before.

She wanted forgetfulness. And she wanted it in Jace's big arms.

MONTANA
★ COUNTRY LEGACY ★

THE COWBOY'S SECRET HEART

New York Times Bestselling Author

Christine Rimmer

Rebecca Winters

Previously published as *The Last Single Maverick*
and *A Montana Cowboy*

If you purchased this book without a cover you should be aware that this book is stolen property. It was reported as "unsold and destroyed" to the publisher, and neither the author nor the publisher has received any payment for this "stripped book."

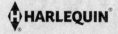

ISBN-13: 978-1-335-50009-0

Montana Country Legacy:
The Cowboy's Secret Heart
Copyright © 2020 by Harlequin Books S.A.

The Last Single Maverick
First published in 2012. This edition published in 2020.
Copyright © 2012 by Harlequin Books S.A.

Special thanks and acknowledgment are given
to Christine Rimmer for her contribution to the
Montana Mavericks: Back in the Saddle continuity.

A Montana Cowboy
First published in 2015. This edition published in 2020.
Copyright © 2015 by Rebecca Winters

Recycling programs
for this product may
not exist in your area.

All rights reserved. No part of this book may be used or reproduced in any manner whatsoever without written permission except in the case of brief quotations embodied in critical articles and reviews.

This is a work of fiction. Names, characters, places and incidents are either the product of the author's imagination or are used fictitiously. Any resemblance to actual persons, living or dead, businesses, companies, events or locales is entirely coincidental.

This edition published by arrangement with Harlequin Books S.A.

For questions and comments about the quality of this book, please contact us at CustomerService@Harlequin.com.

Harlequin Enterprises ULC
22 Adelaide St. West, 40th Floor
Toronto, Ontario M5H 4E3, Canada
www.Harlequin.com

Printed in U.S.A.

CONTENTS

Christine Rimmer came to her profession the long way around. She tried everything from acting to teaching to telephone sales. Now she's finally found work that suits her perfectly. She insists she never had a problem keeping a job—she was merely gaining "life experience" for her future as a novelist. Christine lives with her family in Oregon. Visit her at christinerimmer.com.

Books by Christine Rimmer

Harlequin Special Edition

The Bravos of Valentine Bay

The Bravos of Justice Creek

Visit the Author Profile page at Harlequin.com for more titles.

THE LAST SINGLE MAVERICK

Christine Rimmer

For my readers.

You are the best!

Chapter 1

Family reunions. Who needs them?

Jason Traub didn't. He realized that now. And yet somehow, a few days ago, he'd decided that a trip to Montana for the annual summertime Traub family get-together would be a good idea.

Or maybe he'd just wanted to escape Midland, Texas, and the constant pressure to return to the family business. He should have realized that in Montana it would only be more of the same. Especially given that the whole family was here—and still putting on the pressure.

And why was it that the reunion seemed to get longer every year? This year, it began on the Saturday before Independence Day and would go straight through the whole week to the Sunday after the Fourth, with some family event or other taking place daily.

That first day, Saturday, June 30, featured a late-afternoon barbecue at DJ's Rib Shack. Jason's cousin DJ had Rib Shacks all over the western states. But this one happened to be at the Thunder Canyon Resort up on Thunder Mountain, which loomed, tall and craggy, above the small and charming mountain town of Thunder Canyon.

"Jace." The deep voice came from behind him. "Glad you could make it."

Jason, seated at one of the Rib Shack's long, rustic, family-style tables, glanced over his shoulder at his older brother Ethan. "Great party," Jason said. And it was. If you didn't mind a whole bunch of family up in your face in a big, big way.

His brother leaned closer. "We need to talk."

Jace pretended he didn't hear and held up a juicy rib dripping Rib Shack secret sauce. "Great ribs, as always." With the constant rumble of voices and laughter that filled the restaurant, how would Ethan know if Jace heard him or not?

Ethan grunted—and bent even closer to speak directly into his ear. "I know Ma and Pete want you back in Midland." Pete Wexler was their stepdad. "But you've got options, and I mean that. There's a place waiting for you right here at TOI Montana."

TOI—for Traub Oil Industries—was the family business. The original office was in Midland, Texas, where Jason and his five siblings had been born and raised. Pete, their stepdad, was chairman of the board. And their mother, Claudia, was CEO. Last year, Ethan had opened a second branch of TOI in Thunder Canyon. Jackson, Jason's fraternal twin, and their only sister,

Rose, and her husband, Austin, were all at the new office with Ethan.

"No, thanks," Jace said, and then reminded his brother—as he kept reminding everyone in the family, "I'm out of the oil business."

Now it was Ethan's turn to pretend not to hear. He squeezed Jason's shoulder—a bone-crushing squeeze. "We'll talk," he said.

"No point," Jace answered wearily. "I've made up my mind."

But Ethan only gave him a wave and started talking to the large elderly woman on Jace's right. Jace didn't hear what they said to each other. He was actively *not* listening.

A moment later, Ethan moved on. Jace concentrated on his dinner. His plate was piled high with ribs, corn on the cob, coleslaw and steak fries. The food was terrific. Almost worth the constant grief he was getting from his family—about work, about his nonexistent love life, about *everything*.

Across the table, Shandie Traub, his cousin Dax's wife, said, "Jason, here's someone I want you to meet." The someone in question stood directly behind Shandie. She had baby-fine blond hair and blue eyes and she was smiling at him shyly. Shandie introduced her. "My second cousin, Belinda McKelly. Belinda's from Sioux Falls."

"Hi, Jason." Belinda colored prettily. She had to practically shout to be heard over the din. "I'm so pleased to meet you." She bent closer and stuck her hand out at him.

Jace swiped a wet wipe over his fingers, reached across the table and gave her offered hand a shake. She seemed sweet actually. But one look in those baby blues of hers told him way more than he needed to know: Belinda wanted a husband. As soon as she let go, he grabbed an ear of corn and started gnawing on it, his gaze focused hard on his plate. When he dared to glance up again, she was gone.

Shandie gave him a look that skimmed real close to pissed off. "Honestly, Jace, you could make a little effort. It's not like it would kill you."

"Sorry," he said, even though he didn't feel sorry in the least. He only felt relieved not to have to make small talk with sweet Belinda McKelly.

To his right, the large elderly woman Ethan had spoken to a few moments before said warmly, "Such a lovely young girl." The old lady's warm tone turned cool as she spoke directly to Jason. "But I can see *you're* not interested." He kept working away at his ear of corn in hopes that the large old lady would turn and talk to the smaller old lady on her other side. No such luck. "I'm Melba Landry," she said, "Lizzie's great-aunt." Lizzie was Ethan's wife.

Resigned, Jason gave the woman a nod. "Pleased to meet you, ma'am. I'm Jason Traub, Lizzie's brother-in-law."

"I know very well who you are, young man." Aunt Melba looked down her imposing nose at him. "I was married to Lizzie's great-uncle Oliver for more than fifty years. Oliver, rest his soul, passed on last October. The Lord never saw fit to bless us with children of our own. I moved to Thunder Canyon just this past April. It's so nice to be near Lizzie. Family is everything, don't you think, Jason?"

"Yes, ma'am. Everything." To his left, he was

vaguely aware that the second cousin sitting there had risen. Someone else slipped into the empty spot.

And Aunt Melba wasn't through with him yet. "Jason, you know that we're all *concerned* about you."

"Kind of seems that way, yes." He got busy on his second ear of corn, still hoping that putting all his attention on the food would get rid of her. It had worked with Belinda.

But Aunt Melba was not about to give up. "I understand you're having some kind of life crisis."

He swallowed. The wad of corn went down hard. He grabbed his water glass and knocked back a giant gulp. "Life crisis? No, ma'am. I'm not."

"Please call me Melba—and there's no point in lying about it. I'm seventy-six years old, young man. I know a man in crisis when I see one."

"No, ma'am," he said again. "I mean that. There's no crisis." By then, he was starting to feel a little like Judas at the last supper. If he just kept denying, maybe she would go away.

"I asked you to call me Melba," she corrected a second time, more sternly.

"Sorry, Melba. But I mean it. I'm not having a crisis. I am doing just fine. And really, I—"

"There's a lovely church here in town that I've been attending. Everyone is so friendly. I felt at home there from the first. And so will you, Jason."

"Uh…"

"Tomorrow. Join us. The Thunder Canyon Community Church. North Main at Cedar Street. Come to the service at ten. I'll be watching for you. There is no problem in this wide world that a little time with the Lord can't resolve."

"Well, Melba, thank you for the invitation. I'll, um, try to be there."

"Get involved, young man," Melba instructed with an enthusiastic nod of her imposing double chin. "That's the first step. Stop sitting on the sidelines of life." She opened her mouth to say more, but the white-haired lady on her other side touched her arm and spoke to her. Melba turned to answer.

Jace held his breath. And luck was with him. Melba and the other old lady had struck up a conversation.

He was just starting to feel relieved when a hand closed on his left thigh and a sultry voice spoke in his ear. "Jace, aren't you even going to say hi?"

He smelled musky perfume and turned his head slowly to meet a pair of glittering green eyes. "Hi."

The woman was not any member of his extended family that he knew of. She had jet-black hair and wore a painted-on red tank top. "Oh, you're kidding me." She laughed. "You don't remember? Last summer? Your brother Corey's bachelor party at the Hitching Post?" The Hitching Post was a landmark restaurant and bar in town.

"I, uh…"

"Theresa," the woman said. "Theresa Duvall."

"Hey." He tried on a smile. He remembered her now—vaguely anyway. For Jace, the weekend of Corey's bachelor party and wedding had been mostly of the "lost" variety. His twin, Jackson, had still been single then. The two of them had partied straight through for three days. There had been serious drinking. Way too much drinking. And the night of the bachelor party, he'd gone home with Theresa, hadn't he? Somehow, that had seemed like a good idea at the time. "So, Theresa," he said, "how've you been?"

Her hand glided a little higher on his thigh. "I have been fine, Jace. Just fine. And it is so *good* to see you," she cooed. "I had *such* a great time with you." Theresa, as he recalled, was not the least interested in settling down. In fact, the look on her face told him exactly what she *was* interested in: another night like that one last summer.

He *had* to get out of there. He grabbed another wipe, swabbed off his greasy fingers and then gently removed Theresa's wandering hand from his thigh. "Excuse me, Theresa."

"Oh, now," she coaxed in a breathy whisper, "don't run off."

"Men's room?" He put a question mark after it, even though he knew perfectly well where the restrooms were.

Theresa pointed. "Over there." She gave him a low-eyed, smoldering glance as he pushed his chair out and rose. "Hurry back," she instructed, licking her lips.

It wasn't easy, but he forced himself not to take off at a run. He ambled away casually, waving and nodding to friends and family as he headed for the restrooms—only detouring sharply for the exit as soon as he was no longer in Theresa's line of sight. A moment later, he ducked out of the Rib Shack altogether and into the giant, five-story clubhouse lobby of the resort.

Now what?

Someplace quiet. Someplace where he could be alone.

The Lounge, he thought. It was a bar in the clubhouse and it was exactly what he needed right now. The

Lounge was kind of a throwback really—a throwback to earlier times, when cattlemen had their own private clubs where the women didn't trespass. In the Lounge, the lights were kept soothingly low. The bar was long and made of gleaming burled wood. It had comfortable conversation areas consisting of dark wood tables and fat studded-leather chairs. Women seemed to avoid the Lounge. They tended to prefer the more open, modern bar in the upscale Gallatin Room, or the cowboy-casual style of the bar in the Rib Shack.

The Lounge was perfect for the mood he was in.

He found it as he'd hoped it might be—mostly deserted. One lone customer sat up at the bar. A woman, surprisingly enough. A brunette. Jace liked the look of her instantly, which surprised him. As a rule lately, it didn't matter how hot or good-looking a woman was. He just wasn't interested. Not on any level.

But *this* woman was different. Special. He sensed that at first sight.

She had a whole lot of thick, tousled brown hair tumbling down her back. In the mirror over the bar, he could see that she had big brown eyes and full, kissable lips. She was dressed casually, in jeans and a giant white shirt, untucked. She wore very little makeup.

And the best thing about her? She seemed so relaxed. Like she wasn't after anything except to sip her margarita and enjoy the quiet comfort of the Lounge.

She saw him watching her in the mirror over the bar. For a second or two, their eyes met. He felt a little curl of excitement down inside him before she glanced away. Instantly, he wanted her to glance at him again.

Surprise. Excitement. The desire that a certain woman might give him a second look. These were all emotions with which he'd become completely unfamiliar.

Yeah, all right. It wasn't news that he used to be something of a player. But in the past six months or so? Uh-uh. He was tired of being a ladies' man—like he was tired of just about everything lately. Including finding the right woman and settling down.

Because, yeah, Jason had tried that. Or at least, he'd wanted to try it with a certain rich-girl swimsuit model named Tricia Lavelle.

It hadn't worked out. In fact, the whole experience had been seriously disheartening.

A cell phone on the bar started ringing. The brunette picked it up, scowled at the display and then put it to her ear. "What do you want?" She let out an audible sigh. "You're not serious. Oh, please, Kenny, get real. It's over. Move on." She hung up and dropped the phone back on the bar.

Jace took the stool next to her and signaled the bartender. "Jack Daniels, rocks." The bartender poured and set his drink in front of him. "And another margarita," Jace added. "For the lady."

"No, thanks." She shook her head at the barkeep and he left them alone. Then she turned to Jace and granted him a patient look from that fine pair of enormous brown eyes. "No offense," she said.

"None taken."

"And don't even *think* about it, okay? I'm on a solo vacation and right now, I hate men."

He studied her face. It was such a great face. One of those faces a guy could look at forever and still find new expressions in it. "Already, I really like you."

"Didn't I just say I hate men?"

"That makes you a challenge. Haven't you heard? Men love a challenge."

"I'm serious. Don't bother. It's not gonna happen."

He faced the rows of liquor bottles arrayed in front of the mirror over the bar and shrugged. "Okay, if you're sure."

She shot him a look. "Oh, come on. Is that the best you've got?"

He leaned his head on his hand and admired the way the dim barroom light somehow managed to bring out glints of auburn in her thick, wavy dark hair. "Uninspired, huh?"

She almost smiled. "Well, yeah."

"Story of my life lately. I've got no passion for the game."

"What game?"

He shrugged again. "Any game."

She considered that. "Wow," she said finally. "That's sad."

"Yeah, it is, isn't it?"

She frowned and then looked at him sideways. "Wait a minute. Stop right there, buddy. I'm on to you."

"Oh? What am I up to?"

"You sit there looking gorgeous and bored. I find I have a longing to bring some life back into your eyes. I let you buy me another margarita after all. I go home with you. We have wild, hot, incredible sex. But in the morning, you're looking bored again and I'm feeling cheap and used."

He decided to focus on the positive. "You think I'm gorgeous?"

"That was not my point. It was a cautionary tale."

"I think *you're* gorgeous," he said and meant it. "And that's kind of a breakthrough for me."

"A breakthrough." She was not impressed. "You're kidding me."

"I am as serious as a bad blind date. You're the first woman I've felt attracted to in months. Who's Kenny?"

She shook a finger at him. "You listened in on my phone call."

"Not exactly. I *overheard* your phone call."

"I'm just saying it was a private conversation and I don't even know your name."

"Jason Traub. Call me Jace." He offered his hand.

She took it. "Jocelyn Marie Bennings. Call me Joss."

It felt good, he realized, just to hold her hand. It felt… comfortable. And exciting, too. Both at once. That was a first—for him anyway. As a rule, with women, it was one or the other. He didn't want to let go. But in the end, it wasn't his choice.

She eased her hand free. "My wedding was supposed to be a week ago today. Kenny was the groom."

"Supposed to be? You mean you *didn't* marry him?"

"No, I didn't. And I should have backed out long before the wedding day. But Kenny and I were together for five years. It was going to be a beautiful wedding. You should see my wedding gown. I still have it. I couldn't bear to get rid of it. It's fabulous. Acres of beading, yards of the finest taffeta and tulle. We planned a nice reception afterward at my restaurant."

"You own a restaurant?"

"No. I mean the restaurant I was managing, until I quit to marry Kenny. I gave up a great job for him. Just like I gave up my cute apartment, because I thought I wouldn't need either anymore."

"But then you didn't marry Kenny."

"I already said I didn't."

"Just wanted to be sure. So what went wrong? Why didn't you marry the guy?"

She ran her finger around the rim of her margarita glass. "Who's telling this story, Jace?"

He gave her a nod. "You are, Joss. Absolutely. Carry on."

"It was going to be the perfect wedding."

He nodded once more, to show her he was listening, but he did not interrupt again.

She went on. "And after the wedding and the lovely reception, there was the great getaway honeymoon right here at the Thunder Canyon Resort. Followed by a move to San Francisco. Kenny's a very successful advertising executive. He just hit the big time and got transferred to the Bay Area." Joss paused. She turned her glass by the stem.

He wanted to prompt her to tell him what went wrong, but he didn't. He waited patiently for her to go on, as he'd promised he would.

Finally, she continued. "I got all the way to the church last Saturday. Camellia City Methodist in Sacramento. It's a beautiful church. And I was born and raised in Sacramento and have lived there all my life. I like my hometown. In fact, I didn't really want to move to San Francisco, but I was willing to support my future husband in his powerhouse career. And I would have gone through with the wedding in spite of my doubts."

He'd promised to let her tell it her way, but still. He had to know. "What doubts?"

She shook her head. "Kenny used to be such a sweet guy. But the more successful he got, the more he

changed. He became someone I didn't even know—
and then I caught him with my cousin Kimberly in the
coat room."

"Hold on, you lost me. What coat room?"

She shook her head again, as though she still couldn't
quite believe it. "The coat room at Camellia City Methodist."

Jace let his mouth fall open. "Kenny canoodled with
Kimberly in the coat room on the day of your wedding?"

"Oh, yeah. And it was beyond canoodling. Kimberly
was halfway out of her hot-pink satin bridesmaid's dress
and someone had unzipped Kenny's fly. Both of them
were red faced and breathless. Kind of ruined the whole
experience for me, you know?"

He made a low noise in his throat. "I guess so."

Joss picked up the cell phone, studied it for a moment and then set it back down. "So I threw his engagement ring in his face and got the heck out of there—and
I'm here at the resort anyway. Having my honeymoon
minus the groom."

He tipped his head at the phone. "But Kenny keeps
calling."

"Oh yes, he does."

"What a douche bag."

She sipped her margarita. "My sentiments exactly."

"I hate guys like that. He blew it already. He should
show a little dignity and leave you alone. But instead
it's, 'Joss, *please*. I love you. I just want to work this
out. Come back to me. I'm sorry, okay? And that silly
thing with Kimberly? It meant nothing and it will never
happen again.'"

Joss laughed. She had a beautiful, husky, warm sort
of laugh. "How did you do that? You even captured the

slightly wounded, whiney tone of his voice. Like *I'm* the one with the problem."

Jace stared at her wide, soft mouth in unabashed admiration. "I like your laugh."

She gave him her sternest frown. "Didn't I tell you not to go there?"

He was about to argue that he wasn't "going" anywhere, that he only liked the way she laughed. But before he could get the words out, Theresa Duvall sauntered up behind him and took the stool on his other side.

"Jace." Theresa's hand closed over his arm. He looked down at her fingernails, which were long and done up for the holiday with glittery red stripes and tiny, sparkly little stars. She leaned close and purred, "I'm a determined woman and there is no way you're escaping me."

Okay. He knew he only had himself to blame if Theresa considered him the perfect candidate for another no-strings night of meaningless sex. But he really liked Joss. And he'd never have a chance with her now, not with Theresa pulling on his arm, eyeing him like a starving person eyes a steak dinner.

And it wasn't even that he *wanted* a chance with Joss. Not *that* kind of chance anyway. He just liked her a lot, liked talking with her, liked hearing her laugh. He didn't want her to leave.

Shocked the socks off him when she *didn't* leave. Somehow, she picked up on the desperate look he sent her. And not only did she stay right where she was, she wrapped her arm around his shoulders and pulled him away from Theresa, drawing him close to her side.

Wow. It felt good—*really* good—to have her holding on to him, to feel her softness and the warmth of her. She smelled like soap and starch and sunshine and roses. And maybe a little tequila.

"Sorry," she said to Theresa, her tone regretful. "This one's taken."

Theresa blinked. And then she let go of his arm and scowled. "Jace, what *is* your problem? You should have told me you were with someone. I want a good time as much as the next girl, but I would never steal another woman's man."

He was totally lost, awash in the superfine sensation of having Joss's arm around him. But then she nudged him in the side and he realized he was supposed to speak. "Uh, yeah. You're right, Theresa. I'm an ass. I should have said something."

Joss clucked her tongue and rolled her eyes. "We had a fight. He's been sulking."

Theresa groaned. "Oh, I know how that goes. Men. I don't let myself get serious with them anymore. They're just not worth it."

Joss pulled him even closer. And then she kissed his ear. It was barely a breath of a kiss. But still, with her arm around him and her lips close to his ear, he could almost forget that he had no interest in women anymore. He was enjoying every minute of this and he wished she would never let go. "I hear you," she told Theresa, her breath all warm and tempting in his ear. "But when it's true love, well, what can you do?"

Theresa just shook her head. The bartender approached. Theresa shook her head at him, too. And then, without another word, she got up and left.

Instantly, Joss released him and retreated to her own stool. Jace felt kind of bereft. But then he reminded himself that he should be grateful. She'd done him a favor and gotten Theresa off his back. "Thanks. I owe you one." He raised his glass.

She tapped hers against it. "Okay, I'll bite. Who *was* that?"

"Her name is Theresa Duvall. Last year, she was working at the Hitching Post—it's this great old-time bar and grill down in town, on the corner of Main Street and Thunder Canyon Road."

"She seemed like she knew you pretty well."

"Not really." He didn't want to say more. But Joss was looking at him, a look that seemed to expect him to tell the truth. So he did. "I had a thing with her last summer. A very short thing."

"A thing."

"Yeah."

"What, specifically, is a thing?"

He tried not to wince. "See, I knew you would ask that."

Joss accused gently, "You slept with her."

"Only once. And technically, well, there was no sleeping."

She laughed again. Really, she had the best laugh. "Jace, I believe you're a dog."

He tipped his drink and stared down into it. "Maybe I was. Not anymore, though. I have changed my ways."

She made a disbelieving sound. "Right."

"No, seriously, I'm not the man I used to be. Too bad I'm not real clear on who, exactly, I've become. I lack…direction. Everyone says so. I'm not interested in women anymore. I don't want to get laid. Or married. Also, I've given up my place in the family business and my family is freaked over that."

"You live here in Thunder Canyon?"

"No, in Midland, Texas. Or I did. I have a nice little spread outside of town there. But I've put my place up for sale. I'm moving. I just don't know where to yet. In the meantime, I'm here for a weeklong family reunion—a reunion that is going on right now, here at the resort, over at DJ's Rib Shack."

"I have another question, Jace."

"Shoot."

"Is there anything you *do* want?"

"That, Jocelyn Marie, is the question of the hour. Please come with me back to the Rib Shack."

She was running her finger around the rim of her drink again. "You didn't answer the question of the hour."

"All right. There is nothing that I want—except for you to come back to the Rib Shack with me."

Her smooth brow furrowed a little. "And I would want to go to *your* family reunion because?"

"Because only you can protect me from my family and all the women who want things from me that I'm not capable of giving them."

She shook that head of thick brown hair and sat straighter on her stool. "Before I decide whether to go with you or not, I need to get something crystal clear."

"Fine."

"I want you to listen very carefully, Jace."

He assumed a suitably intent expression. "I'm listening."

"I'm. Not. Going. To. Have. Sex. With. You."

"Oh, that." He waved a hand. "It's okay. I don't care about that."

"So you say now."

"Look, Joss, I like you. You're the first bright spot in

my life in months. I just want to hang around with you for a while. Have a few laughs. No pressure. No drama. Nothing hot and heavy. No big romance."

She stared at him for several seconds. Her expression said she still wasn't sure she believed him. Finally she asked, "So you want to be…friends? Honestly? Just friends?"

"My God, I would love that." He put some money on the bar. "The Rib Shack?"

She downed the last of her margarita. "Why not?"

Chapter 2

Joss surprised herself when she agreed to go with Jace.

But then, she got what he meant when he said that he *liked* her. She liked him, too. And not because he was tall and lean and handsome with thick, glossy dark hair and velvet-brown eyes. Not because he smelled of soap and a nice, clean, subtle, probably very expensive aftershave. Not because he was undeniably hot.

She didn't care about hot. Her life had pretty much crumbled to nothing a week before. Finding a hot guy— or any guy for that matter— was the last thing on her mind.

Jocelyn liked Jason because he made her laugh. Because, even though he carried himself like he owned the world, she could see in his eyes that he really was flummoxed by life, that he used to be one guy and now he wasn't that guy anymore. That he wasn't all that familiar with the guy he was now. Joss could relate to that kind of confusion. It was exactly the confusion she felt.

She entered the Rib Shack on Jace's arm. The casual, Western-themed restaurant was packed. Jason Traub, as it turned out, had a very large family.

"Jason, there you are," said a good-looking older woman with a slim figure and sleek light brown hair. "I was starting to wonder if you'd already left."

"No, Ma," Jace said, his charming smile not quite masking the wariness in his eyes. "I'm still here."

Jace's mother turned a bright glance on Joss. "Hello."

Jace made the introductions. Joss smiled and nodded at his mom, whose name was Claudia.

Claudia asked, "Do you live here in town, Jocelyn?"

"No, I'm from Sacramento."

Jace said, "Joss is staying here at the resort."

"With your family?" his mom quizzed. Claudia had that look, Joss thought, the look of a mother on the trail of every bit of information she could gather about the new girl her son had brought to the family party.

"I'm here on my own," Joss told her. "Having a great time, too. I love the spa. And the shopping in the resort boutiques. And I'm learning to play golf." All of it on Kenny Donovan's dime, thank you very much.

An ordinary-looking man a few years older than Jace's mom stepped up and took Claudia's arm. Claudia beamed at him, her golden-brown eyes glowing with affection. "Darling, this is Jocelyn, Jason's new friend. Jocelyn, my husband, Pete—we're staying here at the resort, too. A romantic getaway, just us two old folks in the Governor's Suite."

Joss was in the Honeymoon Suite, but she didn't say so. It would only be asking for more questions than she was prepared to answer at the moment—which was kind of amusing in a dark sort of way. She hadn't even hesitated to tell Jace that she'd run away from her own wedding. But somehow, with everyone else, well, she didn't want to go there. And she really appreciated that Jace was keeping his mouth shut about it.

He seemed like a great guy. And his parents were adorable, she thought. So much in love, so attentive to each other. There should be more couples in the world like Claudia and Pete.

Claudia said, "I hope you'll join us for dinner tomorrow night, Jocelyn. It will be at the home of Jason's twin, Jackson, and Jackson's wife, Laila. They have a nice little property not far from town."

"Yeah, you should come," Jace said with enthusiasm. "I'll take you."

Joss gave him a look that said he shouldn't push it and asked, "You have a twin?"

Claudia laughed. "A fraternal twin. Jackson is older by an hour and five minutes. That makes Jason my youngest son. I also have one daughter, Rose. She's the baby of the family. Dillon, Ethan and Corey are the older boys."

Joss did the math. "Wow, six kids. I'm jealous. I was an only child. My mother raised me on her own."

Claudia reached out and touched Joss's shoulder, a fond kind of touch. "Sweet girl," she said softly. And Joss felt all warm and fuzzy inside. "You come to dinner tomorrow night," Jace's mom said again. "We would love to have you join us."

"Thank you," Joss said, and left it at that.

A few moments later, Jace led her out onto the Rib Shack's patio where the band was set up but taking a break. They found a reasonably quiet corner where they could talk without having to shout.

"My mother likes you," Jace said.

"You say that like you're not sure if it's good or bad."

"Yeah, well, Ma thinks I got my heart broken and she really wants me to be happy. She's decided I only need to meet another woman, the *right* woman, so I can get married and settle down like my brothers and my sister. Now she'll be finding all kinds of ways to throw us together."

"We'll resist, of course."

"Of course we will."

"Who broke your heart, Jace?"

He hedged. "It's a long story."

"I told you mine," she teased.

He looked distinctly uncomfortable. "Well, you know, this isn't the place or the time."

She got the message. "You don't want to tell me— and you know what? That's okay."

"Whew." He made a show of wiping nonexistent sweat from his brow. "And even though I hate to give my mother the wrong idea about us, I think you ought to come to dinner at Jackson's tomorrow. You know, just to be social."

She gave him a slow look. She knew he was up to something.

And he was. He admitted, "I also want you there because I like you."

"Uh-huh. What else? Give it to me straight, Jace."

"Fair enough. If you come, everyone will think we're together—I mean *really* together, as in more than friends. And that means my family will stop trying to set me up."

"You want me to pretend to be your girlfriend?"

"You don't have to pretend anything. If you're with me, they'll assume there's something going on. It doesn't matter if you tell them that we're just friends. They won't believe you. It doesn't matter that *I* will tell them we're just friends. They'll only be certain we're in denial about all that we mean to each other."

"Still, it seems dishonest."

"Is it our fault if people insist on jumping to conclusions?"

Strangely, she found that she *wanted* to go to dinner at his brother's house. "I'll think about it."

"Good. And don't let my mother get you alone. She'll only start in about the family business and how she needs me in Midland and she hopes that *you* will be open to the idea of moving to Texas because she's already hearing wedding bells in our future."

"What *is* the family business anyway?"

"I didn't tell you? It's oil. Except for my oldest brother, Dillon, who's a doctor, we're all in oil."

She laughed. "Knee-deep?"

"All the way over our heads in it, trust me. We're Traub Oil Industries. I was a vice president in the Midland office. I quit the first of April. I was supposed to be out of there by the end of May. My mother and Pete kept finding reasons why I had to stay. I finally escaped just this past Wednesday. I'm never going back."

"You sound determined."

"Believe me, I am."

"How come you call your dad Pete?"

"He's my stepdad. My father, Charles, was something of a legend in the oil business. He died in an accident on a rig when I was little. My mom married Pete about two years later. Her last name is Wexler now. None of us were happy when she married him. We were loyal to our dad and we resented Pete."

"We?"

"My brothers, my sister and I. But Pete's not only a good man, he's also a patient one. He won all of us over eventually. Pete had a heart attack a couple of years ago. We almost lost him. That really taught us how much he means to us."

"It's so obvious he's head over heels in love with your mom."

"Yes, he is. A man like that is damn hard to hate." He took her arm. "Come on, I want you to meet my brothers."

They wandered back inside. Joss met Dillon and Ethan and Corey and Jace's twin, Jackson. The two did look a lot alike—meaning tall, dark and handsome. But it wasn't the least difficult to tell them apart. Joss also met the Traub boys' only sister, Rose, and Rose's husband, Austin, and she visited with the wives of Jason's brothers. She liked them all, with Lizzie, Ethan's wife, possibly being her favorite.

Lizzie Traub was tall and sturdily built, with slightly wild-looking dark blond hair and a no-nonsense way about her. She owned a bakery, the Mountain Bluebell, in town. Everyone said that Lizzie baked the best muffins in Montana.

And beyond Jace's brothers and sister and their spouses, there were Traub cousins, too: DJ and Dax and their wives Allaire and Shandie. And also Clay and Forrest Traub, two cowboys from Rust Creek Falls, which was about three hundred miles from Thunder Canyon. Joss was starting to wonder how she was going to keep all their names straight when a woman named Melba Landry, who was Lizzie Traub's great-aunt, caught up with them. A big woman with a stern face, Melba possessed a truly impressive bosom. Joss tried not to laugh as the energetic old woman cornered Jace and insisted she wanted to see him at her church the next morning.

"Of course he'll come," Joss told Melba. "There's nothing Jace enjoys more than a good Sunday service."

Beside her, Jace made a low groaning sound.

And Melba turned her sharp hazel eyes on Joss. "Excellent. I want to see you there, too, young lady."

"Well, now, I don't exactly know if I—"

"We'll be there," Jace promised. Joss elbowed him in the ribs, but he didn't relent.

Aunt Melba said, "Wonderful. The service begins at ten." And she sailed off to corner some other unsuspecting potential churchgoer.

The party continued. It really was fun. Joss forgot her troubles and just had a good time. She spotted Theresa Duvall dancing with a tall, lean cowboy, one of Jace's cousins from Rust Creek Falls. Theresa clung to that cowboy like paint. She didn't seem the least upset that things hadn't worked out for her with Jace.

Joss and Jace danced. He was a good dancer. Plus, he kept to their agreement about just being friends. He didn't hold her too close. She swayed in his arms and thought how good it felt to be held by him. His body and hers just kind of fit together. He was a great guy and if things were different she would definitely be attracted to him. Really, the longer they danced, the more she started thinking that she wouldn't mind at all if he did hold her closer....

But no. That wouldn't be a good idea. The last thing she needed right now was a new man in her life. She liked Jace as a person, but still. He *was* a man. All man. And she wasn't trusting any man. Not now.

Not for a long, long time, if ever.

It was after ten when the party broke up. She and Jace were among the last to leave. They wandered out to the lobby together and then kind of naturally turned for the elevators side-by-side.

The Honeymoon Suite was on the top floor. The doors opened and they left the elevator.

At the door, she paused, key card in hand. "If I let you in, you have to promise not to put a move on me."

He looked hurt. "Joss, come on. How many ways can I tell you? I need a friend. You need a friend. That's what we've got going on here. It's *all* we've got going on here."

She chewed her lower lip for a moment. "All right. I believe you." And then she stuck her key in the slot and pushed the door wide.

He followed her in, through the skylit foyer area into the living/dining room, which had floor-to-ceiling windows with a spectacular view. "Nice."

"Hey, only the best for Kenny Donovan's runaway bride." She headed for the wet bar. "How about a little champagne and caviar? On Kenny, of course."

"Got a beer?"

She gave him one from the fridge and grabbed a ginger ale for herself. "Make yourself at home." He took a fat leather easy chair and she shucked off her shoes and curled up on the sofa.

And they talked. About his family. About the party

at the Rib Shack. About how they both thought Lizzie was great and how Lizzie's aunt Melba cracked them up.

"So how long are you here for?" he asked.

She thought how much she liked his voice. It was deep and warm and made her want to cuddle up against him—which she was *not*, under any circumstances, going to do. Ever. "Another week. As long as Kenny doesn't put a stop on his platinum card, I am having my whole two-week un-honeymoon."

"And then?"

"Back to Sacramento. To find a job. And a new place to live."

"We have so much in common," he said. "I'm here for a week, too."

"You told me. The family reunion. And then after that?"

"I suppose I'll have to get a life. But I'm not even going to think about that yet."

"Jace, I like the way you completely avoid anything remotely resembling responsibility. Aunt Melba would *so* not approve."

"Thank you, Joss. I do my best." He tipped his longneck at her. "I'm glad we're friends. Let's be *best* friends."

"All right. I'm up for that."

"Best friends for a week," he declared.

She held up her index finger and reminded him, "No benefits."

He looked at her from under his thick dark brows. "You know you're killin' me here. Have I, in any way, put any kind of move on you?"

"Nope, not a one."

"Then can we be done with the constant reminders about how I'm not supposed to try and get you naked?"

She saluted him with a hand to her forehead. "You got it. I believe you. You are not going to make any attempt whatsoever to get into my pants. Even if you *are* a man."

"Your trust is deeply touching."

The phone rang. It was on the side table next to the sofa, so she reached over and picked it up. "What?"

"Jocelyn, honestly. Is that any way to answer the phone?"

Without even thinking about it, Joss lowered her feet to the rug and sat up straighter. "Mom, hey." She ran a hand back through her hair. "What's up?"

"How can you ask me that? You know I'm worried sick about you."

"I'm fine. Really. Don't worry."

"When are you coming home?"

"I told you. A week from tomorrow." She sent Jace a sheepish glance and mouthed the word *Sorry*.

He shrugged to let her know it wasn't a big deal. Then he got up and went over to the wall of windows. He stood gazing out. She indulged in a long, slow look at him, from his fancy tooled boots, up over his lean legs and hips in crisp denim, his wide shoulders in a beautifully tailored midnight-blue Western shirt. His hair was thick and dark. She had no doubt it would be silky to the touch.

A great-looking guy. And a considerate one. It was kind of him to pretend to admire the view to give her the space she needed to take this unwelcome call. There ought to be more guys in the world like him.

Her mom said, "This is all just a big misunderstanding. You realize that, don't you? Kenny would never—"

"Mom." She struggled to keep her voice calm and even. "I *saw* him with Kimberly. There was no misunderstanding what I saw."

"Kimberly is terribly upset, too. She's hurt you would think such horrible, cruel things about her."

"Oh, please. Don't get me started on Kimberly. I don't want to talk about this anymore, Mom. I really don't."

"Kenny came to see me this evening."

Joss gasped. "He *what*?" She must have said it kind of loud because Jace glanced back at her, those sexy dark eyes full of concern. She shook her head at him. He turned to face the window again and she told her mother, "He has no right to bother you. None. Ever again."

"Honey, he's not bothering me. He loves you. He wants to work things out with you. He's crushed that you left him at the altar the way you did. You've humiliated him, but still, he forgives you and only wants to work things out so you two can be together as you were meant to be."

There was a crystal bowl full of expensive chocolates on the coffee table. Joss resisted the blinding urge to grab it and fling it at the far wall. "Mom, listen. Listen carefully. I am not going to get back together with Kenny. Ever. He and I are done. Finished. As over as it gets."

"If only your father hadn't left us. You wouldn't be so mistrustful of men. You wouldn't ruin the best chance you're ever going to get with a good man who will give you the kind of life you deserve."

She replied through clenched teeth. "There are so many ways I don't know how to respond to that."

"Just come home, honey. Come home right away."

"Mom, I'm hanging up now. I love you very much and I'll be home in a week."

"Jocelyn. Jocelyn, wait…"

But Joss didn't wait. She hung up the phone. And then she stared at it hard, *daring* it to ring again.

But apparently, her mother had come to her senses at least minimally and decided to leave awful enough alone.

For tonight anyway.

At the window, Jace turned. "Bad?"

She covered her face with her hands. "Yeah, beyond bad."

He left the window and came to her, walking softly in those fancy boots of his. She only heard his approach because she was listening for it. "Want to talk about it?"

"Ugh."

"Come on."

She lowered her hands and met his waiting eyes. He was standing across the coffee table from her, his hands in his pockets, accepting of whatever she might say, willing to listen. Ready to understand. She tipped her head at the cushion beside her. He took her invitation, crossing around the low table, dropping down next to her, stretching his arm out along the back of the couch in an invitation of his own.

An invitation she couldn't pass up at that moment. With a sad little sigh, she leaned her head on his shoulder. He smoothed her hair, but only lightly, and then draped his big arm around her.

It was a nice moment. Comforting. He was so large

and warm and solid. And he smelled so clean and manly. And she really needed a strong shoulder to lean on. Just for a minute or two.

She said, "That was my mom."

"Yeah, I got that much."

"I told you she raised me on her own, didn't I?"

"You mentioned that, yeah."

"My dad disappeared when I was two. My mom says he just told her he was through one day and walked out. We never heard from him again."

"That's rough, Joss. Really rough." He squeezed her shoulder, a touch that comforted, that seemed to acknowledge how hard it had been for her. "It can really mess with your mind, to lose your dad when you're only a kid. It can leave you feeling like you're on the outside looking in—at all your friends and their happy, *whole* families. You grow up knowing what normal is. It's what all the *other* kids have."

She realized he was speaking from personal experience. "How old were you when your dad died?"

"Jackson and I were six."

"So at least you knew him, your dad."

"Kind of. He was always working, making his mark on the world, you could say. But yeah, we all looked up to him with stars in our eyes. We felt safe, just knowing he was our dad. He was one of those guys who really fills up a room. Rose always claims it was worse for her than for us boys. She never knew him—well, at least she doesn't remember him. She was two when he was killed."

"Same age I was when my dad left. And I don't remember him either. All I have is the...absence of him." She pulled away enough to meet Jace's eyes. "You really don't need to hear this. You're sweet to be so understanding, but it's old news and it's got nothing to do with you."

He reached for her, pulled her back down to him. She started to resist, but then, well, why not, if he was willing to listen? She gave in and sagged against him, settling her head against his shoulder again—and yeah, she'd promised herself she would never cuddle up with him. But this wasn't cuddling. This was only leaning. And there was nothing wrong with a little leaning when a girl needed comfort from a friend.

"Keep talkin'," he said. "What's your mom's name?"

"RaeEllen. Her maiden name was Louvacek, but she kept my father's name, never changed it back. She always said she only wanted a good guy to stand by her. But I don't think she went looking after my dad left. It was like she…gave up when it came to men. She never dated when I was growing up, not that I can remember. She worked at Safeway, eventually moving up to managing her own store, which she still does to this day. And she took care of me. She was a good mom, a strict mom. And she always wanted the best for me. To her, Kenny seemed like a dream come true."

"So for some reason, she decided she could trust the cheater?"

"He was always good to her—kissing up to her really, it seems to me, in hindsight. When she would have us over for dinner, he would bring her flowers every time and fall all over her praising her cooking. And she knew how well he was doing at work, getting promotions, one after the other. She just…bought Kenny's act, hook, line and sinker. She refuses to believe that the thing with Kimberly even happened. Kenny's convinced her that I've blown an 'innocent encounter' all out of proportion."

"Convinced her? You're saying she's *speaking* to him, after what he did to you?"

"Because she doesn't believe he did anything bad, I guess she figures she's got no reason *not* to speak to him."

"She's your mom and I won't speak ill of her. But I will say she ought to get her loyalties straight."

"Hah, I wish. When it comes to Kenny, she's got on her rose-colored glasses and I've yet to convince her she really needs to take them off. I try to see it from her point of view. She finally decided to give another man a break, to trust Kenny—for my sake. And now she just can't bear to admit she got it wrong again."

"I guess it's understandable," Jace said. "But still. You're her daughter. She should be backing you up."

"Yeah, I wish. You know how I told you I had doubts about Kenny before I caught him with Kimberly?"

"I remember."

"Well, I went to my mom and confided in her. I told her that Kenny wasn't the guy I loved anymore, that sometimes I felt like I didn't even know him, he was so different from who he used to be. She was the one who convinced me my fears were groundless, that I only had a very normal case of pre-wedding jitters, that Kenny was a wonderful man and it was all going to be fine."

Jace touched her hair again, gently, an easing kind of touch. "So your judgment about the guy was solid. And your mom couldn't—and still can't—let herself see the truth. I'm betting she'll get the picture in time."

"I hope so."

"And the main thing is that you didn't go through

with it. You had the guts to turn and walk away. You're a strong woman. And you're going to be fine."

Joss could have stayed in Jace's arms all night. But she'd had her head on his shoulder for several minutes now—too long really. She needed to pull herself together, no matter how good it felt to lean on him.

She sat up and retreated to her end of the sofa. That time, he didn't try to stop her, and she was glad that he didn't. If she was going to have a man for a friend—even just for a week—it was nice to think he was the kind of guy who would know when to put his arm around her.

And when to let her go.

"Mostly," she said, "I think I'm doing pretty well, you know?"

He gave her a slow nod, his dark eyes steady on hers.

"I tell myself I'm getting past what happened last Saturday. But every time my mom calls, she just brings the whole mess into painful focus all over again. Her blindness to the reality of the situation makes me see way too clearly what a huge mistake I made." She held up her thumb and forefinger, with just a sliver of space between them. "I got this close to marrying a guy who cheated on me on our wedding day—and with my own cousin, no less."

"But you *didn't* marry him. Focus on that, Joss."

She braced her elbow on the sofa arm and rested her chin on her hand. "You're right, I didn't. But I did quit my job for that rotten, no-good cheater. I gave up my cute apartment. When I go home, I'll be starting all over again."

"Maybe you can get your job back."

"Maybe I can. We'll see." She straightened her spine.

What she wanted right now was a long bath accompanied by an equally long, totally self-indulgent crying jag. "Thank you for listening—and I need to stop whining."

He gave her a slightly crooked smile. "I have the strangest feeling you're giving me the boot." He picked up his beer from the coffee table and downed the last of it.

"It's only, well, lately talking to my mom really brings me down." She tried to think of something snappy and charming to say, so they could end the evening on a happier note. But right then, she was all out of snappy, totally bereft of charming.

He rose. "It's the great thing about a best friend. Even a best friend for a week. You don't have to explain anything. All you have to say is good night."

Jace thought about Joss all the way out to Jackson and Laila's place.

He hoped she was okay. And he hoped he'd done the right thing by leaving when she asked him to.

What else could he have done? She'd had that look. Like all she wanted was to get into bed—alone—and pull the covers up over head. He'd figured the best thing he could do for her right then was to get lost.

Jackson and Laila had ten beautiful, wooded acres with a big two-story farmhouse, a barn and a paddock where they kept a few horses. When Jace pulled up in front of the house, the lights were off upstairs. But through the shut blinds of the front room's picture window, Jace could make out the faint glow of the flatscreen TV. He figured he would find his brother in there, channel-surfing, waiting up.

Jace was right.

Jackson sat in his favorite recliner, the mutt he and Laila had adopted from the animal shelter snoozing at his feet. Jace entered the room and Jackson turned off the TV. "Beer?"

"No, thanks." Jace dropped into the other recliner and popped out the footrest. "Good party at the Rib Shack."

Jackson grunted. "Ethan get after you?"

"Yeah."

"He thinks he's going to talk you into coming in with us."

"It's not gonna happen."

"Yeah." Jackson set the remote on the table by his chair. "I told him that. More than once. But you know how he can be when he gets an idea in his head."

Jace closed his eyes. He felt comfortable. Easy. It was always like that with him and Jackson. Even when they fought—which they used to do a lot when they were younger—there was a certain understanding between them. They didn't need a lot of words. They just accepted each other.

The mutt's collar jangled as he scratched himself. The dog's name was Einstein. He wasn't much to look at, but Jackson claimed he was really smart.

Jackson said, "You know, I thought you said you'd sworn off women. But you're in Thunder Canyon barely twenty-four hours and already you've got a girl."

"No, I don't." Jace gave the denial in an easy tone, knowing his brother wouldn't believe him.

"Shame on you, Jason. Lying to your own twin brother."

"Joss is great. I liked her the first minute I saw her. But it's not like that. We're just friends."

Jackson chuckled. "Yeah, and if you think I believe that, I've got some oceanfront property in Kansas to sell you."

"I mean it. We're friends. She's here for another week. I'll be hanging around with her if she'll put up with me, but nothing's going to happen between us."

"Hey, whatever you say. I'm just glad to see you taking an interest in a woman again. And she seems like a great girl to me. Laila liked her, too. So did Ma."

Jace made a low noise that could have meant anything and hid his smile. His family—including his twin—were all so predictable. He showed up with a woman at his side, and they couldn't believe there was nothing but friendship going on.

Which suited him just fine.

Jackson spoke again, gruffly this time. "And it's good, that you came back to Montana finally."

Jace knew he'd hurt his brother's feelings by not coming to Thunder Canyon over the holidays—and worse, he hadn't been there for Jackson and Laila's Valentine's Day wedding.

Time to try and get that behind them. "I'm sorry, Jackson, that I didn't come for the holidays when you invited me. And missing your wedding? That was the worst. I know it was wrong of me not to be there."

Jackson didn't answer for a full sixty seconds at least. Finally, he grunted. "I was pretty miffed at the time— especially that you didn't show to be my best man. But I'm over it."

Jace confessed, "I didn't know my ass from up for a while there. I didn't come at Christmas because of Tricia." He said her name and waited to feel miserable. Instead, he realized, he felt perfectly okay. Apparently, he really was putting all that behind him. "The last thing Tricia said she wanted was to 'head for the sticks over the holidays'—her words, not mine. I didn't even argue with her. I was gone, gone, gone. It was 'Whatever Tricia wants, Tricia gets,' as far as I was concerned. And then it all went to hell. For a couple of months after New Year's, I was operating strictly on autopilot. I went to work and I went home. Then you and Laila decided you wanted a Valentine's Day wedding. I was a mess. I just wasn't up for it."

"Sounds like you're better off without Tricia Lavelle."

"I am. A lot better off. I see that now. But at the time, I was one-hundred-percent certain it was the real thing with her. You know how I've always been. Not a guy who ever gets serious over any woman. So when I actually thought it was love, I went for it. All the way. How wrong could I get? It was a rude awakening when it ended, let me tell you."

"Rough, huh?"

"Bad love will do it to you every time—not that it *was* love. Not that I even have a clue what love is."

Jackson slid him a cautious glance. "The whole family kind of wonders if you're really over her yet."

Jace tried to picture Tricia's face in his mind. Somehow, the image wouldn't quite take form. And then he thought of Joss—her great laugh, how much fun it was just to talk to her, those big brown eyes and all that gorgeous cinnamon-shot coffee-colored hair. He had no trouble picturing his new best friend at all. "Oh, yeah," he told his twin. "I'm over Tricia. I'm ready for a brand-new start."

Jackson chuckled. "Good. You quit your job and you don't want to live in Midland anymore, so it looks to me like a new start is exactly what you're going to get."

Chapter 3

The phone by the bed was ringing.

With a groan of protest, Joss lifted her head from the pillow and squinted at the bedside clock. Nine-fifteen in the morning. Not what you'd call early. Unless you'd lain wide awake until the wee hours, stewing over your bad choices, angry at your mother, wondering what you were going to do with your life....

And the phone was still ringing.

Surely, eventually, it would cycle back to the front desk, because she didn't want to answer it. Who could it be except her mother calling to beg her to come back to Kenny—or Kenny calling to demand she stop being "petty" and quit making such a big deal over a tiny little incident that had meant exactly nothing?

Hah.

She reached over and grabbed the phone and barked

into it, "I do not want to hear another word about it. Do you understand?"

The voice of her new best friend answered, "Aunt Melba is going to be disappointed. You know she was really looking forward to seeing you in church."

Joss dragged herself to a sitting position and swiped her tangled hair back off her face. "Ugh. And wait a minute. Did I actually tell her I would be there?"

"No," Jace admitted. "You hedged. Aunt Melba assumed. *I* said you'd be there."

"So thoughtful of you to make my commitments for me."

"Did I mention I brought coffee?"

"Brought? Where *are* you?"

"Waiting in the hallway outside your door."

She grinned. She couldn't stop herself. "That is so not fair."

"Vanilla latte. Just sayin'."

"All right, all right. You sold me." She hung up, grabbed her robe and belted it as she hurried to let him in. When she opened the door, he held out the tall Starbucks cup. She took it, sipped and gestured him inside, shutting the door and then leaning back against it with a sigh. "Yum. Thank you."

"You're welcome." He gave her one of those knock-your-socks-off smiles of his. Really, he was looking great, freshly showered and shaved, in a different pair of expensive boots, tan slacks, a button-down shirt and a nicely cut sport coat.

She grumbled, "At least *someone* got a good night's sleep."

He took in her blenderized hair, the robe, her bare feet—and her grumpy expression. "Sorry to wake you up."

"No, you're not."

"You're right. I'm not." He took her shoulders, turned her around and pointed her toward the bedroom. "Go on. Get ready. We don't want to be late. Aunt Melba would never forgive us."

"Who's this 'we,' cowboy?" She muttered over her shoulder. But she went. And she took her latte with her.

Twenty minutes later, she emerged feeling church-ready in a pink silk blouse and an oyster-white skirt, with a favorite pair of low-heeled slingbacks in a slightly lighter pink than the blouse. She'd pinned her hair up loosely and worn the pearl earrings her mom had given her when she graduated from high school.

Jace said, "You look amazing."

She realized she felt better. A lot better. Jace seemed to have that effect on her. He cheered her up, had her looking on the bright side, thinking that something exciting and fun could be happening any minute. She grabbed her pink purse and off they went.

Thunder Canyon Community Church, Jace explained, was in what the locals called Old Town, with its narrower, tree-lined streets and buildings that had stood since pioneer times.

Joss loved the church on sight. It was, to her, the perfect little white clapboard church, with tall windows all along the sides and a single spire in front that housed the bell tower. A mature box elder tree shaded the church steps and the small square of front lawn.

The doors into the reception area stood wide as the church bell finished chiming. Inside, the organist was playing something suitably reverent, yet inviting. People smiled and said hello. Melba was there, wearing a blue flowered dress and a little blue hat, standing guard over the open guestbook. She greeted them with an approving smile and showed them where to sign.

Joss signed her name and "Sacramento, California," for her address. She felt a little tug of glumness, to be reminded that she didn't have a place to call her own anymore, that all her household possessions were packed up in boxes and stacked in a rented storage unit, waiting for her to figure out what to do with her life.

But the glumness quickly passed when Jace took her arm. They entered the sanctuary and the organ music swelled louder. The sun shone in the tall windows and Jace's brother Ethan signaled them up to a pew near the front. Lizzie, on Ethan's other side, leaned across her husband to greet them as they sat down.

The service was as lovely and comforting as the little white church itself. Joss even knew the words to a couple of the hymns. The pleasant-faced pastor gave a sermon on God's grace, and somehow all of Joss's problems seemed insignificant, workable. Just part of life.

After the service, Lizzie reminded them that she would love to treat them to free muffins at her bakery. Meanwhile, Ethan said he wanted Jace to take a tour of his Thunder Canyon office building.

Jace said, "No, thanks. Gotta go," and herded Joss toward the exit.

Melba was at her post by the guestbook. She told them how glad she was that they had come. "And I want to see you both at the Historical Society Museum very soon. I've been helping out there several times a week. Thunder Canyon is a fascinating place with a rich history. While you're in town, you might as well learn something."

Joss only smiled and nodded. Jace ended up promising he would drop by the museum soon.

From the church, they went over to Lizzie's bakery, where they split a complimentary blueberry muffin and each had a ham and egg croissant and a tall glass of fresh-squeezed orange juice. Jace seemed to know everyone. He introduced her to a guy named Connor McFarlane and his wife, Tori, who was pregnant and just starting to show. Tori taught at the high school. Connor was not only the heir to the McFarlane House hotel chain, but he was also a major investor in the resort.

Joss also met Grant Clifton, his wife, Stephanie, and their little boy, AJ. The child was seventeen months old and adorable, with golden curls and a sunny smile. Stephanie let Joss hold him. He was so sweet and friendly, dimpling at her, laying his plump little hand against her cheek, even leaning his blond head on her shoulder. Joss gave him back to his mom with a little tug of regret. She wished she could have several little ones just like him.

Maybe someday…

Grant Clifton seemed vaguely familiar. When he explained that he managed the resort, Joss realized she'd seen him behind the front desk once and another time at the resort's best restaurant, the Gallatin Room.

That was the great thing about a small town like this one, Joss thought. You could get to know almost everyone. And when you walked down the street, people just naturally smiled and said hi.

After they left the bakery, Jace took her hand. They started strolling west down Main Street, enjoying the sunshine, looking in the windows of the quaint little shops. It felt good to have her hand in his. Really good. Maybe *too* good.

She let him lead her along for another block before she realized they were going the wrong direction and hung back. "Hey, wait a minute. Your car's that way." She pointed over her shoulder. They'd left his fancy SUV back near the church.

"So? It's not going anywhere." He tugged on her hand. "Come on, I want to show you the Hitching Post—you know, that great old bar and restaurant I told you about yesterday?"

She eased her fingers from his grip. "Right, the one where you hooked up with Theresa Duvall."

He stood there on the corner, his dark hair showing glints of bronze in the sun, and looked at her reproach-fully. "What did I do?"

She hung her head and stared down at her pretty pink slingbacks. "Not a thing. Sorry, that was low."

"Yeah, it was. But I'll get over it. Hey, look at me."

Reluctantly, she raised her head. His eyes gleamed. With just a look, he made her want to smile at him. But she didn't.

On that corner was a homey-looking restaurant with flowered café curtains in the windows. The restaurant was closed. He stepped into the alcove by the door and tipped his head at her, signaling her to join him.

"We can't stand here on the corner forever," she groused, as an older couple walked past her and went on across the street.

He chuckled. "*We're* not standing on the corner. *You* are." He waved her into the alcove with him. "Come on. Come here…"

Reluctantly, she went. "What?"

He whispered in her ear, "I love the Hitching Post."

"Whoop-de-do." She spun her index finger in the air.

"Joss, about your attitude?"

"Yeah?"

"Lighten up."

She knew he had a point. "Okay, okay. So why do you love the Hitching Post?"

He sat on the wide window ledge next to the door. "Good memories, that's why. When I was a kid, we always used to go there every time we came to town. My dad would take us. We'd get burgers and fries and milkshakes on the restaurant side, where they allowed kids, and it was a special thing, with all of us together, with my dad relaxed and really *with* us, you know, focused on the family? He used to call us his little mavericks. I thought that was so cool. It seems to me that we went to the Hitching Post often, even though I know that we couldn't have. I was only six when he died. And we only got to visit Thunder Canyon now and then in the summer. But I do remember clearly that on our last visit here before he died, my dad took me to the Hitching Post alone, the two of us. For some reason, Jackson didn't even get to come. It was just me and my dad and I was the happiest kid on the planet." He rose from the window ledge. His eyes holding hers, he took a few stray strands of her hair and guided them back behind her ear. A small shiver cascaded through her and she wanted to move even closer to him—at the same time as she knew she ought to step back.

"Okay," she said softly. "I get it now—why that place is so special to you."

"Good." His caressing tone hovered somewhere on the border between gentle and intimate. "I mean, nothing against Theresa, but she's not what I think about when the Hitching Post comes to mind."

Joss felt rotten, and not only for razzing him about Theresa. There was also the uncomfortable fact that she was starting to wonder what it might feel like to kiss him. Plus, she was flat-out envious of him.

He had a great big, terrific family. And he'd had a dad, a *real* dad, until he was six, a dad who hadn't left him willingly. Then, when he lost his dad, he'd gotten kind Pete Wexler as a stepdad. Her dad, on the other hand, had walked out before she even had a chance to know him. Her family consisted of her and her mom and right now, her mom only lectured her.

He was grinning again. "So come on, let's go to the Hitching Post."

"I don't know. It's past noon. Maybe I should just go back up to the resort."

His grin faded. He blew out a breath. "Okay, Joss. what's up with you?"

"I just… I feel low now, that's all."

"Why? A few minutes ago you seemed to be having a great time."

"I was."

"So what happened? You realized you were having too much fun?"

She opened her mouth to tell him how off-base he was, but then she saw that he might actually have a point. "I keep thinking I can't just hang around in Montana doing nothing forever."

"You're right, but there's no problem. You're only hanging around in Montana doing nothing for another week. Then you can go back home and knock yourself out finding another job and a new apartment."

Now she felt hurt. Really, her emotions were all over the map today. "How can you make a joke of it, Jace? It's not a joke."

"I know it's not." He said the words gently. And then he asked, "Are you bored?"

"No!" She wasn't. Not in the least. "Are you kidding? I'm having a great time—or I was, just like you said, until a few minutes ago. And then, I don't know, all at once I felt low and cranky."

Jace stuffed his hands in his pockets. And then he just stood there next to the glass-topped, café-curtained door of the closed restaurant, watching her, waiting.

She busted herself. "Okay, my life's a mess. And right now, I feel guilty about it. I mean, at least up at the resort I'm busy being defiant, you know? Having my un-honeymoon, hating all men. But here, with you..." She didn't know quite how to explain it.

Jace did it for her. "Here, with me, you're having a good time. And you don't feel you have the right to have a good time. And not only are you having a good time when you don't have the right to, but you're also having it with a *man*." He widened his eyes and spoke in a spooky half whisper. "A man you just met...yesterday." She didn't know whether to laugh or punch him in the arm. Then he put on a look of pretend disapproval. "Face it, Joss. Your mother would never approve."

"This is not about my mother." She said it with way too much heat. "And I really, well, I just want to go back to the resort now. Please."

He gave her a long look. And then he nodded. "All right, but would you do one little favor for me first?"

She resisted the sudden need to tap her foot. "Fine. What?"

"The Town Square's back there about two blocks. It's that small park we passed after we left the bakery?"

"I remember it. What about it?"

"We'll stop there, sit on a bench under a tree and talk a little bit more. And then I'll take you back up Thunder Mountain."

She folded her arms across her middle and looked at him sideways. "Talk about what?"

"I don't know. The weather, the Dallas Cowboys, the meaning of life…"

"Oh, very funny."

"We'll just talk, that's all, about whatever subject pops into our heads. And not for long, I promise. Half an hour, max. Then it's back to the resort for you."

She accused, "I know you're going to try and make me feel better about everything. Don't deny it."

"I wouldn't dream of denying it. Yes, Jocelyn Marie, the ugly truth is I am going to try and make you feel better. That is my evil plan. So what do you say? The Town Square? A measly little half hour of your time?"

He didn't wait for her answer, but only reached for her hand again.

The little park was a lovely, grassy, tree-shaded place. They found a bench under a willow, the drooping branches like a veil, hiding them from the rest of the world.

"Nice, huh?" he asked her, after brushing a few leaves off the bench seat and gallantly gesturing for her to sit first. She did, smoothing her skirt under her, crossing her legs and folding her hands around her knee. He dropped down next to her. "Kind of private. If we whisper, no one will even know we're here."

She laughed. He really was so charming. "How *old* are you, ten?"

"Only at heart. Tell me a secret."

She gave him a deadpan stare. "You first."

He thought it over, shrugged. "Once I kissed a toad."

"Eeww. Why?"

"Jackson dared me. He was always a troublemaker. And I was his second banana, you know? He would come up with these wild-ass ideas and I felt honor-bound to go along. But then, somehow, if there was something gross involved, he would always manage to get me to go first. Then he would mock me. Once I kissed the toad, he told me I was going to get warts on my lips."

"Oh, that's just mean."

"He could be, yeah. But he's also…the best, you know?"

"How?"

"He'd take a bullet for me. For anyone in the family. That's how he is. You can count on him. Even in the old days, when you never knew what stunt he was going to pull next, you always knew he had your back."

"So you're saying he's settled down, then—from the days when he made you kiss that toad?"

Jace nodded. "He was the bad boy of the family. He drank too much and he chased women and he swore that no female was ever going to hogtie him. But then he met Laila. She changed his tune right quick. Now he's got a ring on his finger and contentment in his heart. I've never seen him as happy as he is now." He studied her face. His gaze was warm. She thought how she was kind of glad he'd insisted they come here before he took her back up the mountain, how being with him really did lift her spirits. "Your turn," he said. "Cough up that secret."

"I always wanted to get married," she heard herself say. "Ever since I was little. I wanted…a real family. I wanted the family I never had. A man I could love and trust. Several kids. Growing up, it was always so quiet at home, with just my mom and me. My mom likes things tidy. I learned early to clean up after myself. So our small house was neat and orderly, with a hushed kind of feeling about it. I dreamed of one of those big, old Craftsman-style houses, with the pillars in front and the wide, deep front porch—you know the kind?"

"I do."

"I dreamed of bikes on their sides on the front lawn, of toys all over the living room floor, of spilled milk and crayon drawings scrawled in bright colors on the walls, because the children who lived there were rambunctious and adventurous and couldn't resist a whole wall to color on. I dreamed of a bunch of laughing, crying, screaming, chattering kids, everybody talking over everybody else, of music on the stereo and the TV on too loud. And I saw myself in the middle of all of it, loving every minute of it. Me, *the Mom.* And I saw my husband coming in the door and stepping over the scattered toys to take me in his arms after a hard day's work. I pictured him kissing me, a real, hot, toe-curling kiss, the kind that would make our older kids groan and tell us to get a room."

"Wow," he said. "That's a lot better secret than kissing a toad."

A leaf drifted down into her lap. She brushed it away and confessed, "I always felt guilty about my dream for my life, you know? My mom did the best she could. But all I wanted was to grow up and get out of there, to find my steady, patient, good-natured guy and start having a whole bunch of rowdy kids."

"Joss." He touched her hair again, so lightly, guiding a hank of it back over her shoulder. "I'm beginning to think there is altogether too much guilt going on in your head."

"Yeah, probably. But my mom tried so hard, she *worked* so hard, to do right by me, to make a good life for me."

"Just because you dreamed of a different way to be a mom doesn't make your mom's way bad."

She gave a low chuckle. "You amaze me, you know that?"

"In a good way, I hope."

"In a great way. When I met you I thought you were just another hot guy trying to get laid. But instead, you're a shrink and a philosopher, with a little Mahatma Gandhi thrown in for good measure."

He arched one of those thick, dark eyebrows. "Just don't tell Jackson, okay? Not the part about Mahatma Gandhi anyway. He would never let me live it down."

She uncrossed her legs, folded her hands tightly in her lap and stared miserably down at them. "I have another secret. A bad one."

He teased, "*Really* bad?"

"Yeah, really stinkin' bad. I'm beyond embarrassed to admit it."

He didn't say anything. He just waited, not pushing her.

So she told him. "For the first two days I was here, staying at the resort, I was fully planning to work things out with Kenny, take him back and marry him anyway, in spite of what he did with Kimberly in the coat room." She paused, waiting for him to say how he couldn't believe she would ever give a jerk like that another chance.

But he only sat there, waiting, his expression unreadable, giving her a chance to tell him the rest.

So, grimly, she continued. "Within an hour after I ran from the church, I was already thinking of how I was only going to make Kenny suffer for a while, make him grovel at my feet and beg me to give him another chance. And then, once he'd admitted what a complete jackass he'd been, once he'd sworn never to do anything like that again, I would take him back. I was thinking that he could give me that big Craftsman house I wanted. I was thinking that with him, I could afford to have all those kids. I was thinking that I had chosen him and been with him for five whole years because he was the one to help me live my dream. I told myself all that, even though long before the wedding day, I already knew very well that he wasn't the sweet guy he used to be, that he'd changed, become a smug jerk I didn't even like being around. But still, I had bought my mom's pep talk and gone ahead with the wedding anyway. Because I'm almost thirty and if I didn't settle for Kenny, I might never find anyone better." Deeply ashamed, Joss fell silent.

Jace was silent, too, sitting there beside her on the bench under the drooping branches of the willow tree. Somewhere in the little park, she heard children laughing.

A child called, "Mama!"

And a mother answered, "Right here!"

"Watch me swing high!" the child commanded.

"I'm here. I'm watching...."

Jace asked, "So what changed your mind?"

She'd come this far. She might as well admit the rest. "Kenny failed to grovel. He called six times those first two days. And every time he called, it was only to say the things he said yesterday—you know, in the Lounge, when you overheard me talking to him? He self-righteously explained to me that *I* was being unreasonable, that *I* had completely humiliated *him*, that *I* had it all wrong. That there was nothing between him and Kimberly and I ought to realize there wasn't and quit acting like *I'm* the one who got messed over." She crossed her legs again. "By the end of the second day, I finally had to admit that there was no salvaging things with Kenny, that it was Over, capital *O*, and I was going to need to make myself a whole new life."

"So…would you take him back now, if he wised up and was honestly sorry for cheating on you, if he got down on his knees and swore you were the only woman for him? If he promised he would never even look at another woman again, that he would do anything—*anything*—for one more chance with you?"

She didn't even have to think about it. "No way. I'm through with him. Done. That ship has sailed. It's as Over as Over gets."

He stood. "Well, all right, then." He held down his hand to her.

She stared at those long, tanned fingers of his, puzzled. "What?"

"I'll take you back to the resort now."

A certain wistfulness curled through her. She tipped her head back to look up at him. "Now you want to get rid of me. You're disappointed in me."

"Hell, no. I think you're terrific. You were with that

guy for years. Makes sense it took time to accept that it wasn't going to work out. And in the end, you made the only workable decision about him—after giving him a chance to come clean and make things right. There is nothing to be disappointed about in that. But I did promise you that after we talked for a while, I would take you back up the mountain." He still held out his hand.

She took it. Really, she could get used to holding Jace's hand. He tucked her fingers over his arm and led the way out from under the willow tree, across the grass to Main Street, where they turned back the way they'd come, toward the car.

Twenty minutes later, he pulled into the turnaround beneath the porte cochere at the side of the resort's clubhouse. A valet stepped up to open the door for her. She waved him off and turned to Jace behind the wheel. "I have to ask, did you study psychiatry in school?"

He grunted. "Are you kidding? Petroleum engineering, with a minor in business."

Softly, she told him, "Thank you—for keeping after me until I told you what was bothering me. For listening."

"Hey, what's a best friend for?"

"I had a really good time. At that beautiful little church, at the bakery. Even sitting under that willow tree telling you things you don't even need to know. That part wasn't fun exactly. But it was very…therapeutic, I guess you could say."

He nodded. "Happy to help."

She was suddenly absolutely certain he only wanted to get rid of her now. And why wouldn't he? She had totally blown it with her sulking and feeling sorry for herself, with her icky revelations about how she'd actually thought she might marry Kenny anyway, even if he was a cheating SOB, because he had money and could give her the life that she wanted. Her throat felt tight. She coughed to loosen it. "Ahem. Well, I'll…see you later, then."

"Later."

She hooked her pink bag on her shoulder, pushed on the door and the valet appeared again to open it all the way for her. "Uh, thanks," she said, and got out. The valet gave her a friendly smile and shut the passenger door. Joss stood there, feeling forlorn, as Jace drove away.

His Range Rover had disappeared from sight when the awful realization hit her like a smack in the face. His family was "in oil." He drove an eighty-thousand-dollar car. The price of a pair of his fancy boots would have paid the rent on her lost apartment for a couple of months at least. True, like her, he was between jobs. But Joss Bennings being out of a job and Jason Traub quitting the oil business were two completely different things.

Jason Traub was a rich guy. A very rich guy. She would bet her whole savings account on that—her significantly reduced savings account. There had been a lot more a year ago, before she'd paid for the wedding and the reception that hadn't happened after all. But even if she hadn't spent all that money on her nonwedding, her total savings still wouldn't be more than chump change to someone like Jace. She knew he had to have an inheritance and a nice, fat stock portfolio. He didn't really *have* to work.

And now that she'd told him the truth about her goals, what could he think but that she was trolling for a good provider so she could buy a big house and raise a bunch of boisterous kids? He must be wondering if she'd set out to get her hooks in him. He'd probably decided that she'd been giving him an act, pretending to hate men when she was really looking for a guy with big bucks to replace the no-good cheater she'd left at the altar.

Joss let out a small moan of misery. She *liked* Jace. A lot. She really did want to be his friend. She *loved* being his friend. And she'd been looking forward to spending more time with him before she went back to Sacramento and got to work picking up the pieces of her life.

But now she'd gone and ruined it with him. She just knew that she had. She tipped her head back and let out another moan.

"Ma'am?" asked the valet, looking worried.

She pulled herself together, pasted on a smile and shook her head. "I'm okay. Really."

Another vehicle rolled under the porte cochere and the valet stepped forward to open the passenger door. With a heavy sigh, Joss turned for the glass doors that led into the clubhouse.

Chapter 4

In her suite, Joss tossed her purse on the table in the foyer and went straight to the bedroom, where she shucked off her shoes and fell backward across the bed. As she stared blindly at the peaked ceiling, she tried to make up her mind whether to call Jace and swear to him she wasn't after him in any way, shape or form—or if the wiser course would be to leave bad enough alone.

And then she realized she didn't even have his number, so the question of whether to call didn't matter anyway.

The phone on the nightstand rang. Joss told herself not to answer it. The last thing she needed right now was another lecture from her mother or more crap from Kenny.

But then, as always, she couldn't stand to let it ring.

She reached over, picked it up and put it to her ear. "What now?"

"You're my best friend for the whole week and I don't have your cell number. How wrong is that?"

"Jace." She breathed his name like a grateful prayer. Tears blurred her eyes and clutched at the back of her throat. "Hey."

A silence on his end, then gruffly, "Are you all right? Did something…happen?"

She blinked, swallowed, let out a slow breath. And told him the truth. "I was sure that I'd totally freaked you out. That you had to be thinking I'm some kind of gold digger."

He made a bewildered sound. "Whoa. Wait. *Why*?"

"Okay, now I hear your voice, it all seems completely ridiculous that I could have thought that."

"Joss, why?"

"Because of what I told you. About marrying Kenny anyway, even though he cheated and I caught him in the act, marrying him because he had money and could, um, support me in the style to which I hope to become accustomed."

"Oh, right." He was smiling. She could hear it in his voice. "The big, messy house and all those loud, undisciplined kids who really shouldn't be allowed to color on the walls."

"You can get special paint, you know. Washable paint. And yeah, that would be it—the style to which I can't wait to become accustomed."

"Listen to me, Joss. Are you listening?"

"Yes."

"I don't think you're a gold digger. Not in any way. Got that?"

"Yeah."

"So can I have your cell number?"

She rattled it off. "And can I have yours?"

"Absolutely." He gave it to her. She rolled over and scribbled it down on the complimentary notepad by the phone. "And about tonight," he said, "dinner at Jackson and Laila's? I'll pick you up at five-thirty."

She grinned to herself. She'd never actually told him she would go, but so what? She *wanted* to go, and she was going to go.

"I'll be waiting," she promised. "Outside, under the porte cochere, where you dropped me off just now."

Jackson's house was wall-to-wall family and friends.

To Jace, it looked like just about every Traub in the state of Montana was there, not to mention all the Traubs from Texas. And there were other well-known Thunder Canyon families represented. There were Cateses and Cliftons and Pritchets, all of them related to the Traubs—if not by blood or marriage, then by the bonds of longtime friendships.

Friends and family filled the big living room, the kitchen and spilled out onto the wide front porch and into the tree-shaded backyard. Jackson had a professional-sized smoker barbecue going along with an open grill. The mouthwatering aromas of mesquite-smoked ribs, barbecued chicken and grilling burgers filled the air.

Jace had arrived with Joss just a half hour ago. She was a knockout in dressy jeans that hugged every curve and a silky shirt the color of a ripe plum. He'd whistled at her when she got into the car at the resort. Hey, even a best friend could show his appreciation when a woman was looking good.

His plan had been to keep her close at his side all evening, so his mother wouldn't have a chance to start working on her, pumping her for information about "how things were going" between them, trying to convince Joss that she would love living in Midland, Texas. But within fifteen minutes of their arrival at Jackson's, Laila had dragged Joss off to look at some old picture albums. He'd tried to stick with them, but Jackson had called him outside to help him flip burgers.

And now Ethan had caught up with him. "We need to talk. Come with me," Ethan commanded.

Jace shouldn't have followed, but he knew he was going to have to face his big brother down at some point. Might as well get it over with. Ethan led Jace to the edge of the yard, to a secluded spot beneath a cottonwood tree, where he commenced to put on the pressure.

"I just want you to drop in at the office for a few hours tomorrow," Ethan coaxed. TOI Montana had its offices on State Street not far from the Town Square. "Let me show you around. You can see how far we've come in the past year." Ethan had made the move to Montana only the summer before. "The shale oil operations are surpassing even my expectations."

"I know you're doing a great job, Ethan. I've seen the reports, but tomorrow's a busy day. Remember? We're all taking off in the morning, going riding up Thunder Mountain for that family picnic."

"That's right." Ethan frowned. "I forgot about the damn picnic. Tuesday, then—or come in early tomorrow. The ride up there doesn't get under way until ten or so. We won't have a lot of time, but at least I can show you the corner office that has your name on it."

Jace thought how he'd be happy to admire the new offices. But if he did, Ethan would only be all the more certain that he could talk Jace into coming back to TOI. "I'm out of the oil business, Ethan. I know I've told you that more than once."

Ethan blinked. "Aw, now, Jace. You know you don't mean it. You're an oilman to the core."

"I *was* an oilman. Not anymore."

Ethan reached out and hooked his arm around Jace's neck, getting him in a headlock, then fisting his free hand to scrub a noogie on Jace's head—like he was five again or something. "Snap out of it, little maverick," Ethan muttered, using the pet name their father used to use on them. "What else you plan to do with your time? We Traubs might have more money than we know what to do with, but that's because we're hard workers. We earned every cent and we *keep* earning until they lay us in the ground."

"Let me loose, Ethan." Jace said the words quietly, but he'd had about enough.

Ethan let go. "I didn't mean to get you all riled up."

Jace ran a hand back over his hair. "Oh, right. Put me in a headlock and pull a noogie on me and then say you didn't mean it."

"I'm only trying to help you get your head on straight."

"It's my head. And it feels plenty straight to me."

Ethan gentled his tone. "All I'm asking is for you to come and have a look at what we've built here."

"And I would be more than happy to do that, if that was all you were up to."

Ethan's lip curled, and not in a smile. "You calling me a liar, kid?"

Jason really wanted to pop his big brother a good one, but he valiantly managed to keep his fists at his sides. "In case you've forgotten," he said way too softly, "I'm thirty-three years old. I haven't been a kid for a long time now."

"Well, stop acting like one, then. Ever since you tangled with Jack Lavelle's little girl, you've been moping around, throwing your life away, acting like you don't care about anything anymore."

Again, Jace reminded himself to hold his temper. "Ethan, you don't know what you're talking about."

"The hell I don't."

"You're here in Montana. And I've been in Texas. And Ma and Pete have been filling your head full of their own assumptions about what's been going on."

Ethan demanded, "So what *was* going on?"

"Nothing the least mysterious. I want to find a different kind of work, that's all."

"And Tricia Lavelle didn't break your heart?"

"It's a long story. I don't want to go into it."

"Hah. She did a number on you. You're the last single maverick in the family and it's getting to you."

"Will you stop it with the maverick talk? I'm not six anymore. And Ethan, you're not Dad."

"You fell for Tricia, thought you'd finally found your woman. But she dumped you flat, crushed your hopes and walked all over your tender heart. Admit it."

"I'm not admitting anything. Get off my back."

But Ethan just kept on. "You *love* the oil business. You always did. You love it the most of all of us in the family—next to me, I mean."

"People change."

"I don't believe that," Ethan insisted. "Not for a minute. You got your heart broken and that set you on a downward spiral and all I'm trying to do is help pull you out of it."

"Look, Ethan, how many times do I have to tell you? You've got it all wrong. You've been listening to Ma and Pete. And they don't know what they're talking about."

"They know you were going to marry Tricia Lavelle. And then suddenly, it was over. And you were dragging around like someone shot your favorite hound dog, saying how you were through with the oil industry and getting out of Texas."

"It's not their business. And it's not yours either. Give it up."

"I'm only explaining that I get the picture, loud and clear. You're a mess, Jason, and what you need is to come back to work."

"I have *been* at work. Until last Wednesday, as a matter of fact. I have remained at work well past the time I was supposed to be finished because Ma and Pete pulled every trick in the book to get me to stay. But I'm done now. And I am not going back."

"A man needs to work."

"And I plan to work. Just not for TOI."

"Then doing what, Jason?"

"Something completely different. A business of my own, something hands-on."

"TOI is hands-on. It's *our* company."

"Listen, Ethan, I don't know another way to say it. I'm done at TOI and I don't know yet what I'll be doing next."

"You don't know yet," Ethan echoed in a smarmy

singsong. "Well, that's okay, because *I* know. You're coming to work for *me*, here, in Thunder Canyon."

They were head to head by then, and Jace knew exactly where this discussion was headed. Nowhere. As always, Ethan thought he knew it all. And Jace was not about to be bullied into going back to work doing what he *didn't* want to do anymore. "Back off," he said. "I mean it. Let it go."

"You're my brother. And I love you. And I'll bust your fool head open before I let you ruin your life."

Jace's fists burned to start flying. But what would hitting Ethan prove except that, along with all his other shortcomings, he couldn't control his damn temper even stone-cold sober? They were grown men, for pity's sake. Well beyond the age of imagining they could settle a problem with a brawl. There was nothing more to say here. He turned to walk away.

Apparently, Ethan got the message at last. He spoke wearily to Jace's back. "Aw, come on, Jace…"

Jason wanted to keep walking, but what good was that going to do either of them? Ethan could be a pushy, overbearing SOB, yes. But his heart was in the right place. Jace made himself face his older brother again.

Ethan said ruefully, "You know I only want to help."

"Well, you're *not* helping."

Ethan threw up both hands. "I only thought…a little tough love, you know?" He shook his head. "Lizzie warned me to stay out of it. You have no idea how much I hate it when she's right."

Jason almost grinned. "Why? Because she's right most of the time?"

"She's one hell of a woman, my wife. But she's too damn smart."

"You know you wouldn't have it any other way." His brother's mention of Lizzie had Jace thinking of Joss. He really had to go and find her before Ma did. He said, "The truth is, I'd been thinking about making some changes for a while now—since before I met Tricia, as a matter of fact."

"I...didn't realize that."

"Well, now you know. Ma and Pete hate to see me go. They're going to be on their own in Midland and even though they still want to run the show there, they don't like it that all of us have pulled up stakes and moved on."

"Yeah," Ethan said gruffly, "I get that. They didn't like it much when I left either."

"Whatever they've been saying, I really have changed my mind about the family business. I want another line of work. Something completely different. No, I haven't figured out what yet, but I'm not coming back to TOI. And I really need to go find Joss now."

One side of Ethan's mouth quirked up. "You thinkin' Ma's gotten hold of her?"

"I seriously hope not. Gotta go." He scanned the yard as he headed for the back door. No sign of a hot brunette in snug jeans and a purple shirt. And no sign of his mother either.

He went up the back steps and into the kitchen. "Do you know where I can find Joss?" he asked Laila, who was arranging the food buffet-style in the breakfast nook on a long, wide table covered with a red-and-white striped tablecloth, decorated with flags and red, white and blue candles and sparkly little red, white and blue Uncle Sam hats.

Laila flashed him her dazzling beauty-queen smile.

"Did I tell you I really like her? She's fun and down-to-earth."

"Yes, she is."

"And she loved looking at the pictures of all you Traubs as little kids. She told me she appreciated getting to see some of the old photos of your dad—Charles, I mean. She said you have his killer smile."

"I'll bet she did," he muttered drily. "But where is she now?"

"You know, I think I saw her in the dining room a few minutes ago. She was chatting with your mom."

Jace stifled a groan. "Thanks." He made a beeline for the formal dining room. No sign of Joss in there—or of Ma either. He moved on to the living room.

And spotted them right away, sitting on the sofa, their heads bent close together. His mother was saying something. Joss was laughing and nodding. She didn't look the least overwhelmed. Whatever Ma was filling her head with, apparently it wasn't all that scary.

But still. Joss was kind of jumpy about men—and for good reason. He didn't need his mother freaking her out with too many personal questions and a boatload of assumptions about what was really going on between the two of them.

He headed over there to rescue her.

His mother saw him coming. She gave him a big, wide smile. Joss turned to meet his eyes. He breathed a sigh of relief to see she looked completely at ease.

Maybe Ma was minding her own business after all.

But then he got close enough for her to speak to him. "Jason," his mother said, suddenly looking way too innocent. "Ethan really needs to talk to you. He's been looking all over for you."

"He found me." Jace tried not to scowl. "We had a nice, long talk. I think I cleared up a few…misconceptions for him."

"Oh?" Claudia gave him the arched eyebrow. "What misconceptions do you mean?"

"Long story, Ma. But the upshot is, Ethan understands now that I'm not going to stay in Midland and I'm not going to work at TOI anymore—not in Texas, and not here in Montana."

His mother shot Joss a nervous glance. "Jason, really. This is neither the time nor the place to go into all that."

Oh, right. Now things weren't going the way she'd planned, suddenly it was better if they didn't talk about it now. *Way to go, Ma.*

And he had to give Joss credit. She simply sat there looking gorgeous and completely unconcerned about whatever antagonistic undercurrents might be churning between him and the woman who'd given him life.

He said cheerfully, "Just clueing you in, Ma." And then he bent and kissed her still-smooth cheek.

She grabbed his arm and held him close enough that he could smell the light perfume she always wore. Softly, she told him, "I love you very much. You know that."

"I know. And I love you, too, Ma." He rose to his height again and spoke to Joss. "Hungry? The food's on." He held down his hand.

She took it and rose to stand beside him and he felt like a million bucks suddenly, just holding her slim, smooth fingers in his. "Great getting a chance to visit with you, Claudia," she said.

His mother was all smiles. "I'm so glad we were able to talk a little. And don't forget we would love to have you ride up Thunder Mountain with us tomorrow. The picnic will be such fun, and the views from up near the tree line are stunning."

"Thank you for inviting me," Joss said. "But...didn't you mention that you're riding *horses* up there?"

"Yes, we are. It's a beautiful ride."

"I've never ridden a horse in my life."

"First time for everything," Ma said brightly. "And there are always calm, even-tempered horses available from the resort stables, mounts they keep especially for beginners."

"I'll, um, talk it over with Jace."

"Wonderful." His mother beamed.

He asked, "You coming to eat, Ma?"

"I think I'll find Pete first."

"Well, all right, then." He guided Joss ahead of him. She led the way toward the kitchen. After a few steps he caught up with her and spoke low so only she could hear. "So are you moving to Midland?"

She laughed, a soft, enticing sound. "It was suggested."

They entered the dining room. He pulled her over to a quiet corner where they could talk for a moment or two undisturbed. "What else was 'suggested'?"

"Your mother said she thinks I'm lovely—her word—and she's so glad you and I met and she really has a wonderful feeling about me."

"Well, three things Ma and I can agree on at least."

"Hey, at least *your* mom knows she's meddling."

"Don't be too sure about that."

"But I *am* sure. She wants you back in Texas, but she knows she's out of line to keep after you. She gets that you're all grown up and that it's your life."

"She said all that?"

"Well, not exactly. But I can see it in her eyes."

"Why am I not reassured?"

"You should be. You should take my word for it. Backing Claudia off is going to be a piece of cake—unlike someone *else's* mother I could mention."

Jace wasn't so sure. "Ma filled Ethan's ears with a whole bunch of complete crap about me. He decided he had to come to my rescue with a domineering attitude and some 'tough love.'"

"Yikes. Just now, you mean?"

He nodded, admiring the pretty arch of her eyebrows, the juicy curve of her mouth. She really was easy on the eyes. He'd never had a best friend so good to look at—but then, all his other friends were male and looking at them didn't do a thing for him.

She said, "I hope it all worked out."

"It did. I only *wanted* to punch his lights out."

The brown eyes widened. "But you kept your cool."

"Yes, I did, surprisingly enough. Ethan and I are on the same page now. And I have to agree that siccing Ethan on me was probably Ma's main move. That didn't work, so she'll be about out of ways to get me to come to my senses and get back into life as I've always lived it. But don't kid yourself. She's not finished working on *you*."

Joss tugged on the collar of his shirt. He leaned down even closer. Her warm, sweet breath teased his ear as she whispered, "If she knew the truth about me she might actually believe that we really are just friends."

He whispered back, "Are you saying you're planning on telling her the truth?"

She held his gaze. "Are you?"

"I *have* told the truth, that you and I are just friends. Is it my fault that no one will believe me?"

"I guess not."

"I'm glad you see it that way." Leaning close to her, breathing in the tempting scent of her perfume, it would be so easy to wish for more than friendship. "As for *your* truth, well, it's not mine to tell."

She smiled up at him then, causing his heart to beat harder in his chest. "I appreciate that, Jace. Because I don't want to go into it with everyone. It's too embarrassing."

"That's A-okay with me. I won't say a word."

"Thanks." Now those big brown eyes looked at him trustingly. He felt minimally guilty about that. After all, he did find her way hot. And if she just happened to decide she wanted some benefits in this temporary friendship after all, well, every moment he was with her, it got harder to remember why a few benefits wouldn't be a crackerjack idea. "For some weird reason, I don't have any trouble telling *you* all my secrets—even the shameful ones." Her cheeks flushed pink and she lowered her gaze so she was looking at the second button of his shirt.

He couldn't resist using a finger to tip her chin back up. He stared at her mouth. How could he help it? She had the softest, widest mouth he'd ever seen. He wanted to kiss her. A lot. But he wouldn't. He said, "There's nothing shameful in wanting your dream so much you're willing to compromise to get it."

"That depends on the compromise. Even letting myself *imagine* I might get back with Kenny after he betrayed me with my own cousin…uh-uh. *That* was shameful."

"Listen to me, Joss. I want you to stop beating yourself up about that."

"It's only…"

He put a finger against those soft lips of hers. "Take it from your new best friend. It's over with the cheater. You *didn't* go back to him. That's what matters." From the corner of his eye, he saw everyone filing past, moving toward the kitchen. His brother Corey and his wife, Erin, glanced their way. Erin whispered to Corey. He could just guess what she was saying—something about how Jace had found someone special.

Which was great. It fit into his plan just fine.

He and Joss would have a good time together, enjoying each other's company, taking each day as it came. And his family would leave him alone to pursue what they all hoped was the beginning of a "meaningful" relationship, a relationship that would help him get over Tricia, whom they were all so damn certain had broken his heart.

"Everyone's heading for the kitchen," Joss whispered. "Shouldn't we join them?"

He draped an arm around her slim shoulders. "Let's go."

Chapter 5

"No way. I'm not going anywhere on a horse," Joss informed Jason for what seemed like the hundredth time that evening.

By then, they were back up at the resort in her suite, eating chocolate from the complimentary bowl on the coffee table. She added in a tone she intended to be final, "I'll just take a pass on the family picnic, if you don't mind."

"But I do mind." He put on a needy expression. The guy had no shame when it came to getting his way. "You'll break my heart if you don't go."

She had the bowl in her lap. She fished around in it and found what she wanted. Swiftly, she unwrapped the tempting square of lovely, smooth bittersweet perfection. A groan of pleasure escaped her as she popped it into her mouth. It was fabulous. Too fabulous. Shiny wrappers littered the coffee table in front of them. "Your heart," she said, "is way too easy to break."

Now he looked noble—in a soft-eyed, far-too-appealing way. "It's true. Please. Don't hurt me any more than I've already been hurt. Come to the picnic with me tomorrow. Save me from my family. I'm begging you, Joss."

"So how exactly have you already been hurt?" She *was* kind of curious about that woman who had apparently dumped him.

He actually stuck out his lower lip. "It's just too painful to talk about."

"You know you're totally full of it, right?"

He dug in the bowl for another candy. "What? Full of chocolate, you mean?"

She gave him a slow look of great patience. "You're not going to tell me, are you?"

"One of these days…"

"Which day? By my count, we have five days left and I'm outta here."

"Yeah, but we've been best friends for only about twenty-four hours. I need a little more time to…let down my guard."

"Hah." She kept after him. "So, tomorrow, then? You'll tell me tomorrow?"

"Do you really *need* to know?"

"I'm curious, okay?" And growing more so the longer she hung around with him. "Then again, what does it matter if you tell me all about your recent bad romance, or not?"

"So then, you don't *really* need to know."

She gave it up. "No, Jason. I don't need to know."

He beamed. "Great."

She started to root around for another piece of candy—but no. She really didn't need another piece of candy. Resolutely, she handed him the bowl. "Don't let me near that again tonight."

"Count on me to save you from yourself—and come to the picnic tomorrow."

"Do you *ever* give up?"

"No, I don't. It's not in my nature." He dug in the bowl and pulled out a nutty caramel chew. "Damn, these are good."

"You had to remind me." She reached for the bowl.

He jerked it away. "Uh-uh. Remember? You're not having any more."

"Just one."

"You won't respect me if I don't hold my ground here." He actually put his hand over the top of the bowl, as if she might try to reach in.

Which was exactly what she'd planned to do. "You can be so annoying. You know that, right?"

"It's for your own good," he said oh so nobly. "You said not to let you."

"Well, I *meant*, don't let me until I *want* you to let me."

He cast those bedroom eyes heavenward. "Women. They have no idea what they want."

"Men. They think they know everything." She scooped up the scattered candy wrappers and started firing them at him.

"Hey, knock that off." He ducked and held up the bowl as a shield.

She fired more wrappers. One got stuck in his hair. "Gimme that candy," she demanded, trying really hard to sound scary.

But he only set the bowl aside—his *other* side—and knocked the wrapper out of his hair. "Sorry. No can do." He deflected with his hands that time.

She was out of wrappers. Laughing, she lunged for the bowl.

He caught her by both wrists before she got there. "Behave," he commanded.

"Let me go." She tried to pull away.

He held on. "Say you'll behave."

"No way."

"Say it. Promise."

"Uh-uh. Forget that."

They were both laughing by then, as she struggled to free her wrists and he held on. She got one hand free and she went for it—reaching across him, grabbing for the bowl.

She made it, too. She shoved her fingers in and came out with a nice, big handful. "Got 'em!" she crowed in triumph, holding her prize high.

"Put those back," he instructed in what could only be called a growl.

"What, these, you mean?" She opened her hand and let them rain down on his head.

He sat very still—for a moment anyway—as the candy bounced off his thick hair and broad shoulders and fell to the sofa cushions and down to the floor. Then, frowning thunderously, he glanced around them. "Look at this mess. Wrappers and candy everywhere."

"It's your own fault. You should have given me the candy when I asked for it."

He let go of her other wrist, but then he only captured both of her arms and made a big show of baring his gorgeous snow-white teeth at her. "You're a brat, Jocelyn Marie. You know that?"

"Yes, I am. And proud of it." She tossed her hair and held her head high.

He leaned in, playfully threatening....

And right then, in the space of an instant, everything changed.

One second, they were tussling like a pair of ill-behaved third graders—and the next second, they weren't. One moment she was laughing and teasing and giving him a hard time—and the next, she wasn't.

Out of nowhere, her breath snagged in her throat. Her pulse spiked and her skin felt sensitized and too hot. All at once, she was acutely aware of his big, warm hands gripping her arms, of his dark, dark eyes and the beautiful, way-too-kissable shape of his lips. Of the scent of him, that was a little spicy and a little green and also electric somehow, the way the air smells right before a thunderstorm.

She watched his eyes—saw them track. From her eyes, to her mouth, back to her eyes again...

She knew what was coming. He was going to kiss her.

And oh, at that moment, she *wanted* him to kiss her.

Wanted to feel his powerful arms banded around her, wanted his breath in her mouth and the rough wet glide of his tongue.

Wanted him to guide her back onto the sofa cushions, to press his big, muscled body so tightly against her, to hold her so close and kiss her so long, and so deep and so thoroughly that she would forget...

Everything.

The mess that was her life. All the ways her plans

and her world had gone haywire. All the things she somehow had to fix, to make right, even though she really had no idea how to do that.

She wanted to tear off all her clothes and all of his, too. She wanted to be naked with him, skin-to-skin. Naked with her new best friend who happened to be a man she'd met only the day before.

She wanted forgetfulness. And she wanted it in Jace's big arms.

But then, very softly, he asked, "Joss?" And his eyes were different, clearer somehow, seeking an answer from her.

And she liked him so much then. She liked him more than she wanted the temporary escape his lean, strong, male body offered her.

He was doing the right thing by her. He was giving her the moment she needed.

The choice she needed. The chance to stop now. To say no.

She swallowed, slowly. She pressed her lips together and gave an almost imperceptible shake of her head.

That was all it took.

He let go of her arms and sank back against the cushions. She did the same. Her heart still pounded too hard, her breath came too fast and her body still yearned. But that would pass.

It wasn't going to happen. And that was…good.
Right.

For a long, silent moment, they simply sat there, among the scattered candy and empty wrappers, not looking at each other.

And then, without a word, by a sort of tacit agreement, they both rose and began gathering up the pieces of chocolate. She went and got the wastebasket by the wet bar and they threw the wrappers away.

Finally, he started to turn for the door, but then he stopped and faced her, where she stood by the sofa, still holding the wastebasket, feeling forlorn.

"Tomorrow," he said. "You're coming. Don't argue. Wear old jeans and bring a jacket. Tennis shoes if you don't have riding boots. Do you have a hat?"

Gladness surged through her. Suddenly, she desperately wanted to go. "You'll be sorry. I meant what I said. I do not know how to ride a horse."

"Then it's time you learned." His voice was gentle. Fond. And yet, somehow, an echo of heated excitement seemed to cling to him, to thicken the air between them.

She looked in those dark eyes and she almost wished…but no. It was better this way. Safer. Saner. And lately, she could use all the safety and sanity she could get. She said, "I bought boots and a hat the first day I was here. And a cute Western shirt, too, as a matter of fact."

"I'll be here to get you at nine."

"I think this is a bad idea," she said the next morning when she opened the door to him and he stood there looking one-hundred-percent authentic cowboy in faded jeans and rawhide boots, a worn blue Western shirt with white piping and a blue bandana. He had his hat in his hand.

He gave her a crooked smile that made her feel all warm and fuzzy inside. "You're going to have a great time."

She made a doubtful sound and frowned at his hat. "Is that a real Stetson?"

"Resistol."

She assumed that must be a brand of hat. "Well, all right. Good to know."

He took in her red plaid shirt with its crochet trim and rhinestone studs. "Aren't you the fancy one?"

She tugged on her pant leg, revealing more of her boot. "And don't you love these boots?" They were red, too—beautiful distressed red leather embroidered with hearts and wings and scroll-like flourishes.

"Very stylish."

"As long as I'm going to make a fool of myself, I figure I might as well look good while doing it."

"You look terrific." His eyes said he really meant that.

The memory of that almost-kiss last night seemed to rise up between them. She felt suddenly shy and looked away. "Thank you."

"Joss," he said gently, "it's going to be fine. Ready?"

"No, but I can't seem to convince you what a bad idea this is, so we might as well get going." She grabbed her jean jacket and her brand-new hat and off they went.

They got to the resort stable before the rest of Jason's family arrived, which was great. She would have a little time to practice riding before they started up the mountain.

The horse the groom led out for her was white with brown spots. Already saddled and wearing a bridle, it seemed somehow a very patient horse. It stood there, flicking its brown tail lazily and making gentle huffing noises as Jace checked the strap that held the saddle on and adjusted the bridle.

Joss stood well away from the animal. "Um, does it have a name?"

"Cupcake," said the groom. He was maybe twenty years old, deeply tanned with freckles and a space between his two front teeth.

Joss cleared her throat. "It's a she, then?"

"Nope. Gelding," the groom answered. So very cowboylike. Never use a whole sentence when a word or two will do.

And okay, now she looked, she could see the, er, residual equipment. "Ah, yes."

Jace thanked the groom. The fellow tipped his sweat-stained hat and ambled back to the stable.

"Come on." Jace held out his hand to her.

She eyed that hand warily. "I don't know. I have a bad feeling about this."

"Come on," Jace insisted. He refused to lower his hand.

So she took it.

He showed her which side to mount from and boosted her into the saddle. Cupcake made a soft chuffing sound but didn't move a muscle. Cautiously, she patted the side of his warm, silky neck. "Okay. Can we be done now?" she asked hopefully.

Jace didn't answer. He adjusted the stirrups. Then he gave her some instructions: how to hold the reins, how to use her legs to help guide the animal. And a bunch of other stuff she immediately filed under the general heading, *Things I'm Too Nervous to Remember*.

He took the reins and led her around in a circle for a while, just so she could get a feel for being on a moving horse. It didn't seem so bad really. Cupcake was a prince. He walked along calmly, never once balking or trying to go his own way.

Within a half hour, she was holding the reins and riding Cupcake in a circle, using her knees the way Jace had showed her. She decided that maybe this wouldn't be so bad after all.

His family started arriving in pickups, some of them towing horse trailers. Jace went off to saddle his own horse and Joss kept practicing, continuing in the circle and also stopping, turning and going the other way. Really, it wasn't so terrible. She was actually getting the hang of it, more or less. On a sweetheart like Cupcake, she might even enjoy herself. When Jason's mom, looking trim and young in snug jeans and a yellow shirt, called out a greeting, Joss raised her hand in a jaunty wave.

At a little after eleven, they were all mounted up and ready to go. They formed a caravan and took the road that led to the resort condos farther up the mountain. But before they reached them, Dax Traub, in the lead, turned off onto a tree-shaded trail.

The rest of them followed. It was nice, Joss thought. Not bad at all, riding along at a steady pace beneath the dappled shadows of the trees. There was a gentle breeze blowing and the air smelled fresh and piney. She followed directly behind Jace, who rode a big black horse named Major. A proud-looking creature, Major tossed his head and pranced and required a lot more handling than Joss ever could have managed.

She much preferred the calm-natured Cupcake. With him, all she had to do was stay in the saddle and lightly hold the reins. Every now and then, Jace would glance back at her and she would give him a big smile, just to show him that she was doing okay.

Piece of cake. Seriously. She kind of had a knack for this. Who knew? *Jocelyn Marie Bennings, horsewoman.* It had a nice ring to it.

The trail narrowed, but that didn't seem to faze the sure-footed Cupcake. The mountain, closely grown with tall trees, rose steeply to her left. On the right, the dropoff was dizzying, even with all the trees that might help to block a fall. Joss made a point not to look.

Jace called back to her, "You doing okay?"

"Fine. Absolutely. Doing gr—"

She didn't get a chance to finish saying *great*, because Cupcake took his next step and the downward side of the trail crumbled out from beneath his hooves.

Joss let out a strangled shriek and grabbed onto the saddle horn for dear life. She caught one last look at Jace's stunned face and then she and Cupcake were off, heading straight down the mountain, kicking up a cloud of dust in a high-speed, utterly terrifying slide.

Chapter 6

With both hands, Joss clutched the saddle horn for all she was worth. There was a rushing sound in her ears and her heart beat so hard it hurt. She closed her eyes. She closed them really tight.

Why look? She knew she was done for, that poor Cupcake would lose his precarious balance as they skidded down the mountainside. He would topple and roll and she would roll with him—*under* him. Oh, it was definitely not going to be pretty.

The brave horse stumbled. She lost her seat and felt herself starting to go airborne. But somehow, even though her arms felt wrenched from their sockets, she managed to hold on. Her butt hit the saddle again, knocking the wind out of her, sending a sharp crack of pure pain zipping up her tailbone, jangling her spine.

She might have screamed. She wasn't sure. It was all

happening way too fast and she was so far from knowing what she ought to do next to try and maybe improve her odds of surviving the next, oh, say, twenty seconds.

At least Cupcake remained upright and she was still in the saddle. So far. She dared to open her eyelids to slits, saw the blur of trees as they flew by, heard the sharp retort of hooves beneath her that told her the brave spotted horse was actually running now instead of sliding, that by some miracle, he had gotten his legs under him and started galloping in a zigzag pattern, sideways and downward, switching back and forth, one way and then the other, weaving between the trunks of the tall trees.

And…was it possible? Were they slowing down a little?

She felt dizzy and realized she'd forgotten to breathe. So she sucked in a quick breath and forced her eyes open wider and wished she hadn't dropped the reins when she first grabbed for the saddle horn. Right now, she didn't dare let go long enough to try to get hold of them again.

Knees. She was supposed to use her knees, wasn't she? Kind of press them together to let Cupcake know that stopping would be really, really good—no. Wait. That was to go faster. She really didn't want to go faster.

She needed the reins, but she didn't have them.

All she had was her voice. She used it. "Whoa," she said, "Whoa, Cupcake." It came out in a croak, but the horse actually seemed to hear her.

Triumph exploded through her as he slowed even more with a low snorting sound. She had her eyes open all the way by then and she could see a sort of flat space up ahead, between two fir trees.

She went for it, letting go of the saddle horn, groping frantically for the reins. And she got them! She tugged on them, saying "Whoa, whoa…"

It worked. It totally worked. Cupcake came to a dead stop right there between those two trees.

Actually, it was a really fast stop. Maybe too fast. And maybe she'd been a little rough with those reins. Cupcake rose on his hind legs and let out one of those angry neighs like the wild, mean horse always makes in the movies.

She really should have grabbed for the saddle horn again.

But before she remembered to do that, she was already sliding— right off the backside of Cupcake.

She landed hard on the same place she'd hit when she bounced high in the saddle that one time Cupcake stumbled. Her poor backside. It would never be the same. She let out a "Whoof!" of surprise as she hit the ground, followed by a low groan of pain.

And then she just flopped all the way down onto her back and stared up at the blue sky between the branches of the two big trees as she waited for the agony to finish singing up and down her spine.

Cupcake, making soft chuffing, snuffling sounds, turned around and stood over her. He nuzzled her temple, snuffling some more.

She groaned again and reached up and patted the side of his spotted head. "Good job," she told him, and then qualified, "basically." Reassured, he backed off a little and started nibbling at the skimpy grass between the trees.

"Joss! My God, Joss!" It was Jason. Judging by the

sound of swift hooves approaching, he must have taken off down the mountain after her.

She really ought to sit up and show him that she was okay.

And she would. Very soon. Right now, though, well, her butt really hurt and she didn't have the heart to sit on it yet.

A moment later, she heard him draw to a stop a few feet away. He was off that black horse and kneeling at her side in about half a second flat.

His worried face loomed above her. "Joss... Joss are you..."

"I'm okay," she groaned.

He didn't look convinced. "Can you...move your arms and legs?"

She reached up and touched the side of his face, the same way she had done with Cupcake. "Honestly, I'm fine—well, except for my backside. That could be better."

"I'm so sorry." He looked positively stricken. "I made you come today. I never should have—"

"Shh." She put her fingers against his soft mouth. She really did love his mouth. She almost wished she'd kissed him last night after all, even if it was a bad idea. "It's fine," she said. "*I'm* fine. Cupcake is fine." She laughed a little. "And I have to tell you, *that* was exciting."

He grunted. "Yeah, *too* exciting."

She gave him her hand and he pulled her to a sitting position as she heard more horses approaching.

"She okay?" Ethan asked. Joss glanced over her shoulder and saw Jace's older brother, with Lizzie right behind him.

"Everything works," Joss told them, gathering her legs under her, only moaning a little, as Jace helped her to her feet. "But I'm guessing there will be bruises." She leaned on Jace. He put his arm around her. That was nice. She felt safe and protected, all tucked up close against him.

He said, "There's a doctor available back at the resort. Can you ride back? He can take a look at you."

She put a hand to her head. "My hat…"

"It's halfway between here and the trail," Lizzie said. "We can grab it on the way back up."

Joss stared from Jace to Lizzie and then to Ethan. "I can't believe you guys rode down here on purpose— even to come to my rescue."

Ethan chuckled. "It's really not that bad."

"It only seems that way when the trail breaks out from under you," Lizzie added. "Lucky they gave you a steady-natured mount."

Joss cast an appreciative glance at Cupcake who continued happily munching the sparse grass. "He's a champion, all right."

"Can we cut the chitchat?" Jace insisted, "We've got to get you to the doctor."

She reached back and felt all the places that ached. "Really, it's just not that bad."

"Joss, you could have been—"

"Don't even say it. What matters is I *wasn't*. Cupcake saved the day and I might end up with a bruise or two and there is no way I'm missing the picnic now I've come this far."

"But you—"

She stuck her index finger in the air. "Wait. Watch."

"Joss—"

"I mean it. Wait."

He looked at her like he wanted to strangle her, or at least try to shake a little sense into her. But he did shut up.

She peeled his hand off her shoulder and stepped away from him. "See? Upright and A-okay." She took a step, then another. It hurt a little. And she bet she was going to be sore the next morning. But she was absolutely certain the damage was only superficial. "Really, I'm okay. See?" She held her arms out to the side. "Ta-da!"

"I don't like it," he grumbled.

"Well, too bad. It's my butt and I say it's going to be fine."

Ethan laughed and shared a knowing glance with his wife. "Give it up, Jace. That woman has made up her mind."

The trip back up to the trail was nowhere near as thrilling as the ride down. In fact, going upward, it seemed steep, but not scarily so. And they found her hat about midway, as Lizzie had promised.

Jace jumped down and retrieved it for her, scowling up at her as he handed it over. "You *sure* you don't want to see the resort doctor?"

She gave him her widest, most confident smile as she settled her hat back in place on her head. "I am absolutely certain. And tell you what, you don't have to ask again. If I change my mind, I'll let you know."

"What if you have internal injuries?"

"Thank you for getting my hat. And will you please stop worrying?"

"It's only that…" He pressed those fine lips together.

"If you end up in a coma, I'll hate myself forever and I'll never forgive you."

"A coma? Maybe you didn't notice. It wasn't my head I landed on."

"You know what I mean."

"Hey, you two! Get a move on," Ethan called from several yards ahead.

Jace just waved a hand at him and kept looking up at Joss, a focused, intense, almost angry kind of look. "If anything happened to you, I couldn't stand it...."

His words warmed her. They...touched her, because he really meant them. He really did care. About her safety, her well-being.

Maybe her life was a mess, but at least she'd found Jason. And he truly was her friend.

"Shh." She bent down to him and she kissed him, softly, quickly, on those perfect lips of his. They felt good, his lips. Even better than she had imagined they might. "Stop worrying," she whispered. "That's an order."

He stared up at her for a moment. He didn't look so angry now. Was that a flash of heat she saw in his dark eyes? But then he frowned. "You're fine? You mean that?"

"I am. Yes."

Shaking his head, he turned and mounted the black horse and they continued upward.

At the trail, the rest of the Traubs were waiting. They congratulated Joss on her excellent handling of a dangerous situation. She laughed and told them that her current good health was all due to Cupcake.

They started moving again, following the narrow, winding trail up the side of Thunder Mountain. It was a gorgeous ride. And Joss appreciated it more fully for having survived the headlong tumble down the cliff. She felt a lot easier on Cupcake, too, a lot more confident that even if she was a complete greenhorn, her horse could handle just about anything that fate might throw his way.

Eventually, they emerged from the trees at a higher elevation, where the wind blew brisk and cool and you could look down and see the lower hills and valleys spread out for miles and miles. From up there, the town of Thunder Canyon looked picture-postcard perfect. She could even see the little white church she and Jace had attended two days before. It really was a beautiful little town.

The Traub women had packed a light meal in their saddlebags. They spread blankets in the sun and enjoyed a leisurely lunch. Joss ate heartily. The headlong race down the side of the mountain had given her an appetite.

Jace stayed close. He seemed to be watching for a sign that she might need a doctor after all. She would glance over and catch him looking at her in that same concerned, attentive way. Every time he did that, she felt all warm and good inside. Protected.

Cared for.

She was starting to see that she really would be okay in the long run. Funny how a near-death experience can snap the world into sharper focus. She was young and smart and strong and she had enough money in her bank account to get by until she found another job.

And hey, after knowing Jace, she had to admit that there were still a few good men left in the world. Not every guy was a cheating jerk.

At three, they were back at the resort stables. Lizzie

turned Cupcake over to the groom and felt a little sad to watch him amble away.

Jace said, "I think you like that horse."

"He's the best."

He put his arm around her and she leaned close to him with a sigh. He said, "We can ride again, you know, before the week is out."

"Yes," she agreed, and looked up to meet those velvety brown eyes. "Let's make a point to do that."

That evening Ethan and Lizzie had the big family cookout at their place. Melba Landry was there. She told both Joss and Jason that she was expecting them at the Historical Society Museum.

"Tomorrow, in fact," Lizzie's great-aunt instructed.

Joss had a great time that evening. She helped Lizzie and Rose Traub Anderson in the kitchen. Lizzie was not only a baker but also an excellent all-around cook.

Joss told her about the restaurant she'd managed in Sacramento. "I loved that job," she said. "I hated to leave it. There was something new happening every night. A little bit glamorous, you know? All the customers dressed for a night out, the snowy tablecloths and the good china, floating candles and an orchid in a cut-crystal bud vase at every table. It was a really nice dinner place, with an excellent wine list and to-die-for desserts. I loved the camaraderie between the front and back of the house. And the chef, Marilyn, was a wonder. Not only super creative with a great reputation, but also the calmest, most even-tempered person I've ever met. People say chefs are temperamental. Not Marilyn Standall. I never once heard her even raise her voice, no matter how crazy things got in the kitchen."

Lizzie asked the next logical question. "Why did you quit?"

Joss almost told her. Lizzie would be easy to confide in, but it would have been a downer to get into all that. So she only shrugged. "Time for a change, I guess. I like running a restaurant, though. Most likely I'll find something similar when I get back to Sacramento."

Later, after most of the Traubs had gone home, Joss and Jason stayed to help bring in the extra chairs from outside and stack the dishes by the sink. Lizzie had a housekeeper who would be in to take care of the rest in the morning.

It was after eleven when they climbed into Jace's Range Rover for the drive back up to the resort.

"Did you have a good time?" he asked.

"The best."

"Mind a little detour?" He started the engine.

She glanced over at him and felt a warm glow move through her. "I'm open. Let's go."

Jace's heart sank as he pulled into the parking lot at the corner where Main Street turned sharply north and became Thunder Canyon Road.

The sodium vapor lamp overhead lit a whole lot of empty asphalt. And the rustic, shingled two-story building stood dark in the eastern corner of the lot.

He turned off the engine and leaned on the wheel to stare out the windshield in disbelief. "Not possible. Nobody said a word to me…"

"A word about what?" Joss asked.

He gestured at the darkened building. "The Hitching Post. Looks like it's closed."

"Just for the night, right? It's after eleven."

He shook his head. "In the summer, it used to be open Monday through Saturday till two in the morning."

"Maybe they changed their hours? I see a couple of lights on upstairs."

He leaned closer to the windshield until he could see the glow in the second-floor windows. "There are apartments up there…"

She flashed that gorgeous smile at him as she pushed open the passenger door. "Come on. Let's have a look, see what's going on."

They walked across the empty parking lot together, their footsteps echoing in a way that sounded sad and lonesome to his ears. At the sidewalk, they turned for the front of the building, with its wide, wood-pillared porch and the big wooden sign between the windows on the second floor. The block letters were a little faded but still legible in the streetlamp's glow: THE HITCHING POST.

And the long rail was still there, at the sidewalk's edge, the rail that had given the place its name back when it first opened as a bar and grill in the 1950s. To the present day, folks still used that rail to hitch their horses.

Or they used to, at least last summer, when he'd come to town for Corey's wedding.

There was a big white sign tacked to the doors. FOR SALE, it proclaimed in red letters large enough they were visible even in the shadows of the darkened porch.

Twin signs in the windows that flanked the door proclaimed CLOSED INDEFINITELY in letters as big and red as those on the sign offering the place for sale.

Jace stood on the sidewalk looking at all that darkness, at the sad little glow in one of those upstairs windows. "Closed indefinitely. How is that possible? They did a bang-up business. Everybody in town loved this place. I don't get why it would close. And I can't believe no one even *told* me."

Joss slipped her hand into his and he felt a little better. He was glad for the contact, glad she was there. She said, "You sound like you just lost an old friend."

He turned his gaze to her. There was plenty of light, both from the streetlamp and from the nearly full moon. She'd tipped up her pretty face to him, her big eyes amber-colored right then, and soft with sympathy. Gruffly, he confessed, "I feel like it, too. Damn. I was looking forward to showing you around inside, seeing if that bartender I liked, Carl, was still there. I've been wanting to tell you all about the Shady Lady."

"What shady lady?"

"She was a local legend. Her real name was Lily Divine. She lived in Thunder Canyon back when the town was first settled. They called her the Shady Lady and she owned a saloon by that name, a saloon that stood right here, where the Hitching Post is now. Come on...." He tugged on her hand and she went with him, up the steps, into the shadows of that wide, deserted porch.

She whispered, "Tell me you're not planning a break-in."

He chuckled. "It did cross my mind. But no, I promise. We're not breaking in. I just want a closer look at the For Sale sign." He read the smaller print at the bottom. The Realtor was Bonnie Drake at Thunder Creek Real Estate. Her name was familiar. Hadn't Ethan mentioned her in the past? Maybe she was the Realtor Ethan had used when he bought the building on State Street for TOI Montana.

Joss asked, "Why? You going to buy yourself a bar and grill?"

"Don't laugh. I just might."

She pulled on his hand until he turned and faced her. "You're kidding."

He busted to it. "Well, yeah. What would I do with a bar and grill?" He joked, "Unless you want to show me how to run one?"

She tipped her dark head to the side, and even through the shadows, he saw the ghost of a smile haunting her way-too-kissable mouth. "It's kind of a nice fantasy. Living in this great little town, running the place where all the locals love to hang out..."

A slight wind ruffled her hair, brought the scent of her perfume to him. She always smelled so good. It occurred to him that if he ever tried again, *really* tried, with a woman, he hoped that maybe she would smell as good as Joss did. Clean and sweet, both at once.

She frowned a little. "What?"

He bent closer, whispered teasingly, "I didn't say anything."

She was studying him. "You had the strangest expression on your face..."

"I was thinking that you smell good, that's all. That I like your perfume."

"Oh." Did her cheeks get pinker? Hard to tell in the darkness, but it seemed that maybe they did. "Well, um, thank you."

"The pleasure is all mine, believe me."

Her eyes seemed so wide right then, and filled with

amber light, even in the deep shadows of the dark porch. "Jace?" She sounded slightly breathless.

He encouraged her, "Yeah?"

"You know today, when you came down the hill after me and found me flat on my back?"

"Yeah?"

"I thought how I wished I had kissed you last night." Her words sent a flare of heat moving through him. She added, almost shyly, "I mean life is too short, right? You never know what might happen."

He touched the side of her face. Her skin was so soft. And damn, was she trying to tell him something? "Joss, are you okay? Are you in pain? Do you need to see a doctor?"

She cut him off with a low, sweet laugh. "Stop. I'm fine. That wasn't my point." And then she grew serious again. "It's only, well, in life it always seems like there's plenty of time. But is there really? What if I died and I hadn't even kissed you?"

He gazed down into her upturned face and he never wanted to look away. A moment ago, he'd been kind of depressed, to think that the Hitching Post was closed up, with a For Sale sign on the front door. But suddenly, he didn't feel bad at all anymore. The world seemed full of promise. And hope. Of good things. And every single one of them was shining in Joss's big brown eyes.

"I really don't want you to have any regrets," he said, his voice low, maybe a little rougher than he'd meant it to be.

"But I do have regrets. You know that. About a thousand of them. I've made a lot of mistakes and I—"

"Shh." He touched her sweet lips with his fingers and instructed solemnly, "I want you to let those regrets go."

"I'm working on it."

"And the little problem that we never kissed?"

"Yeah?"

"That's easily fixed."

"You're right," she whispered, tipping that tempting mouth up to him like an offering. "So very easily…"

"We can fix it right now. Here. Tonight."

"Yes." Those bright eyes had a naughty gleam in them. They told him she could be bad—in a very good way. "I think we should."

"Joss…" It wasn't a question. Not this time.

But she answered it anyway. "Yes. Oh, yes."

He lowered his head and tasted her lips for the first time.

Chapter 7

Joss knew that she shouldn't be kissing Jace.

She was almost thirty, for crying out loud. Old enough to know that nothing messed up a perfectly great friendship as fast as sex could. And what did sex start with?

Kisses.

Kisses like this one. Slow, delicious kisses. Kisses that began so gently, with Jace's wonderful soft mouth just barely brushing hers, with the warmth of his big, lean body so close, but not quite making contact with hers.

Yet.

Kisses that led to touching—oh, yes.

Touching just like Jace was doing right now, his big hands cradling her face, holding her mouth up to him. Wonderful hands he had, strong and slightly callused, and warm.

So warm…

He let them wander.

She knew that he would. She welcomed the slow twin caresses along the sides of her neck as his fingers skimmed downward. Oh, she could easily get used to this, to kissing Jace.

For five whole years, she'd never kissed anyone but Kenny. Really, what had she been thinking?

She'd been missing out, big time.

Jace clasped her shoulders. His lips moved on hers, coaxing. She knew what he wanted.

She wanted it, too. She parted her lips for him and let him inside.

He groaned, a soft, low, pleasured sort of sound. She felt it, too. The beginnings of arousal. Already, her body was kind of melty and heavy in the most lovely, delicious sort of way.

She swayed against him and he gathered her in.

Oh. Yes. Perfect. Her breasts were now pressed against his hard chest. They ached, a little, already. A good, rich, exciting ache. An ache that promised to deepen in the best sense of the word.

His arms were nice and tight around her and she felt cherished and safe and very, very good. And his tongue was doing beautiful things inside her mouth, stroking, exploring. Learning all her secrets—well, a few of them at least.

He lifted his mouth from hers. She made a frantic little sound, not wanting it to end. Not yet.

Oh, please. Not yet….

And then, what do you know? It didn't end. He simply slanted his amazing lips the other way and kissed her some more.

Yes. *This*, she thought in a lovely, foggy, heated wordless way. This was it. *The* kiss. The one she'd known she couldn't afford to miss....

Jace's kiss...

He wrapped her even closer, so tight against him.

Tight enough that she could feel his growing hardness, pressing into her. Her response was immediate. She sighed against his warm lips and pressed herself even closer, lifting her hips to him, eager.

For more.

For sex.

With Jace.

Sex...

Oh, she did want to...

But then what?

The annoying question echoed in her brain, stealing her pleasure in this special moment, reminding her that her life was all upside-down and an affair on the rebound was not a good idea. Her world was way too complicated already. She didn't need to make it more so.

He must have felt her withdrawal. He raised his head and he smiled down at her, so tenderly, his dark eyes low and lazy. "You messed up and started thinking, didn't you?"

"Guilty." She put her hands against his chest. She could feel his heartbeat, strong and steady.

He peered at her more intently. "You okay?"

She nodded. "You are a totally amazing kisser."

And he smiled. "Likewise."

"I would kiss you some more, but..."

"...it's not what we're about," he finished for her. His strong arms fell away and she carefully kept herself from swaying back against him. He offered his arm. She took it. "Come on," he said, "I'll take you back up to the resort."

"Not coming in?" she asked, when he pulled up under the porte cochere.

Jace was thinking he would like to go in. He would like it a lot, but it seemed too dangerous after that kiss. She'd felt just right in his arms. And the sweet taste of her lips...

That had been something. The way she'd cuddled up close against him had really gotten him going. They might be best friends and not going there. But he had to be realistic. She did it for him. In a big way.

And he needed a little distance. Tonight, he could too easily be tempted to try and put a real move on her. And he got that she wasn't up for anything hot and heavy with him—or with anyone. Not after what she'd been through.

"Not tonight," he whispered. "Breakfast? We can go down to the bakery and maybe—"

"Yes." She smiled an eager smile. And he was glad. They'd shared an amazing, mind-blowing kiss, but it wasn't going to mess things up between them.

The valet opened her door. She got out and then turned back and leaned in to ask, "Nine tomorrow morning? Pick me up right here, under the porte cochere?"

"You got it."

The valet shut the door. Jace watched her turn for the entrance, admiring the easy sway of her hips, entranced by the way all that lush, shiny hair tumbled down her slim back.

During the drive to Jackson and Laila's place, his

mind kept circling back to the kiss. To the way she filled his arms, to the feel of her breasts against his chest, to the way she pressed her body to him, lower down, to her soft mouth opening under his…

He thought about kissing her again.

He thought about doing a lot more than just kissing.

The house was dark when he let himself in. He went straight up to the guest room and took a shower. A very cold shower, for a long, long time.

When he got out, his teeth were chattering and his lips were blue. But the shower had done the trick. He was freezing and sex was the last thing on his mind.

And he'd learned his lesson. He was not kissing Joss again. He was not even *thinking* about kissing Joss again.

Uh-uh. No way.…

In the morning before he left to pick up Joss, he joined Jackson and Laila in the kitchen.

"So," he asked his twin, "how long's the Hitching Post been closed?"

"Since March," Jackson said.

"You never a said a word." Jace tried not to sound accusing, but it did kind of bug him that no one had told him. "*Nobody* said anything. Joss and I stopped in there last night and everything was dark."

Jackson sipped his morning coffee and answered with a shrug. "It was a shock when it happened. But you were more or less refusing to communicate at that point."

That was true, Jace had to admit. In March, he'd still been pretty down after the whole mess with Tricia. Half the time, when Jackson or any of his siblings called, he would find some excuse to get off the phone fast, and then not bother calling them back. He hadn't felt like talking to anyone—and he certainly hadn't felt like answering any questions as to what the hell was the matter with him.

"Sorry about that," he said and meant it.

"Hey." Jackson gave him a grin. "You finally seem to be coming out of it. That's what matters."

At the stove, Laila asked, "You want some bacon and eggs, Jace?"

"Thanks, but no. I'm picking Joss up and we're going to the Mountain Bluebell." He asked his brother, "So what's the story? I always thought the Hitching Post was a moneymaker. Why would they suddenly close down?"

"Lance O'Doherty died," Laila said somberly.

Jace blinked. "No." O'Doherty and his wife Kathleen had owned the Hitching Post since it first opened in the 1950s. Kathleen had passed away some years back.

"Yeah," Jackson confirmed. "Lance finally went to meet his maker. The old guy was in his eighties. And he was still going strong right up to the end. Story goes that he went to bed on March first and never woke up on the second. There was no one to take over for him."

"I thought there was a daughter…"

Jackson nodded. "Noreen. She's in her fifties. Plays the harp for some symphony in San Diego. Never married, no kids. Has zero interest in coming back to Thunder Canyon to run her dad's bar and grill. So she shut it down and put it up for sale, cheap. At first, we were all sure that someone would snap it right up. I think I heard that there were a few offers made, but I guess those deals never went through."

Jason shook his head. "The Hitching Post out of business. That's just wrong."

"Someone will buy it eventually," said Laila. "It's been only a few months since it went up for sale. It's a great location, with plenty of parking. I heard a rumor a cousin of the Cateses from Sheridan was thinking about buying the property and turning it into a farm machinery dealership."

"Farm machinery?" Jace swore in disgust.

Jackson chuckled. "People need tractors, Jace."

"And this town needs the Hitching Post."

Jackson sent him a sly look. "Why don't you buy it?"

He thought about last night, him and Joss in the shadows next to the locked-up front door with the For Sale sign on it. He'd teased her that he would buy it and she could teach him how to run it.

But it was only a daydream. A fantasy, like Joss had said.

Laila fished bacon out of the frying pan and onto a paper towel–covered platter. "Yeah, that would be great if you moved to town. Your brother misses you, you know? We all miss you. Family matters. It matters a lot."

Jackson and Jace shared a look. Jace had missed his twin, too. He only realized how much now he was coming out of the funk that had gripped him for months.

And Thunder Canyon would be a great place to live. Yeah, it got mighty cold in the winters, but he could deal with that. There were still lots of wild, wide open spaces in Montana. He wouldn't mind exploring them. Plus, he'd have the benefit of being near a lot of the people who mattered most to him. And he *was* planning to move.

But he wasn't ready to decide where yet. And as for the Hitching Post…

"I know zip about running a restaurant," he said.

Jackson got up to refill his coffee mug. "No law says you can't learn."

Joss was moving a little stiffly when he picked her up at nine. But she said she was fine.

She laughed. "Hey, you should have seen me when I first got up. It wasn't pretty. But I'm feeling better now that I've been moving around."

And it did seem to him that her stiffness faded as the day went by. After breakfast at Lizzie's bakery, they walked over to the Historical Society Museum on Pine Street. Aunt Melba was there, behind the little desk in the small lobby area of the old building.

"So lovely to see two young, smiling faces," she said. She charged them three dollars each and then gave them a guided tour.

The rooms were small and dark and packed with treasures from the past. There was a whole display dedicated to Lily Divine, the madam who'd owned the Shady Lady Dance Hall in the 1890s. They learned that some sources claimed Lily hadn't really been a madam at all, but a hardworking laundress who took in women in trouble and helped them to get back on their feet. There was even some dispute as to whether the famous portrait of Lily, nearly nude but for several strategically place scarves, was actually of Lily at all.

Jace couldn't help wondering if that portrait still hung over the bar inside the Hitching Post. He hated to think of someone turning the place into a tractor dealership.

What would happen to the portrait of the Shady Lady then? Would they dismantle the long, gleaming cherrywood bar that had been built over a century ago?

He decided not to think about it.

Times changed and a man had to learn to roll with the punches. He set his mind to enjoying the time he had left with Joss.

It was going by too fast.

That afternoon, they went riding again. He borrowed Major from Jackson and she rode Cupcake. He took her to a small, crystal-clear lake he knew about on the other side of Thunder Mountain from the resort. It was too cold to swim, but they spread a saddle blanket in the sun and stretched out for a while. She said she was feeling better about her life now, about everything. And she thanked him. She told him she didn't hate all men anymore. And she said that was mostly due to him.

He listened to her talk and drank in her laughter and thought about kissing her.

But he didn't. They were friends. Period. And he intended to remember that.

That night, the family get-together was at Dax and Shandie's. Jace took Joss. They had a great time.

The next day was the Fourth. In Thunder Canyon, that meant a parade in the morning, a rodeo in the afternoon and a community dance in the town hall at night. He and Joss spent every moment together.

He thought about kissing her a lot that day, especially at the dance. When he held her in his arms, it was all too easy to start remembering how good her lips felt pressed to his.

But he held himself in check somehow. Even though sometimes, in her eyes, he thought he saw an invitation.

He had a feeling she wouldn't be entirely averse to another kiss. And when he danced with her, he tried not to read too much into the way her curvy body swayed against him.

That night, he took another long, cold shower before he went to bed. It didn't do a lot of good. His dreams were all about Joss, naked and willing in his arms.

Thursday they played golf up at the resort's golf course. Joss was a really bad golfer.

"I'm worse with a golf club than I am on a horse," she said.

He had to agree. Actually, she had some aptitude for riding. But she was a walking hazard with a golf club. Every time she swung it, turf went flying. The ball, however, rarely budged.

After dinner that night at Corey and Erin's, they returned to the resort and hung out in her suite. He told her he kept thinking about the Hitching Post, that he was actually kind of tempted by the idea of maybe buying the place, of moving to Thunder Canyon and learning how to run a restaurant and bar.

She encouraged him. He was just getting around to hinting that maybe she might consider taking a job managing a restaurant and bar in a great little town like Thunder Canyon when the phone rang.

It was her mother, at it again. He couldn't hear the woman's words, but he could see in Joss's face what she must be saying: Come home to Sacramento and work things out with Kenny. When Joss hung up, her slim shoulders were drooping and all the warm amber light was gone from her eyes. He wanted to take her in his arms and hold her, and promise her that everything would be okay.

But she asked him to leave, said she needed a little time alone. She really was down.

He went back to Jackson's and took another cold shower.

That night he dreamed of Lily Divine—except she had Joss's face. In the dream, he stood at the bar in the Hitching Post and looked up at the painting of the Shady Lady.

And suddenly, the painting came alive. The Shady Lady was Joss, so fine and curvy and mostly naked, lying on her side, braced up on an elbow with her beautiful backside to him, sending him a come-and-get-it look over one bare, dimpled shoulder. He stood there, gulping, hard as a rock.

But then she sat up from the pose she'd been stuck in for more than a century. The scarves that covered her breasts and hips wafted in a warm breeze that had come up out of nowhere—right there in the Hitching Post. She stepped out of the painting and down off the wall, her long hair lifted and coiling seductively around her in that impossible breeze. She reached out her slim, bare arms to him, her eyes gleaming with the promise of untold sensual delights.

And then he woke up.

He lay there in the guest room bed and glared at the darkened ceiling and wondered who he'd been kidding, to think it would be enough for him, to be just friends with a woman like Joss.

She called him at seven Friday morning. "Sorry I was such a downer." Her voice was sweet and husky in his ear.

"Hey," he said a little more gruffly than he meant to, "it's not a problem. You know that."

"I want to go riding one more time before I go…."

Her words hit him like a punch to the solar plexus. *Before I go…*

Their time was ending. Tomorrow was Saturday. And Sunday she was leaving.

A week. It was nothing. Gone in an instant. He'd known that, hadn't he?

So why did it suddenly seem so wrong, so completely unfair, that she would be going, leaving him for good?

He schooled his voice to easiness. "So we'll go riding. Today?"

"Yeah. I thought breakfast first at the Grubstake." That was the coffee shop at the resort. "And then we'd head for the stables. I already asked to have Cupcake ready."

He would need to get the go-ahead from Jackson to take Major again. That should be no problem. "Bring something you can swim in," he said.

"But I thought the mountain lakes were too cold."

"I know a little valley. A wide creek runs through it. It's not so high up and should be warm enough for swimming."

"Sounds wonderful," she agreed.

"The Grubstake, then." His voice was rough again, a little ragged with emotions he didn't even understand. "Give me an hour."

"I'll be there. Waiting."

And she *was* there, just as she'd promised, waiting in the coffee shop, dressed for riding in her red boots and jeans and a blue-and-white checked shirt. They ordered pancake specials, with scrambled eggs and bacon. She was animated and smiling, out from under the cloud of misery that had gotten her down the night before.

"Today and tomorrow," she said, her dark eyes gleaming. "And that's it." Did she have to remind him? "I'm going to enjoy every minute of the time we have left."

Don't go. The words were there on the tip of his tongue. He shut his mouth over them and swallowed them down.

He tried to remember what a tangled mess the whole thing with Tricia had been, that he didn't know his ass from up when it came to relationships. That the last thing Joss needed at this point was another man in her life.

A friend, she could handle.

But more?

It wasn't going to happen. She needed time to get over that asshat Kenny, time to put her life back together, to get on her feet. She didn't need to get involved with some ex-player ex-oilman from Texas who didn't know zip about love and was seriously considering relocating to Montana and trying his hand at running a bar and grill.

They finished their pancakes and headed for the stables. By ten-thirty, they were on their way up the mountain. They rode a different series of trails that day, around the mountain, climbing for a time. But then, using a series of switchbacks, heading lower, down into the little valley he'd told her about.

The land belonged to Grant Clifton, the resort's manager, and his wife, Steph. Last year, when Ethan had invested Traub money in the resort, Grant had been kind enough to issue a general invitation to any Traubs who wanted to swim in the creek there.

"It's beautiful," Joss said, when they spread a blanket under a cottonwood at the edge of the creek.

He had a hard time paying a lot of attention to the trees and the clear creek and the rolling, sunlit land. Joss had taken off her jeans, boots and shirt by then. She wore a little black-and-white bikini that looked like polka dots at first glance, but was really tiny white hearts on a black background. She filled it out real nice. He kept thinking about his dream, where she was the Shady Lady and she came down out of the picture and held out her arms to him.

"Jace?" she asked softly. "You okay?"

"Ahem. Fine. Great. Why?"

She laughed then. "Well, your mouth is hanging open."

He shut it. "Is not."

She laughed again and turned and ran to the creek. He watched her pretty, round bottom bouncing away from him and tried not to think about how much he wanted a lot more than he was ever going to have with her. If she had any bruises from her fall the other day, he couldn't see them.

Hugging herself and giggling, she went into the water. "It's cold!" She bent at the knees and got right down into it all the way up to her neck.

"I can hear your teeth chattering," he teased from the bank, admiring the way that thick, long hair of hers fanned out on the water all around her.

"My teeth are chattering because the water is freezing!"

"Don't be a sissy," he taunted.

"You said it would be warm down here in this valley," she accused. "Brrrr."

"It is warm—compared to the lakes higher up."

She rose to her feet, the water sheeting off her body, her hair falling to cling like a lover to her shoulders and the high, proud curves of her breasts. The sight stole the breath clean out of his body and made all the spit dry up in his mouth.

"Well?" she demanded. "Are you coming in?"

He remembered to breathe and he swallowed, hard. "Yes, ma'am." He dropped to the blanket and pulled off his boots and socks. His shirt followed. Then he stood up again to unbuckle his belt. A moment later, he stepped out of his jeans.

Joss gave him a two-finger whistle. "I never saw a cowboy in board shorts before—neon orange, no less." He made a show of flexing his biceps and she laughed some more.

And then he took off toward her at a run. She shrieked as he cannonballed into the water. And when he got his feet under him and stood up, she started madly splashing him.

He dived and grabbed for her legs, yanking them out from under her. Flailing and laughing, she went down, but only for a moment. Then she kicked free of his grip and swam for the far bank.

When he caught up with her, she was trying to climb out on the other side.

He grabbed her shoulders and pulled her back in.

She let out a shriek and went under again.

A moment later, she shot upright. She was quick, he had to give her that. She gave him a shove when he wasn't expecting it. He went down on his back, sending water flying. He heard her laughing as the creek closed over his head.

In a few seconds, he was upright again. They started madly splashing each other, both of them fanning the water for all they were worth, really going to town.

Finally, her hair plastered to her face, water dripping from her nose, she put up both hands. "All right. I surrender. You win. You're the champion."

That made him laugh. "The champion of splashing?"

"Yeah." She swiped a hand over the crown of her head, gathering her hair in one thick swatch, guiding it forward over her shoulder so she could wring the water from the dripping strands. "You don't want to be the champion of splashing?"

He speared his fingers back through his hair. "Depends on the prize."

She made a scoffing sound. "Please. You don't get a prize for splashing the hardest."

He stepped up closer. He couldn't resist. They stood in the shallows by then, not far from the bank and their waiting blanket, with the hobbled horses grazing nearby.

She stared up at him, drops of water caught like diamonds in her long, dark eyelashes, her eyes so bright they blinded him. Damn. She was beautiful. "Jace?"

He couldn't stop staring at her wide, soft mouth. "I want to kiss you."

"Oh, Jace…"

"You'd better tell me not to. You'd better tell me now."

Chapter 8

She drew in a breath—a sharp little sound. And she argued, "But I don't want to tell you not to…"

He took her shoulders. Wet. Silky. Cool. Longing speared through him. Sharp. Hot. "Was that a yes?"

"Oh, Jace…"

"Answer the question."

"Yes." She said it fervently. Eagerly. "That's a yes."

So he kissed her. Kissed her for the second time. Slowly, deeply.

She opened for him and he tasted the sweetness beyond her parted lips. He gathered her close to him, skin to skin, carefully. Tenderly.

The sun was warm on his back and she was so perfect in his arms. He didn't want to let her go.

But he knew he had to. He lifted his mouth from hers with regret. And he opened his eyes to find hers waiting for him.

She searched his face. "Do you know how much I'll miss you?"

Don't go. "Hey, you're not gone yet."

She reached up, touched his lips with her cool, smooth fingers. "That's right. I'm still here. And I'm so glad…" Her eyes shone brighter, wetter. A single tear escaped and trailed down her cheek. He leaned close and kissed that warm wetness away. She whispered, "I'm so glad I met you."

"Me, too." He took her hand. "Come on." He led her up to the bank where he picked up the blanket and moved it out from under the shading branches of the tree.

They lay down side-by-side, faces tipped to the sunlight.

Far off, he heard the cry of a hawk. And then silence, just the rushing whisper of the creek and the wind stirring the cottonwoods.

He closed his eyes. It was one of those moments, so simple. So perfect—him and Joss on a blanket in the sun.

Eventually, they got up and pulled on their jeans, shirts and boots. They ate the jerky he'd brought along in his saddlebag and drank from their canteens. Then they rolled up the blanket and tied it on behind Major's saddle.

They mounted up and started back the way they had come.

That night, they had dinner with the rest of the family at Rose and Austin's. Around eleven, they went back to the resort. He stayed until three in the morning. They talked and they laughed. They ate too much chocolate.

They watched two movies on pay-per-view: a romantic comedy for her and an old Western for him.

The whole night he kept thinking, *Don't go, don't go.* After a while it seemed that the words were there, echoing, in every breath he took, in every beat of his heart.

But he didn't say them.

And he didn't kiss her again either. Not kissing her was almost as hard as not saying "Don't go." But he managed both somehow. He went back to Jackson's in the early morning hours, had his usual cold shower and climbed under the covers to toss and turn and dream of her.

He was up at daylight. He showered fast and dressed faster and headed for the resort. Luck was with him. He caught Grant in the office complex down the hill from clubhouse and took care of the business that had been nagging at him.

Then he went up the hill, got two coffees at the Starbucks on the first floor of the clubhouse and took the elevator to Joss's suite. He had to knock twice before she finally answered, looking sleepy and tousled and irresistible, barefoot in a cream-colored terrycloth robe.

"I see you brought coffee," she said in a sleepy voice. "Smart man."

Don't go. "Mornin'." He held hers out to her. She took it and sipped, stepping back at the same time so that he could enter. "I have a confession," he said to her back as she led the way into the sitting room.

She paused to send him a look over her shoulder. "Nothing too awful, I hope."

"I'm afraid you're going to be mad at me."

She turned around then, and faced him in the archway to the sitting room. "Better just say it." She sipped from her cup again.

It made him ache all over to look at her, to think that she was leaving, that tomorrow, she would be gone. "I stopped in and saw Grant this morning—you know, the resort manager?"

"I remember Grant."

"I caught him down the hill at his office…"

"Yeah?"

"And I paid your bill."

She had her cup halfway to her lips again, but she lowered it without drinking. Her face had a set look to it suddenly, and her dark gaze was steady on his. "Jace. No."

"Come on. It's not a big deal."

"It's a lot of money. And no." She reached out her hand.

He looked at it. "I guess if you're offering me your hand, at least you're not *too* mad. Right?"

"I'm not mad," she said softly. "I promise." She grabbed his fingers. Heat shot up his arm and he had to stop himself from yanking her close to him and slamming his mouth down on hers. "Come on." She towed him into the sitting room and over to the sofa. "Sit." He sat. She dropped down beside him and set her cup on the coffee table. "I'm…well, I could really get emotional, you know? It means so much that you would want to do that for me."

He set his untouched coffee beside hers. "Just say you're okay with it."

She blew out a hard breath. "But I'm not okay with it. It's not right."

"Sure it is." He tried to look stern and uncompromising. "I can afford it, believe me."

"That's not the issue. I mean, I get why you would want to. I do. And it's so sweet of you, really."

"It's not sweet, believe me," he muttered. "Not sweet in the least. I don't think you get it at all."

"But I do get it. It's about Kenny, right?"

How did she know that? He admitted, "I don't want that lowlife, cheating sonofabitch paying your way here. I just don't."

"Jace." She put her hand on his arm. For the second time that morning, he had to steel himself to keep from grabbing her tight and kissing her senseless. "Listen," she said, "I agree with you. I've been thinking about it, too. And I've realized that I really can't have Kenny footing the bill. I don't want *anything* from Kenny."

"Good. There's no problem, then. It's paid."

With a low groan, she let go of his forearm. "You're not listening to me. It's not Kenny's bill. And it's not *your* bill. It's mine. And I will pay it."

He almost wished she'd been mad at him, instead of so firm and sure and uncompromising about it. How does a man get through to an uncompromising woman? "Listen. You like me, right?"

Her eyes held reproach. "Of course I do."

"You even trust me. A little."

"I trust you a lot." She almost smiled. "And a week ago, I would have sworn I would never trust a man again."

"So…can't you think of it as a gift from a friend? From your best friend? When you get settled, with a new apartment and a great job, you can feel free to pay me back if it's that important to you. But maybe, over time, you'll see things in a different light. You'll remember that I said I *wanted* to do this. And I meant what I said. I don't want you owing your ex a thing. I want you free of him. And I don't want you spending every cent you've got to *get* free of him."

She gathered her legs up onto the cushions and tucked them to the side. Then she wrapped the fluffy robe closer around her. "It wouldn't be every cent I've got..." She gave a low, sad little chuckle. "Not quite, anyway."

"Let me do this for you, Joss. Please."

"I really shouldn't..."

"Yeah, you should."

She shut her eyes, hung her head. "Thank you," she said, so softly.

He wanted to touch her, but that would be too dangerous. "Glad to do it."

And then she swayed against him, whispering a second time, "Thank you."

What could he do but exactly what he longed to do? He wrapped an arm around her and drew her close. And when she lifted her sweet lips to him, he kissed her, a light kiss, one he didn't allow himself to deepen.

And then he picked up her cup from the coffee table and handed it to her. "Go on. Get dressed. Let's get some breakfast."

Joss wanted that final day with Jace to last forever, but it seemed to fly by even faster than the ones before it.

They went to Lizzie's bakery for breakfast, and then they dropped in at the Historical Society Museum to say hi to Melba. They took a long drive along Thunder

Canyon Road, all the way to the steep, rocky canyon for which the town was named.

That night, they had dinner in the resort's best restaurant, the Gallatin Room. They ran into Jace's parents there. Claudia and Pete were still staying at the resort.

Jace muttered resignedly, "I suppose we should go and say hi to them."

"Yes, we absolutely should."

So they stopped by the Wexlers' table for a moment. Claudia said how she and Pete would be there for at least another week. And Joss confessed that tomorrow she was on her way back to Sacramento.

"I hope you'll get Jason to bring you to Midland one of these days very soon," Claudia suggested.

Joss didn't give her an answer, only said how much she'd enjoyed spending time with the Traub family while she'd been in town.

They moved on to their table shortly after that. It was in a secluded corner, so it really felt like it was just the two of them. Jace ordered a nice bottle of wine and the food was wonderful, better than ever, she thought.

Jace thought so, too. He told the waiter.

The waiter said they had a new chef.

"Give him our compliments."

"I'll be more than happy to."

The waiter left, and the new chef came out to chat with them briefly. His name was Shane Roarke. He was ruggedly handsome, with black hair and piercing blue eyes. Joss had the feeling she'd met him somewhere before.

When he left them, Jace gazed after him, narrow-eyed. "I could swear I've met him somewhere before."

Joss nodded. "You know, I was just thinking the same thing...."

He looked at her then, his dark eyes so soft and warm, his mouth hinting at a smile. "Did I tell you that you look beautiful?"

Her chest felt a little tight and a delicious shiver whispered across the surface of her skin. "You did tell me. Twice—three times, counting just now."

"I like that dress."

It was snug, black, short and strapless. "You mentioned that, too."

He scowled. "I hate that you're leaving."

"I know. Me, too."

"But we can't go on like this forever."

She grinned. "You're so right. We've been having way too much fun."

He grunted. "It's got to stop."

She laughed. "Yep." She picked up her glass of wine. "Here's to a new life and a great job—for both of us."

He tapped his glass to hers. "To all your dreams coming true."

After dinner, he suggested, "We could go into town. I think there's another dance at the town hall tonight."

She shook her head and took his hand. "Let's go up to the suite."

He must have had a sense of what she was up to because something hot and hungry flashed in his eyes. "Maybe that's not such a good idea, Joss."

She knew exactly what he was doing—or trying to do: the right thing. As usual. "Jace..."

"What?" His voice was rough and low.

"It's our last night. I'm leaving in the morning. We may never see each other again."

"Rub it in, why don't you?"

"Come up to the suite with me." She held his gaze. She refused to glance away, to pretend to be shy about this. She wasn't shy. Not with him. With him, she'd always been able to say exactly what was on her mind.

He muttered something under his breath. She thought it was a swear word, but she wasn't sure.

She kept hold of his hand. "Come upstairs with me. Please."

He touched her cheek, smoothed a few strands of hair out of her eyes. "Are you sure? I don't want you to regret anything about the time you've spent with me."

"I'm sure." She searched his face. "But maybe you're not?"

A strangled sound escaped him. "Of course I'm sure. That's not the point."

"I disagree. I think if you're sure and I'm sure, well, what else is there? And don't start in about regrets again. I will never regret spending tonight with you." She whispered, "Could you stand it if I left without making love to you? I know I couldn't."

He actually groaned. And then he lifted her hand and pressed his warm lips to it. "That does it." He breathed the words onto her skin. "Let's go."

In the bedroom of her suite, they stood by her bed, facing each other.

She felt nervous. Apprehensive.

And yet, at the same time, absolutely sure.

The covers were already turned back. There were chocolates on the pillow.

"Your favorite kind," he said. "Dark and bittersweet."

She grabbed up the candy and set it on the nightstand. "I'll never eat them. I'll save them. To remember tonight…"

He grinned at that. Her heart ached. How would she live without seeing that grin of his? "Uh-uh. You should eat them. I'll feed them to you personally."

She turned her head away a little and gave him an oblique glance. "Now?"

"Later." He growled the word.

She swallowed. Hard. "I'm…on the pill, but I should have bought condoms."

He reached in his pocket and brought out four of them. "Okay," he said roughly. "It's like this. I never planned to put a move on you, I promise you…"

She teased, "But you wanted to be ready, just in case I dragged you up here and wouldn't let you go until you made mad, passionate love to me."

"Right." His dark eyes were bright with humor—and heat. "You being such a total animal and all."

She took the condoms from him and set them on the nightstand next to the chocolates. "So, all right, we have chocolate and condoms. We're ready for anything."

He was watching her so steadily. "Joss."

Her heart stopped still inside her chest—and then started in again, swift and hard. "Hmm?"

He took her by the shoulders, his big hands so warm and firm. And then he turned her around, smoothed her hair to the side and over her shoulder out of his way, and took down her zipper in one slow, seamless glide. Her strapless black dress dropped to the floor.

She looked down at it, in a silky black puddle around

her ankles. Now, she wore her strapless bra, satin tap shorts, black high-heeled shoes. And nothing else.

He whispered her name again. "I never had a best friend like you before..." And he traced the bumps of her spine, so slowly, with one teasing finger, from the nape of her neck all the way down to where her tap pants rode low on her hips. "Beautiful." The single word was more breath than sound.

She stepped out of the dress and bent to retrieve it. There was a slipper chair a few feet from the nightstand. She tossed the dress on that chair and turned to him.

His eyes were dark fire, burning her in the most arousing way.

She said, "I'm so glad you're here. In this bedroom With me." And she reached behind her, undid her bra and let it fall away.

He gasped. She found that ragged sound supremely satisfying, not to mention exciting.

"Your turn," she instructed.

He started undressing. He did it really fast, with a ruthless efficiency, dropping first to the side of the bed to tug off his boots and socks, and then rising again to face her as he stripped away everything else, tossing each article away from him as he removed it.

Within seconds, he was naked. He stood before her, so lean and tall and beautiful—yes. Beautiful. Beautiful in the way only a man can be, a beauty of power, of muscle. Of strength.

He reached for her, gathered her to him. She went with a soft, hungry cry.

His mouth came down to settle on hers and his chest was so hot and hard against her bare breasts, his arms so tight around her.

She kissed him. She opened to him. Her heartbeat, so rapid and frantic a moment ago, settled into a lazier, hungrier rhythm.

He took her face between his two hands, kissing her so deeply, so thoroughly, and then he threaded his fingers into her hair, combing the long strands, following them all the way down in one long stroke. He clasped her waist.

And then lower, grasping the twin curves of her bottom and drawing her up and into him—so tight. He kissed her some more. A dizzying, magical kiss. At the same time, he was turning her, guiding her to the bed, still kissing her as he eased her down. She sat on the edge and he bent to her, his mouth and her mouth, fused in a hot tangle of warm breath, of questing tongues....

He came down to her. She opened her thighs so he could kneel between them.

His strong hands caressed her breasts so gently, at first. He learned the shape of them, cradling them tenderly. He teased her nipples into aching hardness.

She swayed toward him, her mouth fused with his, wanting to be closer, aware of the thousand ways he thrilled her, excited her, made her burn. Awash in sheer wonder, she counted those ways: his touch, the taste of his mouth, the rough rasp of his beard shadow against her palms when she caressed the side of his face.

His dear face...

How had that happened? In the space of a week, he had become so very dear to her. She could no longer imagine her life without him in it.

No. She couldn't.

Not now. Not tonight.

Facing the loss of him would be for tomorrow. In the harsh light of day.

Tonight was for magic. For beauty. For pleasure. For the impossible—her and Jace. Together.

This one time…

For tonight, she could almost be grateful that her world had come crashing down. That her groom had betrayed her. That her dream for her future was shattered. Gone.

She'd lost the life she'd longed for. She was going to have to start over.

But in the middle of her own personal disaster, she'd met Jason. He'd taken her bitterness and transformed it somehow. Made it something so perfect and good and sweet. He'd given her a week she would always remember.

And now, at the end, he presented her with one final gift: tonight.

He broke the kiss, settled back on his knees.

She gave a lost, hungry cry and tried to catch his mouth again.

But he clasped her shoulders, steadying her. She opened her eyes to find his dark gaze waiting. He almost smiled, but he didn't. Not quite.

He let his hands trail down the outsides of her arms, rousing goose bumps of desire, making her sigh.

"Oh, Jace…"

"I dreamed about you…"

She laughed, low, a secret, woman's laugh. "No…"

"Yeah."

"Tell me."

"You were the Shady Lady. It was you in that painting over the bar at the Hitching Post. Remember, we saw a picture of that painting, that day we went to the museum?"

She nodded. "The Shady Lady, lying on her side, draped in nothing but a few scarves..."

His caresses strayed downward. He clasped her waist, molded the outer curves of her hips, and lower. He laid his warm palms on her thighs. "You do remember, then..."

"I do." She moaned a little. "You're driving me crazy."

"Good. In my dream, you were the Shady Lady and you came out of the picture and down into my arms. The wind was blowing out of nowhere, lifting your hair around your face, and lifting the scarves, too, so they kind of floated in the air around you."

"Wait a minute."

He frowned. "You want me to stop?"

"Don't you dare." She let out a shaky breath. "But... the wind was blowing in the Hitching Post?"

"It was a dream after all."

"Ah."

He cradled her calves, one in either hand, rubbing them a little. "And the wind was warm...."

She was on fire by then, yearning. "Ah. Warm. What happened next?"

He took her left ankle, raised it and slipped off her high-heeled shoe. "I woke up."

She sighed. "Oh, no."

"Yeah."

"Sad..."

"Yeah." He lifted her other foot, removed the other shoe, set it aside with its mate. And then he was stroking her legs again, but this time moving upward, over her shins, her knees, her trembling thighs.

Breath held, she watched him as he eased his clever fingers under the loose, lace-edged hems of her tap pants. He touched her, both hands meeting at the place where her thighs joined, delving in, parting her.

She gasped as he caressed her, his fingers moving beneath the black satin. He found her, found her sweetest spot without even half trying. And he worked it, making her burn, making her so wet and ready....

Oh, it was heaven. Jace's touch.

She lay back across the bed and let him torment her so perfectly. She moaned out loud; it felt so right. And she lifted her hips to him, sighing, whispering his name, tossing her head, reaching down to clasp his corded forearms, holding on to him as he stroked her, bringing her higher.

Higher and higher...

"Lift up," he muttered low, pulling on the tap pants, guiding them down.

By then, she was wild with desire, lost in her own building excitement. She moaned and she raised her hips and he slipped the tap pants down and away.

And then he leaned closer. And his fingers were touching her, opening her. She knew she was bare to his gaze and somehow, that only fired her need, made her burn hotter.

"Jace. Oh, Jace..."

And then he leaned closer still. She felt his breath, stirring the dark hair that covered her sex.

His breath.

And then...oh, and then...he kissed her. There. Right there, where she was burning for him. He kissed her and he parted her and his tongue slid in to find that sweet spot all over again. His tongue…

How did he do that? He created sensations that were delicious beyond bearing.

She reached down, threaded her fingers in his dark, thick hair, pulled him even closer. She called out his name, wildly, as he held her in his endless, wet, perfect kiss.

Oh, she was rising, reaching…

And he went on kissing her, his big hands under her hips, tipping her up to him. She didn't want it to end. Not ever.

But of course, the end came. And it was glorious.

With a cry, she hit the crest and went over.

Her body trembled. He held on, drinking from her, doing something impossibly fine with his tongue so that the pleasure expanded, moving out in waves from the core of her, filling her, overflowing, spreading out and out…until it halted, hung suspended on a thread for a world-stopping moment.

And then at last, receding, drawing back, like a shining, perfect wave, retreating to the center of her, where it continued to pulse so sweetly in delicious afterglow.

She lay there, dazed. Wondering.

He eased his hands out from under her hips. He broke that incredible intimate kiss.

And he rose to his feet.

She asked, softly, "Jace?"

He said nothing. She gazed up at him, over his muscled thighs, over the proof of his desire for her, jutting so hard and proud. Over his hard belly and powerful chest.

Beautiful, she thought again. A beautiful man…

Strange. She'd always thought of him as kind. An easygoing, easy-to-know sort of guy.

But he didn't look all that kind right then. And not in the least easygoing.

She saw a roughness, now. A depth of need and emotion she hadn't known in him before. Something that called to the woman in her.

Something undeniably, excitingly, possessively male.

She wanted to reach for him, to beg him to come back to her, but her arms felt so wonderfully heavy, her body limp with satisfaction. Pliant. Slow.

So she simply lay there, watching him, yearning for him, as he turned to the nightstand and took one of the condoms. He had it out of the foil pouch and rolled into place in an instant.

Only then did he come down to her again. She welcomed him, lifting her arms eagerly then, to wrap around his hard, broad shoulders, pulling him close to her, loving the weight of him as he settled on top of her.

He buried his head in the curve of her neck. And he kissed her there, using his tongue, sucking the skin against his teeth. Not hard enough to leave a love bite.

Just hard enough to make her moan.

"Now," she commanded in a ragged, needful whisper. "Please, Jace. Now…"

His hands swept down, along the outer swells of her hips. He guided her legs up to encircle his waist. She hooked her ankles together at the small of his back, and she felt him there, thick and hard and smooth, right exactly where she wanted him.

In one long, sure stroke, he filled her.

She moaned at the wonder of it, and sank her teeth

into his shoulder, but gently. Oh, he did feel so good inside her.

He felt exactly right. He filled her so deep.

She wrapped herself closer around him, tightening her grip with her arms and her legs. She rocked against him.

And he answered her, rocking back, finding first a long, sure rhythm, teasing her with it, bringing her fully out of the soft fade of her own satisfaction.

Into renewed pleasure. Into rising again, this time with him, better even than the time before.

Slow and deep and steady…and then faster, harder, faster still.

And she held on, she went where he took her.

Into the heart of the heat and the wonder. Over the moon, into a velvet black night scattered with bursting stars.

Chapter 9

Later, as they soaked in the suite's jetted bathtub, he fed her the chocolates the maid had left on her pillow.

Leaning back against his broad chest, trapped between his bare, muscular thighs, feeling loose and easy and totally decadent, she let the lovely bittersweet treat melt on her tongue. "I could get used to this."

"Me, too." His voice was a fine, dark rumble in her ear. And along her spine, she could feel the rise and fall of his chest with every breath he took.

She turned her head to him.

He leaned to the side to reach her mouth. And he kissed her. "Um. Chocolate." He offered her a sip of the champagne he'd ordered from room service. She took it, laughing when some of it spilled, those lovely, fizzy bubbles straying down her chin. He said, "I think I'm getting…ideas."

She laughed again. "I feel you." She wiggled back against him. "Oh, my…"

He groaned. "You'll kill me."

"With pleasure…" She rolled, floating up, settling against him again, but this time facing him. "What have we here?" she teased, as she found him under the water and wrapped her eager fingers around him.

He made a rough, wordless sound.

She kissed him as she stroked him.

That didn't last long. A few minutes later, he was gathering her to him, getting his legs under him, rising from the tub, heedless of the water splashing over the sides. He carried her into the bedroom, where he turned so she could reach the nightstand.

She knew what he wanted her to do. Laughing, she grabbed one of the condoms. "We're dripping water everywhere."

So he carried her back into the bathroom, where he boosted her up onto the long counter between the double sinks.

"Oh, my," she said so softly, as he filled her for the second time.

He captured her lips in a long, sweet, wet kiss as he took her over the moon again.

By two in the morning, they had used the last condom. They were back in the bed by then.

She cuddled up close to him and whispered, "I don't want to go to sleep. I don't want to waste a moment of the time we have left."

They spoke of their childhoods. He told her more about his brothers, about the battles between them and also the good times growing up.

She told him about her best friend when she was

twelve. "Her name was Jane Ackerman. She dumped me our freshman year to get in with the popular kids."

"You weren't popular in high school?" He shook his head. "I don't believe it."

"I was shy."

"No way."

"Oh, yeah. And lonely—I told you that the first night I met you."

He answered tenderly. "That's right. I remember."

"I never felt like I fit in, you know? I was something of a misfit, I guess you could say."

"And just look at you now."

She rested her head on his warm, strong chest, where she could hear the steady beating of his generous heart. "You always make me feel so good about myself. Like I could do anything I wanted to do."

"Because you could." His lips brushed her hair.

Her eyelids felt heavy. She let them droop shut. Just for a minute or two...

Joss opened her eyes to sunlight streaming in between the half-drawn curtains.

And to Jason, his strong arms around her, smiling at her sleepily. "Looks like we fell asleep after all."

She snuggled in closer, feeling really good, really relaxed. And really satisfied. "What time is it?"

"Quarter after nine."

"Yikes." She sat straight up and raked her hand back through her tangled hair. "I've got to get moving, get packed. My plane takes off from Bozeman at ten after twelve."

"I'll order room service. You pack. I'll drive you to the airport."

"No need to drive me. I have a rental car."

He looked surprised. "You do?"

She shrugged. "I know. I have taken shameless advantage of you, had you chauffeur me everywhere since that first day we met." She didn't know whether to grab him and hold on for dear life, or burst into tears. "What will I do without you?"

He was braced up on an elbow, looking sleepy and way too sexy. Low and rough, he suggested, "Stay."

Yes! her heart cried.

But then she thought of her mother, of her marriage that hadn't happened, of everything that was so totally up in the air for her. She couldn't run away from her life forever. "Oh, Jace, I wish."

He studied her face for a long, tender moment. And then he said gently, "Well, then you'd better get moving."

She had so much to say to him, but when she opened her mouth, no words came. In the end, she only cleared her throat and answered sheepishly, "Yeah, I guess I'd better." She pushed back the covers. "I'll just grab a quick shower."

"I'll get us some food." He picked up the phone by the bed.

Half an hour later, she was showered and dressed and running back and forth from the closet in the bedroom to the living area, where she had her suitcases spread out on the sofa.

Jace sat at the table by the window, wearing his trousers from the night before and his dress shirt, unbuttoned, in bare feet, putting away a plateful of bacon and eggs. "Come on, Joss. Your food will get cold. Sit down and eat."

She glanced at him, at his beautiful, tanned bare chest between the open sides of his slightly wrinkled shirt. Was there ever a guy as great in every way as Jace? He was smart and fun, thoughtful, kind and generous. Not to mention, superhot and amazing in bed.

Her arms were full of shoes. She wanted to drop them and run to him, grab him, drag him back to her bed and keep him there all day.

He prompted, "I mean it. Come and eat."

That broke the spell. She couldn't run away from her life anymore. She needed to get back to reality. She was going home to Sacramento today. As planned.

He patted the chair beside him.

She promised, "I will, just a minute," as she dumped the shoes into the biggest of the suitcases and then raced back into the bedroom.

Her wedding gown confronted her. She stopped in the open door of the closet and stared at it, so white, so beautiful— a Cinderella fantasy in the classic ballroom style, with a strapless crisscross bodice sparkling with crystal beading and rhinestones, with endless acres of tulle and glitter net over taffeta that made up the fluffy, cloudlike layers of the skirt.

It was her dream dress.

The one that went with her dream wedding—the wedding she'd run from as fast as she could.

She should just ignore it. Just pack the rest of her things and walk away, leave it hanging there for the maid to find.

But somehow, she couldn't. Somehow, it represented way too much that she hadn't really relinquished. She'd got a great deal on it. But still, it had cost what to her was a small fortune.

She wanted it. She…coveted it. She wanted what it seemed to represent, the life she had planned for herself to which her beautiful, perfect wedding was supposed to be the gateway.

The life she would probably never have after all.

She heard knocking from the other end of the suite. Someone at the door.

Jace called, "I'll get it. It's room service with my extra toast."

She took the dress off the hanger and tossed the bodice over her shoulder, far enough that the acres of skirt were well clear of the floor. Then she took the veil. Cathedral length, it was sprinkled with diamanté and edged in lace. She folded it in half and laid it over her other shoulder, so the folded end and the hem end each came almost to the floor in front and in back.

She heard voices in the other room and assumed that Jace was probably overtipping the room service guy.

With one arm wrapped around the dress and the other holding the veil in place, she had all the layers of taffeta and tulle out of the way so that she could see where she was going. She aimed herself at the door to the living area.

She was so busy trying not to trip over all that fluffy fabric that she didn't register Claudia Wexler's voice until she was almost to the sofa and the open suitcases.

"Well, I'm sorry, Jason," she heard his mother say. "I didn't mean to…interrupt."

Joss froze in midstep and glanced toward the arch to the foyer. From where she stood, she could see Jace's back in the open door to the hall and the side of Claudia's face.

Jace said, "Joss is kind of busy, Ma. She's got to get to the airport and she's still trying to pack."

"I only want a word with her."

A word? Oh, Lord. What kind of word? She wasn't up for dealing with Jace's mom. Not right now. Not this morning.

It wasn't even so much that Jace had answered the door barefoot, with his wrinkled shirt wide open, which meant that Claudia had to know he'd spent the night. It was more that Jace's mom would be bound to read more into it than there was—to see it as another proof that Joss and Jace were serious about each other.

And that made Joss feel really bad. Last night had been so beautiful. But look at her now: packing to go. What was she doing with her life? Seriously. Two weeks ago, she'd been about to marry one guy. And last night, she'd done all kinds of naughty, intimate things with another.

Even if he *was* Jace, who just happened to be the greatest guy she'd ever known.

She'd never been the type to go for casual sex.

And last night *hadn't* been casual.

Not exactly.

But it hadn't been the beginning of forever either.

Don't let her see you—or the dress. There was simply no way to explain the dress.

Retreat. Do it now. Joss started to turn.

And Claudia spotted her. "Jocelyn." She craned to the side and put on a too-bright smile. "There you are."

Jace glanced over his shoulder and saw her, too. "Sorry." He mouthed the word.

Joss sucked in a fortifying breath and tried not to think how absurd she must look, buried in a fluffy mountain of taffeta and tulle, frozen in mid-stride just as she was turning to hide. "It's okay, Jace. Really. Claudia, come in."

Now Jace's mom hesitated. Who could blame her? "I honestly didn't mean to butt in."

Jace muttered something under his breath.

His mother glared him. "Well, Jason, I had no idea that you would be here." She aimed her chin high and announced, "Not that there's anything wrong with your being here. You young people have your own ways of doing things. I understand that. I grew up in the seventies. I'm not a complete fuddy-duddy, you know."

Jace stepped aside. "It's all right, Ma," he said resignedly. "Come on in." Looking very uncomfortable, Claudia stepped forward. He asked, "Want some coffee?"

"Oh, no. I won't stay. I have to meet Pete at the Grubstake in ten minutes." Pasting on another smile, she walked past her son and came straight for Joss. "Jocelyn, I only wanted to say—again—that we would love to see you in Midland anytime you care to visit. I have so enjoyed getting to know you. And I'm hoping that even though you're going back to Sacramento, you won't be a stranger. You'll return to see us again and maybe you and Jason..." By then, the fake smile had faded once more. Claudia's voice trailed off. She blinked. "Oh, my goodness." And she stretched out a hesitant hand to lightly brush the frothy skirt of the wedding dress Joss still had draped over her shoulder.

Jace, clearly bewildered at the whole situation, lingered in the arch to the foyer. Joss's frantic gaze skipped from him back to his mother again.

Claudia's face was transfixed. "Is that..." Tears filled her eyes. "Oh, I knew it." She let out a glad cry. And then she was reaching out, grabbing Joss and the Cinderella wedding gown and the endless yards of veil in a hug. "Oh, Jocelyn," Claudia whispered tearfully, her face buried in the dress. "I'm so happy. You two are so right for each other...."

Joss made a sputtering sound. "I, um, well..."

And then Claudia was drawing back, somehow managing to find and clasp Joss by the shoulders, even with the dress and veil in her way. Joss blinked and met the older woman's eyes, which were diamond-bright with happy tears.

"It's a beautiful gown," said Claudia fervently. "Stunning. And I don't really believe in that old superstition that it's bad luck for the groom to see the dress ahead of time. Whatever works, is what I always say. And the two of you...you *work* together. Perfectly. I'm thrilled that you two have realized so quickly how right you are for each other. Jason has been looking for you, Jocelyn—you realize that, don't you? He's been looking for you for much too long now. I think he was giving up hope, if you want to know the sad truth. But now, here you are. Together. In love. Ready to marry and get on with your lives."

"I...uh..." What could she say? How to even begin? *No, see, this is the dress I was going to wear to marry that other guy. As a matter of fact, I've been here on my honeymoon, my* un-*honeymoon. Maybe you noticed I'm in the Honeymoon Suite....*

"Thanks, Ma," Jace said out of nowhere. He sounded sincere. Joss sent him another wild glance. He met her eyes. Held them. And he smiled. The bewildered look was gone. Now he was totally confident. Utterly sure. "We're pretty excited, too."

We are?

This wasn't happening, not really. It wasn't real. Actually, she was still fast asleep in the bed in the other room.

A dream. Yes, it had to be. She wanted to pinch herself, but the dress and the veil and Claudia were all in the way.

Claudia hauled her close and hugged her again. "Have a safe flight to Sacramento. And hurry back. You must come to Midland soon. I can't wait to show you around."

"We're not living in Midland, Ma," Jace said firmly.

We aren't? Joss blinked three times in rapid succession.

He added, "And I'm out of the oil business for good."

Claudia let Joss go and turned to her son. "We'll talk about that."

"No, we won't. There's nothing to talk about. I'm looking into another line of work. And we're staying here in Thunder Canyon."

Claudia sighed. "Oh, Jason…"

"Be happy for us, Ma." He went to his mother and grabbed her in a hug.

Claudia let out another cry and hugged him back. "Well, all right," she said in a tear-clogged voice. "All right. If that's what you really want…."

"It is." He gave Joss another steady, determined look over his mother's shoulder. Joss gaped back at him and didn't say a word. Why speak? None of this was real anyway.

"Then I'm happy for you," Claudia cried. "I am. So very, very happy."

"Thanks, Ma." He stepped back, releasing her.

Still reasonably certain she'd slipped into a dream world, Joss stayed rooted in place, draped in her wedding finery, and went on gaping at the pair of them.

Claudia pulled a tissue from her pocket and dabbed at her eyes. "Oh, I am just so pleased. So very pleased. I can't want to tell Pete." With a delicate little sniffle, she asked Joss, "The wedding will be in Sacramento, then?"

"We're...still in the planning stages," Jace answered for her.

Claudia waved her tissue. "Of course you are." She laughed, a teary, soggy, happy sound. "And look at me. Butting in like this. I can see you were trying to enjoy your breakfast."

"Well, yeah, we were," Jace confessed.

She stepped close to him again and lifted on tiptoe to kiss his beard-shadowed cheek. "I'll leave you two alone, then."

"Thanks, Ma."

She grabbed his hands. "Just...be happy. That's all I want for you. All I've ever wanted for each of my children."

"We will," he answered solemnly. "I promise."

"That's the spirit." She gave his hands a final squeeze and released them. And then she aimed a jaunty wave at Joss. "See you very soon, dear." She was beaming.

"Ahem. Yes. Bye."

Still beaming, Claudia headed for the door, Jace right behind her.

Joss remained where she was, buried in wedding finery, wondering if she was going to wake up soon.

But then she heard the door click shut and the privacy chain sliding into place.

Jace returned and stood in the arch from the foyer again. "Don't say a word."

She didn't, but she did manage a wild, confused sputtering sound.

He put up hand. "I swear to you, Joss. I have a plan. I think it's a good one. Let me explain."

She found her voice and demanded, still not believing that this could be happening, "A plan? You have... a *plan*?"

"Don't look at me like that. Please. Give me a chance. Hear me out."

About then, she realized she wasn't going to wake up. It wasn't a dream.

Jace had told his mother that they were getting married and moving to Thunder Canyon.

And Joss had just stood there and let it happen.

Chapter 10

Jace looked into those big amber-brown eyes of hers and knew she wasn't going for it. He felt like a total fool.

But so what? He wasn't giving up yet.

"Come on," he coaxed. "Put the dress down. Eat your breakfast. We'll talk."

She blinked and stared. "I don't have time for talking. I have a plane to catch."

"No, you don't. You don't have to go. You can stay here. With me."

She wrinkled her nose and shook her head in disbelief. "What *planet* are you from? I can't believe that you… I don't… You just…"

He took a step toward her. "Joss…"

"Don't." She lurched away, almost tripping on the veil that hung down her back, but then she stopped. She stared at him, clutching that giant dress, her slim shoulders drooping. And then, out of nowhere she started to cry. "Oh, Jace." Fat tears trailed down her soft cheeks. "What are we doing? Are we going crazy? What's happening here?"

He felt crappy. Bad. Rotten. And really, for a minute there, he'd thought he'd had a great idea....

And wait. Hold on just a minute. It *was* a great idea. He just needed to convince her of how really perfect it was. "Joss, come on. Don't cry. Please don't cry...." He took another step. She didn't jump away that time, but only stood there, tears dripping from her chin, her nose turning red. "Here," he said gently, "give me all that."

A tiny sob escaped her. "M-my dress, you mean?"

"Yeah. Come on. Give it here...."

She continued to cry, making sad little snuffling sounds, as he eased the big white dress off her shoulder and gently laid it over her suitcases. With a sniffle of pure misery, she asked, "Why did you do that—lie to your mother? It's bad. Very bad. To lie to your mother."

"Give me that, too," he said, and took the giant veil and set it down on top of the dress. He whipped a couple of tissues from the box on the side table and returned to her. "Here, dry your eyes."

She frowned at the tissues, but then she took them. She blew her nose and wiped away the tears. And then she gazed up at him, wearing a shattered expression that somehow managed to be trusting, too. "Now are you going to *talk* to me?"

He took her smooth, slim hand and thought how right it felt in his. She didn't pull away, so he led her to the table and guided her down into the chair in front of her plate. He poured her some coffee, took the warming lid off the plate. "Eat," he said.

She picked up her fork.

And there was another knock at the door.

She stiffened, whimpered, "What now?"

He put his hands on her shoulders, gentling her. "It's nothing. Just the toast I ordered. Eat."

He went to the door, got his toast, tipped the attendant and returned to the living area where Joss was sipping her coffee and staring out the window at the snow-capped peak of Thunder Mountain.

"I'm waiting," she said without looking at him. "This had better be good."

She didn't sound happy, but at least she'd stopped crying.

He set the toast on the table and reclaimed his chair.

She did look at him then. One eyebrow inched toward her hairline. "Well?"

He decided to lay it right out there. "Marry me. We'll buy the Hitching Post. You can teach me how to run it. We'll get a big house with a wide front porch, just like you always dreamed about, on a nice piece of land where we can have a large floppy-eared dog and a couple of horses. And then we'll get to work having a whole bunch of loud, rowdy kids."

She set down her coffee cup and looked at him sideways. "You just want to have sex with me again."

As if he would deny that. "Well, yeah. The sex is great. It's *all* great with us. And come on, think about it. *You* want to get married and have kids. And *I* want you. Here. In Thunder Canyon. With me. And when Ma started in about hearing wedding bells, it all fell into place for me. Why the hell shouldn't we both get what we want? Why should you go? You don't really *want* to go, do you?"

She pressed her lips together and stared out the window again.

He didn't let her off the hook. "Look at me, Joss."

Slowly she turned her head and met his eyes. She wore a slightly stunned expression. "What?" Her voice was more than a little bit husky.

He rose from his chair. Just enough to capture her beautiful mouth. He kissed her. Hard. "Marry me."

She stared at him for about half a century, dark eyes huge and anxious in her amazing face. Finally, she sighed. "Your mother. I think she really is thrilled at the idea that we're getting married."

"Yeah, so?"

"We just met. Shouldn't she be warning us to take it slow?"

"Joss, she sees what you do for me. She's relieved that I'm back among the living again after months of dragging around like a ghost of myself. She thinks we're good together. Why shouldn't she be happy at the thought that we're making it legal?"

Slowly, she shook her head. "She's just so different from my mom, that's all. If we, um, do this, my mom is going to hit the ceiling. She's going to go right through the roof and it is not going to be pretty. You can take my word on that."

"Don't borrow trouble. We'll deal with your mom together when the time comes."

"But really, our getting married, it seems crazy. Insane. I mean, yeah, you're right about things being good with us. You…do it for me. You're the absolute best. On so many levels."

He felt triumph rising. "And *you* do it for me."

"But get real. It's been a week. It's not like it's undying love or anything."

"So what?"

She kicked him under the table—not hard, but right on the shin.

He winced. "Ow, that hurt."

She had her soft mouth all pinched up. "I don't like you dissing love, Jace. I happen to believe that love matters."

He reached down and rubbed where she'd kicked him. "Okay, it matters. I guess. If you say so. But I mean, well, what *is* it anyway?"

She glared. "What do you mean, what is it?"

"Well, I mean, you loved Kenny Donovan, right?"

She sat completely still for a moment, her face somber, her eyes unhappy. And then, with a heavy sigh, she slumped back in her chair. "I thought I loved Kenny." She shook her head. "Now, though…now, I only wonder *how* I could have thought that. I look back and the only good thing I can say about him is that he seemed like a nice guy. At first."

"Exactly. That's it. *I* thought I loved Tricia Lavelle. And what did I love really? *Who* did I love? I swear I didn't even *know* her. I saw her at a party, standing by a grand piano, wearing a short, sparkly red dress, her long blond hair shining in the light from the chandelier over her head. She looked really good in that dress. And what did I do? Out of nowhere, on the spot, I decided it must be love." He made a low, disbelieving sound. "Me, Jason Traub, in love. I mean, come on. Where did that come from? Until I got a look at Tricia in that red dress, all I ever wanted from any woman was a good time and for her to go away when I was ready to go to sleep."

Joss's expression had relaxed a little. She reminded him, "Your mother said you've been looking for the right woman."

He grunted. "My mother said I've been looking for *you*."

"She meant the right woman."

"Okay. Fine. Yeah. I guess I have been looking lately—for the right woman, for the things that really matter in life, the things I never realized how much I wanted. But love? I meant what I said a minute ago. I honestly don't have a clue about love and I don't even want to go there. I'm just a guy doing the best I can to make my life a good one, to…get involved."

She pulled a face. "Get involved?"

"Yeah. With my…community, you know? With *this* community. Like Aunt Melba said the first day I met her, *'Get involved, young man. Stop sitting on the sidelines of life.'* I admit, I just wanted to get away from her when she said that, but that doesn't mean she wasn't a hundred percent right."

Joss almost smiled. "So." Her velvety gaze sparked with challenge. "The mystery woman's name was Tricia Lavelle, huh?"

He picked up a piece of toast, and then realized he didn't want it after all. He set it down. "That's right."

She put her hand on his arm. It felt good there. He wanted to scoop her up and carry her back to the bedroom. He might keep her there all day and into the night.…

But first he had to convince her that they could be a great team in a lifetime kind of way.

"I want to hear about her, about Tricia Lavelle," Joss

said, as he'd pretty much expected she would. "I want the story, all of it."

He groaned. "Now?"

She repeated, "All of it."

He pushed his plate away. "It's pretty damn embarrassing. I acted like an idiot."

"Hey, you're talking to the girl who was going to marry Kenny Donovan, remember?"

He held her gaze. "You're no idiot. You always knew what you wanted. And that cheating creep just had you convinced he was it. And from what you've said, he *was* it. At first."

"Thank you," She said it softly. And then she added, "Now, about the thing with you and Tricia…"

Resigned, he explained, "All that happened with her is that I saw a good-looking girl in a red dress and I had a completely out-there reaction. Instead of admitting I wanted what I always wanted—an overnight, totally *un*-meaningful relationship—I decided that I was in love. Which is a complete pile of crap. I'm just not that deep. I have no idea what love really is and I'm better off not kidding myself that I do. I see now that I need to just go for what works and what's right and leave it at that."

She squeezed his arm. "Tell me about her."

"Ack. You're kidding. You want *more*?"

"I do, yes. More."

He tried to bargain. "Tell me first that this isn't going to ruin my chance of getting you to marry me."

She almost smiled, but not quite. "Talk."

So he did. "I met her through her dad, Jack Lavelle. Jack's rich as Rupert Murdoch, a legendary oilman. He was a real-life wildcatter back in the day. In fact, he was once in partnership with *my* dad."

"You don't mean Pete, do you?"

"No, I mean my birth father."

"And Tricia. Is she in the oil business as well?"

"Are you kidding? She might break a nail. Tricia dabbled in modeling. A couple of years ago, she even made the cover of *Sports Illustrated*. But she's never *had* to work. She has trust funds for her trust fund. One look at her in that slinky sequined party dress, standing by the grand piano in the front sitting room of her daddy's Highland Park mansion, all that blond hair falling in golden waves to her perfect ass, singing 'The Yellow Rose of Texas' for her adoring daddy and all his rich guests, and I was gone, gone, gone."

Joss brushed his shoulder with a comforting hand. "It's not so surprising that you fell for her. She sounds pretty fabulous."

"She did *look* fabulous, I'm not denying that. But what's the old saying about all that glitters?"

Joss smiled at him, a rueful sort of smile. "Go on."

"You sure you haven't heard enough?"

"I'm waiting."

"Fine. All right. We spent the holidays in a series of luxury hotels all over the world. For the first time, I thought I understood what it was to be head-over-heels for a woman. I bought an engagement ring with a rock the size of the Alamo. And on New Year's Eve, I went down on my knees and proposed…." He left it there. Maybe she would let it go.

He wished.

"And?" she prompted softly.

"Tricia got cagey."

"Cagey, how?"

"She said she loved me madly, of course. But she was

only twenty-four. Much too young to settle down, she said. Couldn't we just go on having fun? And then, in a few years, when she got old—that's exactly how she put it. 'When I get old.' Then we could talk seriously about getting married. She said I could move to Dallas and get work with her daddy. Because Tricia was never, ever leaving her daddy—well, except temporarily, for a prime modeling gig in New York or to lie around slathered with suntan oil, wearing a bikini the size of three postage stamps aboard a friend's yacht on the French Riviera."

Joss said, "And the last thing you ever wanted was to go to work for anybody's daddy...."

He chuckled then, even though he knew the sound didn't have any humor in it. "You got that right. Plus, as I said, Lavelle is in the oil business. And by then I was already thinking I might want *out* of the oil business. I was thinking that I wanted..." He frowned as he let the sentence wander off.

"You wanted what?"

"Truth is, at that point, I didn't really know what I wanted. But it wasn't to spend another five or ten years jetting around the world with some spoiled little rich girl. Suddenly I was seeing my supposedly 'perfect woman' in a whole new—and not very attractive—light. I started wondering what my problem was, wondering what I thought I was up to, generally speaking.

"All the things I'd been sure of in my life—my place in the family business, my no-strings-attached lifestyle—I was all at once itching to change. I'd thought Tricia was the solution to the vague unanswered questions that had started nagging in my brain. But within a few days of her blowing off my marriage proposal, I saw that it was never going to work with her. I realized I didn't even *like* Tricia much."

"So what did you do?"

"I felt so stupid. Here I'd been telling her I would love her forever and now all I wanted was to get free of her. So I tried to be really smooth and subtle. I told her that maybe we ought to cool it for a while."

"What did she say to that?"

"She said that was fine with her. She said that ever since I'd started in on her to marry me, I hadn't been any fun anyway."

"Wow, that was kind of cold."

He grunted. "That was pure Tricia. She's a girl who just wants to have fun—and to live near her daddy."

"So that was the end of it?"

"Yeah. It really bummed me out, you know? But not for the reason my whole family assumes. Not because she ripped out my heart and ate it for breakfast like everyone seems to think. By the end, I didn't give a damn about Tricia—in fact, I'd realized I probably never *had* given a damn about her. I was just glad it was over without any big scenes. But all the questions in my head, about the way my life was going, about my work for Traub Oil, about all of it, those questions were nagging me worse than ever. I realized I had no idea what I wanted. I only knew I *didn't* want the life that I had. I went into a really low period after that."

"A depression, you mean?"

"I don't know if I would call it that. It was just, well, I didn't care about much. I blew off Jackson and Laila's wedding, I was so down. I regret that. A lot. I decided to quit the family business. I had no interest in the things that I used to enjoy."

"Like...casual relationships with women?"

"That's right. Can you believe it? I didn't even care about sex. And before the thing with Tricia, I *always* cared about sex."

She did smile then. "You seemed to enjoy yourself last night."

"Yeah." He drank in the sight of her, those brandy-brown eyes, the lush, delicious curves of her mouth, the thick, cinnamon-kissed waves of her dark hair. "My interest in sex has returned at last. It's a miracle. It started about a week ago. The day I met you."

Her expression turned knowing. "Oh, come on. You told me that day that you only wanted to be friends."

"No, I said I would love to be friends and I accepted the fact that you weren't going to have sex with me. That doesn't mean I wasn't interested. I was. From the first moment I saw you. And that was a great moment for me. It's been six months since it ended with Tricia. And until eight days ago, I had nothin' going on with any woman. No dates, no interest. Not even a spark."

She tried to be cynical. "You're working me, right? To get me to say yes to this wild plan of yours. Next you'll be saying you fell in love with me at first sight."

"No way." He put up a hand, palm out, like a witness swearing an oath. "Uh-uh. I told you already. When it comes to love, I've accepted the hard fact that I have no idea what it is or when I'm in it—that is, *if* I've ever *been* in it, which I seriously doubt. When it comes to love, I'd rather just not go there. The whole subject makes me nervous, you know what I mean? I don't understand it and I prefer just to leave it alone."

She studied his face for several long seconds. "So really, what you're proposing is a practical arrangement."

He knew he was getting to her. He tried not to get too cocky, but he couldn't hide his excitement. "That's right. That's it. You and me—together, a team. Getting everything we want out of life. We…pool our experience and resources. We start a family."

"Wait. *You* want a family, too?"

"Haven't I just been saying that?"

"No. You said *I* wanted a family and you were willing to help me have one."

"Then let me correct that. I *do* want a family. A family with you. Remember when you first told me about your dream for your life?"

"I do, yeah. Sheesh, that was embarrassing."

He didn't follow. "Embarrassing, how?"

"Well, I mean, that even after Kenny betrayed me, I actually considered taking him back…."

"But I told you I could see what you were getting at—that you had a dream, and it was hard to give that dream up."

Her expression softened. "Yeah, you did understand. I really appreciated that."

"And I'm trying to tell you now that when you described your dream to me, I started thinking how great that would be—to be a dad, to be a husband to someone like you, to have a big house with a bunch of kids. I realized something about myself. I was tired of being my family's last single maverick. I knew I could go for just the life you were describing. Seriously, I could. Who knew? But it's true. I think part of what's been eating at me the past several months is I've been wanting what a good-time guy like me never wants and I just wasn't ready to admit that yet. But I'm ready now. I promise you, Joss. I want a great big family. I want that a lot."

Her eyes had that special light in them again. "Oh, this is crazy."

"No, it's not. It's the sanest thing two people can do. To get married because they want the same things out of life, because they're good together in all the right ways."

She picked up her coffee cup, looked into it and then set it back down. "So, if we did this, *when* would we do it?"

"You mean, when would we get married?"

"Yeah." She seemed slightly breathless. "When—I mean, I kind of would like a real wedding, you know? I would like to wear my dress."

He sent a wary glance at the pile of white over on the sofa. *"That* dress?"

She bit her lip. "Tacky, huh? To marry you in the dress I chose to marry Kenny in?"

It did kind of bug him. But come on, what did it matter? It was just a dress. And if she liked it so much, why not? "You want to wear that dress, you wear it."

"Oh, Jace. Are you sure?"

"Absolutely." He stuffed his own discomfort at the thought of her coming down the aisle toward him wearing that dress. "You wear your dress. And we get married right here, at the resort. I'm thinking on the last Saturday of the month."

"This month?"

"Yeah. Okay, I know it's quick, but I say we go for it. We put a nice party together for our families and friends in the time we have till then, and after that, we get on with our lives."

Out of nowhere, she jumped up and headed for the bedroom.

He watched her go, too surprised at the suddenness

of her leaving to ask her what was up. But then, a few seconds later, she returned with her cell phone. She tapped it a few times. "That's the twenty-eighth? Saturday, the twenty-eighth…"

So, okay. A calendar. She'd brought up the calendar on her phone. She slanted him a sharp look and he realized she wanted confirmation. "Er, sounds about right."

She narrowed her eyes at the screen. "That's twenty days. Tight."

"Joss."

"Um?"

"Is that a yes?"

She glanced up. "Did I mention this is insane?"

"Repeatedly." He pushed back his chair, captured her wrist, took the phone from her hand and set it on the table. "Is that a yes?"

She looked up at him, a little frown etching itself between her smooth brows. "I mean, this would be for real? This would be a real marriage and we would both give it everything. We would commit ourselves to making it work."

He held her gaze, refused to waver. "That's it. That's the plan."

"You would stick by me always." Tears welled in those fine eyes again.

He knew she was thinking of that bastard Kenny, of how he'd messed around on her. "I would. I swear it. Say yes."

She dashed the tears away. "Oh, Jace…we've known each other only a week. Two weeks ago, I was supposed to be marrying someone else."

"We've been through all that."

"Yes, but—"

"Stop right there."

She blinked. "What?"

"You just said yes. That's the word. Say it again, minus the 'but.'"

"Oh, God, my mother is going to freak."

"Joss, I mean it. Yes or…"

With a little cry, she put her cool, smooth fingers to his lips. "Shh. Wait."

He made a low sound, but he kept quiet. He waited.

And then, at last, she swallowed. Hard. And she nodded. "Yes," she said. "This is so crazy and I can't believe what I'm about to say. But yes, Jace. Yes, yes, yes!"

Chapter 11

The moment she finished saying yes, Jace scooped her up and carried her back to the bedroom again.

"You need rest," he insisted.

She laughed at that. She knew that look in his eyes.

And then he started kissing her. She kissed him back, of course. Making love with Jace was a lot more fun than sleeping anyway.

They stayed in bed until eleven or so, which was checkout time. She called the front desk and asked about extending her stay. The clerk said the suite was hers until Thursday. After that, she would have to change rooms.

She hung up the phone and asked, "What now?"

He was still in bed, braced up on an elbow, looking sleepy and sexy and wonderfully manly. "We need to try and reserve a room for the wedding."

So they showered and dressed and went down to the front desk, where the weekend manager was happy to help them out.

As it turned out, the smaller of the resort's two ballrooms was available. They booked it. The manager told them it would be a simple matter to set up the ballroom for the ceremony first, and then bring staff in again to add tables and reset the room for the reception afterward.

That seemed a little complicated to Joss. Would they have to ask everyone to leave and come back later? Jace said they could talk to DJ, maybe see about having the reception at the Rib Shack, if she wouldn't mind the casual atmosphere.

She grinned. "Our first date was at the Rib Shack—sort of, more or less. Remember?"

He laughed. "How could I forget? It was just last week."

"I love that," she said.

"You mean that our first date was only a week ago?"

"No, that our first date was at the Rib Shack, which means it's the perfect place for our reception because it has special meaning for us."

He faked a scared expression. "It makes me nervous when women start talking about special meanings."

She poked him with her elbow. "Get over it—and okay. Speaking more...practically."

He made a big show of looking relieved. "I'm all for 'practically.'"

"Got that, loud and clear. Where was I? Oh, yeah. We can dress up the ballroom really pretty for the ceremony, and then everyone can just go on over to the Rib Shack for the party after."

He agreed. "I'll get with DJ and see what we can do."

They also wanted to arrange for a consultation with Shane Roarke, the Gallatin Room's new chef, to plan a special menu for the reception after the ceremony. Jace said that since the Rib Shack was right there in the resort, it shouldn't be too much of a problem for the Rib Shack and Shane Roarke to work together.

Joss clued him in that top chefs didn't, as a rule, work all that well with others. However, she was willing to go with it, talk to Grant Clifton about the idea. If Grant said it wouldn't be an issue for the resort, then they could approach Roarke about the idea.

They went to the Rib Shack for lunch. And then they made a trip to Bozeman to drop off her rental car at the airport.

Jace insisted on stopping at a jewelry store next. They picked out a ring. It wasn't a hard choice. One look at the one-and-a-half carat marquise-cut solitaire on a platinum band and she gasped. The price brought a second gasp.

Of course, Jace made her try it on, and then decided it was perfect for her. He handed over his credit card and laid claim to the velvet case. The case still held the matching platinum wedding band, which was channel-set with diamonds.

Back in Thunder Canyon, they drove out to Jackson and Laila's house to share the news of their engagement with his twin. As it happened, DJ and his wife Allaire were there. They'd brought their little boy, Alex. Ethan and Lizzie were there too. So was another of Jace's brothers, Corey, and his wife, Erin.

And Laila's single sisters had come. She had three of them—Jasmine, Annabel and Jordyn Leigh. Laila's other sister Abby, who was married to a local carpenter, couldn't make it that day. Neither could her baby brother, Brody.

Everyone was wonderful, Joss thought. They congratulated Jace and really seemed to mean it. They all told Joss that they were so happy to welcome her to the family. The women made a big deal over Joss's ring. She showed it off proudly.

She also spent some time chatting with Laila's sister Annabel, a librarian who owned a therapy dog named Smiley. Annabel and Smiley spent a lot of time at Thunder Canyon General Hospital, working dog therapy magic on emotionally needy patients. Annabel said how great it was to see the last of the Texas Traubs and headed for the altar.

Yeah, okay. Joss felt a little guilty when Annabel said that. Everybody seemed to think that she and Jace had found true love.

But really, what did it matter what everyone else thought? She and Jace had a great thing going. They would have a good life together. A full, rich life, a life they both wanted.

DJ said he'd be honored to host their reception at the Rib Shack. And if Shane Roarke was up for creating a special menu, DJ would see that his staff assisted the chef with whatever he might need from them.

Lizzie insisted that she would bake their wedding cake personally and they agreed to visit her bakery the next day to put in their order. And then Erin launched into a story of how Lizzie had saved the day for Erin and Corey the year before. Ethan's wife had created a fabulous emergency wedding cake at the last minute when the bad-tempered French baker who was supposed to provide the cake skipped town.

Dinnertime approached. Laila insisted they all stay to eat. She had two Sunday roasts slow-cooking outside on the barbecue. There was plenty for everyone.

After dinner, they lingered over coffee and Lizzie's strawberry-rhubarb pie. Joss enjoyed every moment. It was still a little unreal to her that she and Jace were actually getting married at the end of the month. But she could get used to hanging around with Jace's brothers and cousin and their wives. They treated her like one of the family already.

Before they left, Jace went upstairs and packed up his things. From now on, he would be staying with Joss.

He thanked his brother and Laila for their hospitality. Jackson grabbed him in a hug and said again how happy he was for them. She and Jace drove back to the resort in a happy fog of good family feelings.

Kenny called that night.

It was late. Joss and Jace had just finished making slow, delicious love. She'd cuddled up close to him with his warm, hard chest for her pillow and she was fading slowly, contentedly toward sleep.

The phone by the bed rang.

The sound startled her.

Jace wrapped his big arm around her and whispered into her hair. "Don't answer that…"

She kissed his strong, tanned throat. "I have to."

"No, you don't."

"I do. It's ingrained. The phone rings, I answer it."

He chuckled. With some reluctance, he let her go. She reached for it, cutting it off in mid-ring. "Hello?"

"I called your cell twice," Kenny accused. "Aren't you checking your messages?"

She sat up. "Leave me alone, Kenny."

Jace sat up, too. He wasn't smiling. "Can't that jerk take a hint?"

"Who's that?" Kenny demanded. "It sounds like a man's voice."

Jace instructed flatly, "Tell him to get lost." She reached out and silenced him with two fingers against his lips.

He kissed those fingers. "Tell him."

"It is. My God." Kenny was outraged. "There's a guy with you—in your *room*? Jocelyn, what's happened to you?" He fired more questions at her. "Why is there a man in your room? Why aren't you home? You missed your flight, didn't you?" He heaved an outraged sigh. "This is ridiculous. I've had enough. I thought if I... indulged you a little, you would come to your senses. But this is beyond it. I'm calling my credit card and denying any charges you might incur."

"Go ahead. The bill's already paid."

Kenny sucked wind. "What do you mean paid? I *refuse*, do you hear me? I'm not paying for you to have some strange man in your room. I'll call my credit card company and tell them—"

"I didn't use your credit card."

"What? But—"

"I decided I couldn't stand the idea of taking your money after all."

Kenny made a sputtering sound. Meanwhile, Jace had captured her wrist. He sucked her index finger into his mouth and then ran his tongue around it.

She giggled, mouthed, "Stop that."

He shook his head and sucked some more, using his tongue in a lovely, wet caress. Amazing, really, the things he could do with his mouth. With that tongue...

Kenny demanded, "What is going on with you, Joss? Are you having some kind of breakdown? I don't get it."

She pulled her finger free of Jace's grip—not because it didn't feel really good. It did. But because he made her breathless and she needed all her wits about her to make things perfectly clear to Kenny. "What is going on with me, Kenny, is that I've met someone."

Jace grinned. It was an extraordinarily sexy grin.

"*What*?" Kenny practically shouted.

"I said, I've met someone. He's fabulous. He's asked me to marry him and that is exactly what I'm going to do."

"Joss, you can't. That's completely insane."

Was it? Maybe so. She told herself she didn't care. "Your opinion means exactly nothing to me now, Kenny. I'm getting married the twenty-eighth of this month at five in the afternoon, right here at the Thunder Canyon Resort. As a matter of fact, I'm going to be living here in this beautiful little town with my new husband. We're buying a bar and grill and running it together."

"Wait. No. You're making this up. Just come home. We'll talk. We'll—"

"You're not listening, Kenny. The past couple of years, you never listened. I *am* home. *This* is my home now. I'm never coming back to California, except to get my stuff out of storage and, on occasion, to visit my mother."

"Joss, please—"

"Uh-uh. Forget it. Enough said. Leave me alone. Do not call me again. Goodbye."

"Joss, wait. Don't—"

She hung up the phone. And then she put her hands over her face and let out a groan.

Jace touched her shoulder. "Hey."

She made a vee between her middle and fourth fingers and peeked at him, groaning again. "That was awful. Don't you dare try to cheer me up."

He reached out and pulled her close and settled her head against his shoulder. His beautiful, big body felt so warm and good cradling hers. He even stroked her hair.

She let her hands drop away from her face and allowed herself to lean on him. All of a sudden, she felt totally exhausted. "Ugh. And that reminds me, I should call my mother."

"In the morning."

She let out a short burst of laughter that felt a lot like a sob. "Or maybe never…"

"You just need some sleep," he said. "A little rest and in the morning, you'll feel better about everything."

"What is it with you and all this optimism?"

He chuckled, the sound warm and deep. "It's all going to work out. You'll see."

Was it? Oh, she did hope so. Because seriously, married in twenty days? To this amazing man whom she'd met barely a week ago? Maybe Kenny was right. She'd gone off the deep end—not that she had any intention of backing out of her most recent engagement. No way. If she was crazy, so be it. She wanted to marry Jace.

She sighed. "It's just that we have so much to do."

He captured a swatch of her hair and began slowly wrapping it around his big hand. "Later for all that."

Her mind just kept racing. "And you know, I was

thinking that I really need somewhere to stay—we both do, until we find the house want."

"We can stay right here." His voice had gone husky. She knew that dark, hot look in his eyes.

And in spite of her anxious thoughts, a little spark of excitement bloomed low in her midsection. She tipped her head back, kissed his manly square jaw, and insisted, "No way can we stay here."

"Why not?"

"Because it's ridiculously expensive. Plus, the suite is booked starting next Thursday, remember?"

He unwrapped her hair from around his hand only to raise the strands to his face and rub his cheek against them. "So we'll get another suite."

"Jace." She pulled away enough to catch his dear face between her palms. "It's almost three more weeks till the wedding. And it could be months before we find our place. Months at these rates? Forget about it."

He kissed the tip of her nose. "You're worth it."

She lifted up to lightly bite his ear and whisper, "I like the way you say that, but come on, there has to be another option."

He made a low, growly sort of sound. "I'll see what I can do, okay? But now, you should kiss me."

She caught his earlobe between her teeth again and teased it with her tongue. "I know what you're planning…."

"Kiss me."

She blew in his ear. "I thought you said I needed to get some sleep."

"A kiss," he said gruffly. "Then you can sleep."

So she kissed him.

And that, of course, led to more kisses.

Which led to another thoroughly satisfying hour of lovemaking.

It was after three when they finally went to sleep, and six in the morning when the phone rang again.

"Don't answer that," Jace grumbled in her ear.

More asleep than awake, ignoring her hot new fiancé's wise advice and not stopping to think that the call would probably be someone she didn't really want to talk to without advance preparation, Joss groped for the phone.

"'Lo?" she answered groggily.

"Kenny just called me," her mother said tightly. "He is devastated. He tried not to drag me into this, but what could the poor man do? He spent a sleepless night after he talked to you. And in the end, well, he just couldn't help himself. Jocelyn Marie, you have broken a good man's heart. How could you? I ask you, sincerely, what is the matter with you? Have you lost your mind?"

Joss had dragged herself up against the pillows by then. She must have had a stricken look on her face because Jace was fully awake and watching her, a frown of concern between his brows.

She put her hand over the mouthpiece and whispered, "My mother."

He must have been holding his breath because he let it out slowly. "You want me to talk to her?"

"Oh, no. Uh-uh. I don't think so…"

"Jocelyn, hello?" Her mother's voice grated in her ear. "Are you there? Can you hear me?"

She took her hand away from the mouthpiece. "I'm here."

Her mother huffed. "I asked you several questions. You didn't answer a single one of them."

"Yes, well, Mom, I didn't know where to start."

"Start by reassuring me that this all just a terrible misunderstanding. Tell me you're not marrying some stranger you just met."

Joss swallowed, sucked in a slow breath and counted to five. Jace held out his hand. Gratefully, she took it and wove her fingers with his.

"Jocelyn, will you please answer me?"

"All right, Mom. No, I am not marrying a stranger. I'm marrying a wonderful man named Jason Traub. Jace and I are buying a business together and staying here in Montana to make a new life for ourselves."

Her mother made a tight, outraged little sound. "So it's all true then, what poor Kenny said? You have gone over the edge, lost your mind completely. This is pure craziness. Now, you listen to me...."

"Mom, I—"

"Jocelyn, I'm begging you. I want you to pack up your things and get a flight home. Now. Today. This instant. Call me as soon as you have your flight number and I will meet you at the airport on your arrival. We can—"

"No!" Joss pretty much shouted the word. By then, she was clutching Jace's hand for dear life.

"What did you say?" her mother demanded.

"I said no, Mom. No. I am getting married right here, in Thunder Canyon, Montana, on the twenty-eighth of July. That's all there is to it. I hope you'll come for the wedding. But if you don't, well, that's your choice."

Her mother scoffed outright. "But this is ridiculous. Impossible. It's just all wrong."

"I'm sorry you feel that way, Mom. I'm sorry that lately we seem to be unable to communicate in any constructive way. The wedding will take place here at the Thunder Canyon Resort at five in the afternoon, with a reception in the Rib Shack restaurant, also here at the resort, afterward. I love you and I hope you'll come. Goodbye."

As usual, her mom was still talking frantically as she gently set the phone back in its cradle. "Oh, my Lord…."

"Come here, come on." Jace pulled her close.

She wrapped her arms around him good and tight. "Why couldn't I have a normal mother—say, one like yours? That would be so refreshing."

He pressed his lips to the crown of her head. "Your mom will come around in time."

"I hope so. I truly do. She's not *all* bad, you know?"

He answered gently, "I know she's not."

"She really does love me. I think she truly believes that she's doing the right thing. She just can't let go of the idea that Kenny Donovan is a knight in shining armor and I have to be out of my mind to walk away from him." She let out a low groan. "I honestly have no clue how to get through to her."

He tipped her chin up and pressed a quick, hard kiss on her lips. "I know a copy place on the east side of town, in the mall in what we call New Town. We'll put some invitations together today to send out to the family. We'll send one to your mom, too."

"You think sending her an invitation is going to make a difference with her? Frankly, I can't see how."

He kissed her again, lightly this time. "I just think it's good to remind her that we do want her here for our wedding. By the time she gets the invitation, she'll have had a few days to think it over, to change her mind about coming on so strong. I think once she settles down, she's going to realize that you're what matters to her. She'll want to mend fences by then, to make peace with you."

"Oh, if you could only be right about that."

He stroked her hair. She snuggled in even closer, reveling in the warmth of his body, the strength in his big arms, the scent of him that was clean and manly and managed somehow to excite her and to comfort her simultaneously. He asked, "You want try and get a little more sleep?"

"Hah, as if that's an option at this point. I'm so hopped up on adrenaline, my ears are buzzing."

"So okay, let's get some breakfast."

Over bacon and eggs at the Grubstake, they planned out the day.

It was a busy one.

First they went to the New Town copy shop and ordered some simple, attractive-looking invitations. The clerk said their order would be ready the next day, which was Tuesday.

From the copy shop, they moved on to Lizzie's bakery. Aunt Melba was there, just leaving after enjoying a muffin and morning coffee. She chided them for missing church and then congratulated them on their upcoming wedding.

"Lizzie told me the news and I couldn't be happier about it." She insisted on hugging them both and seized Jace first. Holding him tight against her considerable bosom, she announced, "I am so pleased you'll be making your home right here in Thunder Canyon."

"Uh, thanks, Melba," Jace said, easing free of her grip.

She grabbed Joss next. "Oh, I know you two will be

very happy here." Joss managed a noise of agreement as Melba crushed her closer. "And we need more nice, hardworking young people in this town." She took Joss by the shoulders and held her away at last. "Our youth, after all, are our future."

"So true," Joss agreed. "We'll be sending you an invitation. I hope you can come."

"I wouldn't miss it for the world, my dear."

Melba waved as she left them. They ordered a couple of large coffees. Lizzie joined them and they chose the cake they wanted *and* learned that the two-bedroom apartment over the bakery was vacant.

Lizzie said Joss and Jace were welcome to it until they found the house they were looking for. She took them up and showed them the place, which was charming and fully furnished, right down to the linens in the bathroom, the pretty old-fashioned floral-patterned dishes in the kitchen and the impressive array of pots and pans.

Lizzie explained, "I lived here for a while before Ethan and I got married. It's all pretty much as it was when I stayed here. I keep meaning to have a big garage sale, get rid of everything and put it up for rent. But then, you know, it's kind of nice to have it available, just in case someone in the family needs a place to stay...."

"I love it," Joss told her. "It's perfect."

Jace whipped out his checkbook, but Joss told him to put it away. He gave her a dark look.

She didn't back down. "Come on, let me cover this at least. Please?"

He wrapped an arm around her and they shared a quick kiss.

After which Lizzie informed them that she wouldn't

take money from either of them. She waved a hand. "No way. You're family. I have a successful business *and* a rich husband. I don't need the money. Just take good care of the place, that's all I ask."

Both Joss and Jace promised that they would.

The three of them sat in the apartment's bright living room overlooking Main Street and chatted for a while. Jace told Lizzie about their plans to buy the Hitching Post *and* a new home. Lizzie suggested Bonnie Drake for their Realtor. She said that both she and Ethan had worked with Bonnie before.

But Jace told her that the Drake woman was representing the owner of the Hitching Post and he would rather use someone else. Lizzie whipped out the business card of a guy who came in the bakery every morning early for breakfast.

"His name is Milo Quinn," she said. "An older guy. Seems nice. Steady and dependable. I think you'll like him."

They went to the county courthouse next to see about getting their marriage license. It was a relatively simple procedure, although in Montana, the bride was required to have a test for rubella before the license could be issued. Jace had the solution to that one. He called the family doctor—his brother Dillon—and they drove over to Dillon's clinic to get the test done.

That afternoon, they met with Milo at his office. Tall and white-haired, he wore a Western-cut sport coat, dark brown slacks and tooled boots. He set up an appointment for them to see the Hitching Post the next day. He also said he would find them some houses on acreage.

After that, they returned to the resort and spoke with

Grant, who congratulated them on their upcoming wedding and said that he was certain Chef Roarke would be happy to cater their reception. He took them upstairs to meet with Shane. He was agreeable. They set an appointment for 9:00 a.m. on Wednesday to get the menu planned.

And then they went back to Dillon Traub's clinic to pick up the expedited rubella test results. They made it to the county clerk's office again before it closed. When they left the courthouse, they had their license.

That night, they were so tired that they made love only once.

And they were up bright and early Tuesday morning. They grabbed a quick breakfast and went down into town to meet Milo Quinn at the Hitching Post.

Joss loved the bar and grill from the first moment she stepped through the front door. It was as rustic inside as out and had an old-timey feel about it, with the dining room on one side and the bar on the other. There was plenty of space for a dance floor on the bar side and a small stage in the corner where a band could set up. No wonder the place had always been a hit with the locals. It was a great venue. As long as she and Jace provided good food and good service, they probably couldn't go wrong.

Jace was relieved to discover that the painting of the Shady Lady still hung in the place of honor above the gorgeous antique bar. "She is lookin' way hot as always," Jace said with a grin.

Milo assured them that the painting and all the furnishings and equipment were part of the very reasonable asking price. Lance O'Doherty's daughter, it seemed, really wanted to sell. The place had a full, if somewhat dated, restaurant-style kitchen. And off the long hall-way in the back, there were restrooms and three smaller dining rooms for private parties.

The building could use some updating—of the kitchen and of the restrooms. The main bar and restaurant could stand a little sprucing, too. The idea was to keep all that old-time Hitching Post charm, but freshen things up, make it brighter and more inviting.

All three of them went for lunch together at a pizza place in New Town and then they followed Milo out to see a trio of four-to five-acre properties. None of them were quite what they were looking for.

That evening, they met Lizzie and Ethan for dinner in the resort's Gallatin Room. Over thick, perfectly seared filets, garlic potatoes and curried spinach, they discussed the potential purchase of the bar and grill. Lizzie and Ethan both offered advice.

Shane Roarke emerged from the kitchen while they were devouring a to-die-for dessert of carrot cake and sweet pea ice cream with lavender caramel sauce. The chef greeted Joss and Jason, who introduced him to Jace's brother and his wife. Shane stayed to make small talk for a few minutes and then moved on.

Ethan stared after him. "That guy reminds me of someone...."

Joss and Jason both laughed. Joss said, "We had the same feeling the first time we saw him. We just can't figure out exactly *who* he reminds us of."

The food for the reception, they decided when they met with Shane the next morning, would be buffet-style. They went with mostly finger foods. From the resort, they drove to Milo Quinn's office. After lengthy discussion, Jace offered the asking price on the Hitching Post.

Once they signed the offer, they picked up their invitations at the copy place and returned to the resort, where they spent a few hours scrolling the address lists stored in their smartphones, filling out the envelopes and sticking on stamps. Joss stuck a little note in the invitation to her mother. The note explained that she and Jace had found an apartment to live in until they chose a new home. She gave her mom the address and the phone number at the new place, although she really wasn't expecting to hear from her mother anytime soon—and not expecting her to come to the wedding either.

Every time she thought of her mom, a gray, sad gloom descended. It was a giant rift that had opened up between them over that jackass Kenny Donovan. Joss appreciated Jace's positive attitude about the situation, but she doubted she and her mom would be making peace for a long time to come.

Jace looked up from the envelope he was addressing. "That was a really sad-sounding sigh."

She pulled a face. "It's just, you know, my mother…"

He reached across the table and put his hand over hers. "Hey, she'll come around."

She turned her hand over and clasped his. And then she got up from her seat so she could lean close to him and share a slow, sweet kiss.

Later, they took the finished invitations down to the front desk where the clerk promised they would go out with the morning mail. Back in the suite, they ordered room service. Shandie Traub called. She invited them to dinner the next night, which was great. They wouldn't have to worry about stocking the cupboards at the apartment on their first day there.

It was their final night in the king-sized pillow-top

bed. They made the most of it, enjoying slow, lazy love for hour upon hour.

As always, it was the best. Better than ever, Joss thought, as she sat in his lap, facing him, her legs wrapped around him, holding him deep within her.

Oh, yes! Better every time. Who knew it could be like this? Really, she'd had no idea.

He surged up into her. And she took him. Deeper. All the way. He filled her up so perfectly.

She cried his name. He kissed her, his mouth claiming hers so hungrily as she felt his climax take him.

Seconds later, she joined him. They went over the edge of the world together.

This, she thought. *Yes! Nothing like this. Ever. Not ever in my life before…*

Grant had told them they didn't need to be out of the suite until noon, so they stayed in bed later than usual Thursday morning.

At nine-thirty, as they were lazily dozing and Joss was telling herself they really needed to get motivated and get their stuff packed to move over to the apartment, the phone rang.

Jace said what he always said: "Don't answer that."

And she did what she always did. "'Lo?"

"Is this Jocelyn?"

She sat bolt-upright.

Jace sat up, too. "What the—"

"It's Milo," she whispered excitedly. Then she cleared her throat and tried to sound composed. "Hi, Milo. What's up?"

"You've just bought the Hitching Post," the Realtor announced.

Joss let out a yell and pumped her fist toward the ceiling.

"Give me that." Jace took the phone. "Hey, Milo…" Milo said something. Jace listened and finally answered, "Great. We'll be there." He handed her the phone back.

She put it to her ear, but the Realtor had already hung up. "He's gone." She dropped the phone back on the cradle. "So?"

"We're meeting him at his office at three today to sign the final agreement, give him the earnest money check and talk about inspections. He also said that if everything goes as planned, we close on the property August fifteenth."

"So fast!"

"It's a little over thirty days. That's about right."

She sat there, mouth agape, heart racing with excitement. "Jace, we did it. This is happening. It's really, really happening."

He chuckled, "No kidding."

She swayed his way and planted a big, smacking kiss in the middle of his broad, handsome forehead. He tried to reach for her, but she ducked back, giggling.

"Get back here," he growled.

"No way. I can't sit still." She shoved off the covers and leaped from the bed.

Jace started to go after her, but then changed his mind. He laced his hands behind his head and grinned— possibly because she was totally naked. "All right," he said. "Have it your way. I gotta admit I'm lovin' the view from here."

She let out another joyous shout and then she grabbed her robe from the floor where she'd dropped it the night before. Quickly, she tugged it on and tied the sash. Then she ran around the room chanting, "We did it, we did it, we bought the Hitching Post!"

He just sat there, beaming. "Gee, Joss. You could show a little excitement, don't you think?"

With a long trill of laughter, she ran back to the bed, grabbed her pillow and began hitting him over the head with it. "Oh, this is fabulous! Oh, I just can't believe it…."

"Hey," he protested, still laughing. "Knock that off." He grabbed for the pillow and snatched it away from her. Then he used it against her, trying to bop her a good one.

She played along, leaning in as he took aim, then jumping out of the way when he delivered a blow. "You missed! I'm too fast for you."

He clutched the pillow against his rock-hard, gorgeous chest so she couldn't steal it back from him and threatened in the raspy voice of a villain in some old-time melodrama, "That's it for you, beautiful."

"Hah!"

The bad-guy leer vanished. He gave her the bedroom eyes and crooked his index finger. "Come down here. Nice and close…"

"Forget that noise, mister!" Breathing fast, her heart racing with giddy excitement, she started laughing again.

And then, just like that, out of nowhere, her breath caught.

She could not breathe and her heart had stopped stock-still in her chest.

Twin lines appeared between Jace's dark brows. "Joss, you okay?"

She *was* actually. More than okay.

The breath came flooding back into her chest and her heart started beating again and the hotel bedroom seemed so beautiful suddenly. It seemed to glow with golden light. *Happy*, she thought. *At this moment, I am so perfectly, gloriously happy.* Never in her life had she felt exactly like this. Everything just paled next to this.

She saw it all, her life up till now: her lonely childhood with her brave, determined, damaged mother. Her adolescence, during all of which she'd felt awkward and different; she'd never managed to fit in. And later, through a couple of years of college and her first job in the restaurant business, which she'd discovered she enjoyed. Through her search for a good guy who could help her make the big, loud happy family she'd always dreamed of. To Kenny, who was supposed to be the one, her guy forever, and had turned out to be anything but.

All of it. The whole of her life until she met Jace. It simply couldn't compare to her days and nights with him, to this one shining, perfect moment.

She didn't stop to consider. She just opened her mouth and let the scary words pour out. "I love you, Jason Traub. I love you so much. I never knew that it could be like this, that it could *feel* like this, could fill me up like this, I…" Her throat clogged and the words ran out.

He didn't look happy.

Not in the least. He looked…stunned maybe?

And very uncomfortable.

She felt her face turn blazing red. "Oh, wow." She winced. "More information than you needed, huh?"

Because seriously, hadn't he made it painfully clear upfront that he had no clue what love was, that he just didn't get it and didn't care to get it? That he only wanted to start a business and settle down. That he liked her a lot, but for him, love didn't enter into it.

How had he put it last Sunday when he asked her to marry him?

I have no idea what love really is and I'm better off not kidding myself that I do....

Oh, God. Way to go, Joss. What had possessed her to just blurt it out like that?

He set the pillow aside and sucked in a slow breath. "Uh. Well. Good." And he actually pasted on this fake, too-cheerful smile. "That's great, Joss. I mean, thank you."

"Thank you?"

"Aw, Joss…"

"I say I love you and you say 'Thank you'?"

"Joss…"

She put up a hand. "Okay. Yeah. Bad. Really bad." And exactly what she should have expected, if she'd only had the presence of mind to keep her mouth shut until she'd thought the whole thing through. Duh. Double duh in a big, big way.

"Come on, Joss…" He looked so embarrassed, so totally out of his depth.

And she? Her mouth felt dry as a handful of dust. Her heart felt like a shriveled husk in her chest. She swallowed. With care. And she made herself ask him, "So then, is this going to ruin it for you? Do you want to back out? Because if you do, I would appreciate knowing that now."

"Back out?" He looked totally dazed, beyond confused. And so handsome, she hated him.

Almost as much as she loved him.

Because seriously, he was much too good to look at. It wasn't fair, now she thought about it, how really hot he was. "Excuse me," she said carefully, "are you saying you didn't understand the question?"

He started to push back the covers. "Joss, I—"

"Uh-uh." She leveled a look on him that had him sinking back into the bed. "Do you want to back out? Just say so. Just answer the question."

"No, then. Okay?"

Okay? As a matter of fact, it wasn't. It wasn't okay in the least. "No," she echoed with excruciating care.

"No," he repeated yet again. "It's what I said."

"No, you don't understand? Or no, you don't want to marry me? What are you telling me, Jace? Just do me a big favor and be straight with me about this."

His handsome, square jaw was set. He said, with heavy emphasis, "I *do* want to marry you. I *don't* want to back out."

Relief flooded through her. Yeah, it was tinged with the weight of sadness and mortification and a host of other not-so-fun emotions. But still, it was something. "You mean that? You really do still want to marry me?"

Now he was the one swallowing. She watched his Adam's apple bounce. And then he nodded. "I do. Yeah, it's what I want. You and me. The life we planned. I still want that." He paused. She waited. Finally, he began again, haltingly, "It's just that, well, the whole love thing—"

She cut him off. "Stop. I don't want to hear it, you know? I sincerely do not."

He blew out a slow, cheek-puffing breath. "Wow. Well. Whatever you say."

She wrapped her arms around herself in a meager

attempt to give herself the comfort he couldn't—or wouldn't. "It was…a mistake. To even bring it up, the whole love thing. I know that. I don't know what I was thinking. After all, I understand how you feel about it. And it's my bad. It's not like you didn't set me straight right from the first, not like you didn't make yourself perfectly clear."

"Joss…"

She shook her head. Hard. "No, I mean it. Can we just stop talking about it? Can we just let it go?"

Was that relief she saw in those beautiful chocolate-brown eyes of his?

So what if it was? She could relate. They were both relieved—he that she was giving up the love talk, she because he claimed he still wanted to marry her.

Now her mouth tasted like sawdust. And the luxurious bedroom, aglow with golden light moments before, was all at once dingy and dark.

"Joss, you know that I care for you."

She looked away. "Just don't, okay? Just stop. I said I understand. And I do. There's nothing more to say about it."

The covers rustled as he pushed them aside again. "Damn it, Joss…"

Someone knocked on the outer door.

It was perfect timing as far as Joss was concerned. "What now?" she asked bleakly, turning to look at him again. "You think that's your mother?"

He swung his feet to the floor. God, he was so beautiful. "I hope not," he muttered. "I'll get rid of her."

"No, I'll get it." She tied the belt of her robe more securely.

He didn't say anything. He was looking at her sideways, a concerned kind of look.

Well, he could take that look and shove it. She didn't need his concern. He didn't want to go there—and neither did she. Not anymore. They got along great and they knew what they wanted and that was enough for him.

And it would damn well be enough for her. To show him she was fine with the way things were, she sent him a big, defiant smile, after which she whirled and headed for the other room, pausing only to shut the bedroom door firmly behind her.

The knock came again as she reached the foyer. She ran her hand back through her sleep-mussed hair and peeked through the peephole.

Her heart sank. It wasn't Jace's mom out there in the hallway.

It was hers.

Chapter 12

With a low moan, Joss rested her forehead against the suite's thick outer door. She did not want to open it. She really, really didn't.

Shutting her eyes, she sucked in a slow breath, peeled herself off the door and fled back to the bedroom.

When she flung the door wide, she found Jace right where she'd left him, sitting on the edge of the bed, wearing nothing but a slight frown.

One look at her expression and he jumped to his feet. "What? Who is it?"

She let out a groan. "You'd better get dressed."

"What's going on?"

"It's my mother."

He dropped back to the edge of the bed. "Wait a minute. Your mother. Here at the resort?"

She nodded. As if on cue, her mother knocked for the third time, five swift, hard raps on the outer door.

Jace jumped up again and came for her. Before she could think to jerk away, he caught her face between his hands. "It's okay. It'll be okay."

"Oh, I'm so glad one of us thinks so." She bit back a sob. His touch felt so good. As good as ever. Was that right? Was that fair?

And then he kissed her, the lightest brushing breath of a kiss. That felt good, too. It comforted her in spite of everything. "Now you go on, let her in," he said gently. "I'll put some clothes on."

She laughed, a slightly wild sound. "Great idea. Ahem. I mean, you know. That you should get dressed…" God, she was babbling. Losing it. Holding on to composure by the tiniest of threads.

"There's nothing to worry about," he said. "It's good that she's here."

"Good?" she whispered desperately. "How can it be good?"

"Well, because it means that you two can work everything out now, all the stuff that's been tearing you apart."

"But I…she's not…we can't…" She sputtered into silence.

"It's okay," he said again. "Go let her in." He took her shoulders, turned her around and gave her a gentle push.

She went. What choice did she have?

Quietly, he shut the bedroom door behind her.

And she kept walking, one foot in front of the other, across the living area, back into the foyer, right up to the outer door. She undid the chain, turned the dead bolt.

And pulled the door back. "Mom, hi." RaeEllen had her two large black rolling suitcases, one to either side of her. She planned on a long stay apparently, "It's, um, good to see you," Joss said. She leaned forward and kissed her mother's cheek. Then she stepped back so her mom could enter.

Glancing suspiciously from side to side, RaeEllen crossed the threshold, pulling one of the suitcases behind her.

Joss stepped around her and brought in the other one. She shut the door. "This is…a surprise."

RaeEllen settled her favorite brown purse more comfortably on the shoulder of her cream-colored summer blazer. "You're not even dressed? At this hour? It's almost ten."

Joss kept her smile in place. "Just leave your purse on the table there. And come on into the living area. Things have been so busy. There's so much to do in such a short time." She was babbling again, and she knew it. But somehow, she couldn't seem to stop herself. "We just heard a few minutes ago that we bought the restaurant we offered on and we're very excited that the deal went through, that our plans are—"

"A restaurant? You *bought* a restaurant?"

"Yes, we did. We're so excited. And we've been looking for a house, *and* getting the invitations out, *and* finding a place to stay in the interim. Plus there's all the wedding stuff—arranging for the cake and settling on the menu. It goes on and on. Today's another big day because we'll be moving to—"

"We?" Her mother's pale blue eyes widened.

"Yeah. Jason, my fiancé, and me. We have to be out of the suite by noon and we're moving temporarily to an apartment down in town. I sent you a note about that, along with a wedding invitation. But of course, you didn't get it yet. And anyway, we were both worn

out with all the running around, pulling everything together, so we decided to indulge ourselves and sleep in
a little. We were tired, you know? Just beat."

RaeEllen held on to her brown bag for dear life and
blinked several times in rapid succession. "He's here,
in this room, with you?"

"That's right." Joss reminded herself not to clench
her teeth. "Jason's in the bedroom actually. He's getting dressed."

"Oh. Getting dressed. Then you're telling me he…
well, I mean, that you and he…"

Joss had had enough. "Come on, Mom. Stop acting
like the parson's wife in some Jane Austen novel. Yes,
not only are Jace and I getting married, we are already
living together. And it's working out great." *Well, except for the fact that I love him and he* doesn't *love me....*

"It's working out great," RaeEllen repeated in a tone
that said it didn't sound the least great to her.

"Yes, that's what I said. We're very happy together."

"But you hardly know this man and only three weeks
ago you were supposed to have married Kenny, who is
deeply, deeply hurt by your desertion, who only wants
a chance to make you happy, to—"

"Mom. Whoa. Stop." Joss waved both her hands in
front of her mother's face. "This is kind of a loop we're
into here, Mom. Can we please stop going round and
round about things we've already discussed and don't
seem capable of coming to any agreement on?"

Her mother's mouth drew painfully tight. "Of course.
Whatever you say."

Joss focused on her mother's words and tried her best
to ignore the angry, disapproving tone. "Thank you. I
appreciate that." She straightened her robe, an action

that, for some reason, caused her mother to gasp. Joss was trying to figure out what exactly that gasp meant when RaeEllen reached out and grabbed her hand—her left hand.

"Lovely." Her mother sounded sincere as she studied Joss's engagement ring.

Joss tried to tell herself that maybe there was hope for the situation after all, that her mom might actually try to make the best of things. "Oh, I know. I love it."

RaeEllen glanced up, and delivered the zinger. "It looks real."

That did it. Joss withdrew her hand. "I'm not kidding, Mom. I know you've had a long trip and I would like to be glad you've come, but I've had enough."

"What does that mean?"

"It means I'm not going to sit still and let you run over me. I'm not a little girl anymore. I'm a grown woman and I get to determine the direction of my own life, which you *used* to understand perfectly. Either you start *behaving* in a civil manner and treat me like an adult again, or you can just roll those suitcases right out the door and head for home."

Her mother looked stricken. "But I drove all the way here. As you've already mentioned, it was a very long trip and I'm exhausted."

"Then you'd better stop with the mean remarks, hadn't you? Or you'll be on the road again."

RaeEllen assumed an injured air. "You don't want me here? Is that what you're telling me?"

Joss tried valiantly to form an answer to that one. But what could she say? The truth was she *didn't* want her mother there. Not unless she changed her tune.

RaeEllen spoke again, more gently. "It's only, well,

I felt I should come. I felt we should…work out our differences."

"And that's admirable, Mom." Warily, she eyed the two large suitcases. "So…you were thinking you would stay right through to the wedding?"

Her mother pressed her lips together and nodded sharply. "As long as it takes, yes. I have some family leave stored up."

Joss was stuck back there with that first sentence. "As long as what takes?"

Her mother smoothed her short, fine brown hair. "I wonder, could I have a glass of water?"

Joss resisted the overwhelming desire to lay down the law. She'd already made herself more than clear. Going into it all again right this moment would only be hooking back into the loop she'd accused her mother of falling into. "Of course," she finally said. "Come on into the living area."

"My suitcases…"

"Just leave them here for now." She turned to enter the main area of the suite, her mother close on her heels. "Have a seat." She gestured at the sofa and went to the wet bar, where she filled a glass with ice and opened one of the complimentary bottles of spring water.

Jace appeared, fully dressed in nice jeans, a knit shirt and the usual high-dollar boots. He went straight to her mother. "Mrs. Bennings, hello." He laid on the Texas charm, bowing a little at the waist as he reached across the coffee table. "How great to meet you."

Even her sour-hearted mom couldn't completely resist him. She gave him her hand. He cradled it between his two larger ones, and he hit her with one of those lady-killer smiles of his, the kind that could break a woman's heart at twenty paces.

Her mom sniffed. "It's Ms. Bennings, thank you." Delicately, she withdrew her hand.

Joss hurried to Jace's rescue. "But only to strangers." Jace straightened and slid her a questioning look. Blithely, she went on, "Of course, *you'll* call her RaeEllen." She gave her mother a steely-eyed glance. "Unless you'd prefer 'Mom'?"

"Ahem. Well." RaeEllen nodded at Jace. "Yes. RaeEllen, of course. So nice to meet you." Joss set the glass of ice and bottle of water in front of her. "Thank you, Jocelyn."

Joss nodded, and dropped the bomb on poor Jace. "Mom is planning to stay until the wedding."

Carefully, her mother poured the water over the ice. She said nothing.

Jace said, "Ah. Well, that's great." His smile had slipped a little.

Joss watched him, her heart twisting. She loved him. And he didn't do love.

And now her mother was here with that strange, determined look in her hazel eyes. That couldn't be good.

But she could deal with her mother—if only things didn't go wrong with Jace.

He'd said he still wanted the life they had planned.

But did he really?

Had her passionate declaration changed everything for him? Was he second-guessing now, thinking about how he wasn't really the marrying kind after all? That this was all a big mistake, the two of them? That it had happened much too fast, with her on the rebound—and maybe him, too, when you came right down to it. Because there had been that rich oilman's daughter, Tricia. Even though he said it wasn't love with Tricia, well, he *had* proposed to her. And she'd said no.

And he'd gone into something of a depression after that.

So was he maybe now seeing the future they'd been planning as another trap he needed to escape? Was he...

No.

Uh-uh.

She was not going there.

He'd said straight to her face that he still wanted to marry her. If he'd changed his mind, he could have just said so. She'd given him an opening. A really *wide* opening.

And he'd refused to take it.

If he wanted out, he could tell her. He was a grown man fully capable of speaking his mind.

But what if I want out now? What if I've decided I don't want a marriage without love?

She turned those painful questions over in her mind, and realized that it *wouldn't* be a loveless marriage. At least not on her end.

And she didn't want to back out. Not on her life. She wanted Jace and she wanted everything he offered her—wanted her dream, just as she'd always imagined it might be. Especially now that her dream would include the most important part: the man she loved. He said he still wanted to live her dream with her.

She would have to be crazy to turn her back on that. And she wouldn't. No way.

She let out a heavy sigh.

And realized that both Jace and her mother were

staring at her—Jace kind of nervously, her mom in a measuring, calculating way.

Fine. Let 'em stare. "Mom, there's a second bedroom at the apartment where Jace and I will be staying until we find a house. You're welcome to it." She caught Jace's eye and challenged, "Right, Jace?"

She had to give him credit. He didn't even flinch. "Absolutely. RaeEllen, we'd be happy to have you stay with us."

Whatever her mother's real agenda, she had the grace to hesitate. "Really, I can get a hotel room. I don't want to impose."

Jace stepped right up. "It's no imposition, RaeEllen. You're family, after all."

Milo Quinn's office was only a few blocks from the Mountain Bluebell Bakery and the apartment above it, so Joss and Jason walked to their three o'clock appointment.

An hour later, they left Milo's office with a signed contract on the Hitching Post. Clouds had gathered in the wide Montana sky when they emerged onto Pine Street. A few random drops started falling as they strolled north to Main.

Jace glanced up at the gray underbelly of the thick cloud cover. "We'd better get moving or we're going to get wet."

So they ran around the corner and down the block. They ducked through the bakery's front door just as the sky opened up and the downpour began. One of Lizzie's employees gave them a smile and a wave as they headed up the stairs to the apartment above.

She got to there first. The doorknob wouldn't turn.

She sighed. "My mom's used to city life. She's locked herself in." She raised her hand to knock.

Jace caught her wrist before her knuckles connected with the door. "We have to talk." His voice was so deep and more than a little rough.

Her heart did something unsettling inside her chest. And her skin felt all tingly and warm. Her breath snagging in her throat, she turned to him, met those dark velvet eyes that burned into hers, smelled the spicy, green, electric scent that belonged to only him....

"Talk? About what?" She was pleased that aside from a certain huskiness, her voice betrayed none of her excitement. She didn't *want* to be excited by him. Not now. Not with her new—and unreturned—love so fresh and raw within her.

He looked at her steadily. "It's not the same. You're... distant. Cool to me."

She shrugged. "Be patient. I'll get over it." She wouldn't. But she would get used to it—at least she hoped she would. She'd learn to live with being alone in love.

His gaze burned darker, more intense. "Listen, do you need me to say it? I can just say it if it's what you need."

She took his meaning and whispered low, "You would say that you love me, even though you don't?"

"It's only words."

"To you maybe."

He still held her wrist. And didn't let go. Instead, he guided it back behind her and brought her up close against his broad, rocklike chest. "Whatever you want. Just say it. I'll do it."

Her breasts felt oversensitive, pressing as they did

into the hardness and heat of him. Her body burned. And her heart…

It ached. A deep, thick kind of ache. An ache that was almost pleasurable. She didn't have his love. But he did want her. A lot. It was something. Not enough, but still. Better than nothing.

"Okay, Jace. You go ahead. You say it. You lie to me."

His arm banded tighter and he pulled her even closer. What breath she had left came out in a gasp.

And then he said it, roughly, angrily, his breath warm and sweet across her cheek. "I love you, Joss."

She tipped her head to the side, opened her mouth slightly and ran her tongue over her upper lip, openly taunting him. His eyes burned brighter and a muscle jumped in his jaw. "Hmm," she said with a smile that wasn't really a smile at all. "Somehow it doesn't have the ring of truth, you know? And what good is a lie to me? Not a whole lot."

"Joss…" He said her name very low that time. It was a warning. And also, somehow, a plea. "I just don't want to lose you over this, okay? Over three little words. How stupid would that be? No, I don't get the whole love thing. I think it's a crock. You want to be with someone, build a life with someone, or you don't. And the point is, I want a life with you. And you want the same thing with me."

She hitched her chin higher. "I'm not arguing. We're on the same page with this."

"Are we?" He didn't look convinced.

And she was softening. How could she help it, with his fine, big body pressed against hers, tempting her? And his heated words in her ears, reminding her that he did care, that he wanted her, that he had promised to be a true husband to her. And that she believed him on all those points, believed *in* him.

The L-word shouldn't matter so much. It was what a person *did* that mattered.

"Yes." She let her tone go soft as her heart. "Yes, we're on the same page." She reached up with the hand he hadn't trapped behind her back and caressed the slightly stubbled line of his so-manly jaw. "We just bought our business. We're going to find the right house. We're getting married and we're going to have as many kids as the good Lord will grant us."

"It's gonna be great," he said fervently, the contract in his free hand crackling a little as he tightened his fist on it. "You'll see."

"I know." She gave him a real smile that time, even if it was a little wobbly. "Yes, it will be. Great."

"Joss…" He whispered her name as his fine mouth swooped down to cover hers.

Her knees went loose and she sagged back heavily against the door. Oh, that mouth of his—it played over hers, hitting every sweet, hot, perfect note. It was a symphony he created, every time he kissed her. Slow and tempting, fast and hot. He varied the notes and the rhythms. He swept her away on a warm tide of pleasure. She sighed and surrendered to the spell that he wove.

And then, just she was sliding her free hand up to clasp his neck and pull him even closer, the door behind her gave way.

With a sharp little cry, she stumbled backward.

"What the…" Jace growled.

Somehow, she managed to stay on her feet. She

whirled to find her mother standing there, hazel eyes wide with pretended surprise.

"Oh!" RaeEllen exclaimed. "Well, I'm sorry. I thought I heard a knock...."

"Not a problem," Joss lied, as she straightened her light summer shirt and recovered her dignity.

Jace actually chuckled. "Caught us in the act, RaeEllen."

RaeEllen only pinched up her mouth and smoothed her hair. "I'm glad you're back. I've made a list of the staples we absolutely must have to function around here. And Jason, I was thinking that maybe you could make a quick run to the local supermarket while Jocelyn and I finish putting our things away."

Joss saw right through her mother. It was divide and conquer time. She was sending Jace away so she could go to work on Joss. Not happening. "We can deal with that later, Mom. We're invited to dinner at Jace's cousin Dax's house tonight."

"But we'll at least need eggs and coffee for breakfast tomorrow."

"Actually, we won't. We can just walk downstairs to the bakery. The breakfast croissants have eggs, ham, sausage—whatever you want in them. And they are to die for."

"That could get expensive."

"Mom, it's one day. We'll shop for food tomorrow, after breakfast, when it's not pouring down rain."

Jace spoke up. "Give me the list, RaeEllen. I'll be happy to pick up what we need right now."

Joss whirled on him. "We should talk." She grabbed his hand. "Come in the bedroom." She sent her mother a withering glance. "Mom, we'll be right back."

RaeEllen knew when to keep her mouth shut. She gave a tight little smile and let them go.

Jace went willingly enough. Joss towed him to the larger bedroom at the back of the apartment, dragged him inside and shut the door.

He went over and dropped to the edge of the old-fashioned double bed with its dark headboard and bright log cabin quilt.

She stayed near the door. "You know what she's doing, don't you?"

He didn't even have to think about it. "She wants to get you alone and tell you all the reasons you shouldn't marry me."

"So why are you letting her get away with it?"

"Because you can't avoid her forever. She's staying right here in the apartment with us. You might as well face her down at the gate, let her know you're not running scared and she'd better straighten up and fly right or she can get back in that big old Buick of hers and head home to Sacramento."

He was right, of course.

But still. "I *have* let her know. It doesn't do any good."

"So tell her to go home."

"I'm...not at that point yet. Close. But not yet."

He got up then. He came to her, clasping her shoulders between his strong hands. "You need to show her she doesn't get to you."

"But that's just it. She *does* get to me—and don't tell me you don't know exactly what I'm going through here. Remember that first day we met? When you practically begged me to go to the Rib Shack with you, to pretend to be your date so your family would stop trying to set you up?"

He grunted. "You *would* have to remind me. They were driving me nuts."

"So all right, then. You understand. And I mean it. Don't leave me alone with her."

"Joss, you're only putting off the inevitable."

"That's right. I keep hoping I'll get lucky and she'll decide to back off and be reasonable."

He shook his head. "She seems pretty determined."

She made a face at him. "She's determined, all right. Determined to put a stop to our wedding. Think about that. Out on the landing a few minutes ago, you were all about how you really, really do want to marry me."

"It's true," he said simply. "I do want to marry you." His words touched her. He was such a big, handsome bundle of contradictions. He couldn't say the L-word without scowling. Yet he sincerely wanted to make a life with her.

"My mother is up to no good," she said.

"Joss, she came all the way here to Montana to try and make it up with you."

She wrinkled her nose at him. "That is so not what she's here for."

He caught a lock of her hair, rubbed it between his fingers. "Talk to her."

She could become seriously annoyed with him. "When it's *your* mother, you can't run away fast enough. But when it's *my* mom, I'm supposed to hold my ground and talk it out."

"You're a woman. Women are better at all that crap."

"Crap," she muttered. "A truer word was never spoken."

He slid his hand up under her hair and clasped her

nape. Lovely sensations cascaded through her. And then he pressed his lips so tenderly to hers. "Talk to her."

Five minutes later, he was out the door.

And she was alone with her scheming mother, who took her hands and dragged her into the long, narrow kitchen and down to the little round table at the far end.

"Sit down," RaeEllen said in her warmest, most conciliatory tones. "Let's catch up a little…."

Reluctantly, Joss sat.

"Jason is very handsome," her mother said carefully, a brave soldier in a dangerous field of hair-trigger land mines. "Very charming and very…compelling."

"Yes, he is."

"And I gather he's got money."

"Yes, he does."

"I can understand how he might have swept you off your feet." RaeEllen paused. Presumably so that Joss could agree with her.

Joss said nothing.

Her mother forged on. "But really, how can he possibly be in love with you, or you with him?"

Love. Joss felt the muscles between her shoulder blades snap tight. The last thing she wanted to discuss with her mother was love. It was way too sensitive a subject right then.

And she didn't want her mother to know that. RaeEllen was trolling for weaknesses. Joss refused to show her any. She ordered those tense muscles to relax and she kept her face composed.

RaeEllen kept going, rattling off her list of reasons that Joss and Jace were doomed to failure as a couple. "You met so recently. It's just…well, Jocelyn, it's a fling. On the rebound. And the last thing a woman should ever do is marry a man with whom she is having an affair on the rebound."

Joss couldn't resist. She got in a jab of her own. "Is that what happened with you and my father?"

RaeEllen stiffened. "I beg your pardon. We are not discussing your father."

"I'm just trying to determine how you're such an expert on affairs and flings and getting something going on the rebound. The way I remember it, there was just my father. And when he left, that was pretty much it for you."

"Jocelyn, this is not about me."

Joss let out a slow breath and shook her head. "Mom, you're wrong. I think this is very much about you. About you and your fears and your inability to move on, to try again with a man after Dad walked out."

"No. No, it's not." RaeEllen put a hand to her chest. Two bright spots of color had bloomed on her cheeks. "It most certainly is not. This is about you. About the wonderful man who loves you and forgives you for making a fool of him in front of three hundred people on your wedding day."

"I did not make a fool of Kenny. He did that to himself by rolling around half-naked with my own cousin in the coat room of the church."

"That never happened."

"Mom, it happened. I saw it with my own eyes."

"What happened is that you got cold feet. I remember that you were having second thoughts. You confided in me, don't you recall?"

"Yes, I do recall. Quite clearly. You convinced me

that *all* brides have second thoughts and I should go through with the wedding. You blew me off."

"No, I did not. I helped you to see that you shouldn't let your unfounded fears get in the way of your happiness."

Joss braced an elbow on the table and rested her forehead in her hand. "This is going nowhere."

"We need to talk about this."

"We *have* talked about this. I have no idea why you're so obsessed with convincing me to get back together with a self-absorbed jerk who cheated on me on our wedding day. But I can't argue with you about this any longer. I am finished. I am marrying Jace and I'm never going near Kenny Donovan again and that's the end of it."

"But you—"

"The end of it, Mom. It's over. Stop."

"But I have to—"

Joss dropped her hand flat, smacking the table. The sound was loud and sharp in the small space. "Enough. I've had it. I can't take this any longer. I'm sorry I can't get through to you. And it doesn't matter what you do, you are not going to change my mind."

"Kenny loves you. He loves you so much. And you are cruel and cold to him. How can you be like that? Why can't you see how horribly you're behaving?"

It was the final straw. "That's it. The end. I want you to go back to Sacramento, Mom. I want you out of this apartment. I've got sixteen days until Jace and I get married. They are going to be busy days. I can't have you at me every chance you get, battering away at me, so sure of your righteousness, so certain that eventually you will wear me down. You *won't* wear me down.

What you'll do is ruin what should be a beautiful, busy, exciting two weeks."

"You just want me out of here so you can be alone with that man."

Joss let out a laugh that sounded more like a groan. "You know what? That's right. I do want to be alone with Jace. Why wouldn't I want to be alone with him? Jace is funny and tender and smart." *Even if he isn't in love with me.* "And all he wants is to give me the life I've always dreamed of. What's not to like about that, Mom?"

"What happens when he gets tired of you?"

That hurt. That really hurt. She answered firmly. "He wants to be with me. He's not going to get *tired* of me."

"You are blind. Foolish and blind."

Back at ya, Mom. "I mean it. I want you to go."

Jace returned at twenty after five, his arms loaded with groceries. "There are more in the car. Where's your mom?"

"In her room. Sulking." She took one of the bags from him and turned for the kitchen. "She'll be leaving tomorrow morning." He followed her in there and they set the bags on the counter.

He asked, low-voiced so there was no chance her mother might hear, "You're sending her away?"

"Yes, I am."

"You sure?"

"Yes. I'll make it clear she's still welcome to come for the wedding."

He took her hand, turned it over, wove his fingers with hers. "You okay?"

What happens when you get tired of me? "I've been better."

He pulled her close, into the circle of those powerful arms. She let herself lean on him, breathed in the special scent that belonged only to him, told herself that she wasn't going to let her mother's cruel, misguided words get to her.

But those words were in her head now. Stuck there. Along with the bald facts: She loved him and he didn't love her.

He'd told her right up front that he'd always been a player, that he'd never been one to settle down, not until his whirlwind affair with the rich oilman's daughter. And now, he was doing it again, with her, with Joss.

Could a man really change that much? Or was this just some phase he was going through? He *thought* he ought to settle down, so he'd swept her off her feet and then proposed, just like he'd done with Tricia Lavelle.

He was the last single guy in his family. Maybe that was getting to him. Maybe he was trying to conform to his family's idea of what a man was supposed to do with his life.

Was it only a matter of time before he realized that marriage and a big house full of rowdy kids wasn't for him after all?

The questions spun round and round in her head. She told herself to ignore them. She wasn't going to let them ruin her happiness.

She held on to Jace tighter. It was going to be all right with them. He wouldn't get tired of her. She believed in him, in what they had together.

Everything would work out fine....

Chapter 13

RaeEllen refused to go with them to Dax and Shandie's that night. She said she was tired and needed her rest. "After all," she added loftily, "I have another long drive facing me tomorrow."

Joss didn't try to change her mind. If her mom didn't want to go, fine. At this point, there was nothing Joss could think of to do to ease the bad feelings between them.

Dax and Shandie's big house was packed. All of Jace's siblings and their spouses were there. And so were Laila's sisters Annabel, Jasmine and Jordyn Leigh. Jace's mom and Pete were still in town, so they showed up, too. And then there was DJ and his family as well.

Joss visited with Claudia, who was all smiles over the coming wedding. Joss tried to take comfort in the way Jace's mom treated her. Claudia welcomed her into the Traub family with open arms. If only her own mom could be so accepting.

And if only the bleak doubts would quit dogging her.

She did worry, the more she thought about it, that Jace wasn't really ready for the life they planned together. If he *was* ready, how hard would it be for him to tell her he loved her and to actually mean it?

With half an ear, she listened to Dax and DJ talk about a couple of local crooks, Arthur Swinton and Jasper Fowler. The two men were in prison. They'd committed a series of crimes, including kidnapping Jace's sister, Rose Traub Anderson. The theory was that Swinton had nursed a grudge against the Traub family for decades because Dax and DJ's mom had turned him down flat when Swinton tried to put a move on her. DJ and Dax still couldn't quite believe that Swinton had gone off the deep end because their mom had turned him down. The more they discussed it, the more they agreed that Swinton's reaction to rejection had been way over the top, that there really had to be more to it than that.

Joss thought she could almost feel sorry for Arthur Swinton. It wasn't an easy thing to love someone who didn't love you back.

It was after midnight when she and Jace returned to the darkened apartment. The door to her mother's room was shut and no light bled out from beneath it.

They went to bed. Quietly. In order not to disturb the bitter, confused woman in the room down the hall. For the first time since they'd become lovers six nights before, they didn't make love. Joss just wasn't up for it, not with her disapproving mother right there in the apartment with them.

But Jace did pull her close and tuck her up nice and

tight against him, wrapping that big, warm body of his all around her. Even with her doubts, she felt cherished. Cared for. She dropped off to sleep with a weary little sigh.

Her mom left after breakfast the next morning. RaeEllen and Joss shared an unenthusiastic final hug.

"I sent you a wedding invitation," Joss said. "I hope you'll come."

Her mother held herself stiffly in Joss's embrace. "Of course," she said in the somber tone of someone who'd just been asked to attend a funeral. "I'll be there."

During the first couple of days of the week that followed, Joss and Jace saw five new properties. Wednesday, they made an offer on eight green, rolling acres about two miles from town.

The house would need updating, but it had a little barn and a nice, big pasture for the horses Jace planned to bring up from his place in Texas. On Friday morning, a week and a day before their wedding, they signed the contract on their new home.

Jace took her out to the resort afterward to go riding. She was glad to see Cupcake. The sweet spotted horse seemed to recognize her. He nuzzled the side of her face and kept nudging her hand when she greeted him, urging her to stroke his long, noble forehead.

They rode up the mountain and then down into that valley on Clifton land, where they spread a saddle blanket under the cottonwoods and swam in the creek.

After they swam, they stretched out on the blanket and made out like a couple of horny kids. It was a beautiful day. For a while they lay there side-by-side, staring up at the blue sky, as the horses grazed nearby. They dozed—or at least Jace did.

Joss was wide awake. Her thoughts had turned, the way they did too often lately, to what was missing: his love. She watched a single fluffy cloud float across the blue expanse above and argued with herself, telling herself she really needed to get past this obsession with the L-word. Because, after all, it was just a word and what did a word matter?

"Is something wrong?" Jace asked softly.

"No, not a thing," she said. It was what she'd told him two other times in the past week, when he'd asked if she had something on her mind.

There was no point in going into it again. She loved him. He didn't have a clue what love was. What else was there to say?

Jace waited till they got back to the stables to tell her that he'd bought Cupcake for her.

She threw her arms around him and kissed him long and hard, right there in front of the gaping stable hand. Jace was such a great guy. The best.

Even if he didn't love her.

Even if she kept trying not to worry that someday he would leave her, the way her dad had left her mom.

The next week seemed to fly by. One moment it was Monday and they were making the arrangements for the various inspections at the Hitching Post and on their eight acres of land.

And then suddenly, it was Friday. The day before the wedding.

RaeEllen arrived late in the afternoon. She was actually smiling when Joss opened the door to her.

"Hello, Jocelyn." She held out her arms.

"Mom." Joss made herself smile in return. She acquiesced to the offered hug.

RaeEllen wheeled in her suitcase. "Where's Jason?"

Joss shut the door. "He's out at the new property we bought, following the inspector around. He should be back in an hour or so to say hi. And then he's off to the resort. His brothers and stepdad are throwing him a bachelor party. Tonight it will be just the two of us." Please God, they would get through it without any big scenes. "He'll stay over at his brother Jackson's house. Kind of a nod to tradition. I won't see him till I'm walking down the aisle to meet him tomorrow."

Her mother took her hand.

Joss quelled the urge to jerk away. "Mom, I want this to be a nice evening. Please."

And then her mother said something absolutely impossible. "I've had some time to think about my behavior, Jocelyn. It's been…a lonely time since I left here two weeks ago. And slowly, I've had to admit that I have been losing you, pushing you away by trying to tell you how to live your life. I've had to start facing a few not-so-pretty things about myself. You are the one shining, beautiful thing I've done in all my life. And I've been trying to tear you down."

Joss wasn't certain she'd heard right. "Um. You, um…huh?"

Her mom put her other hand on top of Joss's, so she held Joss's hand between both of hers. "You were right," she said. "It was all about me and what happened with your father. I never trusted a man after him. Not for years and years. And then, finally, I let myself believe that one man could be all right."

"Kenny..."

"Yes." RaeEllen gave a tight little nod. "I couldn't stand to admit that I'd been wrong again. I convinced you to stay with him when you were having second thoughts instead of really listening and trying to understand what was bothering you about your relationship with him. And then I did it again, I refused to hear you when you told me that Kenny betrayed you. I lost sight of what really matters, of what my real job is as your mother now that you're an adult. I treated you like a misbehaving child instead of respecting your decisions and offering my support."

"Oh, Mom..."

"But I want to make things right with you. I want you to know that from now on, I'm not making everything all about me. From now on, I *am* on your side, Jocelyn. It's *your* choice who you marry. And Jason seems like a fine young man. I support you in your choice. I hope—no. I'm *sure* that you and Jason will be very happy together."

Joss's throat locked up and her eyes brimmed. She managed to croak a second time, "Oh, Mom..."

And then they were both reaching out, grabbing each other close, holding on so very tight....

"I love you, honey," her mother said. "I love you and I...support you. Please forgive me for being such a blind, hopeless fool."

When Jace let himself in the apartment an hour later, he heard laughter coming from the kitchen. Joss said something. And then she laughed.

The sound echoed down inside him, warm. Sexy. Good. No one had a laugh like Joss's.

And then another voice answered Joss. Her mother's voice, but lighter than before. Happier. RaeEllen laughed, too.

He followed the cheerful sounds and stood in the doorway to the long, cozy kitchen.

"Jace!" Joss came to him, kissed him.

And then her mother came and gave him a hug and said it was good to see him. She actually seemed to mean it.

RaeEllen, it appeared, had seen the light, which was very good news. It had been so bad the last time she showed up that he'd been kind of dreading her reappearance. Joss had never told him the things her mother had said that afternoon when he'd left them together to have it out. But he knew they couldn't have been good. And he figured RaeEllen must have had a few choice words to say about him.

Sometimes, in the past two weeks, he would catch Joss watching him, a mournful look in her eyes. He figured her mother had filled her head with negative garbage about him, and about the two of them getting married. But when he asked her what was wrong, she said it was nothing.

He didn't believe that. Still, he didn't push her to bust to the truth. There was the whole love thing between them now and he didn't want to get into that again. He knew she wanted—needed—for him to say the words.

And he would. Hell, he *had*. But it hadn't worked out because she read him like a book and knew he didn't mean them.

How could he mean them? He'd told her what he thought of love. He didn't have any idea what love was. But he did want to marry her. He wanted *her*, damn it.

He didn't get why that couldn't be enough for her.

After tomorrow, he told himself, once they were married, things would smooth out. Hey, look what had happened with RaeEllen. She'd had a little time to think over the situation and decided to get with the program and be happy that her daughter had found someone she wanted to make a life with.

It would be the same with Joss. She would see how well things worked out. And she would be happy. He was counting on that.

Jace took a seat at the table and hung around a while. RaeEllen poured him some coffee and he watched the two women bustling between the stove and the counter, putting their dinner together. When he got up to go, Joss followed him to the door.

She whispered, "In case you didn't notice, my mom's come around."

"I kind of had a feeling she might have."

"I still can't believe it. It's like a miracle."

"Hey." He smoothed that wildly curling cinnamon-shot hair of hers. "It's not all *that* surprising."

"It is to me."

"She loves you," he said, uttering the dangerous word without stopping to think about it. "She's figured out that she needs to be on your side."

"Love…" Joss glanced away and then she was tipping her face up to him again, putting on a big smile. "Have fun." She kissed him.

He left feeling strangely regretful. As though he should have said something he hadn't.

As though he'd missed his chance somehow.

The bachelor party went on until after two. It was great, hanging with his brothers and his cousins, getting to know the two Traubs from Rust Creek Falls. Forrest was thirty-one, an Iraq veteran slowly recovering from a serious leg injury. His brother, Clay, was twenty-nine, a single father. They—and Jace—were the only unmarried men at the party. They both seemed like solid, down-to-earth dudes.

But there were a lot of toasts. And Forrest and Clay joined in every one. By the end of the evening, they were both wasted. Jace grinned to himself watching them.

He caught Jackson's eye and knew his brother was remembering how it had been back in June the year before, when Corey had his bachelor party over at the Hitching Post and Jace and Jackson had really tied one on. Jace hadn't slept at all the night of that party. He'd spent a few energetic hours with the one and only Theresa Duvall and then left her to rejoin his brother. He and Jackson had kept drinking right through Corey's wedding and the reception the next day. It hadn't been pretty. In fact, Jackson had started a brawl at the reception.

Jace doubted that the Rust Creek boys would pull any crap like that tomorrow. But he'd bet they would be nursing a matched pair of killer hangovers. Jace didn't envy them.

And he didn't miss the single life at all.

Ethan raised his glass—again. "To Jace, the last single maverick."

His brothers all laughed, in on the joke, remembering the way their long-lost dad use to call them his little mavericks.

Jace wondered what Joss and her mom were doing.

Which he supposed was pretty damn pitiful. It was only one night away from her.

Well, and then tomorrow. He wouldn't see her in the morning either. The wedding wasn't until five, so he'd be on his own for most of the day.

He really needed to buck up. It wasn't going to kill him to be away from her until the big moment when she came down the aisle to marry him.

In the dress she bought to marry that cheating SOB Kenny.

He didn't like that she would be wearing that damn dress. Every time he thought of it, it bugged him more.

But he hadn't known exactly how to tell her that he wanted her to choose something else. And now, well, it was a little late to do much about it.

She would be wearing that dress. Period. End of story.

He decided for about the hundredth time that he would forget how much he hated that damn dress.

At three in the morning, back at Jackson's place, he said goodnight to his brother, gave the mutt Einstein a scratch behind the ear and headed for the guest room.

It was lonely in there. He missed Joss, missed the way she tucked her round, perfect bottom up against him, how she took his arm and wrapped it around her, settling it in the sweet curve of her waist, before she went to sleep. He missed the little sounds she made when she was dreaming. Sometimes he wondered if he was getting whipped.

Because he was completely gone on her.

Every day, every hour, every time his damn heart beat, he got somehow more…attached to her.

And no. It wasn't love. He didn't know what love

was. He was just a not-very-deep guy who'd finally found the right woman for him.

He wanted her with him.

And he would have her.

From tomorrow afternoon on.

At four the next afternoon, wearing his best tux, which he'd had sent up from Midland, Jace arrived at the resort. Lizzie and Laila had taken charge of decorating the small ballroom for the ceremony.

The room was beautiful, set up like a church chapel, with white folding chairs decked out in netlike white fabric, satin ribbons and flowers, a long satin runner for the aisle and a white flower-bedecked arch above the spot where he and Joss would say their vows. Tall vases on pedestals sprouting a variety of vivid flowers flanked the arch, stood at either end of the aisle and on either side of the two sets of wide double doors.

Jace had only Jackson standing up with him. And Joss hadn't chosen any bridesmaids; she wasn't even having anyone give her away. It was going to be short and sweet and simple, which was just fine with Jace. They would marry and head for the Rib Shack to celebrate.

And everything would be good between them. Everything would be great.

He hung around up by the white arch with Jackson and the nice pastor from the Community Church, waiting, nodding and waving at the guests as they entered. He smiled at Laila's single sisters Annabel, Jordyn Leigh and Jasmine. The three came in together, each in a pretty bright-colored summer dress. Forrest Traub limped in wearing his Sunday best, Clay right behind him. As Jace had expected, the Rust Creek Falls Traubs were looking a little green around the gills from partying too heartily the night before.

At five o'clock, almost every chair was taken. Lizzie cued the wedding march. Ma and Pete entered together down the aisle, arm-in-arm, and sat in the front row. RaeEllen came next, escorted by Ethan. He walked her to the front and she sat between him and Lizzie, who was already in her chair.

There was a strange, breath-held moment, when the wedding march played on and Jace's heart seemed to have lodged firmly in his throat and he stared up the aisle toward the small door on the far wall, suddenly scarily certain that Joss had changed her mind about the whole thing. That she'd lifted her white skirts for the second time and sprinted away from the small ballroom and him and the future they had promised they would share together.

But at last, the door opened. And there she was, more beautiful than ever, even if she was wearing that damn dreaded dress. She carried a big bouquet of orchids and daylilies, each exotic bloom more beautiful than the last.

She saw him, there beneath the flowered arch, waiting for her. And she gave him a secret, perfect, radiant smile. And then she started walking, slowly, the way brides always do. Step, pause. Step, pause. He wanted her to hurry. He wanted her beside him. Somehow, as he watched her coming to him, his throat opened up and his heart bounced back down into his chest where it belonged. And he could breathe again.

And still, slowly, so slowly, she came to him. His eyes drank her in and the strangest thing was happening. The craziest, wildest, most impossible thing. The thing that never happened to a shallow, good-time guy like him.

Light. It shone all around her. Golden and blinding, and he couldn't look away.

Why would he want to look away? It was one of those moments. A man like him might not understand it, but that didn't matter. What mattered was that Joss was coming to him, her big, brandy-brown eyes only for him, and there was a light all around her, a light coming from her. She was a beacon, *his* beacon. All he had to do was look for her. Find her.

Follow her light.

All at once, she was there. At his side. And she gave him her free hand and they turned to the nice pastor.

And Jace was *in* the light with her, a part of the light. Should that have freaked him out? Probably. But it didn't. He didn't mind it at all. In fact, it felt great. He knew that being in the light with Joss was exactly the place he was meant to be.

And the pastor started talking, saying the words of the marriage ceremony. Everything was magical and hushed and…more.

More than he'd ever known.

Better than he ever could have dreamed. It was all coming clear to him, all so simple.

And so right.

Until the pastor said, "If there be any man or woman who knows a reason why these two should not be joined in holy matrimony, let them speak now or forever after hold their peace."

And all at once, there was something going on at the entrance, by the twin sets of double doors. The light that held him and Joss was fading.

Joss gasped. And then she groaned. "Oh, no. Not Kenny…and Kimberly, too."

Jace turned toward the doors and saw the tall, fit-looking blond guy in the pricey khakis and the pale blue polo shirt.

"Jocelyn, I'm here," the guy said, noble-sounding as the hero in some old-time melodrama. "Don't do this. Forget that guy. We can work it out. Don't ruin our lives. I know there were…issues. I get that I blew it, but that was weeks ago. We need to get past all that garbage and you need to know that I love you and only you—and look." He gestured at the plump, pretty girl in the yellow sundress, who stood blinking uncomfortably at his side. "I brought Kimberly. She's here to tell you how sorry she is that she's made all this trouble." He jabbed at Kimberly with an elbow. "Tell her," he muttered. "Speak up and tell her now."

Kimberly burst into tears.

Kenny gaped. "Kimberly, what are you doing? Stop that!"

Kimberly cried all the harder. She let out a low wail and covered her eyes with her hands. Everyone in the ballroom was watching them, staring uncomfortably, the way people do when driving by car wrecks.

It was a bizarre moment, so strange that Jace wasn't as angry as he might have been at the sudden appearance of Joss's cheating ex, at the dousing of the golden light.

"Kimberly." Kenny actually took her shoulders and shook her. "Snap out of it. Remember? You're here to help."

"I caaaan't. I just caaaan't," Kimberly wailed. She jerked free of Kenny's grip and whirled to face the flower-decked arch and Joss and Jace standing in front of it. "Joss, I'm so sorry. But, you know, I'm *not* sorry. I've always loved Kenny and we've been seeing each other behind your back for the past six months now."

Kenny blinked and shook his perfectly groomed golden head. "Ahem, Kimberly." He tried to reach for her again but she jumped away. "Now, stop that." He cast a frantic glance at Joss again. "Joss, it's not true. I don't know what's gotten into her."

"But it *is* true," cried Kimberly.

"Of course it's not!" Kenny shouted. Then he caught himself. He lowered his voice and spoke out of the corner of his mouth. "You told me you would *help* me. You are not helping. This is not why I brought you here."

"Oh, Kenny, I know it's not. But I just can't stop myself. I'm sick of it, Kenny. Sick, sick, sick. Sick of the lies, sick of my part in this whole humiliating, ridiculous charade. I can see you for who you really are now. I know that you're not worth crap. And you know what? This, today? This does it. I'm through with you. Finished. And I'm glad for Joss. I'm smiling through my tears that my cousin got away without ruining her life and marrying you, you big butthead, creep-faced, yuppie dirtbag, you giant pile of designer-clad trash."

Kenny made a growling sound. "Why you skeevy little bitch…" His face the color of a ripe tomato, he went for Kimberly.

But Kimberly only grabbed a nearby vase of wedding flowers and hurled it at his head.

Kenny ducked.

The vase kept going until it smacked into the side of Forrest Traub's face. Flowers and water went flying.

"Hey!" Forrest lurched upward, trampling the boots of the cowboy sitting next to him.

"Watch it, buddy." The cowboy jumped to his feet and punched Forrest in the jaw. Forrest punched him back. The cowboy fell on the woman sitting next to him. She let out a scream, which caused the man on her other side to leap up and go after the cowboy.

In the meantime, Kenny was chasing Kimberly around the ballroom as Kimberly ran from him, sobbing and screaming and calling him all kinds of imaginative names.

At Jace's side, Joss made a low, sad little sound. "What a disaster...."

That spurred Jace to action. He'd had about enough, too. Kimberly had run down around the other end of the rows of chairs and started up on the far side, coming toward the flowered arch where Joss, Jace, Jackson and the pastor still stood.

Jace waited until Kimberly fled by him, then he stepped forward between the fleeing girl and Kenny. Kenny tried to sprint around him. Jace only slid to the side and blocked him again.

"Outta my way," Kenny huffed.

And Jace drew back his fist and laid the other man flat with one clean right to his perfect square jaw.

Jace stood over the jerk. "Don't get up until I say so."

The man in the polo shirt groaned and tested his jaw and glared up at Jace. But he didn't get up.

By then, the fight in the chairs had spread to every other short-tempered cowboy in attendance. There were more than a few of them, evidently. The men were fighting and the women were alternately shouting at them to stop and screaming "Look out!" and trying in lower voices to settle them all down.

Over by the double doors, Kimberly was still crying. Melba Landry had gone to comfort her. Joss's cousin clung to Melba and drenched the old woman's flower-patterned purple church dress with an endless flood of desperate tears.

Melba was talking to her in low tones, soothing her, Jace had no doubt. And probably reminding her that there was peace in the Lord.

As quickly as it had started, the brawl wound down.

Things got quiet. Really quiet. The ballroom was in chaos, chairs overturned, vases spilled and shattered, wedding flowers torn and tattered, trampled underfoot. The guests all stood around, clothing askew, hair every which way, looking slightly stunned.

Jace turned to Joss.

But she wasn't there.

"Joss?" And then he spotted her.

She was over by the doors, not far from where Kimberly held on to Melba.

Joss met his eyes. And at that moment, there was no one else in that chair-strewn ballroom. Just him and Joss.

Her eyes shone bright with tears. She said, "This isn't going to work. I can't…" She ran out of words.

"I understand," he answered gently. And he did, though his heart seemed to shrivel to a wasted shell inside his chest. "You're right. It's all wrong."

She threw her bouquet. It sailed over the heads of several shell-shocked guests and into the arms of Annabel Cates, who caught it automatically to keep it from hitting her in the face.

And then, as he'd been secretly fearing she might do for the last couple of weeks now, Joss lifted her froth of skirts, whirled away from him and sprinted from the ballroom.

Chapter 14

RaeEllen appeared at Jace's side. She glared down at Kenny. "Shame on you, Kenny Donovan."

Kenny groaned and started to rise. Jace gave him a look and he sank back to the floor.

RaeEllen turned to Jace. "You have to go after her."

Jace wrapped his arm around Joss's mom. "You okay, RaeEllen?"

Her hazel eyes were dark with concern. "Oh, Jason. I swear to you, I had nothing to do with this. I didn't say a word to Kenny—or Kimberly—about where or when you and Jocelyn were getting married."

Jace patted RaeEllen's shoulder. "I know you didn't. Joss told him, weeks ago, on the phone. She was just trying to get it through his fat head that she really was moving on with her life."

RaeEllen pressed her hand to her heart. "Oh, I just feel terrible about all this...."

"Not your fault," he reassured her. "You and Joss have worked things out. She knows you're on her side."

Jackson, his wife beside him by then, asked, "What do we do now?"

It was a good question. "Hey, everyone," Jace called out loud enough to carry to the back of the ballroom. "Looks like the wedding isn't happening. But there's a party waiting for all of you at the Rib Shack. I want you to head on over there and have yourselves a great time."

People exchanged anxious glances.

Then Clay Traub said, "Great idea, Jace. Come on, everyone, let's head for the Rib Shack."

The guests began filing out.

Jace sent a lowering glance down at Kenny. "*You're* not invited. In fact, you can get the hell out—of the clubhouse, of the resort, of the town of Thunder Canyon. Get out and don't come back. Do it now."

Kenny didn't argue. He dragged himself upright and staggered out.

Jace's brothers, his sister, their spouses and Ma and Pete stuck around to straighten up the ballroom. Kimberly and Melba stayed to help, too, as did RaeEllen. It didn't take all that long. Twenty minutes after they started picking up the chairs, they all left together, on their way to the Rib Shack.

All except Jace. He wasn't going to his own nonreception. Not without his runaway bride.

He found her where he knew she would be—in the Lounge, with a margarita in front of her. She'd taken off her veil and let her hair down. She'd also ordered him a whisky on the rocks.

He almost grinned. "You have a lot of faith in me."

"Yeah," she replied softly, her eyes getting misty again. "I do." She patted the stool beside her. "Have a seat."

He eased her big, fat skirt out of the way and took the stool she offered him.

She picked up her drink and he lifted his. They tapped their glasses together and drank.

When she set hers down, she said, "Got something to say to me?"

"I do." He thought about the golden light, the magic that had happened back there in the ballroom. But then he decided that maybe it wasn't magic after all.

Maybe it was only the most natural, down-to-earth thing in the world. A man seeing what mattered, seeing it fully for the very first time.

A man recognizing the right woman. *His* woman.

And knowing absolutely, without even the faintest shadow of a doubt that she was the only one for him. That he knew what love was after all.

Because he loved her.

"I like you, Joss."

She almost rolled her eyes, but not quite. "There'd better be more."

"There is."

"I'm listening."

"I like you. I want you. You…light up my life. You're the only woman in the world for me. I want the life we planned, want to be your partner in the Hitching Post. I want our eight acres and the house that needs work and the horses and the dog we haven't found yet. I want your children to be *my* children. I want to sleep with you in my arms every night and wake up in the morning with you beside me."

Now her adorable mouth was trembling. "Oh, Jace…"

"There's more."

"Tell me. Please."

"What I *don't* want is to lie to you—or myself—anymore. I not only like you. I *love* you. I'm *in* love with you. It's real and it's forever as far as I'm concerned."

"Oh, Jace…" Her eyes, unabashedly tear-wet now, gleamed like dark jewels.

He dared to reach out to touch her cheek, her shining hair. And he whispered, prayerfully, "Damn if I don't finally get what all the shouting's about when it comes to love and marriage and a lifetime together. It's *you*, Joss. You've shown me that. You've shown me love. I want to marry you. More than anything. I want to be with you for the rest of my life. And I have to tell you…"

"Yes? What? Anything, you know that."

"What I *don't* want is to marry you in that dress you bought to marry Kenny Donovan in—no matter how drop-dead gorgeous you look in the damn thing."

She laughed then, that low, rich, husky laugh that belonged only to her. "Okay." She offered her hand. "Yes, I'll marry you. And I promise I won't wear this dress when I do it."

He skipped the handshake and reached for her, gently sliding his fingers around the back of her neck, under the splendid, rich fall of her cinnamon-shot hair. And he kissed her. "I love you, Joss."

"And I love you. So much. I'm so glad…that you can finally say it."

He cradled the side of her face, oblivious to the

bartender who watched them, wearing a dazed sort of smile, from down at the other end of the bar. "I'm sorry," Jace whispered. "So sorry I was such an idiot. So sorry I hurt you...."

"It's okay now."

"I'll say it again. I love you. I'll say it a hundred times a day."

She laughed then. "Oh, I'm so glad. I *was* a little worried."

"I know you were."

"But I'm not anymore. You have put my fears to rest, Jason Traub. You have given me everything—more that I ever dreamed of. And you know what? I love you with all my heart and it means so much to me to be able to tell you so at last without freaking you out. To know that you love me, too." She raised her glass again. "To love."

He touched his glass to hers. "And forever."

"To the Hitching Post. And the house and the horses and the dog."

"And the rowdy kids."

"And to us, Jace."

"Yes, Joss. To us, most of all."

Not much later, they joined the party that was supposed to have been their reception. They danced every dance, enjoyed the great food Shane Roark had prepared for them, fed each other big, delicious chunks of Lizzie's fabulous cake.

It was a beautiful evening. One of the best.

And after all the guests went home, they took the elevator upstairs to the Honeymoon Suite, theirs for that special nonwedding night, courtesy of Thunder Canyon Resort.

They made love. It was amazing.

Better than ever. So good that when they were finished, they made love again. And again after that.

The next morning at a little before seven, Joss woke alone in the big pillow-top bed.

She sat up. "Jace?"

And then she saw him—in the chair by the bed, dressed in a beautiful lightweight suit, holding a handful of wildflowers. He held them out to her. "Marry me, Jocelyn Marie. Marry me today."

She didn't hesitate. She got up, put on a pretty summer dress, took the flowers from him and off they went, stopping only to collect his parents from their suite and her mother from the apartment over the Mountain Bluebell Bakery.

At the Community Church, the nice minister was willing to be persuaded to perform the wedding ceremony that hadn't happened the day before. And there in the pretty white chapel on that sunny Sunday morning well before the regular service, Joss and Jace said their vows.

And when the pastor announced, "You may kiss the bride," Jason Traub knew that he'd finally found what he'd been looking for. He took his bride in his arms and he kissed her.

And when he lifted his head, he whispered, "I love you, Joss Traub. Forever."

"Forever," she echoed.

It was a great moment. The best in his life so far.

For a while there he really had been the last single maverick, wondering where he'd missed out, envious of his brothers and his sister, who had found what they were looking for, had all gotten married and settled down.

He'd felt left out of something important, and left behind as well. That was all changed now by the woman in his arms. He was part of something bigger now.

The last single maverick was single no more.

* * * * *

Rebecca Winters lives in Salt Lake City, Utah. With canyons and high alpine meadows full of wildflowers, she never runs out of places to explore. They, plus her favorite vacation spots in Europe, often end up as backgrounds for her romance novels—because writing is her passion, along with her family and church. Rebecca loves to hear from readers. If you wish to email her, please visit her website at rebeccawinters.net.

Books by Rebecca Winters

Harlequin Romance

The Princess Brides

The Princess's New Year Wedding
The Prince's Forbidden Bride
How to Propose to a Princess

Holiday with a Billionaire

Captivated by the Brooding Billionaire
Falling for the Venetian Billionaire
Wedding the Greek Billionaire

The Billionaire's Club

Return of Her Italian Duke
Bound to Her Greek Billionaire
Whisked Away by Her Sicilian Boss

The Billionaire's Prize
The Magnate's Holiday Proposal

Visit the Author Profile page at Harlequin.com for more titles.

A MONTANA COWBOY

Rebecca Winters

To my editor Kathleen, who allows me
to write the books of my heart.
What joy!

Chapter 1

Captain Trace Rafferty of the Thirty-First Fighter Wing out of Aviano Air Base was coming home for good, much sooner than he'd expected.

Since leaving Italy, where his squadron had flown F-16s critical to operations in NATO's southern region, he'd been in Colorado Springs, Colorado, for the past few days talking with the higher-ups. Having been forced to retire as a jet pilot from the Air Force at twenty-eight due to an eye injury, he'd decided to accept a flight instructor position at the Air Force Academy.

Trace had been asked to stay on with the Thirty-First as a flight navigator, but after being a pilot, he couldn't do it. The Academy was giving him time to get his affairs in order before he went to work for them. He would use this time to tell his father about his future plans... plans his father wasn't going to be happy about.

Sam Rafferty, known as Doc, was a cowboy and rancher besides being the head veterinarian in White Lodge, Montana. A year ago he'd married Ellen Neerings, a pretty brunette widow from the same town, and they lived in a condo. His arthritic hips had made it impossible for him to live and take care of things on the ranch any longer.

Ellen's husband had died several years earlier. With the sale of their small family home, she'd been able to pay off mounting debts because of her husband's long illness, but she'd been left with little to live on.

Both she and Trace's father had sacrificed too much for their families. His dad should have the money from the sale of the ranch to buy him and Ellen a new house of their own in White Lodge with every convenience. She had two married children and needed more space for them and her grandchildren when they came to visit from other parts of the state.

Since Trace wasn't going to live in Montana, selling the ranch was the only sensible solution to make his father's life more comfortable, but he knew it was a subject that would bring his dad pain. The ranch, located in the south central part of the state bordering Wyoming, had been in the Rafferty family for close to a hundred years. Trace hated the fact that his father had done so much for him all his life, virtually supporting him and his mother, even after she'd remarried. It was Trace's turn to give back.

His parents had divorced when he was eight years old. His mother had settled in Billings, only forty minutes away, taking him with her. She didn't like the ranch's isolation and preferred the amenities of living in town.

His dad had moved heaven and earth to be with his son as much as possible during those years. After living with such a kind, laid-back father, it had been hard for Trace to adjust to being around the rigid-type man his mother married soon after the divorce. When Trace turned eighteen, he joined the air force. His mom now lived in Oregon with her husband.

Trace hadn't come back to the United States very often and traveled home to visit his parents on his infrequent leaves. Over the past year the ranch had stood empty. While no one lived there, his dad had hired a former ranch hand named Logan Dorney from the neighboring Bannock ranch to be the foreman on the place until Trace claimed it for his inheritance. But Trace learned the other man had been accidentally killed by a stray bullet from a hunter in February.

Except for Logan's widow, Cassie Dorney, formerly Cassie Bannock, who came in to do the housekeeping once in a while, the ranch no longer had a foreman. Trace would take over that job until the place was sold. Again, all this had to be discussed with his father who knew nothing yet about Trace's plans.

When the fasten-seat-belt sign flashed on, he'd been deep in thought. It surprised him that the flight from Denver to Montana had been so short. He looked out the window. As the plane made its descent to the Billings airport, he decided summer was the best time to see the patches of wheat and corn fields. Below him lay a different mosaic from the farms dotting the Italian countryside he'd so recently left.

Soon the Yellowstone River came into view under a June sun. The airport itself sat on top of Rimrock, a unique five-hundred-foot-tall sandstone feature rising from the valley floor. It all looked familiar, but Trace felt little sense of homecoming.

After the jet landed and he'd picked up his bags, he grabbed a taxi and asked the driver to take him to the Marlow Ford dealership where he'd arranged to have his new Ford Explorer waiting for him. He inspected the vehicle and liked its Kodiak-brown color.

Trace took off for White Lodge, anxious to spend a little quality time with his father. It had been six months since they'd last seen each other. But when he dropped by the vet clinic, the new vet, Clive Masters, who'd replaced Liz Henson since her marriage to Connor Bannock, said Trace's dad was out on an emergency.

The world he'd once known kept going through changes. You couldn't go back and find everything the same. He understood that, but the thought added to his depression.

"Doc Rafferty has been expecting you. He said if you came while he was gone, he wants you to drive out to the ranch and get settled. When he's through, he'll meet you there."

"Good enough. Nice to meet you, Clive."

"I guess you know your dad thinks the world of you."

"He's my hero," Trace replied, which was only the truth. "See you again soon."

Trace got back in the Explorer and headed for the ranch bordering the Bannock's huge spread outside White Lodge.

For the past few years his dad had opened up the Rafferty property to seasonal hunters with permits. Whenever Trace thought about the ranch, it filled him with remembered pain over his parents' divorce and the move to Billings, wrenching him away from his dad. At least when he started work in Colorado, he'd be able to see his dad a lot more often as Sam and Ellen could drive over to visit him.

The old ranch house with the deep porch was set back from the road in the forested area. Two streams running brook trout and cutthroats ran through it. A perimeter dirt road to the side of the property led past crop land that opened up into pasture where cattle could graze. At one time his father had done it all, and had grown alfalfa and barley besides, but that portion lay fallow now.

To reach the house, you took the right fork in the road. There was only one other road before you reached it. This one led to an abandoned logging site and trailed into national forest land. At least here nothing looked changed about the area until he came in sight of the house.

He put on his brakes. At first he thought he must have come to the wrong place. The old log cabin had been freshly stained. Its big picture window and the attic window were now framed by exterior wooden shutters exquisitely hand painted with wildflowers of every color.

The addition of white wicker porch furniture with pale yellow padding and several large baskets of multi-colored flowers hanging beneath the eaves added bright spots of color. He found that the changes transformed the place, making it inviting in a way it had never been before.

His father must have hired a decorator from town to come out and get all this ready in order to welcome Trace home. The knowledge filled him with guilt over what he planned to do. Those years of working on the ranch with him on visitation were over. Sam Rafferty's cowboy son wasn't a cowboy anymore.

Curious to know who was responsible for the actual transformation of the house, he parked around the side next to an unfamiliar green pickup truck. He jumped down from the cab. The barn in back had been freshly stained, too. Everything looked in fabulous shape!

He walked around behind it where his dad had built a kennel for their dog, which stood empty now. Remembered pain propelled Trace back to the front door of the house. He knocked. Even though he had a key to get in, he'd seen the truck and didn't want to walk in unannounced on whoever was here. While he waited, he admired the professional quality of the artwork on the panels.

They reminded him of the shutters you saw on hundreds of alpine-style homes in the Alps. Trace never dreamed his father would go to this extent to make him excited about being home for good.

When no one answered the door, he left the porch and walked around the other side of the house where he was met with another surprise. The ground cover that had always grown next to the house had been cleared to accommodate a well-tended garden full of strawberry plants and raspberry bushes planted in rows. The strawberries looked ripe for the picking and smelled delicious on this hot Tuesday afternoon.

Trace caught a glimpse of someone working between the rows. Curious to know who was there, he walked down one of them. As he got closer he saw it was a woman with wavy blond hair to the shoulders, gilded by the sun.

"Hello?" he called to her.

She lifted her head and got to her feet, holding a basket under her arm partially filled with strawberries. The raspberries hadn't ripened completely yet. The last time Trace had seen Cassie Bannock she was in her early teens. It strained the imagination that anyone in the well-heeled Bannock clan would be working as a housekeeper.

When Trace could sit down with his father, he'd find out the whole story behind it, but first things first. She was of medium height, her well-endowed body filled out an aqua-colored cotton top she wore over a pair of jeans. On her feet she wore cowboy boots. He found himself staring at her. She was blooming with health. He'd heard the term before, but she personified it.

"Captain Rafferty!"

"Call me Trace."

She laughed gently. "I couldn't resist. I've never met a jet pilot before." Her light green eyes smiled as she moved toward him. "You probably don't remember me."

Her coloring was different from that of her brunette cousin, Avery Lawson, another Bannock who was now married. But they both had the natural beauty of the Bannock genes in the classic shape of their faces and more voluptuous figures. Both were the same age, twenty-six or twenty-seven by now as he recalled.

"Of course I do. The last time I saw you I think you were about twelve to my thirteen. You'd come with your grandfather Tyson to the vet clinic because your pet colt was sick and there was no consoling you. I was helping my dad and went to work with him that day."

"I'm surprised you remembered that. Sam got him all better. He's the best!"

"I agree," he murmured. "I'm very sorry to hear of your husband's unexpected passing."

A shadow crossed over her lovely face for a moment. She studied his features. "Thank you. I'm sorry to learn of your eye injury. Are you in pain?"

"No."

"Thank goodness for that at least." She had a sweetness about her. "Life throws all of us a curve once in a while, one we weren't expecting."

"You're right about that." Their losses were different. Though his career was over, he could still see with a corrective lens. Her loss had to be excruciating. According to Trace's father, they'd been a happily married couple while they'd worked for him.

"Your dad was afraid you might have to stay in the hospital longer for more tests."

"I received excellent care and was discharged the moment the doctor felt I could travel."

"That's wonderful and he's so excited! He said you'd be here today, but I expected the two of you to arrive this evening with you still wearing a uniform."

"The military doesn't usually travel in uniform these days. It's safer." She nodded. "My father said he'd meet up with me here later."

"Then welcome home, soldier. Go on in. Your old bedroom is waiting for you. There's food and drinks in the fridge in case you're hungry or thirsty. Sam said you're a big tuna fish sandwich man, so there's plenty on hand. In case you need anything else, I'll be in as soon as I've filled this basket."

Berry-picking looked fun and Trace considered helping her, then thought the better of it. His gaze fell to her left hand. She still wore her wedding ring.

"Thank you, Cassie. See you shortly."

He retraced his steps to get his bags out of the Explorer. When he walked inside, the delicious aroma of strawberries filled the house. He moved through the foyer and dining room to the kitchen. She'd been making jam. Trace didn't realize her housekeeping duties extended to actually putting up fruit in a house where no one lived.

There were several dozen jars on the counter already filled and labeled. The sweet smell reminded him of times he'd played with the Bannock brothers as a boy before his parents' divorce. The last summer he'd lived here while he was still happy, he remembered going over to their grandmother's house where she was putting up jam and jelly. She'd let them pile butter and fresh jam on homemade bread and feast their heads off.

The wonderful memory pierced him. Soon after that time he'd learned his parents were divorcing and he'd have to move away from friends like Connor and Jarod Bannock, who lived next door. That turned out to be the darkest day of his young life. He'd been searching for happiness ever since. Being a pilot had given him thrills and purpose, but life had a habit of getting in the way.

He left the kitchen and walked across the hall to his bedroom to get rid of his bags. The same framed photographs of family that had always hung there lined the walls. It hurt to look at them. On the way he passed the other two bedrooms. One was his father's. The other was a spare bedroom, but when he looked inside, he received a shock rather than a surprise.

Cassie *lived* here?

Trace had assumed she'd moved back to the Bannock ranch with her family after her husband's death.

Their wealth meant she wouldn't have financial worries. Maybe his kindhearted father had allowed her to stay on for a time while she worked through her grief. That was something he would do. If that were the case, then Trace's plan to sell the ranch would come as a blow to her while she was attempting to get through the worst of her pain. Hell…

That was another subject to talk over with his father when he arrived. But right now Trace was starving. The thought of a tuna fish sandwich on American soft white bread sounded so good, he headed straight back to the kitchen.

Cassie had watched his tall, well-honed physique, dressed in khakis and a crewneck shirt, disappear around the corner of the house. Trace Rafferty had been born an exceptionally handsome man. Judging from the photographs Sam had shown her after his son had gone into the military, time had only added to his male attributes. He'd inherited his mother's black hair and smile. But his rugged features and those searing hot blue eyes fringed by black lashes had come straight from his father.

Sam was so proud of his son, who'd served in many places around the globe. In or out of uniform, Trace Rafferty, still unmarried, possessed killer looks that would always cause him to stand out.

Cassie had been putting up jam for the past week, a little at a time. It always made the house smell good, so she'd decided to put up some more today to make his homecoming a little more welcoming. After that she'd started dinner with a pot roast in the oven and home-made rolls that were still rising.

According to Doc Rafferty, Trace hadn't been out to the ranch since his father had gotten married last year. On his last leave, he'd stayed in town with him and his new wife at their condo in White Lodge.

Perhaps it had been too painful to return to the home that was now empty of all family. But Sam had left it to his son and hoped he would make his life here now that he was out of the air force. She knew Sam's heart. He'd missed his son horribly over the years. To have him back home to stay would thrill him.

After finding as many ripe strawberries as she could, she made her way to the back door through the laundry room to the kitchen. Trace could have them fresh for breakfast if he wanted.

The minute she stepped in the kitchen, the first thing she noticed was the smell of tuna fish mingled with the jam aroma. Looking around she discovered Trace over in the corner at the breakfast table eating sandwiches. He'd already drunk half a quart of milk without the aid of a glass.

He flashed her a smile that gave her an odd, fluttery sensation. "You've caught me."

Troubled that his smile had any effect on her at all, she put the basket of berries on the counter. "It's your house. You're entitled to do whatever you want."

"I didn't know you were still living here."

Uh oh. "After Logan died, I didn't plan to stay on, but your father insisted because he wanted the house kept up while no one was living here. Now that you're home, I plan to leave tonight after I've served you two dinner."

Though she hadn't told Sam yet, she'd already made arrangements with her cousin Avery to stay with her and her husband, Zane, until she found another place to live and work.

He shook his dark head. "Since I just arrived and don't know my own plans yet, I wouldn't dream of asking you to move out."

"But—"

"No buts. You were hired to take care of the house. From what I've already seen, you've done a fantastic job."

"Thank you." She checked on the roast, then started to leave the kitchen, almost faint with relief that she didn't have to give up this job quite yet.

"Where are you going?"

"I'm taking the horses for their daily exercise."

Trace emptied the milk bottle. His eyes played over her. "How do you manage that?"

She couldn't help but smile at the remark. "I ride Buttercup and string Masala along. He goes where she goes."

"So he has a crush on her?"

A chuckle escaped her. "No. But he has no choice if he wants to leave the paddock. He's a wild mustang my cousin Connor tamed and gave to us. Besides Connor and your father, my husband was the only other man to ride him."

He continued to study her. "All you Bannocks are expert horse people. I'm surprised you haven't won that horse over yet."

She averted her eyes. "Masala preferred Logan."

Since when did that matter when according to Trace's father she was an expert horsewoman? He got up from the table. "If you don't mind, I'd like to come with you and take a look around the property. Maybe Masala will let me ride him. If not, I'll hold the rope and lead him around as we walk. After my flight, I need to stretch my legs."

Cassie preferred to be alone, but she didn't see how she could turn down Trace's offer. "Won't your father be here before long?"

"I don't know. Clive Masters said he'd gone out on an emergency. I'll text him to let him know we'll be back soon. If he's hungry, I made enough tuna fish for him to have some, too."

"He'll like that," she said. It seemed Trace had made up his mind. He had the confidence and authority of a man who was comfortable in any setting. "I'll meet you at the barn in a few minutes."

After she left the kitchen, Trace cleaned up the mess he'd made and went back to his bedroom to put on jeans and a T-shirt. His room was exactly as he'd left it. The framed pictures of him, a couple with his dog, some with his parents and some with Jarod and Connor out horseback riding, still hung on the wall.

He found his old pair of cowboy boots and put them on. With the exception of the last time he'd been home, he and his father had always gone riding after chores were done.

His ancient black cowboy hat sat on the closet shelf. He dusted it off and shoved it on his head. Once he'd sent his father a text, he headed for the barn. Cassie was already out in the paddock astride her horse.

Buttercup was well named. Between Cassie's hair and the palomino's golden color that included a white mane and tail, they made quite a sight in the sun. He rubbed her horse's forelock. "You're a real beauty, aren't you Buttercup," he said, struggling not to look at Cassie.

Her coloring was the complete opposite from the Italians he'd spent time with over the past eighteen months.

Nicoletta Tornielli, the olive-skinned woman he'd been planning to marry, had long black hair and large black-brown eyes. After being around her family, Cassie's fairness with that peaches-and-cream complexion was in complete contrast.

While he was deep in thought over the change in his circumstances, her horse pushed against his chest, causing both of them to laugh. She smiled down at him. "Buttercup likes you. When one of the older ranchers in the area told Connor he needed to sell a couple of his horses, Connor took me with him and I ended up buying Buttercup. She's been a wonderful horse so far. Friendly."

"Your cousin has a great eye for horseflesh. One horse down, one to go." Still feeling her smile, he walked into the barn. The smell of the barn brought back memories of getting up early in the morning. He'd repair the fencing bordering the Bannock property with his father, or make certain the planted forage wasn't flooded by the numerous springs. Then he'd ride to the pasture. His job was to look for heifers in trouble while his dad checked on the rest of the herd.

In one of the stalls he found a blue roan with transverse stripes across the withers, marking him a wild mustang. "Hey, big fella." Trace started talking to the horse, touching him, using all the tricks his horse-loving father had taught him years ago. The gentleness paid off. Soon the horse was nickering. Trace went into the tack room for a bridle and brought it out.

At first Masala shied away from it, but Trace continued to talk to him in soothing tones until the horse allowed the bridle to be put on. "It's now or never," he muttered before mounting him. Trace had always preferred riding bareback on his favorite mount, Prince. That seemed a century ago. If this horse didn't like the weight, it was too late now.

Masala tossed his head several times and backed up, but when he realized he wasn't in charge, Trace made a clicking sound and rode him out of the barn.

Cassie's eyes flashed like green gemstones. "I don't believe it! I didn't think he'd let anyone else ride him."

"My father taught me a few techniques." They left the paddock and headed for the deep forest that made the Rafferty property so desirable to Trace.

"You learned them well. He must sense the take-charge pilot in you."

"You think?" he teased.

"I know."

They rode side by side, following a faint trail that wound through the trees. With the temperature at eighty-one degrees, he welcomed the cool of the forest. When the fall hunting season was on, the abundance of wildlife made the property a big game hunter's paradise—elk, moose, mule deer, bison, white-tailed deer, bear and bighorn sheep roamed this part of the state. This ranch had it all. Someone would pay a lot of money for the property. Trace was determined that money would go right into his father's bank account.

He glanced over at Cassie. "Tell me something. Who did the work and staining on the exterior of the cabin? When I first drove in, I thought I'd come to the wrong house. It's so changed I hardly recognized it."

"That was Logan's doing."

"The artwork on the shutters, too?"

"No. That was my contribution."

Trace marveled at her skill. He took a deep breath of the pine-scented air. "And the garden?"

"We both worked on it at the end of last summer to get it ready for spring."

A spring Logan never saw...

It meant Cassie had done all the planting. "You've made the place beautiful."

"Thank you. Your father asked me to pick out some porch furniture so it would look more attractive. When I was young I read all the books in the Little House series. I loved them and envied Laura Ingalls Wilder her life."

He wondered where she was going with this. "I remember watching a few TV shows based on those books."

Cassie flicked him a glance. "Do you know, when I first saw this place, I found myself thinking of it as *Little House in the Big Woods*. You know, it's isolated here. The forest is so pristine and untouched. Anyway, it gave me the same feeling as those books. I was really delighted when your father hired us to live and work here. It's an adorable house in the perfect setting."

Trace was charmed by her. "Well, with what you've done to it, it is now. Tell me—do you plan on writing a series of books about this house, too?"

"Don't be silly."

He eyed her very fetching profile. "You have a real talent for color and design. There are chalets in the Alps with shutters that can't touch the beauty of your artwork. Dad should have hired you years ago. How many other homes have you worked on?"

"None." She sounded surprised. "I'm not an artist, Trace. But a few years ago some of my college friends and I went on spring break to Europe. When we toured through Switzerland, I stayed in a village where all the chalets had decorated shutters and window boxes. I was so delighted by them, I took pictures and thought I'd like to try my hand if I ever got the chance. Your father, bless his heart, was willing to let me experiment."

"He got more than his money's worth. I'm very impressed." He was impressed with a lot of things about her. She was well traveled, could grow a garden and make jam, paint and was an expert horsewoman, as well. Trace had no doubts she could ride Masala if she wanted. He got the feeling she was holding something back where the horse was concerned, but he wasn't about to push his theory about why at this early stage.

"Tell me about your deployment in Italy. What was it like to be a jet pilot?"

His career seemed to be a safe topic for her, so he obliged her. "In a word, *exhilarating*."

"But what was your job exactly?"

"The mission of the Thirty-First Fighter Wing is to deliver combat power and support across the globe to achieve U.S. and NATO objectives."

"I guess you had to memorize that for everyone who asks." He smiled at her perception.

"So what did you do when you weren't fighting?"

"We had to maintain aircraft and personnel in a high state of readiness. That involved a lot of training exercises."

"Did you get your eye injury in combat? I hope you don't mind my asking. When your father received the news, he was too broken up to talk about it."

So was Trace's girlfriend, Nicci. She'd begged him to go to work for her father so nothing between them would change. But everything *had* changed. There was no going back.

For their marriage to take place, she would have to move to Colorado. But she'd been living in denial since his injury and their relationship had hit a plateau.

Not so for the woman riding on the horse next to him. Unlike Nicoletta, Cassie had been forced to face losing her husband and get on with living and working. You couldn't avoid dealing with death. Her life couldn't get more real than that. Since she'd asked the question, why not tell her the truth?

"I was flying a combat mission when a laser beam intersected my eye. If you want the medical version, the light was transmitted through the clear ocular media and imaged onto a small spot on the sensory retina. In a mere moment tissue necrosis occurred. The result being that my vision was impaired."

"A laser? Where did it come from?"

"Lasers are used for different functions in military applications. They serve in targeting guidance systems. Some are fire-control devices, others for access denial systems and communications security. Although the use of lasers as a weapon is a violation of the Geneva convention, the potential for its wrongful use continues to attract international concern. The laser that injured my eye was no accident."

She shivered. "That's horrible. Evil."

"You're right. In military applications, just a few microjoules of laser through the pupils in a 10 to 30 nanosecond pulse can produce a visible lesion. At 150 to 300 microjoules, a small retinal hemorrhage can occur. This type of damage can have a devastating effect on a pilot's vision. It did on mine." His voice grated. "I wasn't blinded, but I have to wear a corrective lens so it prevents me from doing that particular job anymore."

"Though you're no longer top gun, you can still fly, right?"

"Yes. I could be a flight navigator, but once you've done what I do, no other position holds the same excitement for me. That probably sounds selfish to you."

"Not at all," she replied. "There are few careers in this world that demand your specialized kind of expertise. Connor and I had a talk about that very thing last week. Since his injury, his fans have been begging him to get back to steer wrestling and go for a sixth world championship title."

"What did he say?" Trace was curious.

"He admitted that those years of being on top were great, and there was no other thrill like it. But the injury affected him enough that he knew he'd never be that good again. Sure he could train and go for it over and over for a few more years, but he'd never be able to perform at his former level. To be a has-been simply wasn't for him.

"Then he gave me that special smile of his and told me he was glad he'd been injured because he ended up marrying Liz Henson. To quote him, 'The thrill of being married to her has topped anything I've ever experienced.'"

Trace liked hearing that. "He's really happy, then."

"Ecstatic. They both are. From the time we were in high school Liz had a crush on him that never went away."

He nodded. "Dad let on to me about her heartache before she and Connor traveled to Las Vegas together for the National Finals Rodeo. That trip turned their lives around and lost him a great vet in the process."

"It about killed her when he married Reva Stevens. I wasn't surprised when it ended in divorce so fast. Reva loved Connor, but she hated ranch life. Not everyone takes to it. She didn't last long. At the time I was afraid his heart was permanently broken."

"My mother couldn't handle being this isolated either," Trace admitted. "Nine years into the marriage and she asked my dad for a divorce." Would the same thing happen if he and Nicoletta got married, even if they lived in Colorado? He'd been struggling with that question all night.

"For someone who wasn't born to it, your mom lasted longer than most, Trace. That's because she loved your father. At least that's what I heard from people who knew your parents. But I know that's no consolation to you. Anything but. Forgive me for saying something so insensitive."

"There's nothing to forgive. I was the one to bring it up. My mother was frank with me. I knew she loved Dad, but that wasn't enough. I'm glad you told me about Connor. It's great to hear he's found his happiness now."

"I agree, but I'm so sorry about your injury, Trace. It isn't fair," she said in a heartfelt voice. "I'm surprised nothing's been done to prevent such a thing from happening."

"People have tried. There was an international conventional weapons conference in 1995. They announced the latest protocol on blinding laser weapons. The United States signed on to the guidelines. Four of the articles outlined the parameters for the use of lasers in military maneuvers and war.

"They came up with the rule that the employment of lasers solely to cause permanent blindness—or a resulting visual acuity of 20/200—is strictly prohibited. But of course, the enemy doesn't care."

"That is so horrible."

"No more horrible than your husband being shot." Trace wanted to move the subject away from him. "Did the rangers find the person responsible?"

She was quiet for a moment before she admitted, "Not yet. As you know, Avery's husband, Zane, is a special agent for the Bureau of Land Management. While searching for Logan, he found a dead marten near Logan that had been shot on the property that day.

"The slug from a smooth bore shotgun that killed my husband matched the slug in the marten. Zane's still hoping forensics will lead to the owner of the shotgun so he can be brought in for questioning. So far there's no actual proof that it wasn't accidental."

"What do *you* think?"

"I don't know. There's no hunting until April, so whoever was out there in February was trespassing. It could have been an accident, but Zane doesn't think so. A hunter shooting marten would probably have taken it for the fur."

"Did your husband have an enemy?"

They'd come to the first stream running through the property. Both horses stopped to drink. "He was so likeable, I can't imagine it. But *I* have one." She sounded haunted.

"Who is it?"

"My brother Ned."

Chapter 2

Trace scowled. Through his father he knew all about Ned Bannock's instability. "Isn't he in a special mental facility in Billings?"

"He was, but has been getting treatment. In February the doctor allowed him to live at home for a month on a trial basis. According to my older married cousins, he was subdued and seemed to get along well enough. The doctor was pleased with his progress and said if he continued to improve, he'd be able to come home permanently."

"So he was at home during the time your husband was killed?"

"Yes. When he was first put in the facility, the court ordered our family to go into counseling and get therapy. It was painful, but necessary. I welcomed it because I knew that Ned had always resented me. There were times when I felt that he wished I weren't alive. I was able to express those feelings in front of my parents."

Since Trace didn't have a sibling, he couldn't relate, but her admission horrified him. "How did they react?"

"They were oblivious to my pain. Dad said I brought on trouble, that when things went wrong with Ned it was my fault. Mom kept quiet to appease my dad, who claimed that I wasn't sensitive enough to Ned's needs growing up because I was the popular one. I should have included him more in my activities. Their worry over him meant more punishment for me if I didn't coddle my brother. To this day they still believe that. There's no getting through to them."

"I don't see how you've been able to cope. Under those conditions I probably would have run away."

"Once I was out of the house working on my own, I didn't have to be around him nearly as much. What stunned me was to learn in one of the sessions that Ned had hate issues with me because I'd gotten involved with Logan on one of my brief trips home."

"You're serious." Trace was appalled.

"I swear my brother was born a bigot. He felt that a hired hand wasn't good enough to be part of our family. Long before I told my parents I was in love with Logan, Ned had been filling my father with lies about him. Ned was the one who told my parents I was involved with him and it should be stopped."

"Sounds like he was driven by the same kind of hatred that landed Jarod in the hospital."

"Exactly. Dad, who was in a bad way at the time because of what Ned had tried to do to Jarod, wasn't thinking rationally. Like my older brothers, he'd always been afraid of Ned's temper and as usual took his side to placate him. He fired Logan and ordered me not to marry him in order to keep the peace."

"He *ordered* you?" Trace was incredulous.

"Dad used the very word. Shocking, isn't it? But I couldn't obey him. At that point he told me that if we went ahead with our marriage, then I no longer had a home with the family. Out of fear, Mother backed Dad by not saying anything at all. My other brothers took their cue from mom and stayed out of things."

Incredible. "I had no idea of the stress you've been through." And here Trace had been wondering why she hadn't gone home to her family after her husband was killed. She'd never want to go there again unless a miracle happened.

"No one knew. It isn't something you want other people to know, but I'm aware of your close friendship with my cousins and realize you probably know everything."

No, not everything. Not this.

She let out a deep sigh. "I loved Logan, so that was that. We got married in a civil ceremony and took a job with your father to run the ranch for him. I broke down and told him my whole situation. He's such a wonderful man. Mostly I checked hunting permits and collected fees while Logan monitored the hunters' activities throughout the season. Thanks to your dad, this job saved our lives."

So many people loved and respected Trace's father. He was an exceptional man. "I take it nothing has changed with your family?"

She hunched her shoulders. "Absolutely nothing. Though extended family and a lot of neighbors came to Logan's funeral in White Lodge, my parents didn't come near or even try to talk to me."

"I can't conceive of it. There's something very wrong with him, Cassie."

"I know. The doctor has urged me to stay in therapy. I'm glad I have because I've since learned that along with their other emotional problems, my parents are battered people and need a lot of intensive counseling."

"I could have used therapy when I was young," Trace admitted in a moment of self-reflection.

"Everyone could. In the case of our family I've learned that Ned irritated our older brothers to the point they didn't want to be around him. Ned had already felt abandoned when Sadie, the girl he'd always loved, married my cousin Jarod. In his jealousy he almost killed Jarod in order to get rid of him."

Trace nodded. "It was very tragic."

Cassie grimaced. "When I married Logan and moved away from the ranch, Ned began nursing an unhealthy hatred toward me."

"You think he could have killed your husband to hurt you?"

"It's possible," she said, "but I don't know how he could have left the ranch without someone knowing about it. Zane did an investigation. None of my father's firearms were missing or had been fired close to that time. In any event, Dad had people keeping an eye on my brother."

"But if he went off his meds, he might have found a way to make it over to this ranch. Is that what you're thinking?" Trace asked.

"He could have. One of the guys he hung around with in high school is still his friend and visits him. Through him it's possible he got hold of a gun or rifle he hid somewhere before he'd been committed. I try not to think about it or I get ill."

"That's why the military disqualifies a person with a history of mood or behavioral disorders."

"Exactly. But home isn't the military, and my parents want him back to help around the ranch."

"That's hard on everyone."

"I've talked this over with Zane. If Ned was the one responsible, Zane will find out in time. After the shooting, he advised your father to close the ranch to hunting and keep it closed until more proof of what really happened came to light. As you know, he was a tough Navy SEAL before he started working as a special agent for the BLM."

"I know him by reputation. Let's hope he has an answer for you soon."

"Yes. Avery said Ned is going to be coming back to live with my parents again on a permanent basis." The anxiety in her eyes spoke volumes.

Trace cringed for her. "With restrictions, of course."

"I don't know what they'd be as long as he keeps taking his medicine."

"Cassie, I'm sorry you've had to live through such pain." To lose her husband and be afraid that her brother might have been the one to shoot him was horrendous. Worse, he could tell she was worried that Ned might come after her one day when he got the chance. That frightening possibility was going to keep Trace awake nights from here on out.

He couldn't begin to imagine the pain of Cassie's loss, but she was obviously handling it. She was a strong woman to have married for love despite her father's wishes. Trace admired that strength and her will to get on with her life.

Just then his cell rang. He checked the caller ID. "It's my dad. He's on his way to the ranch now."

"Then let's get back. I have a pot roast with potatoes and carrots cooking."

"I could smell it before we left the house. Did he tell you that's my favorite meal?"

She smiled. "That's why I made it. To welcome you home. He's so happy you're going to be living here from now on, you can't imagine."

Trace was afraid he could and didn't look forward to the conversation he was about to have. When they reached the barn and dismounted to take care of the horses, he turned to her. She was removing Buttercup's bridle. "I want to thank you for what you and Logan have done."

"We were just doing our job."

"It was a lot more than that and you know it. You've eased my father's mind while I've been away and made the place beautiful. There's no way to repay you. I'll feed and water the horses while you go into the house. It's the least I can do."

Once dinner was over, Trace went out on the front porch with his father. He sat on a chair while his dad settled for the swing. "That Cassie could make her living as a cook."

"Agreed. I can't remember the last time I had a meal that good."

His dad studied Trace. "You're talking home cooked. Nothing like it." Trace nodded. "Do you have any idea how good it feels to be sitting on the porch with my son after all these years?"

Trace's throat thickened. "I do," he murmured. *More than you can imagine*.

His dad's hair was a sandy color mixed with gray. Lines from years of outdoor living gave his rugged features character. He'd dressed in one of his familiar plaid shirts and jeans, and he wore a belt with a silver and turquoise buckle, his trademark.

One of the tribal elders from the reservation had presented it to him for saving their horses from dying during an equine flu epidemic. The tribe had bought some horses in Mexico and had them transported. But several of them had the virus. Afraid all the horses would die, they came to Trace's father.

Trace, who had been only eight years old at the time, remembered going out to the reservation with him to test the horses. Sam told the elders all they could do was rest them for a month in fresh air in a shady, confined area. Walk them for short periods to maintain circulation during the fever and coughing. Keep them away from dust and hay to minimize the risk of bacterial infections of the lungs. Then give them an antibody vaccine booster every three months.

The horses looked and sounded miserable to Trace. He couldn't imagine his father's treatment working. But in a month's time the tribe hadn't lost one of them and he'd become a valued friend of the Crow.

Tears smarted Trace's eyes just remembering the day they presented his dad with the belt buckle, handmade on their reservation. His father was held in high esteem by a lot of the population around White Lodge, including members of the Crow nation.

Soon after that experience, his parents divorced. Remembered pain still lingered to think his mom would want to leave the man who was Trace's idol. So what did Trace do? After he'd turned eighteen, he'd left his father, just like his mom had done.

"You probably won't believe me, but I've missed being here. I've missed you, Dad." His voice was thick with emotion. "More than you'll ever know."

Sam leaned forward with his hands on his knees. "When your mom left, the heart went out of our home. You couldn't take it."

He shook his head. "That's not it. At first I was angry at her. Later I was angry at you for not making her come back."

"You can't hold somebody who doesn't want to be held, son."

"I know that now. Forgive my anger."

"It was natural. Divorce means an automatic whammy for everyone involved. No one escapes. I'm proud of you for what you've done with your life even when it threw you some curveballs. Is it killing you not to be a pilot anymore?"

"If you'd asked me that when I was rushed to the hospital, I would have told you I'd rather have been killed. But after a few days I realized it would be the coward's way out and I thought about something you said the day our collie's paw got caught in a snare and had to be amputated."

"Poor Kip. He was the best dog we ever had."

"I loved him. While I was having hysterics, you told me he'd be able to get around just fine with three legs. That's why God gave him four, just in case."

A quiet laugh came out of his father. "Did I really say that?"

"That's why everyone in Carbon County puts their

favorite vet on a pedestal. Before I phoned you from the hospital to let you know what had happened to me, I figured you'd say something like, 'Son? God gave you two eyes so if you lost one of them, it didn't matter.' Even if you didn't know what went through my mind before our phone call, your wisdom helped me through that dark period. So, the answer to your question is no, it didn't kill me."

"Thank God for that."

"But during my recuperation I had to think about how else I could earn my living. On the way home, I spent a couple days at the Air Force Academy in Colorado Springs. They've offered me a teaching position on their staff, but I've been given five to six weeks to get my affairs in order before I report."

At that piece of unexpected news his dad—hurt to the marrow as Trace had anticipated—got up from the swing and walked over to the porch railing. He looked up at the stars. "What about the woman you said you wanted to marry in Italy? How does she feel about that decision?"

Trace couldn't stay seated either. He wandered over to his father. "You're the smartest man I ever knew, so you already know the answer to that question."

"Which means *if* she's willing, you'll live in Colorado Springs."

The hollowness of his father's voice stung Trace. His eyes closed tightly for a minute. It was a big *if.*

"That's the plan, but these are early days. Nicci needs to fly to the States. I want her to meet you and Ellen, then we'll fly to Colorado Springs and let her get a feel for where we'd live."

Trace waited for the next question. It was a long time coming. "What about the ranch?"

This was the part he'd been dreading. "I'd like to use the time while I'm here to find a buyer. With the sale of the house and property, you'll have plenty of money to spend on you and Ellen.

"All these years you've sacrificed for me, for mom. Now it's time you thought about yourself. You can go on some cruises, buy a house. I was hoping you might invest in a motor home. Then you and Ellen could come and visit us in Colorado whenever you wanted."

His father slowly turned to him. In the semidarkness he looked older than he had earlier in the evening. "This ranch is your legacy, son."

Here Trace went again, stabbing his father in the heart once more. "Not when I won't be able to live here. Since you have health issues and can't work the ranch anymore, the only sensible thing to do is sell it. Maybe one of Ellen's married children would like to buy it."

His dad's body had gone still as a statue. "You know what? It's getting late. I don't want Ellen to worry, so I'm going to leave. I've already said good-night to Cassie. But you tell her again how much I appreciated dinner."

He started for the porch steps. Trace walked with him to his truck. After he got in the cab, he lowered the window. "Didn't she do a great job on those shutters?"

The question only added to Trace's pain because he knew the renovations had been done expressly for Trace's homecoming. "They're exquisitely done."

His father nodded. "Come on over to the condo anytime. Don't be a stranger."

This wasn't the way their reunion was supposed to go. "What are you talking about? I'll see you tomorrow at the clinic. Love you, Dad."

"Love you. Always."

In agony, Trace watched his father drive away. If it weren't late, he'd head over to the Bannock ranch to look up Connor or Jarod. They'd understand his impossible position. Letting out a groan, he went back in the house for his wallet and keys. A restlessness had come over him. He'd never be able to sleep.

Cassie had already disappeared to her room for the night. Not wanting to disturb her, he left a note on the kitchen table that he was going into town and probably wouldn't be back till late. He supposed he didn't need to say anything, but it seemed the courteous thing to do. She'd gone the extra mile to make Trace comfortable today. No one had fussed over him like this in years and he appreciated it.

The Golden Spur Bar in White Lodge didn't close till one in the morning. He needed the canned country music, a lot of noise plus a beer to drown the condemning voice in his head. Too bad the laser's damage hadn't burned the guilt out of him at the same time.

He found a parking spot around the corner. Summer brought the tourists in droves and the place was crowded. Trace made his way through to the bar. After a five-minute wait he grabbed a vacated stool and signaled the bartender.

"Trace Rafferty?" The man on his left had spoken to him. When he turned, the guy said, "It *is* you. You're the F-16 pilot. What do you know about that."

"Sorry. Have we met before?"

"Yeah, but it was a long time ago and I'm the forgettable type according to my ex-wife. The name's Owen Pearson."

It rang a bell, but Trace couldn't place him. Between

the empty whiskey glass and his self-pity, Trace could see Owen was getting wasted fast. The bartender asked Trace what he wanted. "A beer please."

Owen raised his empty glass. "Another one of these while you're at it." Then his gaze swerved back to Trace. "You in town on leave?"

"Something like that." It was no one else's business.

"Haven't figured it out yet, have you?"

"Pardon?"

"You remember Ned Bannock. He and I have been buddies for years."

At the mention of the name, the hackles went up on the back of Trace's neck. It all came back to him. Owen Pearson was the one who lent Ned the truck that had bashed Jarod's truck years ago almost killing him. "Your dad's ranch is right next door to the Bannock's."

The conversation with Cassie was still fresh in Trace's mind. His teeth snapped together. "That's right." Ned and Cassie's parents lived on the Bannock property owned by Ralph and Tyson Bannock, the two brothers who raised their families side by side.

"Then you'd know all about the shooting."

"My father filled me in. Did you go to the funeral?"

"Hell, no. Logan Dorney was a no-account. Ned's dad fired him when he found out he'd been doing Ned's sister on the sly. I'm surprised your dad hired them."

Sickness started to rise in Trace's throat. "That's my father's business surely."

"The Doc didn't know Logan the way Ned did."

Trace let the remark pass. "Any idea who shot him?"

"Some hunter."

Yup. "How is Ned these days? I haven't seen him in years."

"He had some family problems for a while. His sister was nothing but trouble for him. But he's doing much better now and will be home before long. We're going to go into business together soon."

"Is that right? What kind?"

"A stud farm for feral horses."

That was the business Connor had been building with Liz. "Where?"

"My dad's ranch."

The conversation robbed Trace of any interest in his beer. It was still sitting there untouched. He put some money on the counter and got to his feet.

"Hey—you haven't drunk your beer."

"I discovered I'm not thirsty. It's all yours. So long."

In a different frame of mind than before, Trace drove back to the ranch. After he reached the house, he tore up the note in the kitchen and wrote another one. She'd see it first thing in the morning.

Cassie—

I've gone to Billings and will be in and out of the house at odd hours for the rest of the week. Dad and I agree your food is out of this world, but please don't do any more cooking for me since I don't have a schedule you can count on.

T.

When Friday the twenty-second came around, Cassie kept her afternoon appointment with her OB. Dr. Raynard did an ultrasound and handed her the picture of the sonogram. "Your little girl has a healthy heart and measures the right size. So far everything looks fine."

Tears streamed down her cheeks. "I can't believe that's my baby. Oh, I wish Logan were here."

"Of course you do."

"You're sure she's all right?"

"Yes, but to make certain she stays that way, I'm going to insist you stop your horseback riding altogether."

"Since my last appointment I've stopped riding Masala, but Buttercup is gentle. I love riding so much."

"At twenty weeks, you're too far along to take any chances. That isn't a great deal to give up. Go on walks instead."

"Okay. I haven't felt the baby move yet. How come?"

"It's been moving for a long time, but too small for you to notice. I imagine you'll feel it within the next couple of weeks."

"I hope so."

"And I hope you mind me. I know you're an expert rider, but a horse can do the unexpected. Do you hear what I'm saying? This is for your own good. If your husband were alive, he wouldn't want you to ride now."

"Probably not."

He smiled. "I'll see you in a month. That'll make it Friday, July 22. Remember to go easy on salt and caffeine, and put your legs up for a few minutes every day."

"I will. Thanks so much."

Cassie left the White Lodge Clinic where Dr. Raynard practiced and did a little shopping. She couldn't hide her pregnancy any longer. She needed to buy another couple of pairs of maternity pants and a few more tops she could layer. Now that she knew she was having a daughter, she would pick up a few things for the baby at the same time.

When Logan was killed, Cassie hadn't known she was pregnant. Later she became ill and went to see the doctor because she'd thought she'd come down with the flu. The news that she was pregnant had sent her into shock again, but a wonderful kind. A part of Logan was growing inside her.

To know she had their baby to live for pulled her out of the dark depression she'd been in. The doctor gave her medicine to help with the morning sickness. Since that stage had passed, she'd never felt better.

Later tonight she would drive over to Zane's ranch and show Avery the new things she'd bought for the baby while they talked. Avery was the closest thing she had to a sister. Her cousin was the only one who knew she was pregnant, but Cassie wouldn't be able to keep it a secret from now on.

When she returned to the ranch, there was still no sign of Trace. No doubt he was spending a lot of time with his father in town. She hurried inside to change into her new clothes that gave her more room to breathe. After grabbing a sandwich, she went out to the barn to take the horses for a late afternoon walk, mindful of her doctor's advice.

"Come on, Buttercup. You first."

If her horse thought it strange Cassie didn't mount her, Cassie would never know. She walked her as far as the stream, then left her to graze in the paddock. It was Masala's turn next. He was used to trailing behind her. When they returned to the paddock, Masala joined Buttercup. To Cassie's amusement, her horse moved her head against his neck.

"I think you two like each other!" she exclaimed. "Liz said it could happen, but I can't believe it!"

"So I wasn't wrong," spoke a deep male voice right behind her. She spun around in surprise and discovered Trace's blue eyes eyeing her as if he could see right through her. A rush of warmth enveloped her.

"I didn't know you were home," she said, out of breath for no good reason. She'd begun to think he was never coming back. It surprised her how much pleasure she felt at seeing him.

"I got here a little while ago."

"You've been making yourself scarce."

"I'm back for the weekend. When I looked out the kitchen window and saw that you weren't riding Buttercup, I wondered if my first suspicions about you were correct. Now I know."

Her heart fluttered like the wings of a darning needle she could see flitting around. "First suspicions about what?"

"That you're pregnant. When you told me Masala wasn't your horse, I wondered if pregnancy was the reason you wouldn't ride him. You've hidden your pregnancy so well, no one would suspect."

"*You* did, though," she remarked.

"Well, that's because we went riding on Tuesday and I was close enough to you to notice. Does my dad know?"

She averted her eyes. "No one does except my doctor and Avery. But your dad is a doctor who has delivered a lot of foals. He has probably guessed. I'm quite sure it's the reason he's let me stay on here without saying anything. He's such an understanding man. You can't hide much from him."

His eyes smiled. "Nope." He cocked his head. "I don't mean to pry, but why have you kept it a secret?"

"Because I'm trying to make my way on my own. My parents never forgave me for marrying Logan. Once they find out I'm having his baby—and they will—they'll write my child off completely, too."

"But you're carrying their grandchild!"

"They don't want one from a lowlife like Logan. That's what Ned called my husband because Logan was an orphan. In my family, if you don't have a pedigree dating back to the turn of the last century, you're not acceptable."

A grimace marred his handsome features. "Your brother's a sick man."

"I know. Ned had no idea how much I loved Logan. Neither did my parents. It's their loss now." She was all fired up at this point. "I intend to prove that I'm independent and will make a good mother even if it kills me—"

"I'm already convinced nothing could do that."

She let out a laugh. "Sorry I got so heated."

"It's understandable. When are you due?"

"October 14."

"You must be about five months along. Do you know the gender?"

Cassie nodded. "I found out today."

His lips twitched. "Are you planning to keep me in suspense?"

"I'm going to have a girl. I bought some baby clothes for her in town after my doctor's appointment. He gave me a picture of the sonogram."

"I've never seen one. You'll have to show it to me."

"As it happens, I have it right here because I can't

stop looking at it." She reached in her jeans pocket and pulled it out. He moved next to her so they could look at it together.

"That's incredible," he said in a husky voice.

"I know. While he took the picture, her heartbeat was so strong and loud, it made everything real for the first time."

"Did you and Logan pick out names for the baby before he died?"

Cassie put the picture back in her pocket. "I didn't learn I was pregnant until a few weeks after his death."

"That's tough. I'm sorry," he murmured. "You really are doing this on your own."

"It's all right. Finding out I was pregnant gave me a whole new lease on life."

"You're a remarkable woman, Cassie."

Her eyes met his searching gaze. "Say that to me when I'm old and have raised a terrific daughter, and I'll believe you." Surprised they'd spent this long talking she said, "I've got to go in and finish putting up the strawberries I picked this morning." She would prepare a meatloaf and potatoes to go in the oven at the same time.

"While you do that, I'll take the horses back to the barn and settle them in."

They weren't his responsibility, but there was no point in fighting him on it. "That would be great. Thank you."

Much as she appreciated Trace's help, she felt guilty. Now that he knew she was pregnant, it changed everything. Cassie could tell he had a protective streak in him like his father. She didn't want him treating her any differently, but it was too late because he'd already figured it out just by looking at her blossoming figure.

Trying not to think about how excited he'd sounded when he'd looked at the baby picture, she prepared the dinner, then continued to make jam. Her raspberries would be coming into season soon. White Lodge had a fair in the fall. She could sell her wares and hopefully make enough money to buy a crib and the basic items she'd need for the baby.

Trace had asked her about a name. She didn't know yet, but the fact that he'd asked told her he was a caring, sensitive man. Cassie was thinking too much about him. What on earth was wrong with her?

While she was pouring the hot paraffin wax over the filled jars to seal them, she heard him come in the back door. He didn't pause to talk so she didn't say anything. *Forget he's here, Cassie.*

Chapter 3

Trace walked down the hall. The meeting with the therapist in Billings earlier today had gone as he'd imagined. He didn't need a doctor to realize he'd been in a morose state since his eye injury. It was all part of his PTSD. But Dr. Holbrook had emphasized that there was one thing he needed to do before all else. Deal with Nicci. No other decision should be made until he knew if he was going to live in Colorado or Italy.

The therapist made a lot of sense. It was time for a heart-to-heart.

Now that Trace was on the ranch and had spent two full days with his father, it was time to pay Nicci some attention. A month had passed since he'd last seen her. They'd spoken several times since, but nothing had been resolved. His call to her yesterday had gone downhill. They needed to talk when her father wasn't around.

She picked up on the fifth ring. *"Caro—"* she answered in a sleepy voice.

"Nicci? Sorry for calling you in the middle of the night, but this can't wait. Our conversation yesterday wasn't good."

"That's because I'm miserable," she said in heavily accented English. "Papa wants to know if you have come to your senses yet. Please say yes. Is that why you're phoning while I was dreaming about the two of us in our own villa overlooking the water?"

Clearly nothing in her mind had changed since he'd left Italy. His eyes closed tightly. "I can't say yes. All I know is that I miss you."

"I think not enough, or you would take the job my father has offered you. I never knew anyone so obstinate." That was her temper talking because she was in pain. So was he.

Trace paced the floor. "Listen to me, Nicci. I have to use my expertise. As I told you, the Air Force Academy has offered me a position as a flight instructor. Colorado Springs is a beautiful city. You'll love it there. We'll buy a house and start a family. You'll be able to visit your family often. They'll visit us. We'll visit my father and his wife. They'll come to us. We can have the life we wanted."

The silence on the other end was tangible. "But it's *not* the life we planned."

"Only the location and the kind of work I do have changed. *We* haven't."

"I don't know. What would I do all day while you're at work?"

"We talked about that yesterday. You can find a job here you like. I have contacts."

"But it won't be like helping Papa."

"Of course nothing would be like that, Nicci." She was his social princess and did things for him only a daughter could do, but you could never call it a job. Even Nicci was honest enough to admit that. He turned on his other side. Naturally he couldn't blame her for her fears, but the conversation was unraveling fast.

"You won't know how you feel until you try. When can you fly over?"

"I'm not sure."

He was used to her pouts, but since he'd been to the therapist he was more immune to them now. "This is hard on me, too, Nicci. Plan a time and I'll meet your plane in Denver. We'll drive to Colorado Springs so you can get a feel for it. We'll look at houses and plan. Then we'll fly to Montana so you can meet my father and his wife. What do you say?"

"I say I miss you so much, I feel like I'm going mad."

He could just picture her stomping the floor in one of her spiky high heels. Trace wouldn't be getting a definitive answer out of her yet. Maybe never. "I love you, too. Phone me when you've picked the date to fly over."

"What are you going to do now?"

"Eat dinner and go to bed. It's been a long day and I'm exhausted." But that exhaustion was of the mental kind.

"That's where I wish we were right now."

He inhaled sharply. They'd always communicated well in bed. "Then hurry and make arrangements. I'll pay for your ticket."

"Papa will do it!"

"You know how I feel about that. I plan to take care of you."

"We're not married yet. He can afford it."

Yes he could. Benito Tornielli, who owned a company that constructed some of the largest cruise ships on the Adriatic, was a multimillionaire who spoiled his children. Trace almost said she would need to get used to living on his salary, but he caught himself in time.

She was so headstrong in favor of spending her father's money, this was one fight he couldn't win over the phone so there was no point in trying.

"Good night, Nicci. Come to me soon."

After they hung up, he lay back staring at the ceiling. Nicci still wasn't ready to fly over, which made their conversation more troubling to him than ever. She was a fiery, exciting woman who'd been pampered all her life and felt perfectly safe in her sheltered environment.

The accident that had changed his life had shaken her to the core. To live with him in Colorado away from her family was so frightening to her, she couldn't face it.

He understood. This would ask a lot of any woman from another country. But Nicci wasn't just any woman. The more he thought about it, the more he feared that marriage to her wouldn't work unless it was on her terms, which meant living in Italy.

For her sake he'd been wrestling with the idea of being a flight navigator since his injury. But enough time had passed during his recuperation that he knew in his heart it wasn't what he wanted. He'd expressed that sentiment to Cassie on Tuesday, and to the therapist today. He couldn't do that job, not even for love. Trace had to be true to himself. His father had taught him that much.

To work for Nicci's father—to be under his thumb for the rest of their lives—was out of the question. So until she came to the United States to see if they could make a new life here work, then a marriage between them wasn't possible. She needed to be true to herself, too. Knowing his own mind helped him to deal with matters closer to home.

Trace left the bedroom and walked out to the kitchen to wash his hands. Cassie eyed him. "I was just going to call you to dinner."

His gaze darted to the table. She'd fixed him a plate of meatloaf and potatoes, but it looked like she was ready to disappear. "Since you've gone to so much trouble, why don't you eat with me?" It upset him that she felt she had to stay away when he was home for the evening.

"I can't. I have plans. Just leave everything when you've finished and I'll be back to do the dishes."

An unaccountable feeling of disappointment passed through him as she walked out the front door. He'd looked forward to talking to her. More important however, there was something he needed to discuss with her tonight. After his therapy session he realized it couldn't be put off.

His plans to sell the ranch had made her circumstances more precarious because she was pregnant. He hated the idea of bringing her added distress, but she needed to know his plans so she could think about making other work and living arrangements.

When he'd finished eating, he cleaned up the kitchen. Still at a loose end, he went to the bedroom for his laptop. After going to the living room, he looked up some real estate websites for Billings. From the long list, one name stood out he recognized. Over the years he'd seen

Hawksworth Realty signs around the White Lodge area and figured they must be a reputable company.

While he jotted down the phone number, he heard the front door open and turned his head. The sight of Cassie brought him more pleasure than it should have. "Home so soon? You weren't gone long."

"No. I went to Avery's to show her the new baby clothes, but she and Zane weren't there so I came home."

"I'm glad you're back early. Since it's Friday night and not time for bed, would you like to drive into White Lodge and see a movie with me? I haven't done it in years. It might be fun." He'd broach the serious subject later.

She gave him a speculative glance. "This must be hard for you."

"What do you mean?"

"Being back here twiddling your thumbs after the life you spent overseas. Don't tell me there isn't a woman you left behind. Some time ago your father mentioned a particular woman you were crazy about. Do you still feel the same way about her?"

"You don't miss much, do you, Cassie."

Her eyes smiled. "It's not hard to pick up on the news when your dad talks about you all the time." At this point Trace's guilt weighed heavily on him. "What's her name?"

"Nicoletta Tornielli. I call her Nicci."

"I love that name. Italian and gorgeous?"

"As a matter of fact she is. Before my injury we were planning to get married and live in Italy. Now I'm afraid everything is on hold."

"Why?"

"Because I'll be working in Colorado."

"If she loves you, she'll go where you go."

"You don't know Nicci. She comes from a privileged background."

"Logan accused me of being privileged. He didn't believe I would leave my family to marry him and work here with him, but I did."

"But your family lives on the ranch next door."

Her features closed up. "As you know, they might as well be in Italy since my marriage to Logan."

"I forgot. That was insensitive of me."

She smiled. "Then we're even. What kind of work does she do?"

"Nicci waits on her father, but she doesn't work in the sense you mean by drawing a paycheck."

"What does he do?"

"His company builds ships that travel the Adriatic. He owns a huge villa and estate in Monfalcone overlooking the water."

"Um, that sounds fabulous."

"It is. I'm afraid Colorado Springs won't be able to compete."

"Has she been here before?"

"Only New York. I'm expecting her to fly over next week so I can show her around. But I'm not holding my breath. My instincts tell me she knows she won't transplant well."

"Give her a little more time."

He shook his head. "In her case I don't think time is going to make a difference."

Cassie's eyes filled with concern. "When you're in love, even a week sounds more like an eternity." After a pause, "If you want to see a movie tonight, I'd be happy to go."

Her comment pleased him no end. "So you're taking pity on me?"

"Why not? I could do with some diversion myself."

"You deserve it. We'll celebrate the news that you're expecting a daughter."

That brought a radiant smile to her face. She really was a beautiful woman. "I am! I can hardly believe it."

"You're not too tired?"

"Not yet."

"We'll go in my new car. You'll be the first person to ride in it."

"That sounds exciting. Do you know what's playing? All the years you've been away there are still only two movie theaters in our little hamlet."

He chuckled. "I remember, and I checked earlier. *The Amazing Spider-Man 2* or *Draft Day*."

"I've heard about the second option. I like a good football story. Let's go with that one."

So far there wasn't anything about Cassie Dorney he didn't like. "You're on."

"I'll meet you outside in a minute."

He waited for her on the porch steps to help her to his car. On the way to town she said, "You didn't need to do the dishes. I would have done them."

"I think I can handle putting a plate and glass in the dishwasher." A chuckle came out of her. "The meatloaf was so good I'm afraid I ate all that you cooked."

"You must have been starving."

"Since coming home I've noticed my normal appetite is back."

"That's good to hear. Your father was so worried while you were in the hospital."

"Sounds like you and Dad have gotten close."

"He's been a wonderful friend to Logan and me. I—" She stopped talking.

"I know what you were going to say, Cassie. How could I have chosen a career that kept me away from him all these years?"

"No. I was just going to say that you were lucky to have been raised by a father who loves you so completely."

The situation with Cassie and her father was tragic. "I wish my anger over the divorce hadn't carried me down a path of separation for as long as it did." The laser injury dictated more separation, but not as far away from home as before.

They drove into White Lodge. Summer tourists had invaded the place. When he'd parked and they'd walked to the theater, he discovered it was packed. They were lucky to get seats on the next to the last row. Cassie refused the popcorn Trace bought them. "I'd love some, but the doctor told me to watch my salt intake and put my feet up every day for a while."

"I'll remember that and we'll bring our own unsalted version next time."

There wouldn't be a next time, but Cassie didn't say anything. The woman he planned to marry would be here before long. Cassie couldn't imagine his girlfriend letting him get away from her. It was just his depression talking.

After he'd helped her down from his elegant new Explorer, he'd cupped her elbow as they'd walked to the movie theatre. Because she was pregnant and wearing maternity clothes that showed her bump, people no doubt thought they were a married couple. If anyone recognized her, word would get back to her family, but it had to happen sometime. She couldn't worry about it now.

This was the first time Cassie had been anywhere with another man since Logan. Oddly enough she didn't feel uncomfortable, probably because Trace wasn't just another man. He was Sam Rafferty's son. Cassie had known them since she was a young girl.

She and Trace had already confided in each other over the traumas in their lives. The unconventional situation of them being thrown together had forced secrets to be divulged, putting them on a more intimate footing.

Most of the females who saw her with Trace couldn't take their eyes off him. Even before he'd arrived at the ranch, Avery and Liz had commented that he was one of the most attractive men they'd ever seen in their lives, but they'd said it out of earshot of their husbands.

Cassie agreed with them. Endowed with dark hair and those blazing blue eyes, Trace turned heads, especially in his black cowboy hat. He looked the part, but she'd seen the pictures of him in uniform. He looked the part of a pilot, too. With his intelligence and charisma, he could be anything he wanted.

His Italian girlfriend was lucky to be loved by a man like him. Nicci was so blessed that Trace was still alive, but until tragedy happened, you couldn't appreciate what you had. Tears smarted Cassie's eyes. She blinked them away, disturbed by a tumult of emotions attacking her.

It hadn't been a good idea to come out with Trace tonight after all. She'd been giving way too much thought to his life and situation. Worse, she felt guilty that she was enjoying herself. Logan had only been gone half a year. To her chagrin she sensed an attraction to Trace deep down she couldn't explain. It was starting to disturb her.

She could blame it on hormones or the fact that she was a widow. Cassie could blame it on whatever she wanted, but the fact still remained she found Trace appealing. On the walk to the theater she'd become aware of his touch. Sitting next to him in the dark, she could hear him breathe and discovered herself listening for his deep laugh. She smelled the soap he'd used in the shower. It was all too much.

How could this be happening to her? She was pregnant with her husband's child, and Trace was planning to marry another woman in the near future. Why was she so susceptible to him? Maybe she would feel this way around any attractive man now that Logan was gone. All Cassie knew was that at this point she needed to stay away from him whenever possible until he left for Colorado.

"Hey, Cassie?" A married friend who worked at the saddlery shop called to her as they left the theater.

"Hi, Mandy!"

The other woman, always cheerful, headed toward them. She was yet another female who'd seen Trace and couldn't resist. Cassie was forced to introduce him to her.

"You're Doc Rafferty's famous ace son!"

"Is that what I am?" His eyes danced, but he'd directed his question to Cassie, not Mandy. This shouldn't be happening either. Cassie was sure he didn't mean to, but he was behaving as if they were a couple. It gave the wrong impression. No, no, no.

Mandy smiled. "Modest, too." She whispered to Cassie. "I didn't know you were pregnant."

"I only found out after Logan died."

"Oh, wow. You've really been through it, but I'm so happy about your baby."

"So am I. It's a great blessing."

"Of course. You look terrific." She turned to Trace. "See you around, hotshot."

His male laughter followed behind Cassie as she hurried over to the Explorer. She would have climbed in without his help, but he'd locked it so she had to wait until he'd activated the remote. Though she didn't want his assistance, he helped her in anyway, then walked around and got in behind the wheel.

"At least she didn't call you Maverick," Cassie quipped to ease the effect his nearness had on her. "You know, the pilot in the film *Top Gun*. I'm afraid you're in for it because everyone knows your dad. You're all he ever talks about."

"I'm a legend before my time. Is that what you're saying?"

"Something like that."

"My father's the legend. Unfortunately I'm his greatest disappointment, but he's done his best not to let it show in public." Since Cassie knew how her dad felt about her, who was she to tell Trace how wrong he was if that was his perception. "Would you like to stop at the drive-thru for something?"

"Sure. A lemonade sounds good to me. Thanks."

They stopped long enough for drinks, then headed back to the ranch.

"Tell me something, Cassie. If Logan hadn't died, what were your plans for the future?"

She let out a deep sigh. "To make enough money to buy ourselves a modest little ranch somewhere in the Pryors where the horseback riding and fishing is good. Maybe run a head of cattle. And of course raise a family. It was a lovely dream while it lasted."

Once they reached the house, she got out before he could help her and hurried to unlock the front door. He was right behind her. "Thanks for the fun evening," she said without looking at him. "I really enjoyed it."

"So did I."

"See you in the morning."

"Cassie?"

She paused in her tracks and looked back at him. "Yes?"

He acted as if he was on the verge of saying something important, then apparently changed his mind. She discovered his eyes playing over her with disturbing intensity. "Please don't worry about getting my breakfast or dinner tomorrow. After I exercise the horses, I'll be out all day."

"All right. See you later, then."

Since Cassie knew he'd lock up and turn out the lights, she went straight to her bedroom. After being with him tonight, she realized how difficult it would be to live in the same house with Trace. It was a good thing he would be leaving for Colorado soon. She was conscious of his presence whenever he came near her. Mandy had already seen her with Trace and would be speculating on their relationship. It didn't look right and didn't feel right.

No more jaunts out in public with him. When she'd made the decision to go to the movie, she'd been trying to cheer him up. And honestly she was glad to get out and away from her loneliness for a little while. But her good intentions had backfired. Bumping into Mandy had been a wake-up call for her. Sam had hired her to keep up the house, not to entertain his son.

Saturday morning Trace took Buttercup for a ride. After leaving her in the paddock, he put a bridle on Masala, whose ears pricked when he heard Trace coming. "Good news, big fella. We're going for a ride." He gentled him before putting on the bridle.

"It'll be your turn again tomorrow, Buttercup." Cassie's horse nickered, causing him to smile as he mounted Masala and they took off for the Bannock ranch. It had been a year at least since he'd been over there. Not only was he eager to see the Bannock brothers again, Trace was anxious to talk to them about the sale of the ranch. Following that conversation he needed to express his concerns about Cassie and what would happen to her when he sold the property.

Maybe Connor, his friend who'd become a legend as the world's greatest steer wrestling champion, knew someone in the region who'd like to buy the ranch. But when he reached the big corral on their property, it was Jarod he saw ride up in his truck.

The second he laid eyes on Trace, he got out of the cab and started toward him with a smile. Trace, in turn, jumped off Masala and tied him to the fencing before they gave each other a bear hug.

"Welcome home, Trace. We heard from your father that you were coming. You've been missed around here. Those visits home over the years weren't long or often enough."

"I agree. It's good to see you." He eyed Connor's

older brother, whose long black hair tied back with a thong emphasized his half Apsáalooke heritage. "You look like fatherhood agrees with you."

"Sadie and I have never been happier." Those black eyes studied Trace for a moment. "You'd never know you suffered an eye injury as serious as yours. I'm sorry about what happened to you."

"It's life. When you go in the military, you take a risk."

They stared at each other before Jarod said, "Life's a risk under any circumstances as we've all found out."

"No question about it. How's Ralph?"

"Would you believe our grandfather is stronger and happier than I've seen him in years? He'll want to see you."

"I promise to stop by and visit him soon."

"Good. In the meantime come on over to our new house and meet our son Cole. Between him and Sadie's half brother Ryan, they've put fresh life into him."

"I'd love to, but I need to talk to you and Connor about a couple of things in private first." He was worried about Cassie for several reasons and wanted their input. Three heads were better than one.

"Connor will hate missing you, but he's up at the wild horse refuge office and probably won't be back till dinner."

"I knew it would be too much to hope for that you'd both be around at the same time, but I'll catch up with him later."

"What's on your mind, Trace?"

"Sure you have time?"

"For you, I'll always make time."

"Ditto."

Trace looked around to be certain they were out of earshot of the ranch hands. "You and Connor have known my situation from the beginning. Dad has sacrificed his whole life for me. Now I have a chance to pay him back. I'm only going to be home long enough to sell the ranch. He deserves to buy himself and Ellen a house they'd both love. With the money from the sale, they can have whatever they want. Their condo is too small and confining."

Jarod stood there with his arms folded. "I hear you. Where are *you* going?"

"Colorado Springs. I've accepted a position as a flight instructor at the academy."

His friend nodded without saying anything. Because of the partly stoic side of Jarod's nature, at times it was hard to read what was going on inside him.

"I'm afraid Dad didn't take the news well."

"He wouldn't. You're the bright spot in his life."

"Unfortunately I don't have a choice since I have to work at something I know. I'm expecting my Italian girlfriend Nicoletta to be flying over shortly. Before my eye injury, we were planning to be married and live in Italy. Now she's got to find out if she can adapt to living in Colorado before we make plans. As you can see, everything's up in the air."

Jarod had that faraway look in his eyes. "There was a time when I came to a crossroads after my accident and had to face difficult decisions. Sadie had fled to California to be with her mother. It felt like my life was over. My uncle Charlo knew my thoughts and warned me to think outward to seven generations before making any new plans."

You couldn't resent Jarod's words. There was wisdom in everything he said. Raffertys had only been here for four generations. According to Jarod's counsel, there were three more to go, taking him beyond his life span. Trace knew what his friend was saying, but he couldn't see another way out.

"Your uncle gives excellent advice."

"But hard to swallow. I know all about it." By the thick tone in Jarod's voice, Trace knew Jarod had been through years of torture before Sadie came back to him. "Have you forgotten you were a cowboy long before you became a pilot?"

Trace took a deep breath. "Life is different now. Dad will be doing vet work until he keels over, but with his arthritis he shouldn't have to worry about the ranch anymore. The problem is, I can't take care of things long distance when my future isn't here. Before I contact a Realtor, I'm wondering if you know anyone around here who might be interested in buying it."

Jarod took his time answering. "Your great-great-grandfather Rafferty picked out that prime piece of land to settle down for a reason." Guilt swamped Trace at the reminder, but circumstances were forcing him to sell. "Once the news is out, you'll be besieged with offers."

"That's what I'm hoping, but since our land borders yours, I want the right person living next door to you. I'd like to use you and Connor for a filter."

After a long silence Jarod said, "The right person is already living there."

Trace knew what he meant. "I appreciate those words, Jarod, but if Nicci can be happy with us living in Colorado, then that's what I need to do for both our sakes. Which brings me to my next concern. I didn't realize until I got home that Cassie was still living on the ranch taking care of the house since Logan's death. Somehow I'd taken it for granted she'd gone back to her parents' house. Since she didn't, this will mean a move for her which I hate to do to her considering the fact that she can't go home."

Lines darkened his face. "She wouldn't want to even if she were allowed."

"I know," Trace muttered. "She confided a lot to me yesterday."

His black eyes narrowed. "Does she know about your plans to sell the property?"

"No. I told her I'll be going to work in Colorado, but I've said nothing to her about finding a buyer for the ranch. As far as she knows, she's doing the job Dad hired her to do, which she's doing admirably well I might add."

"I'm glad you haven't told her yet. Cassie has always been a hard worker and I know she thrives on keeping the place up for Sam. But *I'm* not happy to learn you're selling the ranch. Connor won't be either." Jarod had always had a stubborn streak when he felt strongly about something. In ten years that hadn't changed.

"I don't see another way to handle this, and I'm worried about something else. I guess you know she's pregnant."

"I've had my suspicions, but you've just verified them."

"Then you understand my concern. Cassie intimated that Ned will be coming back to live with her parents one of these days. I saw fear in her eyes. She told me about the problems with her parents and the suspicious circumstances of the shooting during Ned's last visit home. I've been horrified by the things she told me."

His friend grimaced. "We're all worried about Ned, but I don't imagine he'll be allowed home for quite a while yet."

"Then you need to hear the news I got from the horse's mouth last night."

Jarod looked surprised. "About Ned?"

For the next few minutes Trace told him about the encounter with Owen Pearson at the Golden Spur. "He'd already had too much to drink when I got there. Everything that came out of his mouth verified Cassie's conviction that her brother hates her and hated Logan. According to Owen, Ned is going to be coming home any day now for good."

"That could be Ned's wishful thinking talking. But if it's true, then we're all in for a new nightmare sooner than we thought."

"There's more. Owen says they're going into the feral stud farm business on his father's ranch."

Jarod's features hardened. "So now he wants to compete with Connor? His jealousy is over the top, always has been. It'll never happen, Trace. That's another pipe dream of Ned's. Uncle Grant wants his son working around here, but Ned gets out of work any way he can. As for Owen, he's been in so much trouble because of Ned, his father would never allow it."

"He told me he's divorced."

"Yup. His short-lived marriage was another mistake. He keeps making them, and sticking like glue to Ned isn't helping. Zane needs to hear all this from you, but it's Saturday, which is his day to go out to the reservation with Avery. They probably won't be home until late."

"I'll try to get together with him tomorrow."

"Sunday will be a good time to find him home. Trace—do me a favor? Until you've talked to Zane, don't breathe a word of your plans to anyone about selling the ranch, especially not to Cassie. For reasons you don't know about, he'll want to hear everything you told me first."

That sounded cryptic. "Except to explain the situation to my father, I won't say anything. But I'm anxious for the opportunity to talk to Zane about Logan's death. Once Ned is home again, whenever that happens, I'm afraid Cassie could be in danger."

"My thoughts exactly."

"Don't let me keep you, Jarod. After I take Masala back, I need to drive into town and discuss Cassie's situation with Dad."

"Let's exchange phone numbers so we can stay in close touch."

"Good idea."

Chapter 4

Cassie left the house wearing a clean, pale green smock over her clothes and got in her truck. Every Saturday she volunteered at the White Lodge Wildlife Sanctuary. It was one of several public refuges in Montana to save animals that were too sick or injured to be returned to the wild, or were too humanized to survive there.

Today she was going to join her married friends Paul and Lindsey Shaw, also volunteers, to paint the railings in front of the outdoor wolf enclosures. The sanctuary was adding new sections to accommodate the animals and birds found struggling. If they recovered and could handle it, they'd be released to live in their former habitat. Otherwise they were well taken care of.

Every Saturday there was a different assignment to tackle. Cassie had been helping out for close to a year. More and more tourists stopped to see the wildlife.

She could understand why. She loved the animals, too, and through perseverance had made friends of some of them.

As Cassie started the engine and backed up, Trace, wearing boots and Stetson, rode into her line of vision on Masala. She put on the brakes. Like his father, he was such a natural on a horse you'd never have guessed he was also an ace pilot whose career had been cut short.

Her pulse raced when the hard-muscled male astride the horse walked them right up to her open window. She was almost blinded by the intensity of his hot blue eyes. "Where are you going in such a hurry?"

"To the White Lodge Wildlife Sanctuary."

"I've heard of it, but have never seen it."

"You'd love it. I'd tell you more about it, but I volunteer there and I'm late. Have a nice day, Trace."

Without waiting for his response she took off down the dirt road. Seeing him had changed the rhythm of her heart. Until now she'd managed to put him out of her mind for a little while. It was astonishing how fast everything changed the minute he came near.

She was determined not to let him affect her day. Once she'd reached the area of the sanctuary closed off to tourists during renovation, she started painting with a vengeance.

Today's project happened right outside the fencing where the wolves were enclosed. Paul had been sanding the surfaces of the railings, so the paint went on evenly. The old structures were being refurbished. The brown color was a great improvement over the weathered wood that had never seen a coat of paint.

One of the gray she-wolves came up to the fence and howled at Cassie when she got to work.

"Don't be upset, Lulu. I know the smell is a hundred times stronger for you than for me, but it won't hurt you. We'll be gone pretty soon." The minutes turned into a couple of hours.

Lindsey was painting the last railing. "Can you believe that constant yipping? It's coming from Annie who went into her house to get away from Paul. She hasn't stopped."

Cassie nodded. "Lulu is defending her. The sound of the sander frightens them. I didn't realize our work would stress them out so much. They're usually so calm. We'll be gone in a few more minutes, Lulu. Don't worry."

"Can anyone help?" spoke a deep, familiar male voice behind Cassie.

She turned around with brush in hand and almost dropped it. The man she'd been trying her hardest not to think about had come to the sanctuary. "Hi! What are you doing here?"

"I dropped by my Dad's for a while and thought I'd check out the sanctuary before heading back to the ranch. What's wrong with these wolves? They look healthy."

"They are now, thanks to your dad. Two winters ago someone found them near dead in the forest just outside the town. Sam tested them for mange. Mites had burrowed under their skin and the scratching caused so much hair loss, they almost froze to death. Unfortunately they're too domesticated now, so they have a permanent home here."

"Did he name them?"

"No. That was the owner of the sanctuary. She passed away a year ago at the age of ninety-five. I heard she loved the Little Lulu comic books as a child so she named these sister wolves Lulu and Annie. Aren't they beautiful?"

"They are," he murmured, but he was looking at her. She could hardly breathe.

"We're finished with the painting for today."

"I bet your OB would tell you not to get around paint."

"It's okay. We're outside, and this paint is VOC proofed. As long as you're here, you need to see my favorite animal. Let me put my things away first." She put the brush in the can of turpentine and sealed the paint can. As she started to pick them up, Trace took them from her and carried them down to the box at the end of the railing for her.

"Thank you," she said. "See you next week, guys," she called to her friends.

They waved her off.

"You won't believe how darling this little female fox is. Logan found her in the forest behind your house. He said she acted disoriented, so we took her to your dad's clinic. He discovered the poor darling was close to blind. Wait till you see her."

Trace followed her around to the next enclosure. "Right now she's housed in a special raptor mew waiting for new animal quarters. The owners call it the 'fox condo.'"

A low chuckle escaped him. Cassie felt it to her bones as she approached the fox. Her little goldish-red head lay propped on the grassy platform. "Look, Trace. That sweet face with all the white below. Have you ever seen anything like it? She's elegant. You would think she was gazing out at the whole world, seeing everything.

"Giselle?" The fox's ears pricked like Buttercup's. "Giselle? It's Cassie." The animal lifted her head and put her black nose to the fence. Cassie touched it with her finger. "I brought a friend. His name is Trace. Do you know what? He owns the ranch where you were found. Isn't that amazing?"

The fox moved its head as she talked.

"Good heavens. That animal understands you," Trace said under his breath. "I never saw anything like it."

"Then you haven't watched Liz talking to her horses. It's almost spooky the way they know everything she's saying. On her last round barrel racing at Finals, she had to ride Polly because Sunflower had gotten stall cast. She spoke to Polly the way I'm talking to you and told her they had to win for Connor. I swear that horse knew exactly what she had to do."

Their eyes met. "I wish I'd been there."

"You can't be everywhere while you're protecting our world from the air. But now that you're here, why don't you say something to Giselle? Let's see what she does. Touch her nose at the same time."

Trace moved closer and put his index finger on it. "Hello, Giselle. You don't know me. I'm Trace."

"Trace rhymes with Ace, Giselle. Guess what? Would you believe his eye got hurt, too? You two have a lot in common."

The man standing next to her threw back his head and laughed. It was a marvelous sound. Happy. Cassie wished he'd do it more often. When he quieted down he said, "Are you the one to name her Giselle?"

"Yes. The woman who ran this incredible French auberge in Switzerland had that name. I think it's beautiful, and it just seemed to suit my precious fox. I wanted to take her home with me to raise, but of course that was impossible. She was turned over to the sanctuary. That's when I started coming on a regular basis to help where I can.

"You should see all the animals and birds. They've got a rough-legged hawk that's only half-flighted, and a lynx that can only see light and dark. Then there's a vulture with an amputated wing. The list goes on and on."

Trace smiled at her. "Pretty soon you'll be occupied with your own little daughter. Maybe if the fox lives for a long time, you can bring her to see Giselle and tell her the story of how her daddy found the fox."

The tenderness in Trace's voice was too much. She felt her eyes smarting and fought tears. "Maybe."

"I'm sure you're tired. I'll follow you home. You've worked so hard, you need to put your feet up."

"You're not supposed to remember everything I tell you." Trace was way too attentive.

"My former commanding officer would tell me the exact opposite." He walked to her truck. "Drive safely." His eyes narrowed on her face. "Remember there are two of you to consider."

"As if I could forget," she said, sounding out of breath to her own ears. The things Trace said shook her world.

He got in his truck just as Paul called to her from outside his car. "See you next Saturday."

Cassie wheeled around. Lindsey smiled, giving Cassie a knowing look that said she approved of the attractive cowboy who'd come to the sanctuary looking for her. This town was too small for Trace and Cassie. Gossip would build. There'd be a price to pay if he didn't leave for Colorado soon.

"I'll be here, you guys. What will we be working on next?"

"That's anyone's guess. Let's go for pizza after."

"I'd love it."

Adrenaline spilled into her system as she drove back to the ranch. Out of her rearview mirror she noticed how Trace stayed behind her. She'd been alone just long enough without Logan that she'd forgotten what it was like to have someone watching out for her.

Cassie had to admit it was a nice feeling. She couldn't understand why Trace's girlfriend hadn't arrived here already. A man like him didn't come along every day. The Rafferty men were exceptional.

When she finally reached the ranch house, Trace pulled up alongside her and opened his window to talk to her. "Jarod called me a minute ago and asked me to meet up with him. Before I go, I want to make sure you get in the house safely."

Her spirits didn't know whether to be relieved or disappointed he was leaving. "I'm fine, Trace. Don't forget I've been doing this for a long time. But thanks for caring." She climbed down from the cab and hurried up the porch to the front door.

"Wait, Cassie—before you go in let's exchange cell phone numbers in case we need to get hold of each other."

"That's a good idea." She pulled the phone out of her purse and programmed his number. He did the same thing with his phone. After opening the front door, she waved him off.

Who knew when he'd be back? *Please don't care, Cassie. Please don't.*

Once she showered, she'd grab a bite to eat and

watch a little TV before going to bed. Maybe because she knew he would be coming back, even if it was late, Cassie was able to fall asleep faster. For the first time since Logan's passing, her husband didn't fill her thoughts. She found herself thinking about Trace and what an amazing man he was. Any woman loved by him would feel cherished.

Trace drove over to Jarod's to pick him up. Jarod had talked to Zane after he and Avery had returned from the reservation. She was eager to visit her grandfather and tell him about her day, so Jarod thought this was the best time to drop in on Zane.

They took off for the Corkin-Lawson Ranch bordering the other side of the Bannock spread. "What does Avery do at the reservation?"

"She's a historian, writing a book on Crow folklore. On Thursdays she teaches classes on Crow culture at the college."

"You must be very proud of your sister."

"I am. The tribe has given her a special name. Winterfire Woman."

"What does it mean?"

"Because she does her research on the reservation year-round, not just in summer, the tribe considers her an authentic teller of their histories. She reminds them of the storytellers of old who gathered children around the fire on long wintry nights. Avery doesn't make them feel used."

"That's a phenomenal compliment. Are she and Zane happy?"

A smile broke the corner of Jarod's mouth. "You

ought to see them together. I know she'll be anxious to see you."

It didn't take long for them to pull up in front of the small, one-story ranch house. They got out and knocked on the front door. Only one other time had Trace ever been over here. His father had been called out on an emergency and fifteen-year-old Trace had gone with him.

The owner of the ranch, Daniel Corkin, was in a drunken rage because his best horse had broken a leg. When his dad told him they needed to put the animal out of its misery, Daniel ordered him off his property. If he didn't leave, he'd shoot him.

Trace still remembered that day and understood why Daniel's daughter Sadie had fled to California to live with her mother, who later on remarried. His thoughts drifted back to Cassie. Her father Grant Bannock may not have been in a drunken rage, but he was unstable enough to drive his flesh-and-blood daughter out of his home and his life. Considering Ned Bannock was his son, it proved the adage that the proverbial acorn didn't fall far from the oak tree.

Trace's thoughts were jerked away when a striking man, Trace's height, in cowboy boots with dark brown hair answered the door. He wore a plaid shirt and jeans. "Thanks for coming, Jarod."

He nodded. "Zane Lawson? Meet Trace, Doc Rafferty's son."

His gray eyes swerved to examine Trace. Dimples formed when he smiled. "Your fame is legendary. Avery will be sorry she wasn't here to welcome you home, Trace. She's thrilled to know you're back to stay for good."

That meant Jarod hadn't told him about Trace's plans.

Everyone assumed he was home to take over the ranch. "It'll be great to see her again."

"I'm finally shaking hands with the Ace!"

Trace liked him right away. "I'm a has-been. You're the famous SEAL."

"You couldn't be talking about me. My nephew Ryan has reduced me to Deputy Dawg status, isn't that right, Jarod."

All three men chuckled before Zane grew serious. "I know you have other things you'd rather do tonight, but I felt this visit couldn't wait, not after talking to Jarod. Come on in. Can I get you a drink?"

"No, thanks." They walked into the living room and sat down on the couch and chairs placed around the coffee table.

Zane eyed Trace. "Jarod said you've got something to tell me pertaining to Ned I need to hear. He said it would be better coming from you. What's going on?"

For the next ten minutes Trace told him virtually what he'd told Jarod about his conversation with Owen Pearson, plus his own plans to sell the ranch. "Whoever the buyer is, I want all of you to approve. That includes Connor."

He saw Zane eye Jarod. "I can see why you felt this was important." Then his gaze switched to Trace. "I'm glad you haven't spoken to a Realtor yet. For your ranch to be put on the multiple listings, it could rip off the Band-Aid of a very old wound that has never healed."

"What do you mean?"

"How much do you know about the history between the Bannocks and the Corkins?"

"My dad told me Daniel Corkin has always had it

in for the Bannocks. Something about oil, but he never knew the details."

"Then let me fill you in. Silas Bannock, a Scottish Presbyterian, drilled for oil on his property in 1915. At the time it was part of the Elk Basin Oil Field, and he hit a spewing gusher. Since it was on private land, he claimed all the money and built up the Bannock ranch. With wise investing over the years, Ralph Bannock has turned it into one of the wealthiest cattle ranches in Montana originally funded by oil."

Trace had no idea.

"In 1920, Pete Corkin, an English Methodist and neighbor of Silas Bannock, established the Corkin Ranch, the one we're sitting on right now. He drilled on this land and made some strikes that fizzled. In that same year Congress established a law that you had to lease federal land from the government and pay a royalty. Over the years, the Corkin descendants couldn't get rich by drilling for oil so they turned to cattle, and thus began a jealousy and a rivalry that developed into hostility."

Jarod sat forward and picked up the story. "Over the years this envy on the part of the Corkin family over our family's success escalated. Daniel Corkin swore he heard a story from one of his hands that a Crow Indian saw a vision about oil being under Corkin land.

"Convinced he'd be wealthier than the Bannocks when he made his strike, he became so obsessive about more drilling, his wife, Eileen, Sadie's mother, divorced him and went to her family in California. But he threatened to kill Eileen if she tried to take Sadie with her."

Trace couldn't believe what he'd just heard. "So that's why Sadie spent so much time with Liz's family."

Jarod nodded. "Daniel left the raising of Sadie to the Hensons, his foreman and wife. When Daniel died, he left nothing to Sadie in his will, and he made it impossible for any Bannock to buy the ranch. But that didn't hold up in a court of law. When the ranch was put on the market, Ned Bannock wanted it and was determined to buy it."

"Ned?"

"That's right. He was still in love with Sadie and wanted her, too. Using his father's and grandfather's money, he put in his bid with the Realtor. But my grandfather went to his attorney and we found a way to outbid him so Sadie could keep her property."

"They did it by helping me so I could buy it in my name," Zane interjected. "By that time I'd come from California with Sadie to help her raise Ryan, who is my brother Tim's son. I wanted to start a new life here after both Tim and my wife died. This property is now called the Corkin-Lawson Ranch. It'll be my nephew Ryan's legacy one day." His voice grew husky. "I'll be indebted to Jarod and his grandfather forever for what they did for Sadie and for me."

"But we still have a big problem," Jarod interjected. "Like Daniel, Ned is still convinced there's oil under all our ranches. On his last birthday three weeks ago, he came into his inheritance. The second he hears that you've put the Rafferty ranch on the market, he'll forget his idea to go in on a feral stud farm with Owen, and use the money to buy your ranch. In his sick mind, he'll want it so he can drill for oil and be wealthier than anyone. Then Sadie will want him."

"That's really sick, Jarod."

"You don't know the half of it."

"Jarod's right," Zane said. "In my mind Ned is a sociopath. Maybe he didn't kill Logan. That I have yet to discover. But he tried to kill Jarod."

"I know. Last night Cassie told me about the therapy sessions. They revealed that Ned has always hated her."

"He's been jealous of his sister and brothers, my cousins, and me for as long as I've known him," Jarod murmured.

Trace eyed both men. "I can tell she's afraid."

Zane grimaced. "With good reason."

Jarod said, "The other day Grandfather told me and Connor that according to Uncle Grant, Ned has been a model patient and his doctors feel he's ready to come home for good. But none of us believes it. There's something wrong in Ned's nature. If he gets upset, he'll go after anyone who gets in his way."

"After what happened to Logan, Cassie has to be terrified," Trace said.

"That's why Uncle Grant has always been afraid of Ned. We have a situation we're going to have to handle." Jarod got to his feet. "Sorry to have held you up, Zane, but I felt this was important for you to hear."

"It's vital," Zane replied. "If you're intent on selling the ranch, Trace, get it done discreetly by private sale. Hopefully Ned won't find out about it until long after it's a fait accompli. As for Cassie, she knows she'll always have a home with us."

"Or me or Connor," Jarod exclaimed. "Now that she's pregnant, she's going to need family. We're all going to have to help keep her safe."

Trace got to his feet. "You two have given me a lot to think about."

Zane walked them outside. "Let's keep in close touch from here on out. Now that you're retired from the Air

Force, I know Avery wants to give a party to welcome you home."

"That sounds terrific."

"Words can't tell you how sorry we are about your eye injury."

"It's nothing compared to the many guys who've lost lives."

Trace waved Zane off before they drove away and headed for Jarod's house. The conversation had increased his fears for Cassie's welfare. Jarod slanted him a piercing glance.

"With you back, it feels like the circle is complete once more."

Emotion thickened his throat. "It's great being with you again, Jarod. I'd forgotten just how much I've missed my oldest friends."

"Then prove it and stay put." He got out of the truck. "We'll talk again soon."

"Yup. Tell Sadie hi for me."

Trace drove back to the ranch, hoping Cassie was still up. There was a lot he needed to say to her. But when he walked inside, it was quiet and he knew she'd gone to bed. After talking with Jarod and Zane, he could see things were more complicated than he would have imagined. Nothing was black-and-white.

When he got ready for bed, he remembered what his doctor had said about working things out with Nicci before he made any decisions. Trace fell asleep frustrated that she hadn't called him today. His last thoughts were of Jarod telling him to stay put.

Late Sunday morning he came awake to the smell of strawberries drifting through the house. Cassie was at it again. He was glad she hadn't gone anywhere yet.

He was glad her brother wasn't back living on the Bannock Ranch yet.

Content that she and the baby were safe for the moment, Trace could relax while he thought about the conversation with his father yesterday. "Before you make a decision you can't take back, why not rent the house for the next year, son, to give yourself time?"

In the light of morning his father's suggestion made sense. The right renter would pay a lot for the use of the house sitting on prime hunting land. If Trace charged enough money, his father would receive substantial monthly payments that would add appreciably to his income.

Once he was working in Colorado Springs, Trace could fly to Billings for a weekend once a month to see his father and inspect the property. It could work. How would Nicci feel about it? He needed her to come! The doctor in Billings was right. There was no way he could make definite plans about anything until they were together and could make a decision about getting married.

He rolled onto his side and reached for the phone to call her. To his chagrin it went through to her voice mail. Trace asked her to get in touch with him as soon as she could. Had she refused to answer his calls on purpose? They needed to talk before any more time went by.

Once he'd showered and dressed, he walked through the house and heard voices in the kitchen. One of them was male. Connor! A smile broke out on his face as he entered. "Well if it isn't the king of the rodeo!"

"Dude!" His dark blond friend made a beeline for him and gave him one of those hugs he was famous for—one that could throw a bull to the ground in a couple of seconds. No one had ever called him that but Connor.

"I thought you were injured at finals, but I swear you're tougher than ever."

Connor let out a bark of laughter. "Don't I wish, but you're looking ripped. How in the hell did you run into a laser?"

Cassie stood in the background, dressed in a blue-and-green print top and jeans. The pregnant woman was beautiful no matter what she wore. Her gaze swerved from Trace to her cousin. "It ran into *him*, Connor. Kind of the way that steer bucked upward and tore your shoulder. Talk about the walking wounded around here, but no one would ever know looking at the two of you!"

Both men chuckled. Connor's blue eyes twinkled as he studied her. "I guess you thought you could keep *your* condition a secret, sweetie pie. But Jarod and I had our suspicions a month ago when we saw you leading Masala around instead of riding him. Liz and Sadie are already fighting over who's going to get to babysit your daughter."

Trace eyed Connor. "Did she show you the ultrasound picture yet? It's like a miracle."

"No." Connor shot him a speculative glance. "I haven't had that privilege. Cassie? Can I see it, too? Liz and I are trying for a baby."

"I know."

"What do you mean you know?"

"At your wedding reception Liz whispered to me that giving you a child would be her top priority in the foreseeable future."

"Apparently there are no secrets."

"Nope—I'll run to the bedroom and get it."

In another minute she was back. Trace smiled at her before he took the picture from her and showed it to Connor. While they tried to pick out all the parts, Cassie finished a batch of jam.

Connor let out a whistle. "Your baby's going to be a real knockout."

"You're full of it, cousin."

"That wasn't nice. I may not have been born with Jarod's gift of vision, but I can say without any doubt that your baby's going to be just like her mother. You brought every cowboy in Carbon County to your doorstep in high school."

"Stop, Connor. You're embarrassing me in front of Trace."

"Why? You know it's true and Trace is practically family. You broke so many hearts when you went away to Missoula, it took me and Jarod at least a year to pick up the pieces you left behind. I think Russ Colby still hasn't married because of you."

"That's absurd."

"Nope. He stopped me at the supermarket the other day, wanting to know how you were getting along since the funeral. I could swear he was nervous and it wouldn't surprise me if you hear from him one of these days. I know what you're going to say. That it's too soon since Logan's passing, but I just thought you ought to know."

Trace wouldn't be surprised either. When he'd taken Cassie to that film on Friday night, every male in creation was aware of her. It wasn't just her exceptional looks a man found appealing. She glowed.

When he'd first seen her in the garden at the side of the house, he was drawn to her in a way he hadn't been to another woman besides Nicci. But he could tell Connor's comments were getting to her.

He put the picture on the table. "Have you got time to ride with me this morning?"

"That's why I'm here." Trace could read between the lines. Connor had already been in communication with his brother and Zane.

"Good. Then we'll get out of your hair for a while, Cassie."

She darted Trace what could be a grateful smile. "When you get back I'll have lunch waiting for you."

"I'm looking forward to it already," Connor said over his shoulder. They left through the back door and headed for the barn. The sky had become overcast. "It might rain later."

"Maybe."

"Jarod told me you handled Masala like he was your horse. You ride him while I take Buttercup."

In a few minutes the horses were bridled, but both men rode bareback. They headed for the forest and rode as far as the second stream crossing the property. "When I think of the years we used to ride all over the Pryors..." Connor murmured. "It's great to have you back, Trace."

"I'm afrai—"

"Save it," Connor cut him off. "I know all about your plans to get out of Dodge, but you can't do it."

"I'm planning to get married."

"I know all about that, too. You don't honestly think you'll be happy at the Air Force Academy. It won't work. I'll give you a month at best before you want out. Anything less than flying again and you'll hate it. You're a crack pilot, Trace, but those days are over."

"But if I stay here and work the ranch, I've a feeling in my gut Nicci won't like it."

"How soon is she coming?"

"I don't know. I'm waiting to hear any day now."

"Well don't do anything about the ranch until you've spent time with her here. It would be a waste to take her to Colorado Springs. You're a cowboy to the roots, Trace. What would you have done if there'd been no injury? What if you'd finished out all those years as a pilot? Then what? Stay in Italy for the rest of your life away from your father? Doing what?"

Trace took a swift breath. "I've been asking myself that question since I was released from the hospital. I know what Nicci would want. She'd expect me to go on living there while her father found work for me."

"No way," Connor muttered. "When I married Reva, I thought I had it all figured out until she came home with me for a time. Our marriage took a nosedive. We could never get it back because it never worked in the first place. The ranch was my life. Hers was in the city."

"I know. Cassie told me. Reva and my mother had a lot in common."

"That's right, but with one difference. We weren't pregnant so it was easier to say goodbye. So learn from my mistake and take a leaf out of my book while you're still free. Forget Colorado. You don't really want to teach other guys how to fly. You've been there and done that.

"Bring Nicci to the ranch and let her get a taste of what life will be like with you. This is your home. Ask her to stay here and find out if she takes to it. Otherwise I can promise you'll be miserable, and that's without the benefit of Jarod's special gift telling you the same thing. We don't want anyone else living next door."

"You and Jarod know how to make a guy feel good. I'll think about everything you've said. But there's still the problem of Cassie to worry about."

"It's been solved. Liz has already talked to her mom. Millie and Mac are going to keep Cassie with them until after the baby is born. She'll be close by all of us and safe with them."

"That's a terrific solution, but Cassie won't do it. She's too independent."

"She will when Zane talks to her. Jarod found out from our grandfather that Ned is being released from the mental facility a week from Thursday." *Eleven more days…* "Because of the suspicion surrounding the reason for Logan's shooting, he wants her away from your ranch. Mac Henson will be the best body-guard she could have."

Trace pondered everything. "When were you going to talk to Cassie?"

"After lunch I was hoping to take her over to our house where Liz and I will broach the subject."

"Do me a favor and let me discuss that with her, Connor?" Several ideas were rolling around in his head now that he'd heard the date of Ned's release from the facility. A new, possible option had opened up in his mind, but he wasn't prepared to address it yet. "I need to tell Cassie about my plans for the ranch before she hears it from anyone else. Dad and I owe her that much after the fabulous way she and Logan have taken care of everything."

After a moment of quiet, "Sure, Trace. We just want you to know we're here for her in any capacity. And you."

"Thanks, Connor."

"That's what best friends are for, right?"

"You know it."

They headed back to the barn to give the horses water and fresh hay. When they entered the kitchen, Cassie had made them tuna fish and peanut butter sandwiches. She'd also put two quarts of milk on the table, unopened, and a bowl of potato chips. Trace couldn't help but smile at her. "Trust you to know exactly what to fix."

"It's easy when you're feeding a bunch of ravenous cowboys," she quipped.

Did she really see Trace that way?

After they'd eaten, Connor thanked Cassie and excused himself to get back to Liz. Trace walked him out to the porch and waved him off. When he returned to the kitchen, the clock on the wall said it was ten after two.

Cassie had cleaned everything up and was packing her jam jars in some cartons.

"Need me to help?"

"Oh, no. I'm all done. Thanks, though."

She wouldn't look at him. "Who's the lucky recipient?"

"Hopefully my baby. I plan to sell these at the White Lodge Fair in the fall so I can buy some essentials. You know. A crib and an infant car seat. Things like that. My time will be here before I know it. I need to be prepared."

"Cassie?"

"Yes?"

"If you don't have plans, how would you like to take a Sunday ride with me? Not a long one. I haven't been up to Yellow Bell Lake in years. There won't be many people around in case you're worried about that." He figured they'd beat the rain if it came.

She turned her head to look at him. "I'm sure you have other things you need to be doing."

He stared at her through veiled eyes. "Talking to you is at the top of my list."

Chapter 5

That sounded somewhat ominous because there was no levity now that Connor had gone. Trace would never invite Cassie to go out with him unless he had a heavy reason.

"You want to leave right away?"

"If it's all right with you."

"Of course. I'll just grab my purse."

In a few minutes they'd both freshened up. He brought a bottle of water for each of them. After helping her into his Explorer, he walked around to his side and they took off. After they pulled out on the highway, he turned at the next left leading up the mountain to a number of lakes hidden in the pines.

The small circular lake was named for the yellow bells that blossomed there in the spring. But when Trace pulled into the area where he could park the car, he could see that time was over for this year.

"I'm afraid it's too late for the flowers to be in bloom," she said, reading his mind.

"It's still a beautiful spot, even with the cloud cover. Your cousins and I used to ride our horses up here when the ground was covered in a mass of tiny yellow bells. We'd swim and have rock-skipping contests."

She nodded. "I rode up here with my high school friends, too. Marsha Porter's dad would drive up with the inner tubes so we could float and sunbathe. I'm sure the music scared away every wild creature in sight. Those were fun, lazy days until—"

When she didn't finish the sentence Trace glanced at her. "Until Ned ruined things?"

"I don't want to talk about him."

"I think we're going to have to at some point. What do you say we get out and sit on that log the guys and I dragged over there once upon a time."

Her eyes widened. "You did that?"

"It was either that or sit in the wet grass."

Cassie chuckled and got out before he could come around to help her. "It's lovely up here. I'd almost forgotten." She made her way over to the log. "Oh, my gosh—your initials! TR, CB and JB." Cassie lifted her head. "Okay. Truth time. How many girls did you bring up here?"

His lips twitched. "We swore an oath we'd never tell."

"Well, we all know who Jarod brought, so that's no mystery. Connor probably had dozens up here at one time or other. Besides Liz, Marsha had a terrible crush on him. Then there's *you*. Since you went to high school in Billings, you were the mystery man of the three amigos. Did you have a special girlfriend?"

"I dated, but didn't bring anyone up here." His eyes zeroed in on her. "You're the first. To prove it, I'll carve your initials next to mine."

"No, Trace. Stop!"

But he'd pulled out a Swiss army knife and carved so fast she couldn't believe it.

"There—CBD."

Her heart pounded like a runaway train.

"I think you're trying to sweeten me up before you drop a bomb on me."

He put the knife back in his jeans pocket and straddled the log near where she was sitting.

His right boot almost touched hers. Being with him like this away from the world caused her to think forbidden thoughts. She despised her vulnerability and—heaven help her—her susceptibility to everything male in him.

Cassie sneaked a glance at his handsome features made more severe by whatever serious thoughts were going on inside him.

"You need to know something important. I can't put this off any longer. It wouldn't be fair to you. My father gave me the ranch as my legacy, but my intention is to sell it."

She averted her eyes, too shocked by his announcement to make a sound. Poor, dear Sam.

"By the crestfallen look on your face, I can tell this has come as a blow. If I tell you the reason why, I know it won't take away the shock, but I hope you'll understand this is something I have to do. Dad and Ellen need the money to buy themselves a house."

"You don't owe me an explanation, Trace. It doesn't

have anything to do with me. Logan and I were lucky to find work here for as long as we could."

"Cassie—" he said in an urgent voice. "Please realize it won't happen right away. I want you to stay on and earn your living until I find a buyer. Or maybe a renter. Probably within four to six weeks. Hopefully that will give you enough time to make other arrangements. I'm prepared to help you with that. So is your family."

"What do you mean?"

"Connor told me that Mac and Millie want you to live with them until after your baby is born where you'll be safe. That's the reason he came over earlier, but I told him I'd rather tell you myself."

"I see." She got to her feet and walked over to the water's edge. "That's all very kind of the family, but I'll make my own arrangements."

She felt him behind her. "I told Connor that's what you'd say because you're much too independent."

"You know me well. Do you mind if we go home now? It's going to rain." They'd heard thunder, so it wouldn't be long.

His hands slid to her shoulders. He pulled her back against his hard-muscled body. The unexpected action caused a small gasp to escape her lips. "I meant what I said about helping you. The Realtor I'm using can find you a place to live at the same time."

"I'm sure he could, but I'll be fine." Before she turned around and crumbled in his arms, Cassie eased away from him and walked back to the car. By the time he'd joined her, she'd put one of the bottles of water to her lips.

"Cassie—"

"I want to thank you for being frank with me so I

can handle this on my own. Four to six weeks gives me enough time to find work and a place to live that suits me. I knew this day had to come. It's another wake-up call after being in a deep sleep. You and your father have been so kind and wonderful to me, I'll never be able to thank you enough."

Fat drops of water started to hit the windshield as they started down the mountain. Slow at first, they picked up speed until there was a downpour. By the time she and a tight-lipped Trace reached the ranch, she felt as if they'd been enclosed in their own secret world. She was unbearably aware of him. Something about the rain made everything more intimate. His chiseled profile haunted her.

When he stopped the car, she jumped out, needing to get away from him. Once in the house she rushed to her bedroom and shut the door. Hoping to shrug off the feel of his hands on her shoulders, Cassie got undressed and took a shower.

She washed her hair and pampered herself, but the imprint of his body against her back still stayed with her. When desire hit, there was no mistaking it for anything else. She desired Trace Rafferty. How long had he been at the ranch? Six days? Up at the lake he'd carved her initials in the log and she'd responded like a love-struck teenager instead of a twenty-seven-year-old pregnant woman.

When she finally left her room in a clean pair of denims and a cotton sweater, the house was quiet. After looking out the living room window she discovered his Explorer was still there, but he wasn't inside the house. With the storm activity, he was probably out at the barn to settle the horses. Thank heaven. She needed some breathing space.

While he was gone, she fixed them each a sandwich and left a covered plate on the table for him. She took her sandwich back to her room. How long ago had Trace dropped his bomb on Sam? Had it happened while the two men had sat out on the front porch swing that first night?

She was still trying to recover from the direct hit she'd taken after learning about his plans. Doc Rafferty would be sick over his son's decision to live in Colorado, but as she'd told Trace, it was none of her business.

Cassie should be thankful he'd been up-front with her this afternoon. Trace had given her enough time to find a new job she badly needed. Her college degree in wildlife conservation from the University of Montana in Missoula could open doors for her. She would hunt for jobs with the government, but her first choice would be to work in the private sector.

The White Lodge Wildlife Sanctuary might be a good place to start looking since she already had a connection there. It depended on one of their paid staff leaving, but she didn't know what the odds were of that happening. If she found a decent apartment to rent in town, the location would be perfect.

She could approach the owners at the sanctuary and find out if they were planning to hire someone else. With her college credentials and her work with the American Prairie Reserve after she'd graduated, it was possible they might hire her. The two years she'd spent on the High Plains in northeastern Montana helping facilitate and maintain water rights along with livestock and wildlife had given her invaluable training.

It was on one of her brief trips home she'd met Logan Dorney, the new hired hand on the Bannock Ranch. Technically speaking, Jarod had done the hiring. When Cassie's father had fired him, Jarod didn't override the decision. Sadie confided to Cassie that her husband felt it was wise to leave it alone. Everyone, especially Jarod, knew how fragile Cassie's father had become because of Ned.

If Cassie and Logan hadn't fallen in love, she'd still be working in the northeast part of the state. With that on her resume, it was worth it to find out if the sanctuary would be interested in her.

Tomorrow after breakfast she'd drive into town and make a start. If there was no opening, she'd run by the fish-and-game office to see what they'd posted locally. After that she'd drop in at the Bureau of Indian Affairs.

A water conservancy group was doing a project out on the Pryor Crow Reservation an hour away from White Lodge. Maybe she could get hired on there, but they preferred to employ an Apsáalooke. She understood that. Still, if they needed someone qualified and no one else had applied, she could get lucky and be hired.

Cassie was desperate for a good job and wouldn't stop until she found one.

For the next hour she looked up all kinds of positions in her field on her laptop. Helena and Kalispell had half a dozen wildlife conservancy openings, but she didn't want to move to either place away from Avery and her cousins' wives. Sadie and Liz had been her friends from grade school. With Logan gone, she needed them, even if they didn't get together very often.

Though Trace had said she could stay here until the

new owner moved in, she knew she was living on borrowed time. Tomorrow she'd go to town and start looking for an apartment. The small nest egg she'd saved from the insurance money would make it possible for her to put down a cleaning deposit, plus first and last month's rent.

As soon as she could move in, hopefully next week with Avery's help, she'd drop by the vet clinic and turn in the house key to Sam. If her applications for work didn't produce results soon, then she'd get a temporary job in town until the right one came along. Having made up her mind, she could finally settle down to sleep.

But when she got ready for bed and crawled under the covers, she soon broke down in agony and reached for the picture of her husband she kept on the bedside table. "Logan…why did you have to die? I need you more than ever now. I don't know how I'm going to make it." Tears soaked her pillow as she fell, finally, into a fitfull sleep.

Trace checked on the horses to make sure the storm hadn't bothered them. There'd been some lightning and thunder. Content they were all right, he went back in the house and found a couple of sandwiches waiting for him.

She was amazing. He decided there wasn't anything she couldn't do in spite of her pain.

After he'd finished eating, he started down the hall to his room when he heard anguished sobs coming from the other side of Cassie's door. It tore his guts out. He felt guilty as hell.

Not only had he devastated his father with his unwelcome news on that first night, Trace was now forcing

Cassie to find a new job while she was still grief-stricken over the loss of her husband. But no one could bring Logan Dorney back.

No one could give Trace a new eye so he could continue to fly.

No one could make his father ten years younger so he and Ellen could enjoy the ranch together.

No magic formula could take away Nicoletta's pain because the work he needed to do was here in the United States. Their dream to live in Italy had been shattered by that laser.

No wrinkle in time could put Trace's family back together before the divorce.

Some things weren't fixable.

Full of grief himself, he left the house and walked around to the garden, thankful his father had Ellen to cling to at this time in his life.

The rain had stopped and the storm clouds had moved on. In the distance loomed the shadow of the Pryor Mountains. They were sacred to the Crow Nation whose people called them the Hitting Rocks Mountains because of the abundance of flint.

The Pryors weren't as high or as spectacular as the Italian Dolomites where he'd done a lot of mountain climbing and skiing, but they had their own unique beauty. Over the years he and his father had ridden into them hundreds of times. They would wind around the canyons where wild horses like Masala roamed free. The sight of them thundering through a gully took your breath.

Trace walked down one of the rows of fruit and reached for some strawberries that had ripened. The rain hadn't hurt them. They were delicious. Cassie's jam was to die for. So were her rolls and the roast and meatloaf she'd cooked last week, the kind he'd eaten as a boy. He hadn't had much of an appetite since his injury. But the food he'd enjoyed since coming to the ranch had conjured memories of home long ago when his life had been intact, and he'd found he couldn't get enough of it.

Food could do that to you—send you to a place in your mind. Trace had been around the world. Every country had its own specialties. But only one place served food that reminded him of his childhood. Today at the lake, tonight in the barn tending to the horses, he was shaken by emotions he hadn't allowed to surface for a long time. They would smother him if he didn't do something concrete about his situation.

First thing in the morning he would contact Bud Hawksworth, the Realtor in Billings, and ask him to keep his sights out for someone who wanted to buy a ranch like Rafferty's. No putting it on the multiple listings. With the fall hunting season coming up, this time of year would be the best time to make the most of a profitable sale.

Cassie had turned him down flat when he'd suggested the Realtor would be able to help her find a place. It could kill two birds with one stone, but she wasn't having any of it. He shouldn't have said it. Cassie was fiercely in charge of her own life. His respect for her continued to grow. *So did his attraction.* That alarmed him.

When he'd pulled her against him at the lake, it had taken every bit of willpower not to turn her around and kiss her whether he had her permission or not. To do that would end any trust and she'd be out the door and gone in a shot.

He needed to put the desire to make love to her behind him. They'd start fresh at breakfast. But when he got up the next morning and eventually went to the kitchen after a shower and shave, he discovered a note she'd left on the counter.

Trace,

I didn't want to wake you, so I left your breakfast in the oven. If you feel like strawberries, they're in a bowl in the fridge. There's some ham and rolls for lunch if you get hungry before my return. I made a fresh pot of coffee before I walked out the door. I'll be back by afternoon to do your wash and anything else you might want done. You already have my cell phone in case you need to get in touch with me.

C.

He shook his head. Trace had never had service like this in his life. She took the role of housekeeper to a new level.

When he opened the oven door he discovered bacon and scrambled eggs just the way he liked them. Her husband had been a lucky man. After pouring himself a cup of coffee, he took everything to the table and phoned the Realty company while he ate. The secretary said Bud would return the call once he was free.

When Cassie had gotten up early on Monday, she'd been relieved to discover Trace's Explorer was still out in front, which meant he was in bed. After making breakfast for both of them, she got on the computer to see what rentals were listed. Instead of printing out the ones she wanted, she could pull them up on her smartphone and leave for White Lodge now. She was determined to find a place to live ASAP so she could start planning a nursery.

By midafternoon she'd found an eight-plex apartment house near the center of town with floor plans she liked, but the ground-floor apartment she wanted wouldn't be vacant until two weeks from now. But before she paid money, she needed to see it empty. The landlord agreed to hold it for her if she left a refundable deposit in case she didn't want it. They made an appointment for her to come back then. If all went well she'd sign a year lease.

Tomorrow being Tuesday, she'd spend part of the day putting up more jam. When she'd finished she would drive over to Connor's ranch house. Since she was moving, she couldn't keep her horses. If he didn't know someone who would like to buy them, he would know how she should advertise to get the best results.

Trace was home when she returned. She found him in the living room eating potato chips while he watched a rerun of an NFL football game on TV. The second he saw her, he turned it off and got to his feet. He looked amazing in a black crewneck shirt and jeans. "You've been gone a long time."

She bit her lip. "I had a lot to do. How was your day?"

"Good. I spent most of it with my Dad."

"How is he?"

"Fine."

"I'm glad." She turned to leave.

"The horses are happy."

"That's good."

"How are you?"

"Tired. I'm going to bed. Have a nice evening."

"Cassie? Wait—" he said as she started for the hallway.

Her heart pounded. She glanced at him. "What is it?"

"Have I offended you in some way?"

"Of course not!"

His hands went to his hips in a male stance. "Something's bothering you. Can we talk about it in more than monosyllabic words?"

That was her fault. She was being rude. "Sorry if I came across uncommunicative. Let's agree we both have a lot on our minds."

"Do you want to talk?"

She shook her head. "No."

"Well *I* do. Today I happened to see your truck in front of an apartment complex with a for-rent sign in the manager's apartment window. Has my presence made you so uncomfortable, you're considering moving out right now?"

Oh, boy. She should have known. White Lodge was such a small town, you couldn't get away with much.

Cassie lifted her head and stared straight at him. "After Mandy saw me out with you the night we went to the film, I realized how it must have looked to her. Your dad is a prominent man in town and people are finding out you're back home. Friends like the people I volunteer with know I'm still living here on your ranch. But all it takes is one troublemaker to spread rumors about you and me living under the same roof together. They don't know you're moving to Colorado."

She watched him rub the back of his neck. It meant he was listening.

"You know what I mean, Trace—the grieving widow and the hotshot bachelor pilot. Soon it will be all over town that I'm pregnant. I can just imagine the spin some people will put on it, saying that the last time you came to visit your father, you must have hooked up with the housekeeper when her husband wasn't around."

"No one would think that!"

"Yes they would and you know it."

His silence said it all.

"There's a base element of society that exists every-where, Trace. We can solve the problem by not being seen together. The damage may already have been done when Ned hears about it from his friends. They visit him and have regular contact. Once he finds out you're back and were seen with his pregnant sister, it could start a wildfire of gossip. I've told you he hates me. You'd be surprised just how ugly it could get."

Trace stood. "I know you're frightened of him, but since he's still living in the mental health facility, you don't need to be in a rush. I had a long talk about him with Zane and Jarod. When and if Ned is released, you have a home with your cousins who plan to protect you."

Her face went hot, something it had been doing a lot since Trace had shown up in the fruit garden. "I know my cousins would do anything for me, but I would never impose on their lives that way because of Ned. They're all newlyweds for heaven's sake!"

"But you're forgetting one thing. If Ned is released soon, they're not going to let you live in town by yourself."

"Then I'll move to another part of the state!" she fired back.

Trace shifted his weight. "We're getting ahead of ourselves. For now I'm here to keep an eye on you until I leave for Colorado Springs. Until then, this is your home."

"It's *not* my home!" Cassie exclaimed. "Your father left the ranch to you. Hopefully I'll be able to move to the apartment in two weeks when it will be vacant."

"Have you put money down yet?"

"A deposit. I want to see it without any furnishings. If I like it, then I'll sign a year's lease."

"Where are *your* furnishings? None of your things are here."

"They're in storage," she lied.

Trace's eyes looked pained. "I can't let you leave because of what a few people might say, Cassie."

"Please stop feeling guilty. I can handle anything but that."

"If I'd known what was going to happen, I would never have suggested we drive into town to see a film."

"Please don't say that. Don't you know I'm glad Mandy saw us together? It got me going sooner on finding my own place to live. I need to get ready for the baby. This is all for the best. In four or five weeks when this place is sold, I'll be another month along. I'd rather move now while I'm in good shape. That apartment is perfect for me."

His dark brows furrowed. "But you don't have a job yet."

"I'll get one. I know almost every store owner in White Lodge. If I can't work in my chosen field for a while, I can always get a job at one of their businesses. Today I saw a dozen help-wanted signs in the shop windows."

"That kind of work isn't for you, especially not at this stage in your pregnancy."

"Don't be ridiculous. I'm perfectly healthy."

"And I want you to stay that way."

"I *am* over twenty-one and in charge of myself. You're sounding like a husband—" she blurted before she realized her mistake. Heat washed over her in waves. "I—I'm sorry," she stammered. "I didn't mean to say that."

The faint glimmer of a smile hovered on his lips. "I'm sorry I provoked you. Chalk it up to the picture of your sonogram. Since looking at it, your pregnancy is very real to me. I don't like being the person who is causing these sudden drastic changes in your life. I want to fix everything. Since learning more about Ned's instability, I intend to keep you safe."

Cassie knew he meant it, and it touched her heart. "That's not your job. When I move, everything's fixed. It's that simple. Tomorrow I'm going to ask Connor if he knows anyone who would like to buy the horses."

"When the time comes, I can help with that. While I have time on my hands waiting for a potential buyer, I'll move everything from your storage unit into your apartment."

"You mean you've decided I'm allowed to make my own decisions and move out of here?"

He shrugged his broad shoulders. "It appears there's no stopping you."

"Good. I'm glad we understand each other." She took a deep breath. "Just so we're clear, I won't need your help during the move."

He walked closer to her. "Naturally your cousins will

be there for you, but I'm the one creating all the distur-
bance, so I intend to repair the damage."

"There's no damage, Trace, and I'd rather you didn't."

"Why?" he demanded in a quiet, yet compelling,
tone. She knew he'd keep it up until he got the answer
he wanted.

"Because there *are* no furnishings."

He frowned. "What do you mean?"

"I didn't want you to know. Logan and I moved into
this house without any possessions of our own except
our clothes and a few personal items. My father forbade
me to take one thing from my home."

"I don't believe a parent could be that cruel."

She clenched her hands. "He thought that if I left des-
titute, I'd cave and decide not to marry Logan. Luckily
my husband owned his own truck. We lived at a motel
for a week before moving into your father's completely
furnished house. All of the furniture and pictures must
be heartbreakingly familiar to you."

Fists formed at his sides. "He literally threw you
out?" Trace had ignored her comments about the house.

"Yes," she whispered, blinking hard to keep her eyes
from tearing.

"Didn't your brothers want to help you?"

"Afraid not. We have a dysfunctional family with
a capital *D*."

"So when you rent the apartment, you have nothing to put in it?"

"Nothing, except for personal possessions. But that's
not a problem. I'm planning to make the rounds of the
yard sales and find what I need."

"Then we'll do it together."

"What? And cause even more gossip?" Her questions

bounced against the walls of the house. "I have friends to help me. It's not your concern. I'll buy a new bed and crib from the furniture store and have them delivered. It will all work out."

"The hell it will."

"Careful, Captain. You're not in the military now." The second the words left her mouth, Cassie wished she could call them back. "I'm sorry, Trace. That was another terrible, thoughtless thing to say to you. I keep doing it. Forgive me."

"It's my fault," he said in a quiet voice. "I've done a terrible thing by badgering you."

"Neither of us is at our best. I'm missing Logan who's never going to come back. You're missing Nicoletta, but you're fortunate because she'll be flying over soon."

"Cassie—"

"Don't interrupt me. Please," she begged. "Can't you see how much better it will be when I'm gone so she can stay here with you alone? The two of you will be able to make plans for your future."

"I'm afraid it won't be that simple."

"Give her some time to get acquainted with your world, Trace. Take her to Colorado Springs, then come back here. Who knows? Maybe she'll love it here more and want to be a rancher's wife. I guarantee that seeing you again, she'll want to marry you on the spot."

His head lifted. "That's because you grew up a Montana girl and love of the Pryors is burned deep inside you, but it's not for everyone. My mother never took to this life."

"I always wondered about her. How did your parents get together?"

"They met in Yellowstone Park while she was on vacation with some friends from Denver. Dad had just finished attending a veterinarian conference in Salt Lake and stopped there on his way back to Montana. He urged her to come and see him in White Lodge. One thing led to another and they got married, but she missed living in a big city and complained a lot."

"That would have been incredibly painful for you."

"It was. When she asked for the divorce, Dad begged her not to move so far away he couldn't see me when he wanted. So she moved to Billings and eventually met a man from there. They married, and now he works for a company in Portland."

"Your father never met anyone else?"

"There were women, but his hurt went deep. It made me glad when he met Ellen and wanted to marry her."

"Your dad seems to be so happy."

"He was until I came home and hurt him all over again."

"Not deliberately, Trace."

"You're very sweet, Cassie." He lounged against the back of the couch. "How's the job hunting coming?"

"I've made applications at several places. Now it's a waiting game. All I can do is hope to be contacted for a first interview. You know how that goes. Except that *you* never went through that process. The Air Force wanted you immediately."

"Where did you get an idea like that?"

"Your father."

He shook his head. "What did you study at the university?"

When she told him about her college degree in wild-life conversation and experience with the American

Prairie Reserve, he said, "I should think any of those places where you applied would be eager to hire you. With all those credentials, you blow me away."

"Thanks. I'm hoping someone will give me a call back."

"If Jarod knew about your application for the job on the reservation, he'd do whatever he could to help you."

"I know, but I need to do this on my own merits."

He smiled. "If I didn't know anything else about you, I know that."

"So is anyone interested in buying the ranch yet?"

Trace had hesitated talking about it, but since she brought it up, he might as well tell her the truth. "I heard back from my Realtor this afternoon. He's going to put out some feelers, but not on the multiple listing. I've decided to keep this as quiet as possible. Naturally I'll let you know when he's found someone who wants to come out to the ranch to look around."

"It's a choice piece of property and this house is darling." Her voice throbbed.

"That's because you and Logan made this place your own and it shows. I feel worse than ever over the new situation facing you."

"Please don't. With that eye injury you have your own cross to bear. For your sake, let's hope the ranch is taken off the market in no time."

"We'll see. Now I've kept you up too long. Get a good sleep."

"You, too. Good night."

Chapter 6

Tuesday morning Trace had just come in after a ride on
Masala when his cell rang. Hoping it was Nicci phoning
him, he jumped down from the horse and let him run
in the paddock. But when he looked at the caller ID, it
was the Realtor. He clicked On.

"Mr. Hawksworth?"

"Bud, please."

"All right. I didn't expect a call from you this soon."

"Are you kidding? A ranch like yours will be a piece
of cake to sell. I've got some great news already."

Trace braced himself. "Go ahead."

"I keep a list of preferred clients who want to be no-
tified if something they've been looking for suddenly
comes on the market. One in particular is a potential
buyer with money from the East Coast whose family is
into the manufacturing business. His name is Lamont

Walker. When I called him about your property, he said it was exactly what he was looking for and can meet your ballpark price. In a word, he was *ecstatic*."

The unexpected news twisted unpleasantly in Trace's gut. This was all happening too fast. "Tell me about him."

"He's a big game hunter who would use the ranch for hunting parties with his friends throughout the year when he's not off to Africa."

Already Trace didn't like the sound of him. The man had no plan to do any ranching. No interest in raising crops or running cattle. He'd have to hire someone to look after the place when he was gone on safari.

"Mr. Walker has his own company jet and is already on his way to Billings after being in Chicago on business. He'll come to my office tomorrow before we drive to your ranch."

Tomorrow? "Does he have family?"

"He's forty-seven and divorced. That's all I know. I have to tell you that this is absolutely the right kind of buyer who knows what he wants and is ready to strike while the iron's hot. I'll let you know what time you can expect us at the ranch."

Trace wasn't ready for this, but it was too late to put him off now. Bud Hawksworth was a go-getter. Probably the best in the business.

"I'll look out for your call, Bud. Thank you."

Cassie loved her cousins and Liz. No one had a more loving extended family than she did, but she didn't expect them to solve her problems.

"Thank you for dinner, Liz, and everything you're trying to do, but I could no more impose on Mac and

Millie than I could any of the rest of you. You're all newly married with plans and dreams of your own."

Cassie got to her feet, having been at their new ranch house too long already. Liz still had veterinarian work waiting for her. "I'll be moved into an apartment in town within two weeks. I want to get ready for the baby in a place of my own." She smiled at her. "No amount of generosity on your part will get me to change my mind."

"But you're going to let us give you a baby shower, right?"

"I'd love that!"

"Good. Then it's settled. I'll talk with the others to plan a date and call you."

Thankful she had her own transportation, Cassie was able to leave so Liz and Connor could enjoy the rest of the evening. After leaving the Bannock ranch, she drove to White Lodge and bought a pot of white mums at the supermarket. From there she went to the cemetery at the northeast end of town.

Logan's grave was in the newer section. It would be several years before the planted trees grew to a significant size. She pulled up near his flat marker and got out of the truck with the flowers. One day when she had enough money, she would have a granite stone erected.

She walked over and knelt down to put the pot at the bottom of the marker. "I haven't been here for two weeks, Logan. Forgive me. So much has happened since my last visit. We're going to have a little girl, but I bet you already know that. Sam's son, Trace, is home from Italy to sell the property, so I'll be moving to town within the next two weeks.

"The family wants me to live with Liz's parents. Can

you believe how wonderful they all are to me? But I could never do that to them. I've got to make my own way. It was always you and I against the world. Now it's our daughter and I facing it without you. In four months I'll be a mother."

Tears welled in her eyes. "I promise to tell her all about her wonderful daddy and keep your pictures around her forever. I'm praying that by the time she's born, Zane will have found out who shot you and can rule it an accident." She shuddered. "For so many reasons I don't want to hear it was Ned." She started crying and buried her face in her hands.

"I've asked Connor to take care of the sale of the horses. Trace said you did a beautiful job on the house. He's planning to move to Colorado to be a flight instructor for the Air Force. I love the house so much I—I just know it will sell fast. We were so happy there."

Tears dripped everywhere. "While our dream lasted, you were such a marvelous husband to me. I loved every second we were together. I'm having a hard time leaving our little house in the forest. I've taken dozens of pictures inside and out so our little girl will know how happy we were there.

"Trace asked me what you and I had decided to name her. I told him neither of us knew I was pregnant before you died. Since we don't know who your parents were, I can't name her after someone from your family's side. I'll just have to keep thinking about it. One day the right name will come to me." She wiped the tears off her face and got to her feet. "Goodbye for now, Logan."

She turned and started for the truck. Evening had fallen. But this time as she left the cemetery, everything was different from all the other times because Cassie felt as if she'd reached the end of an era. All the way back to the ranch she thought of the new troubling era looming before her.

Trace owned the home she'd been living in. When she arrived at the house, he would be there instead of Logan. He'd been the first person to see the ultrasound picture of the baby and ask the baby's name. Besides her cousins, he'd been the one and only man to take her to a movie or anywhere since the funeral.

Cassie had been preparing Trace's meals, doing his wash. He'd walked and ridden the horses with her while they'd talked about the intimate, private issues of their lives. They'd been thrown together so hard and fast, it felt as if they'd skipped the normal period of getting acquainted. Last night during a heated conversation she'd actually accused him of sounding like a husband. To think she would even entertain the thought seemed like a betrayal of Logan's memory.

When she pulled to a stop in front of the ranch house and saw that Trace's car was gone, Cassie resented the fact that she even noticed. What was worse—for that infinitesimal moment, she experienced disappointment. What did that mean?

It means you need to move out of there pronto, Cassie Dorney. Two weeks couldn't come soon enough.

The second she'd showered, she got into bed and went to sleep. When she awakened late Wednesday morning, she had no idea when Trace had returned or if or when he'd gone to bed. Once she'd dressed in fresh maternity jeans and a blouson-type blouse, Cassie went to the kitchen for a glass of juice and some toast. She found a note from Trace sitting on the kitchen table.

> Good morning, Cassie. Just wanted you to know that I've gone to town for some supplies. I'll be back by eleven. The Realtor Bud Hawksworth and a potential buyer will be coming to the ranch around noon.
>
> T.

A buyer already?

At the mention of the ranch being sold, there went that pain again. Not only her pain, but pain for Sam Rafferty, too. He had to be broken up over his son's intention to live in Colorado. It wasn't just because the property was going to pass into other hands, but because he'd wanted this for Trace's legacy.

Cassie appreciated Trace giving her warning and hurried through the house to be sure everything was clean and in order. After she'd fixed her breakfast and had eaten, she went out to the barn and led the horses to the paddock. While they enjoyed the morning sun, she mucked out their stalls, put fresh hay in the nets and made certain there was fresh water.

Once that chore was done, she went back to the house for the basket and spent the rest of her time picking any ripened strawberries. She didn't want anything left undone.

Her watch said it was close to eleven when she heard a car pull up to the house. Her heart raced to realize Trace was home even sooner than she'd expected. While she was coming to the end of the last row, she heard men's voices behind her and turned around.

"Sorry to startle you, Mrs. Dorney. I'm Bud Hawksworth and this is Mr. Walker. Did Trace tell you we were coming?"

The Realtor wore a summer suit and glasses. "Yes, but he's not here yet."

"Mr. Walker's plane landed early so we've come ahead of time. I told him you've been looking after the place since your husband passed away. I'm very sorry to hear about your loss."

Mr. Hawksworth had taken a liberty coming early, one Cassie thought inappropriate. She took a steadying breath. "Thank you."

"The exterior of the house is charming and so unexpected. Mind if we walk around until Trace gets here?"

"I guess that's all right."

"We'll take a look at the barn. Maybe the horses he mentioned are for sale, too?"

"They're my horses," she murmured, disliking the way Mr. Walker was eyeing her.

"I see."

To her chagrin the other man said, "You go on, Bud. I'll catch up with you in a minute." The potential buyer was probably in his late forties and somewhat attractive with blond hair and burnished skin. In khaki shorts and a T-shirt, his lean build reminded her of a golfer. "Your garden is thriving. Looks like you're going to have raspberries soon."

"One hopes."

"How long have you worked here?"

"A year."

"Then you know all its secrets."

She didn't care for the way his brown gaze seemed to leer at her. "Like all hundred-year-old properties, it needs constant upkeep, as Mr. Rafferty will tell you."

"If I buy this place, I'll need someone to take care of it when I'm not here."

Cassie knew what the offensive man was getting at. He could see she was pregnant, but her condition didn't make a difference to him. "That's something for you to take up with Mr. Hawksworth. If you'll excuse me."

She headed for the house with the basket, aware of his roving eyes on her retreating back. There was nothing she detested more than a man who looked at her as if he was undressing her. It sickened her. He obviously had money or he wouldn't be wasting the Realtor's time. But already she was hoping Trace wouldn't sell to him.

As for the horses, Cassie wouldn't let such a disgusting man get near them. She marched into the house in a mood and ran right into Trace, who must have been on his way out the back door. As the basket dropped, a small cry escaped her lips. He grasped her upper arms.

"I'm sorry, Cassie."

"I'm the one who needs to apologize." She tilted her head back to look at him. Their faces were so close, she felt his warm breath on her lips and had to stifle a moan. "I wasn't watching where I was going."

"You're upset. I can feel you trembling. What's happened? I saw another car out there."

"Mr. Hawksworth came early with Mr. Walker."

"So I see. And?"

"It's nothing."

"The hell it isn't," he muttered in a deep voice.

Reeling from his touch, she eased out of his arms and reached for the basket. Luckily it hadn't tipped over.

She put it on the counter. "They're waiting for you. Trace. While you show them around, I've got some errands to run."

It was the best excuse she could come up with at the spur of the moment. She knew he wanted an explanation, but she couldn't tell him the whole truth. Otherwise he'd find out she didn't want him to sell the ranch, never mind that it was none of her business. And what would he think if she said Mr. Walker reminded her of a predator? Trace would decide she was as unstable as her brother.

She dashed out of the kitchen and down the hall to her room for her purse. Once again as she started to leave, Trace blocked the doorway, but this time they didn't collide. He looked good in his Western shirt and jeans. Better than good. All of him looked so-o good.

"I'm not going outside until you tell me what happened."

She let out a sigh, resigned that she needed to say something to appease him. "I have an idea he'd like me to work for him if you sell him the ranch."

"What else?" he demanded. Emotion had turned his eyes a darker blue.

"There's nothing else."

"Cassie—"

"Oh, all right. It was just the way he looked at me. It made me shudder." Cassie could tell when a man found her attractive, but not in an offensive way. This man's probing gaze was something else. "Maybe I could be wrong, so please don't let that color your judgment."

His body tightened. "Say no more."

"Trace—"

But he'd bolted down the hall and out the back door. She'd done it now. Part of her thrilled to his protective instincts. The other part felt terrible if it meant the sale he needed wouldn't go through because of something she'd said. She should have left the ranch after seeing to the horses. But there was nothing holding her back now!

Grabbing her purse, she rushed through the house and flew out the door to her truck. She was so shaken, she knew her blood pressure had to have spiked. What she needed was something to calm her down.

When she reached town and drove by the Clip and Curl beauty salon, she decided a visit there would be therapeutic. After turning around she parked in front. You could walk in and wait for someone to wait on you. The place was bursting with customers of course. The redheaded owner, Mildred Paxton, sat behind her counter.

"Hey, Cassie— I haven't seen you in ages. You're pregnant! I didn't know."

"Neither did I until after Logan died."

"You look wonderful. How do you feel?"

"Frazzled. I need pampering, but this place is so busy I'll come back later."

"No, no. I'll do your hair myself."

"Really?"

"For a favorite customer, anytime. What do you want?"

"A shampoo and style."

"Come on over to my chair."

In a minute Cassie was draped in a smock. For someone else to do her hair was the height of luxury. "My kingdom to have my hair washed every day by you. This is heavenly, Mildred."

"I hear you."

"How's your daughter?"

"Rosie's fine, but her husband had to move to Billings so I've lost my helper. You don't know anyone who's looking for a part-time job, do you?"

Cassie gripped the sides of the chair. "What kind of work?"

"Running the desk, making appointments, taking the money. I usually come in at three to finish up the day, but so far no takers. Everyone wants full-time work. I don't blame them." Mildred finished the rinse and wrapped her hair in a towel.

When Cassie sat up she said, "I might know someone who could do it until her baby's born."

The older woman stared at her. "You need a job."

She nodded. "For the next four months. After the baby gets here, I'll need it more than ever." No one needed to know Trace's plans for the ranch. "I'll be out of a job in another month."

"I don't get it. You're a Bannock."

"Every Bannock I know works hard." Except for Ned who treated work as a joke.

"You know what I mean, Cassie. For you to work in the salon…"

Cassie had met with this kind of mind-set before. "Tell you what, Mildred. I've put out feelers for work in several places. Even with a college degree, it hasn't helped produce results yet. If nothing pans out by morning, do you mind if I call you for an interview?"

"You're serious!"

"I am. I did the accounts, took money and handled reservations for hunters while Logan and I ran the Rafferty ranch. I'm friendly with quite a few of your regular customers. This job would be perfect since I'm an early morning person. By late afternoon I can go home and put my feet up the way the doctor told me to."

"Tell *you* what. I won't hold my breath because I can't imagine you not getting snapped up by someone else. This job doesn't pay that well."

"But you'll give me a chance if I phone you tomorrow? Provided you haven't found someone else?"

"We'll see. Between now and tomorrow anything can happen."

At least Mildred hadn't said no.

After she left the beauty salon, Cassie went to the drive-through for a hamburger and a lemonade. On her way back to the ranch she felt energized after her talk with Mildred, who'd done a great job on her hair. If she hired Cassie and she could move into that apartment soon, she would have solved all her problems for a while.

Trace was at the root of her guilty turmoil. Earlier today when he'd grasped her arms, she'd felt desire for him arc through her body again more intense than at the lake. To experience such a yearning this soon after Logan's death filled her with sorrow over her weakness. She couldn't allow it to go on happening.

Once she was out of Trace's house for good and they didn't have to see each other again, maybe she could forget how he made her feel.

When she reached the house, his Explorer was gone. Thankful for the respite she hurried inside, eager to get busy and put up the last of the strawberries. But when she walked into the kitchen and read the note Trace had left on the table, she had to sit down so she wouldn't fall.

Cassie—

I should never have left you alone when I knew Bud was coming over. It won't happen again. For your information, Mr. Walker has been told I'm looking for a family man who plans to be a full-time rancher.

Can I count on you to hold down the fort for a while? After hearing from Nicci again, I've decided nothing can be resolved over the phone so I'm flying to Italy and talk to her face-to-face. I don't know how soon I'll be back, but with you in charge I have no worries.

The guys know my plans and they'll check in on you to make certain you're all right. If there's any problem at the ranch, call my father and he'll take care of it. My main concern is you. Please take very good care of yourself and that baby.

T.

Cassie sat there in a daze. What was it Mildred had said? Anything can happen between today and tomorrow. She struggled for breath. Trace was on his way to Monfalcone. *He's in love with Nicci.* From the looks of it, he would be married before long and probably live in Italy after all.

Whatever feelings Cassie struggled with, they were on her part, not his.

She ran to the bedroom and buried her face in the pillow, heedless of her pregnancy or her new hairdo. His note had left her in complete limbo.

The white Tornielli villa gleamed in the sun. One of the staff told Trace he'd find Nicoletta by the pool. He wanted to surprise her and made his own way beneath the purple bougainvillea overhanging the portico to the deck.

He found her lounging in a minuscule black bikini. She wore sunglasses and was talking on the phone, probably to her friend Bianca. If she was in pain, it didn't sound that way to him. She hadn't seen him yet. After a month's separation, the sight of her playing with the strands of her black hair should have excited him. She was at once so familiar to him.

All that animation bequeathed from the genes of her dynamic family was in evidence. Nicci was a beautiful creature of her unique environment. But Trace had been away from her and removed from this world for quite some time. He knew in his gut that to take her out of it would kill the part of her that was so scintillating. The part that had drawn him to her.

The fact that she still couldn't bring herself to fly to the United States meant she understood herself well and had done both of them a great favor. Their separation had given her second sight, too. Unless he came to her and melted into her world, they wouldn't work.

"Nicci?"

She turned her head and threw off her sunglasses. *"Caro!"* But she didn't come running yet. Instead she got up off the lounger and took in his Western shirt, jeans and cowboy boots. Her dark brown eyes played over him. "I don't recognize you like this. You've turned into a Montana cowboy." Her strong Italian accent made her words sound so charming in English.

"I'm afraid this is the real me. For ten years I forgot."

Nicci looked lost. He couldn't blame her. "What do you mean?"

"When I joined the Air Force, I was running away from my past because I was in pain."

"Your parents' divorce did that to you."

"Yes. You've never known that kind of pain. You have an intact family. But since I've been home, my past has caught up with me. I never really wanted to leave it."

Her eyes filled. "So what are you saying?" she cried. "Are you glad that laser almost blinded you?"

"With hindsight I can say yes because it brought me to my senses sooner. I've come to tell you that I've decided not to take the position at the Air Force Academy. Ranching is what I love to do." When he realized what Lamont Walker planned to do with his property, Trace had had an epiphany. He didn't want anyone living there but him. "If you could live with me on the ranch and like it, then I could see us getting married because I love you, Nicci."

She shook her head. "I love you, too, but I don't want that kind of life, *Caro*."

"I know, and I respect you more than you can imagine for being totally honest with me. Our happiness depends on it. I owe you so much. That's why I'm here so we could say these things to each other in person."

"I'm remembering what you told me about your mother. She never liked being a rancher's wife."

"It's true. Ranch life isn't for everyone." But there was one person he knew who loved that life.

Visions of Cassie had been in his mind from the first time he'd seen her in the garden. Though she was still in mourning for Logan, she loved every minute of her time on that ranch. She'd been born into a ranching family.

After hearing her tell him what Lamont Walker had intimated and how'd made her cringe, Trace had been more than annoyed. In truth, he'd felt like decking the guy before the two men had driven away. His feelings for Cassie had grown so strong, they refused to go away.

"As long as we're being truthful, why did you never want an engagement with me?"

"Because I knew I could never work for your father. Not that he isn't a fine man, but I have to be my own boss."

"But I'm talking before your injury, *Caro*."

"Maybe because of my parents' history, in my subconscious I was afraid of commitment."

"What are we going to do?" came her plaintive cry.

"Marriage isn't the answer for us, Nicci."

"But I can't bear to lose you. I'll get dressed and we'll go to your hotel."

"I didn't check into one."

"Why?"

"Because I didn't think it would be a good idea."

"Since when? Something about you has changed." She moved closer and slid her arms around his neck. "Kiss me, *Caro*. It has been such a long time."

In ways it had seemed like an eternity since they'd made love. He pulled her close and kissed her, but the driving passion he'd always felt for her was missing. To his shock he found himself wishing it was Cassie in his arms. She'd been so shaken by that lowlife Bud had brought out to the ranch, Trace had wanted to kiss her until she forgot everything else and clung to him.

As gently as he could, he removed Nicci's arms from around his neck and kissed her hands. "I'll never forget you, Nicoletta Tornielli. Meeting you, knowing you, was the best thing to happen to me after I was deployed here. You brought happiness into my life when

I didn't think it could be found. I wanted to marry you, but our dream wasn't meant to be. You have to know I enjoyed every minute of it. Now I have to go. A taxi's waiting for me."

She looked stung by his words. "You planned to leave so soon?"

He nodded. "We both know it has to be this way."

"After flying all that distance, why are you in such a hurry to get away from me?"

"This is difficult enough without prolonging it, don't you think? Do we really want to make things harder on ourselves?"

A silence surrounded them. "You've met someone," she accused quietly, summoning his guilt.

"Nicci…"

"You have! I can feel it. Who is she?"

This was one time he wished Nicci didn't have such an intuitive nature. "Give my best to your family. They're wonderful people. As for you, I want your happiness more than anything in the world."

The tears trickled down her cheeks. "You haven't answered me."

"Goodbye, Nicci." He kissed her cheek.

Her perceptive comment trailed him as he headed for the portico and hurried outside to the taxi. Contrary to what he'd thought, driving away from Nicci and the villa wasn't the traumatic experience he'd expected. Trace's mind went over his session with Dr. Holbrook.

His expert advice to straighten things out with Nicci first had cleared Trace's emotional vision. Instead of more pain at seeing her again, he was filled with a sense of wonder over the relief he felt that this chapter in his life had come to an end. A whole new world awaited him back in Montana. A familiar world he'd tried to put behind him during his time in the Air Force, but he hadn't succeeded.

You're going home, Trace.

On his way to Montana, he'd make a stop in Colorado Springs to let the brass know he wouldn't be taking the teaching position after all. Once that was done, he'd head for Oregon to see his mother. Dr. Holbrook told him he needed to get rid of his anger for past hurt if he really wanted to heal, more advice Trace intended to take.

Then he'd return to White Lodge and have a big talk with his father. It was long past time Trace begged his forgiveness for being so blind.

What an irony that it took his eye being scarred by a laser to see what had been right in front of him all the time.

On Wednesday he flew into Billings, realizing he'd been gone a week. His feelings were so different from the first time he'd looked out the window two weeks ago, he couldn't believe he was the same person. The excitement missing before was in full evidence now. He picked out familiar landmarks that told him he was home. Everything he held dear was down there. Everyone...

Once he'd landed and gathered his suitcase, he picked up his car in the long-term parking and headed for White Lodge. He'd phoned his father from Portland and had asked him to meet him at the ranch at two in the afternoon. It was important.

Sam was already there on the front porch of the house reading a magazine, no doubt the latest veterinarian medical journal. Cassie's car was gone. Knowing her, as soon as his dad told her Trace would be arriving, she'd taken off so she wouldn't impose. For once he was glad she wasn't there. This gave him private time with his father.

He pulled to a stop and levered himself from the front seat. His dad got up from the swing. Trace took the porch steps in one leap and embraced his father. Tears smarted his eyelids.

A surprised laugh came out of Sam before he let him go. "What's this all about? A goodbye hug because you've decided to marry Nicci and live in Italy? Is that why she isn't with you?"

"Dad? We've got a lot to talk about."

"That's what I thought," he murmured, sounding defeated.

"You have no idea what I'm going to tell you. Sit down and I'll explain."

When his father did his bidding, Trace perched on the porch railing opposite him, too full of energy to sit. "I went to see Mother before I flew here. She sends her love."

His dad's head lifted. "How is she?"

"Good. I asked her to forgive me for being so angry with her over the divorce."

His dad sat back in obvious surprise. "That must have been quite a conversation."

"It was cathartic for both of us."

"Nothing could please me more than to hear that." He wiped his eyes.

"Not even if I told you I flew to Colorado Springs to tell them I'm not going to take that job after all?"

"You mean you're going to work for Nicci's father in Monfalcone."

"No, Dad. I mean I've come home for good. I don't want to sell the ranch. I want to work it and run cattle again, put in some crops."

One sandy brow lifted. "Is Nicci okay with that?"

"We're not getting married and we've said our good-byes."

"What?" He was clearly in shock.

"You heard me. Oddly enough it was something she said when she saw me walk out to the pool that reaffirmed my own feelings. It proclaimed the end of our relationship because in her heart she knew a marriage between us wouldn't work."

"What did she say?"

"Nicci took one look and exclaimed, 'I don't recognize you like this. You've turned into a Montana cowboy.' Her soul was speaking to my soul, Dad.

"The truth is, I went into the Air Force because of anger over the breakup of the family. But the cowboy was always there. When I came home two weeks ago, I fought its pull. But I discovered these Rafferty roots grow so deep, you can't get rid of them. I'm here to stay. Can you ever forgive me for taking my anger out on you?"

"Oh, son…" He got up from the swing and gave Trace the biggest bear hug of his life. In a tug of war, his father always won. "Welcome home."

Both of them had to wipe their eyes. "Do you know where Cassic is?"

"She's at work."

Trace did a double take. "What work?"

"She got a part-time job at the beauty salon Mildred Paxton owns in White Lodge."

He couldn't believe it. "I didn't know she was a beautician, too."

"Oh, no. She runs the counter and makes appointments. It's only two blocks from that apartment she plans to move into. I believe it will be ready in another week. That girl is a go-getter if I ever saw one. She's up early to see to the horses before getting to the shop at nine."

"What are her hours?" Trace was stunned how fast she made decisions.

"Nine to three. She'll be home pretty soon unless she has other plans. Speaking of getting home, I've got to tell Ellen the wonderful news. We're going to have to celebrate!"

Chapter 7

Cassie was happy to see Mildred come in through the back door of the shop. It was close to three-thirty. The owner was running late. Normally it wouldn't matter, but today Cassie wanted to get to a couple of yard sales before everything was already picked over. She was looking for a playpen in good condition.

"Sorry I got held up."

"No problem, Mildred."

"How are things?"

"Just fine!"

"How do you stay so cheerful when we both know most days it's a royal pain?"

"Not to me."

"You're so great at this job I hope you never leave. Now go on home and relax."

"Thanks, Mildred. See you tomorrow."

Cassie had parked out in the back alley. She was glad the owner was pleased with her work. So far it had gone smoothly on her new routine. She'd taken her doctor's advice and went home every afternoon to put her feet up and check her emails or watch television.

She ate the second half of a peanut butter sandwich while she drove to the first yard sale. But she didn't even get out of the cab because there weren't any baby items. Cassie would probably end up having to buy a new one. Still, there was one more sale she'd seen advertised and drove by it.

A painted wood high chair caught her eye, but after seeing all Sadie's new paraphernalia, Cassie couldn't make a decision yet. The issue of safety was a factor to consider. In the end she drove back to the ranch without having made any purchases. The budget she'd allowed herself wasn't big enough for her to acquire everything she wanted. Not when she needed a couch, bed, a TV and a dozen other things first.

Functioning on autopilot at this point, she wasn't prepared to see the brown Explorer parked in front of the house. *Trace...* He was back! She was sick with excitement and afraid, too.

He'd been gone so long, maybe he'd brought Nicci with him so she could see the ranch and they could make wedding plans. If that was the case, Cassie would sleep at Avery and Zane's until she moved to the apartment.

Not wanting to walk in on them, she knocked. When no one answered she knocked harder. After no response she unlocked the door and poked her head in.

"Hello? Trace? Are you here?"

She got brave and walked in. When she passed his

bedroom she saw his suitcase next to the bed. Maybe Nicci wasn't with him after all, unless she was staying with Sam and his wife. Curious at this point, she reached for two horse snacks and walked out to the barn.

Buttercup nickered from the paddock. Cassie went over to the railing. "Hi there, Buttercup." She patted her forelock and undid the wrapper so her horse could eat. She chomped it down. "Did Masala desert you?"

"We're right here."

Trace's deep voice had her spinning around. He looked down at her with a smile that reached his brilliant blue eyes. "You don't have something for Masala, do you?"

"Of course I do." She patted the horse's head and took the treat out of the paper to feed him. "There you go." He was a chomper, too. "They're noisy eaters." It made both of them laugh. "When did you get home?"

"I drove in to the ranch around two this afternoon to meet with my dad."

A dozen questions sprang into her mind. Had he come home to tell his father he and Nicci had set a wedding date? Or had he married her while he'd been in Italy? A strange pain shot through her at the thought of either possibility. "After I saw your car out in front, I thought you might have brought Nicci home with you."

"She's not coming."

At those words Cassie's heart almost failed her. What did it mean?

While she was groping for something intelligible to say, he opened the gate and walked Masala into the paddock. Once he'd removed the bridle, he patted his rump before closing the gate. He hung the bridle over the post.

"Come in the house with me. You and I need to talk. Dad tells me you're working at the beauty salon in town. No other job offers came through while I was gone?"

"Not yet, and Mildred needed help. It's a perfect job for me while I'm pregnant."

"If you're happy, that's all that matters. How was your Fourth of July?"

"Fine. My cousins took me to the White Lodge fireworks celebration at the park. It was fun. I'm sure you would have enjoyed it."

"When I was a kid, I lived for fireworks."

"You and every male I know."

"Connor and I put on our own shows when no one else was around. Jarod helped."

"I'm not surprised."

He opened the back door for her and followed her through to the kitchen. "Why don't you sit down while I wait on you? It's hot out there and your cheeks are rosy. Want a soda?"

She wished he wouldn't make personal comments. "A lemonade sounds good."

"Your favorite drink." He handed her one and reached for a cola. His gaze panned the kitchen. "You've put up more jam. I can't believe the abundant yield from your garden."

"The weather has cooperated."

"Only with the help of a green thumb like yours."

"I used to help my mom in the garden."

Trace snagged a chair with his boot and sat down. His eyes centered on her. "You never talk about her, but I know you miss her, especially with the baby coming."

The conversation had started to border on painful issues she'd rather not discuss. "I miss the mother I loved before she started siding with my dad in order to keep the peace with Ned. But I'd rather talk about your news." Her heart was thudding. "Did your trip to Italy help you and Nicci figure things out?"

He drained his soda and put the empty can on the table. "There isn't going to be a wedding. We're two halves of the wrong whole."

The blood hammered in her ears. Trace wasn't going to marry her? "I—I'm sorry," she stammered.

"Don't be. It would never have worked. We both knew it and avoided the mistake of getting married and then having to end it, maybe with a child involved."

Cassie drank some of the lemonade while she assimilated what he'd just told her. She must have been born with some evil gene to be happy with his news. Her mind pounced on her next question. "Have you heard from your Realtor? Does he have more buyers lined up?"

He sat back in the chair with his arms folded. "Nope. When I flew into Billings earlier today, I dropped by his office and told him I was taking the ranch off the market. It's not for sale. Ever."

Hearing that news made Cassie positively giddy. It was a good thing she was sitting down or she might have fallen over in shock. "Did you tell your father?"

"Yeah. He was pretty happy about it."

"Pretty happy—I'm surprised he didn't go into cardiac arrest."

Laughter poured out of him.

"Do you plan to rent the property, then?"

Her question caused his laughter to subside. "No."

She didn't understand. "Then, what?"

"I'm going to live here."

That did bring her out of the chair. "You mean you're not going to Colorado Springs after all?"

Trace put his hands behind his head and stared up at her. "Nope. I stopped there on my way home and told the brass I've decided to go back to ranching."

"Are you telling me the truth?" Her voice had come out more like a squeak.

He'd tipped the chair back as far as it would go before there was an accident. "Scout's honor."

"Don't tease me, Trace."

His dark brows suddenly furrowed. He jumped out of the chair. "You went pale just now. I forgot how this news would impact you, but you don't need to worry about losing your housekeeping job."

That wasn't why she'd gone pale. It was the idea that he'd come home to live and they'd see each other coming and going. "Of course I do!"

"I want you to stay on and work for me."

She clung to one of the chair backs. "With you living here, too?"

"Why not? Unless you have designs on me."

"Be serious, Trace—" she snapped. He'd hit a nerve that ran the entire length of her body.

"Better me to be your bodyguard than Mac Henson or your cousins. They're all married. Since Zane's responsibilities prevent him from serving that purpose, I'm the logical choice."

Cassie didn't understand. "What do you mean bodyguard?"

"Ralph told your cousins that Ned will be coming back to the ranch tomorrow."

Her gasp filled the kitchen. She gripped the chair back tighter.

"When I was at the Golden Spur last week I bumped into Owen Pearson at the bar. He mentioned that Ned would be released shortly." Cassie groaned. "Ralph's news confirmed it."

"If our grandfather confirmed it, then it has to be true."

"Afraid so. Your name was mentioned during my strange conversation with Owen. I can tell you now that you won't be safe from harassment if you live in that apartment. We know what Ned is capable of, but we don't know what will set him off next, or what he'll do even on his medication. There's only one place for you, here where I can protect you."

"I'm not your responsibility, Trace."

"You are now. Dad hired you and Logan to look after the property. The shooting took place on our ranch. Now that I'm back, I want you to stay put and do the same things you've been doing. It's worked so far, hasn't it?"

"Yes! Because you were in Italy and I thought you were moving to Colorado."

"Cassie—my father thinks the world of you and doesn't want anything to happen to you or the baby. This isn't just my idea."

Incredulous she said, "You mean Sam approves of us living under the same roof?"

"Yes, and your cousins will all be for the idea, too. They don't want you to be on your own either."

She shook her head. "I couldn't consider it."

One dark brow lifted. "Because of what other people will say?"

Adrenalin surged through her veins. "It's because *I* don't believe it's right!"

"Not even to protect your unborn child?"

She closed her eyes tightly for a minute. "After I move to the apartment I'll figure out a way to keep us safe."

"How?"

"If I decide it's necessary, I'll buy a handgun and take lessons out at the shooting range like Avery. You know what they say about an ounce of prevention. It's something I'll talk over with her and Zane the next time we're together."

"That's not going to stop your brother if he gets it into his mind to stalk you." Cassie shuddered. "You're in a unique and dangerous situation. The father you should be able to go to isn't there for you."

"How many times do I have to tell you this isn't your problem?" she asked in frustration.

"What if I want it to be?"

"That's because you're like your father and play the Good Samaritan even when your world has been turned upside down. You shouldn't be worrying about anything but your own affairs."

"Are you afraid of me, Cassie?"

"Of course I'm not."

"Do you trust me?"

"What a question to ask."

"Do you?" he persisted. "Because you'd be foolish to move into town, let alone move to another part of the state, when you're this far along. There'd be no one to lean on. It would make no sense. Let all of us help you. We're in this together. Everyone has a vested interest in shutting Ned down. He's been a menace to you, Jarod, Zane and now Connor."

Fear pierced her. "What has he done to him I don't know about?"

"It's what he plans to do to antagonize your cousin that has us worried. Owen told me they're going into the feral stud farm business."

"Ned?"

Trace nodded.

"That's the biggest joke I ever heard, but I know you're not joking. He's always been in competition with Connor. Whatever my cousin did, Ned tried to do and failed miserably, especially at steer wrestling. He'll probably steal some wild horses which is against the law."

"Or try to put Connor out of commission like he did Jarod."

She let out a cry. "I just can't believe he's coming home this soon. It's a nightmare."

"It doesn't have to be if you'll let me help you. Jarod assumes they're planning to use Ned's money from his recent inheritance for their latest scheme. But he says Owen's dad would never allow him to set up business on his ranch."

"I don't know. Owen has walked over his father all his life."

"Sounds like Ned and Owen are two of a kind."

"Like two peas in a pod."

"Your cousins are worried that if Ned is thwarted on that score, he and Owen will think of some other scheme that will be up to no good."

"Dad shouldn't have released that money. If my Grandfather Tyson were still alive, he wouldn't allow it. All my father does is placate Ned. There's something wrong with him, too!"

"Is your father still in counseling?"

"He was in the beginning. Unfortunately I don't know anything at this point."

"That's why Zane and your cousins are so concerned. Let's not worry about that right now. Why don't you go in the living room and put your feet up while I cook us dinner. Any suggestions? I won't use salt."

When Trace was around, he watched out for her constantly, endearing himself to her in ways he didn't realize, but this was his home. He could do what he wanted and shouldn't have to look after her, too. "There's some hamburger in the freezer."

"Great. I'll thaw it and make spaghetti. How does that sound?"

"Sure. I haven't had it in a long time," she said before leaving the kitchen. But food wasn't on her mind. Trace had given her so much to think about, she felt like she was on an emotional seesaw.

After taking a shower, she dressed in a pair of maternity jeans and a short-sleeved top in a tiny pink print on white. Bed sounded so good, she lay down on her side. Two things he'd said stood out above all else. He wasn't getting married, and he wanted to get back to ranching.

Cassie still had a hard time believing any of it. She'd thought Nicci would go to the ends of the earth for a man like Trace. Was he in pain that she couldn't bring herself to come and see where he'd lived? Even if he was certain a marriage with Nicci wouldn't work, his heart had to be aching.

She closed her eyes. His insistence that she continue to live in the house was out of the question. Cassie had made her plans and wouldn't change them. As for her brother, she didn't want to think about him coming home tomorrow. It was only a possibility that he'd killed

Logan. Without proof, maybe they were all being too paranoid. The doctor wouldn't release Ned unless he felt the therapy and medications were working.

Cassie didn't like to think of her brother confined to a facility for the rest of his life if it wasn't absolutely necessary. Her parents had suffered over Ned for so many years. But when she remembered what he'd done to Jarod, and his cruelty to her and Logan, she shivered and refused to think about it.

For now she was happy to know that Trace had made peace with his past. Sam had to be euphoric that his long-lost son had found his way back home. While she lay there pondering this afternoon's unexpected events, she felt a flutter in her stomach. At first she thought it could be a hunger pain, but when it came again and again, she knew it was her baby moving.

Her heart leaped for joy. There was no other feeling like it. The sensation could be a butterfly's wing brushing against your skin, but on the inside. At her ultrasound, the doctor had told her she'd probably feel something pretty soon.

She felt beneath her top to put her hand against the bare skin of her tummy. For a few minutes she lay there absorbing the flutters that meant her daughter was alive and getting ready to be born. Pregnancy was a miracle. Full of hormones, she broke down sobbing in happy tears.

Just then Trace knocked on her door. "Cassie? Dinner's ready."

She sniffed. "Thank you."

"You sound different. I know I upset you."

"I—I'll be there in a minute," her voice faltered.

"Something's wrong. Are you in pain?"

"No."

"I can hear you crying. If anything has happened to that baby because of me, I'd never forgive myself."

"You don't understand."

"Do you need a doctor?" He sounded panicked. "Whether you're decent or not, I'm coming in."

Before she could get into a sitting position on the bed, he opened the door. One look at her lying there and he said, "I'm calling 9-1-1."

"No—" she exclaimed. "I'm crying because I felt the baby move for the first time."

In an instant the lines in his face disappeared. "You did?"

She nodded. "It's beyond incredible. I was so afraid something was wrong because I'm almost twenty-two weeks along and should have felt movement by now. But I'm getting lots of it at the moment."

He stood in the doorway watching her. "What does it feel like?" When she told him, the most tender smile she'd ever seen broke out on his face. "I'm not often around a pregnant woman."

Cassie smiled. "Being a former Ace, why doesn't that surprise me?" Motivated by a force she hardly understood herself, she told him to come over to the bed. "Give me your hand." He hunkered down so she could place it against her belly. Their faces weren't that far apart. "Just wait a minute and you'll feel it." Their eyes studied each other. "She senses a male presence."

"You think she knows the difference?"

"Not only your touch, but your voice. She heard it when I showed you her first photograph. Move your hand a little. Maybe that will stimulate her."

Trace's touch was stimulating Cassie so much, she could hardly breathe. "There—did you feel that?"

A look of wonder broke out on his face. "Like the merest whisper."

"That's exactly what it's like."

Another minute of amazing sensations they could both feel passed before he suddenly took his hand away and got to his feet, breaking the intimacy they'd shared. "Thank you, Cassie. That's one experience I'll never forget."

Bombarded by new emotions, Trace strode through the house and out the back door to get a grip while he put the horses in the barn. Since seeing the sonogram, he'd almost felt as if he was the father of Cassie's baby. For those precious moments just now, he'd forgotten he *wasn't* the father. Was there any woman alive sweeter than Cassie? More generous?

But in his line of vision Logan Dorney's face in the framed picture had stared back at him, bringing him to his senses. Naturally she kept his photograph on the table next to her bed. That was the first time he'd seen her husband. He was attractive and had a clean-cut look in the dressy Western shirt he'd worn for the picture.

Because of a fatal gunshot wound, the man would never see the fruition of his efforts in the garden. He would never see the little baby growing inside Cassie. He'd never hold his wife in his arms again.

When Trace had felt the evidence of new life inside Cassie, a primitive need had been born inside him to protect her and the baby at all cost.

She was on the phone in the kitchen when he went back inside a little later. He served up two plates of spaghetti with bread and butter. Knowing what her doctor said, he gave her ice water while he drank coffee. After she hung up, she joined him at the table to eat. The sparkle in her eyes was back.

"That was Avery. She called to plan a baby shower for me. When I told her your latest news, she was so thrilled she's decided to have a big barbecue on Saturday night. It will be your welcome-home party, plus a shower. She'll invite your father and Ellen and anyone else you'd like to be there."

"Everyone I care about will already be on her list." Starting with the gorgeous female seated across the table from him.

"So is Saturday night okay for you? You're supposed to let her know."

He finished his coffee and pulled out his cell phone. "I'll call her now to thank her. I have no plans for Saturday night." *I'm not going anywhere.*

The living room of the Corkin ranch house was packed. Everyone had turned out to welcome Trace home. After the feast out on the patio, Zane and Avery had assembled the crowd inside so Cassie could open her shower gifts.

"It's time for bed, Ryan."

"I don't want to."

"Come on, honey." Sadie had already put her baby down with a bottle in the guest bedroom, but Zane's nephew was fighting going to sleep, not willing to miss out on the fun.

"Auntie Cassie?" He ran over to her. "Mommy says you and Trace are going to have a baby. I want to see all the presents."

Trace was sitting across the room from her, but he didn't miss the blush that filled her cheeks. She'd worn an attractive khaki skirt with a cream-colored cotton knit sweater that blended with her golden-blond hair. "I'm having a baby, but Trace isn't the daddy."

"How come?"

"You remember Logan?"

"Um, I think."

Jarod saved the moment and swept him up in his arms. "Come on, Tiger. It's way past your bedtime."

"I hope it's a boy like Cole," he said over Jarod's shoulder.

"I'm afraid it's going to be a girl."

"A girl—" He frowned, causing everyone to laugh, including Trace. "What's her name?"

"I haven't decided yet."

Jarod carried him out of the room before he could say anything else. Trace loved it. He'd loved every moment of tonight and it wasn't over.

Avery and Liz started the gift giving. By the end of the evening, Cassie had everything she'd need for the well-dressed, well-equipped baby. By the time it was over, she was in tears. The guys cleaned up the mess before carrying everything to Trace's car. Pretty soon people were saying good-night.

While they'd been inside, a wind had started up that hadn't been present during the barbecue. The weatherman had forecast some rain, but it wouldn't hit until later. Cassie walked out of the house holding Ralph's arm while Connor held the other.

Trace's father and Ellen followed. They headed for Jarod's car, parked next to Trace's. "I wish your Grandpa Tyson had been here tonight."

"So do I," she murmured and kissed Ralph's cheek. "I'm so thankful you're alive and could be here. Thank you for your gift. To start a college fund for my daughter is beyond wonderful."

"No one deserves it more, and I wouldn't have missed tonight for the world." He flicked a glance to Trace, who was holding the front passenger door of Jarod's car open for him. "The good Lord brought you back to us, Trace. Now that you're home, be sure you take good care of my Cassie. She and her baby are mighty precious to me."

Trace smiled at her. "I will if she'll let me."

Ralph looked at her. "Of course you will. I don't want to hear about you living in town in some apartment. You stay put, young lady." Jarod's exact words to Trace.

"I'm afraid she's a Bannock with a mind of her own," Trace said when he could see Cassie was uncomfortable. She must have heard that a dozen times throughout the party.

"Don't you let her do it," Ralph warned in a serious tone.

Connor exchanged a wordless message with Trace before helping his grandfather into the car. They were all aware Ned was home but no one more than Ralph, who feared for Cassie.

As Trace opened his own car door for her, his father gave her a hug. "You mind Ralph, Cassie. He knows what's good for you."

"Thanks for the advice, Doc."

His father shut her door, then hugged Trace hard before leading Ellen over to their car.

Trace waved to the others and got behind the wheel, anxious to be alone with Cassie. He hadn't known this kind of contentment in years. They didn't have far to go. The weather was definitely growing more blustery, adding to the excitement at the thought of the two of them being together in his house.

He glanced over at her. "Are you tired?"

"A little, but it was such a wonderful party I don't care."

"That Ryan was the life of the party. Jarod and Sadie have their hands full with two children."

"They do, and they love it. Little Cole, or Sun in His Hair, is absolutely adorable."

"Just like your baby is going to be. I guess she can't be given a Crow name," he teased.

"Only Jarod's offspring are entitled."

"He always did love his Crow heritage. It's a shame he never got to know his mother."

"I agree. But he has everything he wants now with Sadie and the children."

Trace swallowed to get rid of the lump in his throat. "After tonight I think your child won't want for a single thing."

"No." He heard a big sigh. "Everyone was so generous, I don't know how to repay them."

"They don't expect anything. All they want is for you to be happy and safe."

"I know. I swear if one more person had told me to stay on your ranch…"

"Did their remarks upset you?"

She shook her head. "I have the dearest family and friends in the world. But they're so focused on me and what happened to Logan, they're not considering your situation."

"I don't have one, Cassie. I'm eager to get started

on some projects. It would be a relief to me if you were there doing the things you always do. I could keep a better eye on you after you get off work at the beauty shop. If you move to that apartment, everyone who attended the party will be checking up on you all the time, including me. Ralph knows what goes on in his son's household with Ned and he's worried enough to warn you to be careful."

"That's what I'm afraid of, Trace. I don't want to be anyone's project."

"If you stay with me, then everyone can get on with living."

"But it's not fair to you. I'm a liability, and you're too much of a gentleman to admit it."

He scoffed. "You couldn't be more wrong. If anything I'm the intruder in your world. You were getting along just fine until I came home. Don't you know I love getting up to the smell of strawberry jam? I'm crazy about your cooking. I like walking into a clean house and I sleep better knowing someone's in the house when I go to bed. Flying can be a lonely business and I've done it for a long time."

"I've wondered about that."

"Have you ever heard of Pauline Gower?"

"No."

"She was a British pilot during WWII. She said that 'to be alone in the air at night is to be very much alone… cut off from everything and everyone. Nothing's "familiar" any longer.'"

"Is that how you felt at times?"

"Exactly like that. Another of her quotes was right on. She said that 'one feels rather like Alice in Wonderland after she has nibbled the toadstool that made her grow smaller—and like Alice, one hopes that the process will stop while there is still something left."

"Sounds like she was a writer, too."

"Yes."

"Do you miss it? Flying I mean."

"No. I didn't live for it like some pilots do. It provided an escape for me at a time when I was floundering. I wanted to get far away."

"You weren't alone, Trace. I had those same feelings at a very young age and couldn't do anything about them until I went away to college. There was a time when I swore I'd never come back. If I hadn't met Logan on a visit, I'd be living somewhere else in the state."

"Well I for one am glad you ended up right where you are."

Trace left the highway and drove along the dirt road to the ranch house. He'd left the two outside lights on. Cassie's description of the little house in the woods came to mind. "With your painted shutters at this time of night, you'd think we'd stumbled on to the Hansel and Gretel house."

A small smile appeared. "It does kind of remind you of that old fairy tale."

He parked and turned off the engine. "You don't really want to move to an apartment when you have a home here for the present. Do everyone a favor and stay until after the baby is born. By then we'll have a good idea about Ned's state of mind. It will give you time to find the kind of job you really want."

"But—"

"No buts, Cassie. Don't pressure yourself to make a decision you might regret. Who knows? Maybe an apartment won't look good to you once the baby is here.

You may want to rent a house for you and your daughter. Promise me you'll think about working for me, at least until Christmas. Then you can reevaluate."

She didn't answer him. He hoped that was a good sign.

Chapter 8

"Come on. Let's go inside with your haul."

"That's exactly what it is!" Cassie exclaimed.

"Dad won't be staying here so why don't we store everything in his room."

"But what if he and Ellen want to sleep over one night?"

"All they'll need is the bed."

Without saying anything, she got out of the car before Trace could help her and reached for one of the sacks in back filled with baby clothes. The wind was blowing harder now.

"You must be tired after volunteering at the sanctuary earlier."

"I'm not that tired."

As his father had remarked, Cassie was a hard worker. "How's Giselle by the way?"

"As precious as ever."

"She probably waits for your visits."

"I think she's happy when I call to her."

He smiled. "You only think?"

"Everyone loves her."

"But I wager you're her favorite. I'll go by there again soon and see if she remembers me. In the meantime if you'll open the front door, I'll bring in all the rest of the things."

Trace handled the heavier boxes with furniture that had to be put together. After several trips he got everything inside the bedroom. "What did you work on today at the sanctuary?"

"We painted the new fox condo. Paul did the roof and sides while Lindsey and I worked on the legs."

"The same brown color?"

"Yes."

"Does it have shutters?"

She chuckled. "No."

"I think you should add two and apply your terrific artwork to brighten things up."

"I'm afraid it would be a little much."

"You're so expert at it, we can't let that talent go to waste. If you noticed, I didn't give you a gift at the party. Why don't you open the closet door?"

Cassie stopped emptying the bags and walked over to do his bidding. "Oh—a little wooden toy box." She leaned over and opened it. "How darling!"

"It's unfinished. I thought you could paint it and decorate it yourself."

She stood up before her eyes darted to his. "You do too much, Trace."

He hunched his shoulders. "If you don't want it—"

"You know I do! I'm just overwhelmed by your thoughtfulness. You're too generous for your own good."

"And you're too stubborn for yours." He opened the top dresser drawer. "This is empty. Shall we put the clothes in here?"

Cassie walked over to the bed and lifted a little white bodysuit from the sack. They both chuckled. "Trust Connor to find this eenie-meanie bull outfit. Look at the size of that steer's horns!"

"How about Liz's contribution?" He pulled out the little pink-and-white bodysuit dress with two cowboy boots on the front. "I can't wait to see her in this. Or this." Trace drew out another bodysuit. "Super cowgirl."

"That was Mac and Millie's contribution. I never saw so many cute baby clothes in my life." She started folding them and the receiving blankets in the drawer.

Trace never saw a cuter mother-to-be in his life. While she got busy doing that, he opened the box containing an ivory-colored crib. He had it assembled before she turned to look at him.

"You shouldn't have set that up."

"Too late. It's done. Don't you want to see what the mobile looks like attached to it? Jarod says Cole is already intrigued by his."

After a slight hesitation, she opened the box and pulled it out. He knew Cassie couldn't resist. A horse, bear, cowboy boot, dog and bull dangled from a tan cowboy hat. A laugh escaped her lips. "What won't they think up next?" She put it at one end of the crib.

"Every little well-brought-up cowgirl should have one of those." Trace took the crib mattress out of the other box and fit it inside the crib. "The padding with the cowboy boots is here somewhere." He found it and set it around. "All this crib needs now is your baby girl."

Cassie stood there clutching the crib rail with a pained expression. After such a great evening, his spirits plummeted to see it. "I realize Logan is the one you wished were here doing this with you. I'm so sorry, Cassie."

He left the bedroom and walked through the house to the back door into the wind. A ride on Masala was what he needed, and he didn't care if it started to rain on him. In practically begging Cassie to stay on at the ranch, he'd added too much pressure by erecting the crib. He should never have done that. It hadn't been on purpose, but he'd been so carried away by the events of the night, he hadn't stopped to think. She had every right to resent him. *Damn and damn.*

In a few long strides he reached the barn, but the left door was open and banged against the structure with every gust of air. Trace had closed the doors before they'd left for the party. In all the years he'd lived here, he'd never seen the wind blow one of them open. They were heavy.

Whether it had been left open on purpose or not, he was convinced someone had been here.

Walking inside, he turned on the overhead light and headed for the horses' stalls to check on them. Speaking in low tones, he examined them to make certain they were all right. They nickered back and forth while he inspected the other two empty stalls and the tack room. Nothing seemed amiss, but he wasn't convinced a force of nature had been responsible.

Without hesitation he phoned Zane who'd probably

gone to bed by now. He picked up on the third ring. "Trace? What's up?"

"After the great party, I'm sorry to bother you, but this couldn't wait." In the next breath he told him what he'd discovered when he went out to the barn. "If we had an intruder over here, he could have left a fingerprint or two. I haven't touched the handle or the door."

"I'll be right over."

While he stood inside the opening to get out of the wind, Cassie came out of the house. "Trace?"

He stepped outside. "I'm right here."

"What are you doing? Why is the light on?"

"Come inside and I'll tell you. Don't touch anything."

When she reached him, her hair was in beautiful disarray. "I thought you'd gone out to the front porch."

"Actually I was going to take a ride on Masala before going to bed, but I found the barn door open the way you see it right now. Before we left tonight, I closed both of them. I could be wrong and it was just the wind, but I think we might have had an intruder while we were at the party. So I phoned Zane. He should be here in a minute to lift any prints he might find besides yours and mine."

She bit her lip. "The wind wouldn't do that unless the door had already been ajar."

"I'm inclined to agree."

Cassie left him long enough to go over to the horses. While she was talking to them, Trace saw headlights in the drive coming toward him. Zane got out of his truck with a bag. Jarod was with him.

"Thanks for coming."

"I'm going to test for fingerprints. Let's go in the house first so I can get a set of yours and Cassie's.

Then I'll test for prints on the front and back door of the house, window frames and the doors of Cassie's truck before we go to the barn."

"While you do that, I'll take the barn door off the hinges and set it inside," Jarod offered. "It'll be easier to work on out of the wind."

"Good idea." Zane handed him a screwdriver from his bag before Trace and Cassie went in the house.

An hour later everything had been done and the door was put back and shut. "I'll get all this off to the crime lab in Missoula first thing in the morning. It ought to be interesting to see what they come up with. You know what this means if we find what we're looking for."

Cassie's anxious eyes revealed her fear. "Will it be enough to send him back to the facility for good?"

Jarod hugged her around the shoulders. "No question about it, cousin."

After they left, Trace walked her back in the house and locked the door. "Cassie?" he said as they reached the kitchen. "Do me a favor? Zane says he'll ask for results ASAP. If I'm right and Ned was bold enough to trespass tonight, he'll do it again once you're in that apartment. Promise me you'll stay here where I can protect you."

An odd sound came out of her. "You don't have to say anything more, Trace. When I came looking for you earlier, it was to tell you that I'll stay and work here.

"Neither Ralph or your father minced words with me tonight. I'm not going to let my pride make everyone so nervous for me, they lose sleep over it. I've already left a voice mail with the landlord of the apartment that I won't be wanting it after all. I'm sure he'll refund the money.

"Ralph's health has been so much better since Sadie first came back, I don't want to be the one to put him in bed again. He made a promise to my Grandfather Tyson to watch out for me. No one takes responsibility more seriously than he does."

Thank heaven.

"Then you know how I feel because my father put me under the same mandate where you're concerned."

"I'm sorry, Trace."

"For what exactly?"

"For being a liability. And for the heartache you must be feeling because your marriage plans didn't go through. While you were putting the crib together, all I could think of was you, wishing this baby was yours and Nicoletta's."

That's what had put the pain in her eyes? Not the memory of Logan?

"I *was* wishing your baby was mine, Cassie," he whispered. "Yours and mine."

Her green eyes widened.

"I found myself envying your husband. If you remember a certain conversation before I left for Italy, I challenged you to stay with me, unless you had designs on me and were reticent. That was my way of teasing you. But even as a tease, you let me know in a hurry that nothing could be further from the truth. A love like yours doesn't come along every day. You left your family to be with Logan. As I've told you before. He was a lucky man."

"If Nicoletta couldn't leave her family, I can't blame her, not when she comes from such a different world. But it ruins your dreams of a family with her."

"Once the injury happened, I believe it brought both

our dreams to an end. In truth, I don't think I was ever in love with her enough, or I would have done what she'd wanted and live there." He'd loved Nicci. If things had worked out differently, he might have married her and then regretted it because deep down he'd always longed for home. It would have caught up with him.

"With hindsight I can see that if you don't love someone with every fiber of your being, then how can you expect to make it through the difficult times of marriage? You and Logan had that kind of tenacity."

"It wasn't perfect. Deep inside he was insecure because he'd been orphaned. When Ned put him down to Dad, it did a lot of damage though he didn't show it in front of other people. I had to beg him to let us try for a baby. Without a role model, he was convinced he'd make a terrible parent."

"How sad."

She nodded. "He'd been in half a dozen foster homes before he turned eighteen and could be on his own. I told him it didn't matter that he didn't know his father. It was in the doing of being a father himself that he'd find out how to be a great father. We'd learn together. But it wasn't meant to be."

"Are you the one that found him in the forest?" he whispered. Trace had wanted to know the details, but had never dared ask until tonight.

"No. When he didn't come home for dinner and it got later and later, I called your father in alarm. He in turn called my cousins and Zane. They all went out with flashlights and found him facedown near one of the streams. I told you about the dead marten that lay nearby."

"I don't know how you lived through that."

"I don't either," she laughed sadly. "Those first few weeks are a complete blank to me. Avery and the girls took turns staying with me. When I discovered I was pregnant, it was like I'd been brought back to reality and had something to live for again."

"His little girl…" He took a deep breath. "Was Logan Dorney his birth name?"

"He never knew. It was the one given to him at the orphanage in Dillon. He never did find out if they just assigned him that name, or if it was the name of one of his birth parents."

"Well he may not have known his parents, but he was married to a wonderful woman."

Tears filled her eyes. "But that so-called wonderful woman had a brother who wouldn't leave him alone." Trace saw her hands tighten into fists. "He jeered him and mocked him and—" But she couldn't go on and broke down.

Not immune to her pain, Trace pulled her into his arms and rocked her while she poured out her grief. Cassie had been holding all this in for such a long time, she had difficulty quieting down. It was past time for her to let it out. Trace was fiercely glad he was the one she'd turned to. They had a connection that was growing stronger.

When she eventually eased away from him and lifted her tear-ravaged face, it was all he could do not to protest. "The front of your shirt is wet. I'm so sorry to do that to you."

"Hey—you're pregnant and have the right to fall apart anytime you want."

Cassie laughed. A good sign that she didn't resent

him. When he'd gone out to the barn earlier, he'd been convinced he'd blown it with her.

"Just call me water works. I exhibit every pregnant hormone-filled symptom in the book. I'll probably have momnesia after the baby's born, too."

"Momnesia?"

She nodded. "Pregnancy brain. They say there's forty times more progesterone and estrogen marinating in my brain right now affecting the circuits. The IQ doesn't change, but priorities do. Something about so many shelves in the brain and the top three are filled with baby preoccupation."

Trace grinned. "I learn something new every day living around you. Maybe it'll be contagious. Now I think you've had enough excitement for one day and ought to get to bed. I'll lock up and turn out the lights."

"Thank you." Her voice trembled. "For absolutely everything." She kissed the corner of his jaw and left the kitchen.

He touched his fingers to the spot where her lips had been. Next time she had one of those urges, he'd help her find his mouth.

The next Friday Cassie had a dental appointment at noon. A filling had come loose and it was the only time her dentist could fit her in before he left on a trip. She called Mildred who told her to lock the salon. Rosy, her daughter, was visiting and would open it and cover the counter while Cassie was gone.

At one-thirty she returned and entered the shop through the rear door like she always did. When she reached the counter, Rosy stood up and gave her a hug.

"It's been a long time, Cassie, and you're more beautiful than ever."

"So are you."

"It isn't fair to look like you do when you're pregnant."

"Thanks for the lies. In my condition I can use them. You're really great to come in and help me out."

"Anything for an old friend. Mom says you run this place with the precision of a Swiss clock."

"Is that good or bad?"

They both laughed. "When my mom says it, you know it's good. Everything has gone smoothly. Oh—I almost forgot. You're not going to believe it. Remember Owen, your brother's old friend from high school?"

Suddenly her heart was racing like a runaway train. "Yes?"

"He came inside for a second, looked around and left. I heard he got divorced. Maybe he was looking for his ex. But don't you think that's weird? He's still that same smarmy, squinty-eyed loser."

"That doesn't surprise me." Cassie felt sick to her stomach. The news had sucked all the air out of her lungs. "Thanks for covering for me, Rosy. I'll take over now so you can get back to your mom's house."

"Let's get together the next time I'm in town."

"We'll do it."

They hugged again and she left, waving to several customers on the way out. Cassie sat down on the chair and phoned Trace.

Pick up. Please, pick up.

When it went to his voice mail she said, "Trace? I'm at the salon. After I got back from a dental appointment, Rosy said Owen Pearson came in the shop, looked around and left. I'm sure he was on some errand for Ned. You were right about my not moving to the apartment. At least here I'm surrounded by other people. Call me when you can."

The next hour got busier as it wore on, which helped keep her fears at bay. Trace had to be out doing something that kept him from phoning her back, but she knew he would when he could.

Mildred relieved her at three. Cassie chatted with her for a minute, then left through the back entrance. The first thing she noticed was the glorious sight of Trace lounging against the side of his SUV with his arms folded. Beneath his cowboy hat those shocking blue eyes filled with concern took stock of her. He straightened.

"I'd been out exercising the horses and didn't check my messages until after I'd put them back in the barn. Rather than phone you, I decided to come here and make certain you get home safely. I'll follow you, then we'll talk."

The knowledge that he was behind her filled her with relief. If she'd seen Owen skulking around the apartment, she would have been panicked. Now that there was no urgency to leave the ranch yet, she'd been sleeping so much better since Saturday night.

Though the threat of Ned was out there, she was comforted to know Trace was in the house. It seemed as though overnight he'd turned back into the rancher with new energy and plans. Cassie could tell he was happier than before. Contrary to her initial worries about living under the same roof with him, they'd slipped into a comfortable routine. By tacit agreement they respected each other's boundaries, keeping her desire for him sheathed.

She entered the house first and walked through to the kitchen. Before she could open the fridge he said, "Zane got back to me earlier today."

Cassie turned around. "What did he find out?"

"We got lucky if you can call it that. One set of prints on the inside of the barn door was a match for Owen's."

She let out a gasp.

"Zane thinks he probably got spooked and ran without securing the door and the wind did the rest. After his first arrest, he wouldn't want to be nabbed again. The police have both Owen and Ned's fingerprints on file because of the investigation into Jarod's truck accident. What we don't know is why Owen went into the barn."

"He was spying for Ned," she almost hissed. "My brother would have been furious because Masala was Logan's horse. He probably wanted to know if that horse was still in the barn now that my husband was dead. I think he plans to steal it as part of his absurd plan to run a feral stud farm."

"Ned wants to know your whereabouts, too," Trace said. "He probably heard that you are working at the beauty salon. They wanted to know your hours. It would explain Owen's brief appearance."

Cassie threw her head back. "He's up to his old tricks running surveillance for Ned. Owen does whatever Ned tells him to do. It's sick and twisted."

"I've given this a lot of thought. Ned had time to think and plan while he was in that facility. He has enjoyed harassing you over the years, but no one can predict a timetable for him to do something destructive *if* he's going to."

"Oh…he's going to. Just give him time."

"Zane and I talked about putting a restraining order

on Owen, but it's Ned we want to catch in the act. To serve Owen with an order would let Ned know we're watching them. To do this right Zane feels we need to wait a little longer before netting them at the same time."

"You mean carry out a sting?"

"That's how Zane operates, but a sting takes patience. To reduce the anxiety level I have something in mind, but you'd have to be totally on board with it, too."

"What is it?"

"I was wondering how you would feel about keeping a dog around here to alert us when someone comes on the property."

His suggestion couldn't have thrilled her more. "I'd *love* a dog, Trace."

He looked pleasantly surprised. "You're not just saying that?"

"Not at all. When I was young we had a terrier, but he didn't like Ned because Ned teased him without mercy. Mother was the dog lover in the family. I begged her to give him away so Ned wouldn't hurt him. One day he was gone and mother never replaced him. I was glad, but I missed Dex horribly. He guarded me everywhere I went."

Trace's expression sobered. "Do you think Ned had something to do with his disappearance?"

"I'll never know." She turned and got a lemonade out of the fridge. "Do you want a cola?"

"Not right now, thanks."

She pulled the tab and took a long drink. "What kind of dog were you thinking of?"

Trace rested against the counter. "A sheltie."

"I adore shelties! They look like little collies."

One corner of his mouth curved upward. "Our family had a collie once named Kip."

"I bet you loved him."

"To me he was the greatest dog on earth."

"I know. I felt the same about Dex. Every dog owner feels that way, like they're another member of the family."

"Yup. Dad thinks Mr. Ogilvie's sheltie kept him alive after his wife died. He was one of my father's clients who passed away this week, leaving Dusty who was with him for eight years. His daughter lives in California. She came here to plan the funeral and sell the house. She can't take the dog with her and asked if Dad could help find a home for him."

"Oh, the poor thing." Already Cassie's heart went out to the sheltie who'd lost his owner. "No doubt he's still waiting for him to come home. I saw a documentary recently where one dog was in such great mourning, someone found it lying on the ground of its owner's tomb."

"It's a heartbreaker all right. Dad has taken care of that dog since it was a pup and knows its history. He's a blue merle with a blue eye and a brown eye."

"You're kidding—"

"Scout's honor. We could run by the Ogilvie home after dinner and see what we think."

"Why don't we go now?"

He chuckled before cocking his dark head. "Because you're supposed to put your feet up and rest."

She rolled her eyes. "Thank you for reminding me."

There was a time when she wouldn't have liked him minding her business. But in the past three weeks a change had come over her. She had to admit she loved being watched over by him. He was an amazing, caring man whose company she craved more and more.

"You're welcome. While you do that, I'll call Dad and ask him to make the arrangements for us to see the dog. I need an address."

Cassie hurried to her room and took a shower. Afterward she put on a skirt, which made a nice change from jeans, and teamed it with a summery print blouse with three-quarter sleeves. Then she lay down on the bed and propped her feet for half an hour.

Trace's suggestion that they get a dog had taken hold. She and Logan had talked about getting one when they could get their own place. It would have been so comforting to have one after he'd died, but she wouldn't have dared broach the subject to Sam. This ranch house wasn't hers.

It still isn't, Cassie.

She got up off the bed to apply lipstick and brush her hair. After putting on a mango-scented lotion, she left her room and went to the kitchen, but Trace wasn't there. She found him in the living room watching the news on TV. His black hair was still damp from the shower. He'd put on a dark blue shirt over light gray chinos. No other man could possibly match his looks or his charisma.

He got to his feet while his gaze swept over her. "You look rested. How's your appetite?"

"I'm hungry."

"So am I. Have you been to that new place called Smoky's?"

That's why he'd dressed up. "I've been meaning to try it."

"Well I'm in the mood for ribs. How about you?"

"That sounds fattening and wonderful."

"There's no fat I detect on you anywhere," he murmured. The personal comment did dangerous things to her pulse.

"Liar," she teased.

"No argument that we might be seen in town together?"

"Since I'm sure my parents know about my pregnancy by now, I'm too grateful for your help to care," she answered honestly.

A glint of satisfaction entered his eyes. He turned off the TV with the remote. "Shall we go?"

Smoky's turned out to be another restaurant with a Western motif and a live band of cowboys cranking out country music. The place was crowded. While they had to wait to be seated, Cassie looked so damn beautiful, Trace couldn't keep his eyes off her. Whatever fragrance she wore was heady stuff.

Less than a month ago, he'd flown into Billings at the lowest ebb of his life. If anyone had told him that in three weeks he'd be head over heels in love with Logan Dorney's pregnant wife...

At the time it would have been beyond the realm of possibility, or so he'd thought. But he knew in his gut this was the real thing. If she was compelled to live in Siberia, he'd follow her there.

The host showed them to a table and soon they were served baby back ribs with side dishes. Trace smiled at her. "They're good."

"Very tasty. Tonight I can't worry about the salt."

"Do you really notice a difference?"

"I will when I get up tomorrow. My hands and feet

swell. That's why I removed my wedding ring last week." She'd done it while he'd been in Italy. "Marsha had to call 9-1-1 to get hers cut off during her pregnancy, so I'm not taking any chances."

"It was that bad?"

"It was starting to cut off her circulation. The fireman had her lie down on the kitchen table while one of them used a ring cutter that had to be inserted."

"What a painful experience."

"She said it was excruciating. Having the baby was nothing in comparison."

Trace chuckled. "I'm glad you're cautious, then. Would you like dessert?"

"Nothing more for me. I'm too full and will waddle out of here as it is, but please order some for yourself."

He shook his head. "Your strawberries are so sweet, they make the best dessert. I'll eat a bowl of them later." Trace put some money on the table to pay the bill. "Shall we leave?"

Her green eyes danced. "I thought you'd never ask."

"Too excited about the dog?" She was a true animal lover.

"I can't wait."

"Since you can't keep Giselle, maybe Dusty will be the next best thing." He stood up and helped her from her seat. They walked out to the Explorer and left for the Ogilvie home on the other side of town.

He pulled into the driveway of the small L-shaped bungalow. Before they could get out of the car, the woman came out the front door with the sheltie on a leash. Trace cupped Cassie's elbow as they walked to the front porch. They introduced themselves to the woman named Grace and expressed their sympathy for her loss.

"Thank you. You bear a certain resemblance to your father."

"I hope he doesn't mind."

Cassie laughed at him. "You know very well you take after your handsome father." Trace liked the sound of that.

Grace nodded. "I agree."

He noticed that the whole time they'd been talking, the dog stood back. "Is Dusty naturally shy?"

"Let's just say he's more reserved around strangers, but he's a dear."

"I can see that." Cassie hunkered down in front of him. "Dusty? I know you're sad to lose your best friend. How would you like to come home with us? I can tell you're a sweetie. We'd take very good care of you."

Connor had told Trace that Liz was a horse whisperer. As he watched the way Cassie talked to the dog, he sensed she had that special gift, too. The dog's ears pricked up. Like the little fox, Dusty's head moved with the sound of her voice. It was touching beyond belief.

"Do you mind if I pat your head?" She put her hand out palm down and let Dusty smell her before she scratched his ears. "We'd like to take care of you if you'll let us."

Dusty lifted his head and licked her wrist.

Trace hunkered down next to her. "What do you think, Dusty? Will you let us be your friend?" The dog cocked his head.

Cassie said, "His name is Trace, and I'm Cassie. Do you know what? I think you have a smile on your face and your blue eye looks like Trace's eyes. It's as if you belong together. Isn't that amazing?"

The dog made a little moaning sound as if he understood. His tail waved slowly back and forth.

Grace was beaming. "I'd say you've already won Dusty over. He's usually hand shy. My father would be in tears if he knew."

Cassie's eyes were full as she stood up. She looked at Trace. "What do you think?" she whispered wearing her heart in her expression.

He got to his feet. "Grace? Will you hand me the leash? Cassie and I will walk him around the front yard and see how he does."

"Come on, Dusty." The dog went with them, but after a few seconds he worked himself between them and they chuckled. When Trace made a turn, Dusty barked.

"Dusty's afraid you're going to take him back in the house," Grace called to him. "He loves walks and rides in the car."

"Do you love walks?" Cassie leaned over and rubbed his head and ears. "So do I."

This time the dog licked her everywhere he could.

"I think we'll take this dog with us, Grace. I'll get his dish and dog bed." Trace handed the leash to Cassie.

"Don't forget the toys," Cassie reminded him. "We'll wait right here for you."

Before long Trace came outside with the dog's things. Dusty walked right over to him smelling everything. When Trace opened the rear door, Cassie got in first and Dusty followed. He sat on the seat next to her. There was no question Cassie had already bonded with him.

With a smile, Trace walked around and put everything on the floor in the front before getting behind the wheel. "I told Grace not to come out in case it created more anxiety."

"That was smart."

"Are you buckled up?"

"Oh—I forgot. We're ready now, aren't we, Dusty." He barked.

When they got back to the ranch, Trace set up the dog's bed in one corner of his room with a couple of his toys. Grace had given him the doggie treats she had left, along with his bag of food and bowl.

He and Cassie took a couple of the treats out in front and exercised him to wear him out. When it was time for bed, Trace gave him a treat. "It's outside time." He walked around the side of the house to train him where to go.

"Good dog," Cassie patted him.

They went in the house and removed the leash. Dusty took off running everywhere and sniffing everything, causing them to laugh. Trace eyed Cassie. "One day your little girl is going to be able to crawl around and explore. This dog is going to break you in."

"I'm already picturing it."

Trace walked through to the kitchen. After he filled one of the bowls with water, he put it down in the corner. Dusty came running and lapped up most of the liquid. "You were thirsty."

"You seem to know exactly what to do, Trace."

"With a vet for a father, you pick up a few tricks, but it's going to take time to train Dusty to our lifestyle. So far I'd say he's doing great. You need to get to bed. I'll turn out the lights."

"Thank you for an unforgettable evening. I'm thrilled you got a dog."

When Dusty started to follow her out of the kitchen, Trace told him to stay. He stopped in the doorway and made a few strange sounds, but he didn't take another step. Mr. Ogilvie had trained his dog well.

"Good night, Dusty. See you in the morning." She patted his head before disappearing.

"Okay buddy, let's lock up." Dusty stayed by him as he walked around before going to his room. "Here's your bed." He stood by it until the dog curled up in it with one of his toys that looked like a weasel.

Trace got ready for bed and wore the bottom half of his navy sweats. Before he got in, he knelt down to gentle the dog. "We need you a lot more than you need us, Dusty. That woman in the next room needs all the protection we can give her."

After turning out the light, he slid under the covers with a deep sigh. He didn't envy the dog who had undergone a huge change in his life. But as Trace's father had told him, even if a dog had a long memory, he would adjust fast if given love and attention. He and Cassie could supply that in abundance.

He drifted off with visions of Cassie running through his mind. But sometime during the night he was awakened by low moans that made him jump out of bed. Dusty wasn't in his bed. Trace left the bedroom and found the dog outside Cassie's door. He'd put his paws as far under the slit as possible. Trace had to smother his laughter.

I know how you feel, he spoke to himself. *I want to crawl into her bed, too, but we can't. You have to be invited.*

"Come to bed, Dusty." The dog made another moaning sound, but he obeyed Trace. "Stay," he said after he got back in his little bed.

Ten minutes later the moaning started up again. Through the slits of his eyes he noticed the dog was missing again. Once more he got up and walked down the hall. But this time Cassie opened her door dressed in a robe that revealed her swollen figure. Her hair was beautiful, all disheveled and golden.

"Are you lonesome tonight, Dusty?" She darted Trace a glance. "I know he needs to learn his place, but do you think it would be all right if I sit by his bed for a few minutes so he'll settle down? Otherwise you're not going to get any sleep either."

How could he possibly tell her no when she looked at him with eyes as pleading as the dog's?

"Come to bed, Dusty," he told him. Cassie followed them to his bedroom and sat down on the floor next to the doggie bed. Dusty lay down on his back with his paws up, another peculiarity they found endearing. Trace sat next to her. The dog had gotten his way. In the end he was thankful for Dusty because an hour later, Cassie had fallen into a sound sleep against Trace's shoulder.

He put his arm around her and lowered her head to the floor, leaving his arm there for a cushion. She turned into him, bringing her body breathlessly close to his.

The world in his arms.

That's what it felt like. In a minute he'd waken her so she could go back to bed. But for this moment he wanted to savor her sweetness a little longer.

When the sleeping dog whimpered, Cassie stirred and her eyes opened. "Trace?" she whispered, sounding disoriented.

"You fell asleep."

Her free hand had been resting against his chest. Now that she was waking up, she started to touch him experimentally. "For how long?"

"About an hour."

"I'm sorry."

"I'm not. You were out like a light and needed the sleep."

"You're so good to me."

Their mouths were achingly close. He brushed his lips against hers out of need. "It's because you're so easy to please I want to do everything for you."

"Trace..." This time she took the initiative and pressed her lips against his. That was all it took to deprive him of his last shred of self-control. Maybe he was dreaming, but her mouth seemed to welcome his, urging him to kiss her and hold nothing back.

He pulled her against him, loving the shape of her, the fragrance of her hair, the softness of her skin. She'd aroused his passion on so many levels, he didn't know how he was going to stop, but he had to. He could feel her baby. Much as he wanted to make love to her, he couldn't. This wasn't the time, and the floor wasn't the place. Cassie needed to be able to trust him.

Let go of her now, Rafferty.

As carefully as he could, he eased her away from him and got to his feet. "Even with the carpeting, the floor is hard. Come on. Now that we've got Dusty to bed, it's your turn." He helped her to her feet. She weaved in place. Trace clasped her upper arms until she felt steady.

Her eyes looked glazed as she stared at him in the semidarkness. "I won't pretend I thought you were Logan when I first woke up."

Her honesty slayed him. "Believe it or not, Nicci wasn't in there either."

"Attraction is a dangerous thing."

"Only if it's wrong, but there's nothing wrong with what we just shared."

"Thank you for having more discipline than I do."

He smiled, loving her frank speaking. "If I had control, I wouldn't have let you fall asleep on my shoulder. That makes us even. Let's blame it on nerves over becoming new parents tonight."

To his relief Cassie smiled back. "I like that excuse better than anything you could have come up with besides the truth. I'm going back to bed now. If Dusty whines at my door, I won't open it. He has to learn discipline. Unfortunately his new parents have to teach him 'do as we say, not as we do.'"

But for the dog, Trace would have burst into laughter. Long after she went to her bedroom, Trace lay in his bed knowing he might not get any sleep for what was left of the rest of the night. Cassie had fanned the flame tonight. It was all part of the same fire he'd felt ignite when he'd first found her in the garden.

He knew in his gut she'd felt it, too.

Chapter 9

Dr. Raynard helped Cassie sit up on the examining table. "After you're ready, come into my office. I want to talk to you."

She hoped nothing was wrong. A little alarmed, Cassie got off the table and straightened her skirt. After reaching for her purse she went into his office and sat down opposite his desk.

"Is there anything wrong?" she asked immediately.

"Your baby is doing fine and we want to keep things that way. But you've developed a condition called pre-eclampsia. For one thing, your blood pressure is higher than I'd like to see it.

"Are you under any undue pressure lately that could have contributed to it since your last exam?"

"Yes." Ned had come home, but she didn't want to talk to the doctor about her brother. Everyone in her family was trying to do something about it. Trace had gotten them a dog to ease her anxiety. She loved that man to distraction.

"I'm sorry to hear it. You must have noticed you have more swelling."

"Yes. What can I do?"

"Don't salt any food and lie down between your normal household activities."

"But I've got a job at a beauty salon."

"I'm afraid you'll have to quit. We want to keep your blood pressure from elevating."

Cassie couldn't believe it. "Can I take walks with my horse and dog?"

"Once a day. A short walk. Ten minutes, no longer."

"I've been doing volunteer work at the wildlife sanctuary on Saturdays."

"No more of that, no grocery shopping, no rides in the car. Let someone else do any errands."

I can't do that to Trace.

"What aren't you telling me, doctor? This is really serious, isn't it."

"It can be if you ignore it. But if you'll mind me, you'll be fine. As a precaution I want to see you weekly for a urine sample and blood pressure check until the baby is born. You're at twenty-four weeks now. I'm hoping you can go as close to term as possible."

Panic had taken over. "What if I can't?"

"If it looks necessary, we might have to do a Cesarean. There's only one cure for this condition. That's to give birth. Until then we take every precaution to ensure a healthy mom and baby. Go home and relax as much as you can. You're in excellent condition in every other way. Continue to take care of yourself and I know things will be fine."

She wished she had his faith.

"Do you have any more questions I can answer?"

"What are the chances of the baby surviving if you have to take her early?"

"Don't worry about that right now, Cassie. Just concentrate on rest. Watch TV, read some good books, listen to music. Those are distractions that will alleviate some of your stress."

Nothing was going to relieve her fear while Ned was out there. She got to her feet. "Thanks, Dr. Raynard. I'll follow your advice. This baby means everything to me."

"Of course it does. See you next Friday."

Cassie left the clinic in such a different frame of mind, she didn't know which foot to put in front of the other. For the moment she had to get back to work until Mildred relieved her. Then Cassie would drop her bomb. She hated having to let the owner down. It meant Mildred would have to advertise for someone else, but Cassie's precious baby had to come first.

At three-thirty she left the beauty salon for the last time. Mildred had been so kind and understanding. Cassie drove her truck down the alley and headed for Zane and Avery's ranch. She needed to find out if their offer still stood to let her stay with them until the baby was born. To put any more burden on Trace was out of the question.

After what happened the night they'd brought Dusty home, she needed to put space between them anyway. When Trace had started kissing her, she'd spun out of control. It still embarrassed her that he'd been the one to bring a halt to the rapture she'd experienced for those unforgettable moments in his arms.

For the past week they'd been friendly and had spent any free time together playing with Dusty. The dog was a great buffer to prevent her from getting too close to Trace, who kept his distance without being obvious. Despite the desire they both felt, he respected her pregnant condition. His gallantry was a revelation.

She'd been so happy since he'd come home from Italy. Who could have foreseen a health problem this serious that forced her to seek Avery's help after all? If not hers, then maybe Millie Henson would be willing to let her live with them and pay rent until after the baby was born.

Cassie should have known this past heavenly month with Trace couldn't continue. Tears rolled down her cheeks while she took the turnoff for Zane's ranch. If Avery wasn't home yet, she'd wait for her out in front. Maybe she ought to seek out Millie right now, but Cassie needed someone to talk to first. Avery was like a sister.

When she turned in to the ranch her heart leaped to see the Explorer just leaving. Trace put on his brakes and drew alongside her. He was the last person she'd expected to see. She didn't have time to wipe her wet face before he scrutinized her.

His brows furrowed. "What's wrong? Did Owen or Ned do something while you were at the salon?"

She wiped her cheeks. "No. I came to see Avery."

"Zane said she wouldn't be home until later." Cassie groaned. "How did your doctor's appointment go?"

"Fine. What are you doing here? Where's Dusty?"

"In the kennel for a little while. If anyone comes around, he'll bark and hopefully warn an intruder off.

I've just picked up some surveillance cameras Zane bought for me to install on the property. When we're both away from the house, anyone who trespasses will be caught on video. I'll follow you home and mount them."

Trace was doing everything in his power to relieve her fear. The only thing she could do to repay him for his goodness was to move out so he could get on with his life. She couldn't bear for him to have to wait on her because she knew he would treat her like a princess. Since she wanted to talk to Avery before she did anything, Cassie turned the truck around and drove back to the ranch.

Once parked, she hurried inside the house and ran to her room. After sitting on the side of her bed, she phoned Avery but had to leave a message on her voice mail. Cassie asked her to call her when she could, then hung up.

She made one more call to the sanctuary. When she told the owner she wouldn't be able to volunteer until after the baby was born, Adrian thanked Cassie profusely for all her help and wished her the very best. She made Cassie promise to visit with the baby when she was able to go out.

Lindsey wasn't home when Cassie phoned her. She left a message telling her the doctor told her not to volunteer anymore until after the baby was born. With those phone calls made, she went to the kitchen for a cold lemonade and a bologna sandwich. She made an extra one for Trace.

After reaching in the bag for a doggie treat, she grabbed the leash and went out the back door to find Dusty. He barked excitedly when he saw her approach the kennel. She gave him a peanut butter doggie bone, then let him out and walked him around the front of the house.

Trace was up on the ladder mounting one of the cameras. Between his powerful legs sheathed in jeans and the muscles that played across his back beneath his white T-shirt while he worked, she was mesmerized.

The dog led her around the ladder. "Dusty wants to be with you."

He looked down at her, impaling her with those blue eyes. "I know, but this isn't the right time. We'll play in a little while, Dusty."

The dog barked.

"He understood you! He's so affectionate."

"We have Mr. Ogilvie to thank for that."

And Trace's kindness. "When you're hungry, I've made you a sandwich. I hope you like bologna and cheese."

"I like everything you fix."

Cassie knew he was waiting for an explanation of her earlier tears, but she would wait until Avery called her back. When she told Trace everything, she wanted her plans to be a fait accompli.

"Come with me, Dusty."

She climbed the front steps and sat down on the swing. The dog jumped up next to her and put his head in her lap. There wasn't much room for him and the baby, too. She played with him. Anyone looking in on the situation would think they were a real family enjoying a lazy summer evening together.

A pain pierced Cassie's heart. There was so much wrong with this picture. Trace only had partial vision in one eye and was attempting to get over a broken heart.

Cassie had to quit her job so she could hope to keep the baby Logan would never see. Her brother was out there somewhere stalking her. Dusty was grieving for his original owner.

Hoping Avery would return her call soon, she put her head back and closed her eyes. Long before she heard the sound of a truck, Dusty started barking and jumped to the porch floor. That pulled the leash out of her hand, bringing her fully awake.

"Dusty! Stay!" she called to him, but he'd already run out to the parking area and barked at Zane and Avery who got out of their truck. Cassie walked down the steps and caught hold of the leash. "It's okay, Dusty. These are friends."

Zane grinned. "That's a great little watchdog you've got there."

"Come and meet him."

After Dusty sniffed them, he stayed by Cassie.

"Look at that," Avery murmured. "He's adorable. I love his coloring."

"He has a blue eye and a brown eye."

"I noticed. You're an original aren't you?" Avery patted his head and he licked her hand.

"While you three have fun, I'll go see what Trace is up to."

Once Zane disappeared around the side of the house, Avery glanced at Cassie. "You sounded serious on the phone earlier. Tell me what's wrong."

The tears started again. "I'm so glad you're here."

Avery hugged her before they went up the steps to the swing and sat down. Dusty sat at Cassie's feet. "I went to my doctor's appointment today. The news wasn't good."

For the next few minutes she poured out her heart to Avery, who was the best listener in the world. "It was one thing to stay here as housekeeper for Trace until the baby came, but I can't do that now. Would you still be willing to let me stay with you? I'll pay rent."

"Do you even have to ask? As for rent, you're crazy. I told you that when I learned you were pregnant, you would always have a home with me and Zane until you were on your feet again. Have you told Trace yet?"

She averted her eyes. "No. He saw me crying earlier and knows something's wrong, but I needed to talk to you first."

"Are you prepared for him to protest your going anywhere else?"

"That'll be the Good Samaritan in him talking. But you don't know Trace the way I do. He'll become a full-time caretaker, doctor, nurse, cook, breadwinner. He didn't sign on for that kind of responsibility when he decided to go back to ranching again. I was hired to keep the house up and fix his meals, not the other way around."

"What if he wants to be all those things?"

"You're not serious!" she exclaimed.

"Maybe it's because you're too close to it, but Zane and I have noticed a change in Trace over the last few weeks, a contentment. I think helping you has pulled him out of that deep depression since his injury. Zane told me he isn't the same morose man he was a month ago when he dropped in with Jarod, determined to sell the ranch.

"Frankly, you're not the same depressed woman, either. You'll have to look at the video Mac took of everyone at the shower. Anyone watching the two of you wouldn't have a clue there was any sadness in either of you. Something tells me that if you tell him you're leaving, his PTSD could act up."

"You know about that?"

"A lot."

"What does that mean, Avery?"

"Only my brothers and Zane know what I'm about to confide. Since you're like my sister, I'm going to tell you. I was assaulted by a man who's in prison now. It happened when I went to college in Bozeman."

"Avery—" Cassie hugged her for a long time. So many things suddenly made sense that had never made sense before she married Zane.

"I've had to live with my PTSD and Zane's. We've seen it in Trace. It wasn't just the injury to his eye. He suffered severe trauma when his parents divorced. Not all children of divorce react that way. My psychiatrist told me you don't just get PTSD in war. I can tell that living with you is helping him to heal."

Was it true?

"Cassie, when I've talked to my therapist about you, she told me you've been dealing with PTSD, too. The trauma of your family life was bad enough. But when Uncle Grant ordered you out of the house, you went through a life-changing crisis. Logan's death only added to it. You need to heal. I've seen how you respond to Trace. It's my belief you two need each other. Don't worry about the future. Just take it a day at a time."

Avery didn't know what she was asking. But since she'd been through the most horrific experience a woman could face, Cassie knew there was a lot of wisdom in her cousin.

"I'll think about what you've said." She hugged her hard.

"Good. But like I said, you can come home to us if that's what you decide."

"Thank you. Have you had dinner yet?"

"No."

"Then come in the house. I'll make some more sandwiches and whip up a salad."

"That sounds good."

"Come on, Dusty. Let's go inside. I'm sure you need water." He barked, causing Cassie to laugh. "Trace swears he understands everything."

Avery's eyebrows lifted. "Did he suggest getting the dog?"

"Yes. He had a collie years ago."

"I remember. Sounds like he's over the pain of losing his dog. Connor told me he was so broken up, it changed him into a much more serious guy. He swore he'd never own another one again."

Cassie's breath caught. "When did it happen?"

"Soon after his mother moved to Billings and he had to go with her."

Dusty echoed Cassie's moan as they went in the house.

Around nine, Trace walked in the back door. Dusty rushed out of the kitchen to greet him. "The last camera has been mounted on the exterior of the barn."

"Great!" Cassie was sweeping the kitchen floor. Zane and Avery had just left after he'd helped mount a camera over the back door. "Between those and Dusty, you've got us covered."

"That's the plan." He walked over to the sink and

washed his hands. While he dried them, he looked at her. "Want to take in a late movie in White Lodge? A James Bond film I understand. I never did see all of them."

She put the broom in the closet. "I'd like to, but I can't."

"Why?"

Cassie had been mulling over Avery's words in her mind all evening. "Why don't we go in the living room?"

In an instant, stress lines marred his striking features. He went ahead of her, but he didn't sit when she sank down on the couch. Dusty wandered around the room with a toy. "I've been waiting until we were alone to find out why you were in tears earlier."

"No one deserves an explanation more than you do. Today at my appointment, the doctor told me I've developed a condition called preeclampsia."

"I've heard of it. One of the pilots in my squadron had a wife who suffered from it."

"How did it turn out for her?"

"Fine. But she had to go to bed for eight months of her pregnancy."

Eight?

"So I guess you have a good idea of what my doctor told me I have to do."

"Yup. I'm going to turn into Mr. Mom."

His comment was so unexpected, she laughed. "I'm being serious now, Trace."

"So am I. Did he tell you to quit your job?"

"Yes. I already did it today."

"Good."

"Trace—if I continue to stay here, my activities are

limited." She listed everything so he'd understand exactly. "I'm supposed to be working for you, remember?"

He smiled. "Did your doctor know he was talking to the most independent mother-to-be in Montana? Does he know how drastic this is going to be for you to let someone else help take care of you?"

Trace knew her better than she knew herself. "I don't imagine any woman likes hearing it."

"Especially you, but I'll help you pass the time. It won't be so bad." If only he knew how heavenly that sounded.

"You don't have to do this, Trace. I talked to Avery and can move there tomorrow."

He rubbed the back of his neck. "Knowing how your mind works, whom would you rather inconvenience? The Lawsons or yours truly?"

"That's not a fair question because there's no good answer."

"Why don't you think about where you'll be happiest and give me your decision tomorrow? But I'd rather you stayed here so you can walk me through the process of putting up raspberry jam. They're starting to ripen. I'll set up a sun lounger in the kitchen. You can lie there with your feet up and give me instructions."

"You'd actually do that?"

"Whatever it takes to entertain you until your daughter arrives. Have you thought of a name yet?"

"I *have*." While he was mounting the camera in front, it came to her.

"And?"

"I'm going to think about it for a while before I say it out loud."

"So you're superstitious?" he asked playfully.

"No. I've just got to be sure. Trace—if I stay here, you have to promise you'll let me pay you the money I was going to use for the first and last month's rent on that apartment. I have it and more saved in the bank."

"Agreed." He answered too fast. "Do we have a deal?"

Her heart pounded so hard she felt sick. "Only if *you're* sure."

He flicked her another glance. "Do you honestly think I would have bothered to get a dog if I hadn't planned on you being here throughout your pregnancy? Dusty will go into mourning if he can't find you to-morrow."

Trace knew how to apply emotional bribery to her exact vulnerable area.

"Any other conditions before I send you to bed where you should have been an hour ago? Considering everything you've done since you left the doctor's office, you've already disobeyed his instructions."

"I'm aware of that."

"If you want to know the truth, I've been hoping you won't leave. I like having you around. That first day I got home from Italy, I dreaded driving out here knowing I'd be bombarded with too many memories I didn't want to think about. But the minute I saw you in the fruit garden and realized the pain you were living with, they seemed to vanish.

"Now that we've got Dusty and your pregnancy is coming along, it feels good to be alive despite my bad eye, your brother and maybe even momnesia."

Avery had been right about everything.

"I'd like to stay, but only on the condition that if it gets too hard, Avery will insist on taking over."

* * *

Connor and Trace rode Buttercup and Masala to the pasture to exercise the horses. Before Cassie had been put to bed, he'd planned to have a herd of cattle unloaded. But the situation had forced him to put any of those ranching ideas on hold.

"I went to the checkup with her this morning. While she was in the restroom, I spoke to Dr. Raynard. After eight weeks of virtual bed rest, her blood pressure is even higher and there's too much protein in her urine. He's given her a medication to help. If it can get her to last another week, then he'll perform a Cesarean."

"That's too early," Connor muttered.

"He says that at thirty-three weeks the baby will be in good shape. I need to be on hand because once she's born, the baby could be in the hospital a month or longer and Cassie will want to be right there with her. He wants me to bring her in day after tomorrow to see if the medicine is helping. That's why I haven't done anything about the cattle yet."

"I hear you."

"What's the word on Ned?"

"We've noticed him riding around the ranch with my uncle. Jarod caught sight of him headed into the mountains alone the other day and followed him until he came back. I saw him driving with Owen in Owen's truck yesterday."

"Did they leave the ranch?"

Connor nodded. "I followed them into White Lodge. They hit the supermarket. I'll give you one guess what they bought. Then they drove to the Pearson ranch. I stayed hidden and followed them after they left to bring Ned back. Jarod and I are doing our damndest to keep an eye on him. It's clear my uncle hasn't put him to work yet, which means he's still afraid of his son and Ned is the same old Ned."

"Cassie never believed he would change. Now he's free to come and go. I check the video on the cameras every day. So far, neither Ned or Owen have trespassed, unless they're aware of the cameras and move out of the line of vision."

"We simply don't know what Ned's up to. I've talked to Zane. He's no closer to finding the person who shot Logan, but we're all keeping a close eye on Ned."

"You can't do more than that, Connor. If he gets into one of his manic moods, he'll make a mistake and we'll be ready for him."

"Liz and her mom are planning on taking turns with the girls to help when the time comes."

"You've all done so much already bringing food and keeping her company. Cassie is so grateful."

"My cousin didn't deserve all that's happened to her. Thank God she has you, Trace. Let's get back to her."

"Do you ever talk to Cassie's mother?"

"No. She stays away. The only time I see her is when she leaves the ranch. Her mother still lives in Bozeman and she goes there a lot."

Trace shook his head.

"Don't try to figure it out, Trace. It's Cassie she should be visiting and giving comfort to. I think living with my uncle and Ned did something to her mind a long, long time ago. Jarod's convinced of it."

On that tragic note they galloped back to give the horses a workout. When they reached the paddock, Connor took off in his truck. Trace watered their mounts and left them to graze while he hurried toward the house. He could hear Dusty's bark before he entered through the back door.

"Hey, buddy. Let's go see how Cassie's doing."

He found her on the couch in the living room with her jean-clad legs propped. Her blond hair fanned around her head on the pillow. She was one woman whose body hadn't looked that pregnant at six months. But over the past two the baby had really grown.

"Sorry we were gone so long. Are you ready for dinner?"

"Whenever you are. It's disgusting how I can lie around all day and still be hungry for every meal. Did I tell you my little girl has found a new place to jab me? She did it during the night and now she's at it again. Here. Feel *this*."

His pulse raced. Trace had been hoping she'd let him feel the baby again. He hadn't dared touch her since the night he'd wanted to go on kissing her senseless. That seemed like a century ago. After she'd left his arms to go to bed, he'd forced himself to put his desire for her in cold storage.

But now that she'd just given him permission, he hunkered down next to her. She took his hand and put it on the side of her swollen belly. He felt movement at once, hard and strong. "Good grief. That has to hurt!"

"It kind of does now that she's been doing it in the same place for so long. I need to shift positions." He had to give her credit for trying. "Do you have any idea how difficult it is to move when you feel like a beached porpoise?"

"Don't you mean whale?"

Her eyes rounded. "Do I look that huge?"

He chuckled over her hurt expression. "No, Cassie.

No. You look good enough to eat," he whispered. Without waiting for permission, he covered her mouth with his own, breaking the rule he'd set for himself two months ago. He couldn't help it.

For a pregnant woman who was more or less stuck in that position, her hungry response sent *his* blood pressure spiking through the roof. Neither of them could get enough of the other. Cassie was with him all the way. His patience was paying off.

Don't blow it now, Rafferty.

He finally lifted his mouth from hers, struggling for breath. She made a little groan of protest that thrilled him. But he was far too conscious of her medical condition to take advantage of the moment. Instead he gripped one of her hands.

"You're so lovely, I couldn't resist. Don't say another word about how you look. There's a glow about you I find irresistible. You're going to make the most stunning mother."

"I hope you know your compliments are spoiling me."

"Good. Connor said you were the most popular girl at high school and I believe it."

"He made that up."

"Nope. I heard it from Jarod, too."

"Thanks for trying to cheer me up." Fear had entered her eyes. "You really think the baby will be all right being born premature?"

"Believe your doctor. Even if it came today, he said both of you would be fine." Overwhelmed by love for her, Trace drew her into his arms and pressed his cheek against her hot one. "You're going to have a beautiful baby."

"I just want her to be healthy," she said as Dusty started barking.

"Someone's at the door."

Trace had been so involved with Cassie, he hadn't heard a knock or the doorbell. "Just a minute and let me see who it is." He sprang to his feet and strode to the front door. When he opened it, he discovered his father and Ellen standing there with food they'd brought. He invited them inside. No sight could have been more welcome.

While they hugged, Dusty brushed up against Sam who leaned over to pet him. "You remember me, don't you, boy. Do you like your new home?" The dog barked.

"He was talking to you, Sam." This from Cassie.

"Cassie has me convinced he really does talk," Trace exclaimed. "How did you two know Cassie and I were hungry for dinner? Something smells delicious."

Ellen smiled. "I'll fix a plate for everyone and we'll eat in here."

A few minutes later they settled down to enjoy the fajitas she'd made. Trace told them what the doctor had said. His father leaned forward in his chair.

"Cassie? I understand your fears, but thousands of women face this and come out of it fine. Your doctor knows what he's doing. Remember—you've been through the worst part having to stay on bed rest."

"I disagree. Your son is the one whose life has been living torture. He's worn every hat there is taking care of me and has listened to me cry and worry until I'm sure he's ready to scream. Both of you should get a medal."

Sam looked surprised. "What do I have to do with it?"

"You raised him to be as exceptional as you are."

"She's right," Ellen chimed in.

Trace had rarely seen his father blush. He was glad his dad had come over tonight. Cassie had never needed reassurance more. When they were ready to leave she said, "Ellen? Take one of those jars of raspberry jam home with you. Trace made it."

"He did?"

"She told me what to do," Trace explained. "It all sold at the White Lodge fair, but I held a few jars back for us."

"We're both impressed." Sam gave Cassie a kiss on the cheek. After hugging Trace, they left. He could tell their visit had relaxed her.

"What can I do for you?" he asked after shutting the door.

"You and Dusty can watch football to your heart's content while I go to bed." She got up from the couch with some difficulty. "Your dad and Ellen are the greatest. See you in the morning."

He didn't try to detain her. Trace could tell she was tired. Hopefully she'd fall right to sleep and not brood over her condition.

Chapter 10

The next afternoon Cassie lay on the couch watching TV. She'd worn a robe over her nightgown because she was more comfortable like that at this stage in her pregnancy. Dusty suddenly sprang from the floor where he'd been lying in front of her and flew out of the living room, barking so loudly it startled her. She sat up as carefully as she could.

When he came back, he headed straight for the front door and wouldn't stop barking.

"What is it, Dusty?" For the dog to go investigate meant someone had been walking around the outside of the house. Trace had driven over to Connor's and said he'd be right back. Dusty would never react like that if it were Trace returning in the truck. She would have heard the engine.

The dog darted from the door to the front window.

His front paws rested on the window sill. His bark had turned into a primitive growl, his tail high in the air. It caused the hairs to lift on the back of her neck. She shut off the TV with the remote.

Someone had been prowling around that Dusty didn't recognize. Cassie hadn't heard the bell or a knock. Whoever it was had started rapping on the big window, obviously enjoying baiting the dog. She got to her swollen feet.

When she padded over to the window to look out, she got the fright of her life. A man stood there on the front porch in front of the window, pressing his face against the glass. Though his features were distorted, she'd know him anywhere.

Ned.

Her body started trembling with fear and wouldn't stop. Any meds he'd been on either weren't working, or he hadn't taken them. His manic side was in full evidence. She moved away from the window and flattened her back against the wall where he could no longer see her. Dusty stayed on point, growling with menace.

Fear caused her body to break out in a cold sweat.

Come home, Trace. Please, God.

"I already saw you through the window, Cassie. Don't you know you can't hide from me?" he taunted. "Especially when you're fat as a French hen with that bastard's baby."

Knowing he was out there made her physically ill. "What are you doing here?" she called to him, praying not to show how terrified she was. Her cell phone was on the end table, a couple of yards away. If she lunged for it, he would see her.

"That's a fine way to speak to your brother. Not even a hello after all this time?"

"Go away, Ned. You're not welcome here."

"It's no sin to come and see my sister, is it?" Suddenly he was trying to open the front door. He kept it up, trying to force his way in with the strength of his body. Snarling, Dusty dashed to the door and barked his head off. But neither of them would be a match for her brother, who was like an animal gone berserk. There was no reasoning with him.

She hurried over to the table and grabbed the phone to call Trace. Her fingers shook, making it difficult to press the digit. *Answer it!* But it went to his voice mail.

"Help, Trace—Ned's here! He's trying to break in!"

Ned was at the window again and could see her. "I know what you're doing, little sister. But there's no Logan to help you now. I should have gotten rid of him before you disgraced our family with his kid."

So he *had* killed Logan!

"Now it's time to get rid of you."

Her brother was in a full rage. Cassie had the sure knowledge that he was going to kill her, too. Forgetting she was pregnant, she ran over to the fireplace. She had to stretch to take the rifle from the rack. Trace didn't keep it loaded. The ammunition was in the drawer of the credenza, but Ned didn't know that. It could buy her some time until Trace got here.

The dog kept up his blood-curdling growl until she heard glass shatter, then a yelp. Ned had used the end of a shotgun to break the pane.

"Dusty!"

Her brother pushed out the rest of the glass before climbing inside the living room. He stepped over the dog who lay moaning in pain and lifted the shotgun to his shoulder. Out of self-preservation she dropped to the floor with Trace's rifle and turned on her side away from him.

Not my baby. Not my baby.

She shuddered in horror as Ned walked around so he was facing her with those soulless eyes glittering down at her. "You have no idea how many years I've wanted to do this." He pointed the shotgun straight at her. "The perfect sister who always did everything right. The popular one. But you made a big mistake when you married Logan."

Somehow she found the strength to send the rifle hurtling against his knee caps.

He let out a groan. "Damn if you aren't a regular little hellcat. Let's see if you like the way *this* feels." Turning the butt end of the shotgun around, he moved toward her with only one intention. To smash her and her unborn baby to pulp. She got up from the floor and ran screaming Trace's name at the top of her lungs.

"I'm here!" came the beloved voice.

Trace had come in through the front door. He swept her into his arms and rocked her close to him. "You're safe now, sweetheart."

She could hear her cousins' voices mingled with Ned's threats in the background, but nothing mattered because Trace had come for her. "I'm getting you to the hospital right now." He carried her out of the house to his Explorer parked in front.

"Thank God you came when you did," she said after he'd settled her in the front seat. "I think I've hurt the baby."

"You're going to be fine. Dr. Raynard is meeting us there."

Tears streamed down her cheeks. "Ned admitted he killed Logan."

"He's not ever going to hurt anyone again. The camera videotape will have caught him climbing the porch steps with the shotgun. It will provide the positive proof Zane has been looking for. He and your cousins are taking care of Ned right now."

She shook her head. "To think my only brother is so mentally ill. I'm having a hard time conceiving it. I wonder what my parents are going to think now," she half moaned.

"Cassie—your mother called Connor and told him Ned sneaked out of the house. He's been refusing to take his medication. Your dad went to look for him. She was worried sick for you and begged everyone to find Ned and stop him before he reached you."

"Mother did that?"

"Yes. We have her to thank that we got to my ranch in time to save you."

"I—I can't believe it."

"Believe it, Cassie. She loves you and is devastated by what has been going on all these years. Now that Ned is going to be taken care of, she can concentrate on loving and helping you."

"I want that more than anything." She wiped her eyes. "What about Dusty? I'm afraid the glass really hurt him."

"He'll be all right after Dad takes a look at him. Hang on, Cassie. We're almost there."

"Because it's you, I'll hang on for as long as it takes."

She felt him grasp her hand and hold it the rest of the way.

* * *

Twenty-four hours later the nurse wheeled Cassie down the hall to the NICU. Trace's tall, hard-muscled physique was waiting inside the unit. He'd been gowned, gloved and masked. So much love poured out of her, there were no words to describe how she felt about him at this point.

Dr. Raynard had done a Cesarean after she'd reached the hospital. Cassie's baby weighed in at four pounds, elating her and the doctor. The pediatrician proclaimed her in excellent health considering her early arrival.

Cassie had started to pump her breast milk. They fed it to the baby through a tube in her mouth. The incubator kept her warm. Both Trace and Cassie could reach in the holes to hold the baby's little fingers and talk to her.

Beneath his black hair and brows, Trace's eyes were a brilliant blue above the face mask he wore. "She's so tiny and perfect. With her fine blond hair, she looks a lot like you, Cassie."

"I just can't believe she's here," she said through the mask. "It's over. Thanks to you, I have her and my life." Her voice shook. "I owe you everything, Trace."

"Everyone pitched in. It was a team effort. Even Dusty tried to help."

"How is he?"

"Dad had to put a couple of stitches in his left ear. He's doing well, but is going to stay with my father and Ellen for a while."

"The poor little darling. You can't believe how fierce he was when he saw Ned out on the porch. He's really a great watchdog." After a pause she said, "So are you." Emotion had caught up to her. "Where did you come from, Trace Rafferty? How was I ever so blessed?

You've had to wait on me day and night for months and have put up with me when I was grumpy and out of sorts. You have the temperament of a saint."

"Really? Then it's good you didn't hear me when I reamed out Lamont Walker."

"He was awful."

"I didn't like him on sight. But let's not talk about unpleasant things anymore. How soon does the doctor think you can take her home?"

"Maybe two weeks. She has to be able to suck on a bottle. They're watching her sleep habits and checking for infections."

"How soon can *you* come home?"

Cassie didn't have a home yet. She was living in Trace's home out of the goodness of his generous heart. "I think tomorrow after the doctor does his rounds, if he thinks I'm recovered enough. But I'll only be there to sleep before I go back to the hospital and be with the baby."

"We'll do it together."

Though music to her ears, he had other obligations. Now he could start putting his plans for the ranch into action. But she refrained from reminding him. Her momnesia had taken over and she couldn't think about anything but this miracle that had happened.

Ten days later Trace brought her and the baby home. When they entered the nursery, she saw a new rocking chair in the corner the same color as the crib. "Oh, Trace—I love it!"

"This is my welcome home present to you. Now you'll be comfortable feeding her."

He'd turned the bedroom into a nursery for her precious daughter who was putting on a little weight every day. As Trace helped her put the sleeping baby in the crib and she realized there was nothing more to fear from Ned, Cassie felt euphoric. Forget that the Cesarean had caused her any discomfort and made her a little slower on her feet, she couldn't complain about anything.

Cassie looked at him. "You've been here from the beginning. I owe you my life, Trace."

"I was just thinking the same thing about you. When I came home from Italy, my depression was so bad at the time, I knew Nicci and I wouldn't be able to work things out. I figured I'd never have the experience of being a husband and parent. But you let me be a part of yours. Whether right or wrong, that sonogram picture did something to me."

"It felt natural to show it to you," she admitted.

"The times you let me feel the baby moving brought me alive again. At the hospital you asked the doctor if I could come in to watch the procedure."

"You'd been with me every step of the way. I couldn't imagine you not being a part of her birth."

"It felt like you were pregnant with my child. When I saw the baby lifted out of you and heard your cry of joy, it touched something in my soul."

"Mine, too." Her fingers gripped the crib railing. "I want to show you something. If you'd go to my bedroom and look in the closet, the little wooden toy chest is there. Would you bring it in here?"

Trace had wondered where it had been all this time. He couldn't imagine why she'd put it in there. Though her request seemed odd, he didn't question it. "I'll be right back."

He hurried down the hall to her bedroom and opened the closet door. Mystified, he found it at the back hiding behind some clothes. When he pulled it out, he saw that she'd transformed it with her unique artwork. She must have painted it whenever he left the house to do errands.

But when he brought it out of the closet, he stopped because he saw the name she'd painted on the center of the lid.

Tracey.

He needed a minute to get himself under control before he carried it to the nursery. She looked up at him with a hint of anxiety. "Do you like her name?"

Trace was overcome. "I don't know what to say." His voice sounded husky to his own ears.

"I painted it right after you gave it to me. In my heart she's been Tracey for a long time."

Her eyes glistened. "It's to honor the most wonderful man I know. I've known quite a few, but your name is at the top of that remarkable list. When my daughter is old enough, I'm going to tell her how I came to give it to her."

He put the toy box down on the floor and pulled something from his pocket. "Come here." He drew her over to the rocking chair, but he sat down first before pulling her onto his lap. "Cassie?" His breath was warm against her neck.

By now she was trembling like crazy. "Yes?"

"I have something for you. Hold up your left hand."

Could this really be happening?

"I've waited a long time to do this." He reached around and pushed a diamond set in gold on her ring finger. "You're going to marry me, right? You *have* to. I'm madly in love with you and I want to adopt Tracey. My two Montana cowgirls. If you don't tell me what I want to hear, I won't be able to handle it."

She didn't answer him right away. He shouldn't have done it yet, but he hadn't been able to hold back.

"Cassie?" he prodded her. "Say something—"

Hearing his uncertainty, she got up from his lap and turned around, placing her hands on the arms of the chair. Her eyes had ignited with little green fires. "After we're married, I'll have the birth certificate amended to read Tracey Dorney *Rafferty*. How does that sound?"

"Sweetheart—"

Before she knew it, he'd picked her up and walked her the few feet to the bed. He followed her down on it, taking care not to hurt her.

"Cassie—if you only knew how long I've wanted to be able to just hold you like this and not worry that you'd tell me it was too soon."

"Too soon?" She laughed for joy. "I've been desperately in love with you from the moment you walked out to the fruit garden. Sam Rafferty's son was home. When you smiled at me, that was it. There will always be that place in my heart for the Logan of my past life. But when you walked into my world that day looking so gorgeous and wonderful, you changed my life."

He kissed her long and hard. "When shall we get married?"

"Whenever the arrangements can be made."

"Thank heaven. I don't want to waste any more time. Dad once told me that God's mills grind slowly, but they grind. We've been through the hard part and can attest to it, beloved. Now it's time to live."

After a passion-filled wedding night, Cassie woke up before Trace. His legs had trapped hers and his arm held on to her possessively even though he slept.

She looked around Connor's trailer. This had been his home on the road with Liz while they were building their new ranch house. Since he knew Cassie couldn't be far away from Tracey for a while longer, he offered his trailer as a temporary wedding night solution. He and Liz wanted to take care of the baby for them at Trace's ranch.

Cassie loved this tiny house on wheels. Everything you needed was right here. Best of all it was totally private and so cozy.

At her six weeks' checkup, Dr. Raynard had proclaimed her well and healthy. *Hallelujah*, Trace had shouted before giving her a husband's kiss, hot with the passion they no longer had to hold back. Cassie shared his sentiment so completely all night long, she hardly knew herself.

Trace was the most satisfying lover she could ever have wanted or imagined. Anxious for him to wake up so they could make love again, she started kissing him. He had a compelling mouth that could send her into rapture.

"Um," he moaned before his eyelids opened. "Is my little wanton awake already?"

Cassie actually blushed.

He chuckled and kissed her neck. "Don't ever be embarrassed for making me the happiest man on earth."

"I hope you'll always feel this way." She covered his eyes and nose and mouth with kisses.

"I sense a new happiness in you, sweetheart. Your mother has turned a corner in her own emotional recovery. You can tell she wants to start over to be your mother and a grandmother to Tracey. With Ned back in the facility for good, maybe your dad will change and start to come around, too. There's always hope. Deep down I know it's what you've wanted."

"You know me so well, it's scary."

"I'm still learning exciting new things about you," he whispered into her profusion of gold hair.

Her whole body went hot. "I think I love you too much."

"Don't ever say those words again. Just show me instead." He rolled her on top of him and the divine ritual of loving and being loved started over again. And again. And again.

* * * * *

**WE HOPE YOU ENJOYED
THIS BOOK FROM**

Believe in love. Overcome obstacles. Find happiness.

Relate to finding comfort and strength in the
support of loved ones and enjoy the journey
no matter what life throws your way.

6 NEW BOOKS AVAILABLE EVERY MONTH!

HSEHALO2020

SPECIAL EXCERPT FROM

⊕ HARLEQUIN

SPECIAL EDITION

*An explosion ended Jake Kelly's military career.
Now his days are spent alone on his ranch, and his
nights are spent keeping his PTSD at bay. But the
ex-marine's efforts to keep the beautiful Skylar Gilmore
at a distance are thwarted by his canine companion.
Every time he turns around, Molly is racing off to the
Circle G looking for Sky. Maybe the dog knows that two
hearts are better than one?*

Read on for a sneak peek at
The Marine's Road Home,
*the latest book in Brenda Harlen's
Match Made in Haven miniseries!*

"Actually, I think I'll try a pint of Wild Horse tonight."

She moved the mug to the appropriate tap and tilted it
under the spout. "Eleven whole words," she remarked. "I
think that's a new record, John."

He lifted his gaze to hers, saw the teasing light in her
eye and felt that uncomfortable tug again. "My name's
not John."

"But as you haven't told me what it is, I can only
guess," she said.

"So you decided on John...as in John Doe?" he
surmised.

She nodded. "And because it rolls off the tongue more easily than the-sullen-stranger-who-drinks-Sam-Adams, or, after tonight, the-sullen-stranger-who-usually-drinks-Sam-Adams-but-one-time-ordered-a-Wild-Horse." She set the mug on a paper coaster in front of him. "And I think that's a smile tugging at the lips of the sullen stranger."

"I was just thinking that next time I'll order a Ruby Mountain Angel Creek Amber Ale," he said.

"Careful," she cautioned with a playful wink. "This exchange of words is starting to resemble an actual conversation."

He lifted the mug to his mouth, and Sky moved down the bar to serve a couple of newcomers, leaving Jake alone with his beer.

Which was what he wanted, and yet, when she came back again, he heard himself say, "My name's Jake."

The sweet curve of her lips warmed something deep inside him.

Don't miss
The Marine's Road Home *by Brenda Harlen,*
available August 2020 wherever
Harlequin Special Edition books and ebooks are sold.

Harlequin.com

Copyright © 2020 by Brenda Harlen

IF YOU ENJOYED THIS BOOK
WE THINK YOU WILL ALSO LOVE

✦HARLEQUIN
DESIRE

*Luxury, scandal, desire—welcome to
the lives of the American elite.*

Be transported to the worlds of oil barons, family dynasties,
moguls and celebrities. Get ready for juicy plot twists,
delicious sensuality and intriguing scandal.

6 NEW BOOKS AVAILABLE EVERY MONTH!

HDXSERIES2020

SPECIAL EXCERPT FROM

⒣ HARLEQUIN

DESIRE

*Successful architect Rani Gupta has sworn off all men.
So when she begins working with hotelier Arjun Singh,
India's hottest bachelor, she vows to keep it professional.
But he won't ignore the attraction they share, especially
when she needs a fake fiancé...*

Read on for a sneak peek at
Marriage by Arrangement *by Sophia Singh Sasson*

Rani's pulse raced. *Is this really happening? I'm going to lead a big contract?* The best she had hoped for was to get the promotion to senior architect and be allowed to work on this high-profile project. She wasn't prepared to manage a big client like Arjun Singh. Arjun's eyes sought her out and he lifted his chin. *Is he asking me if I'm okay with this? Can't be!* Wealthy Indian men didn't ask permission; they took what they wanted. Panic seized her. Could she really work with a man like Arjun? While she had legally freed herself from Navin, the scars from his verbal assaults still tore at her soul. Would Arjun be a reminder of what she'd worked so hard to leave behind?

She met his eyes and gave a slight nod of her head, trying to look nonchalant, as if she was asked to lead big projects every day. *I'm not going to let Navin get in my head. I can do this.*

"I'm willing to do a limited contract with your firm for the construction of the owners' suites, plus blueprints and a 3D interior design for the lobby that mimics the one Ms. Gupta presented for the owners' suites." Arjun stood and left the room without even a goodbye handshake.

Rani slipped out and caught up with Arjun at the elevator banks, her heart beating so hard she was sure he could hear it.

"I look forward to working with you, Mr. Singh." She held out her hand and he looked at it for a second before taking it. Her hand felt small enveloped in his firm grip and a delicious current danced through her body. She was five foot four and wearing two-inch heels but had to tilt her head to maintain his gaze. She met his eyes and her legs turned to Jell-O.

"Call me Arjun." His lips twitched. "Is it okay if I call you…Rani?" He said her name slowly, like it was a sip of fine wine tantalizing his tongue.

"Um, sure." She tugged on her hand and he let it go, but his eyes stayed on her. The man vibrated with sexual charm. *Careful, Rani!*

"How much of the owners' suites did you personally design?" he asked.

Rani resisted the urge to look back at the boardroom. "All of it."

He smiled. Not the clipped polite smile he gave when reporters thrust a microphone in his face or the fake one he gave at the meeting. This one was wide, revealing a tiny dimple in his right cheek. Rani's stomach flipped, and then flipped again. She'd looked at hundreds of photos of this man in the course of her research and there wasn't a dimple in any one of them. *Oh my God. Can this man get any hotter?*

"I've been meeting with architectural design firms for months and no one has come close to what I wanted. You're quite talented, Rani. I can't wait to see what you come up with for the lobby."

Now it was Rani's turn to smile.

"I already have your lobby designed. I think you're going to like it."

His lips twitched. The elevator doors dinged opened and he stepped through, then turned to face her and smiled. A full-watt smile with the little dimple. "I think we're going to work really well together." He joined his hands as the elevator doors closed. "Namaste, Rani," he said in a silky voice that melted her insides.

Namaste, temptation! Rani stared at the closed doors.

Don't miss what happens next in
Marriage by Arrangement *by Sophia Singh Sasson.*

Available August 2020 wherever
Harlequin Desire books and ebooks are sold.

Harlequin.com

Copyright © 2020 by Sophia Singh Sasson

HDEXP0720

Heartfelt or suspenseful, inspiring or passionate, Harlequin has your happily-ever-after.

With new books published
every month, you are sure to find the
satisfying escape you know you deserve.

SIGN UP FOR THE HARLEQUIN NEWSLETTER

Be the first to hear about great new
reads and exciting offers!

Harlequin.com/newsletters

HNEWS2020